Locked Down

A Nicole Grant Thriller, Volume 1

ED KOVACS

Published by THE PHOENIX GROUP, 2021.

PRAISE FOR ED KOVACS

LOCKED DOWN

"Some guys just write about it, but some guys live it. THIS guy lives it. A trip to Hong Kong with an author who knows where the bodies are buried." —*JAKE NEEDHAM, USA TODAY BEST-SELLING AUTHOR*

"*Locked Down* is a riveting read." —*AWARD-WINNING NOVELIST DEAN BARRETT*

"*Locked Down* is a brilliant techno-thriller teeming with suspense."—*SP REVIEWS*

. . . .

GOOD JUNK

"...the scenes of New Orleans are rich and real. Kovacs hopeless, elegiac vision of the city is touching, and his quick studies of hidden landmarks like the outré bar in the French Quarter that calls itself Pravda, and Pampy's, a purveyor of soul food to politicians, are written with true affection and terrific humor." –*THE NEW YORK TIMES BOOK REVIEW*

"Powerful prose that evokes a city still struggling to recover its infrastructure and identity elevates this well beyond most other contemporary PI novels." –*PUBLISHER'S WEEKLY, BOXED, STARRED REVIEW*

. . . .

STORM DAMAGE

"A sleeper here, a beautiful spin on hard-boiled fiction, and it's all done with style and energy."— *BOOKLIST*

"Kovacs noir take on the thriller will hook readers."—*ASSOCIATED PRESS*

"Kovacs is a vivid addition to the thriller genre." —*STEVE BERRY, NEW YORK TIMES BESTSELLING AUTHOR*

"Kovacs writes like a master." —*GAYLE LYNDS, NEW YORK TIMES BESTSELLING AUTHOR*

"Highly recommended."—*JONATHAN MABERRY, NEW YORK TIMES BESTSELLING AUTHOR*

• • • •

THE RUSSIAN BRIDE

"This is a thriller packed so full of action, it leaves readers breathless. Kovacs does an incredible job at being technically accurate and easy to understand, so readers of all levels are engaged throughout. A must-read for fans of fast-paced stories that don't let you go till the very end."—*RT BOOK REVIEWS*

"Brisk, easy-to-read thriller" – *PUBLISHER'S WEEKLY*

"Quick, entertaining action." – *KIRKUS REVIEWS*

• • • •

BURNT BLACK

"The vibrant description of occult doings mixes well with the movements of the earthbound characters, making this Cliff and Honey's best outing to date." —*KIRKUS REVIEWS*

"The rough around the edges locale will be catnip to some readers, like myself. The book has more twists and turns than the streets and back alleys of New Orleans."—*CRIMINAL ELEMENT*

• • • •

UNSEEN FORCES

"Indiana Jones on steroids."—*COL. JOHN ALEXANDER, AUTHOR OF "FUTURE WAR"*

"A spellbinding thriller that will keep you riveted well past midnight." — *THE ST. LOUIS POST-DISPATCH*

"A real page-turner rivaling *The Da Vinci Code*." — *PHENOMENA MAGAZINE*

"A taut, suspenseful story that keeps the reader riveted until the very end." — *MIDWEST BOOK REVIEW*

"Will keep you up nights with anticipation." — *RANDALL FITZGERALD, AUTHOR OF "COSMIC TEST TUBE"*

"Terrific debut novel that deserves to be on the bestseller lists." — *THE DAILY GRAIL*

"I couldn't wait to get back to it after I put it down." — *PAUL SMITH, AUTHOR OF "READING THE ENEMY'S MIND*

• • • •

Please visit Ed's Website[1] to learn more about his novels.

---

1. http://www.edkovacs.com/

ALSO BY ED KOVACS

DEDICATION

This one's for those who must remain unnamed.
With profound gratitude and heartfelt thanks for everything, and
more.

ACKNOWLEDGEMENTS

Sincere thanks to a terrific editor, Ed Stackler, who believed in this book from beginning to end and whose support never wavered. Ed always sticks to his guns when we cross pens, and that's one reason he commands my ultimate respect.

I'm deeply indebted to Carl Scholl who time after time proves with his actions what a great friend he is.

In Hong Kong my deepest gratitude extends to JL, who made everything happen like a maestro with a magic wand. Bravo! And to LC, who first introduced me to Hong Kong decades ago, and whose intrigues with the Middle Kingdom could fill several fascinating volumes, if only she would write them.

Heartfelt gratitude to David Reeves, Tony Ritzman, David Tseklenis, Ernest Norman (for the barstool diagnosis that was a lifesaver), Tom Hansen (for keeping things running), Christopher Graham (my Webmaster and IT genius *par excellence*),kindred spirit and kind soul Warren Sessler, and Paul and Vicky Hasse. Thanks to Allan Jackson and Gordon Danby for all the stuff you guys generously left for me at the "hotel" in Eastern Europe. And I tip my hat to all of the U.S. Navy MAs who served hardship duty with me and provided such good company during difficult times as I rewrote this book in my spare time while deployed.

The biggest thanks go to my wife and children. I must beg their forgiveness for my long absences and for the time I spend at my writing desk instead of being fully engaged with what's really important in this world: sharing our love for each other in a thousand different ways.

AUTHOR'S NOTE

I prefer to write about places that I have personally visited. Hong Kong and mainland China are exciting places to do research and I have spent a lot of time there and all over Asia learning about and trying to understand the ways of the Far East.

Most of the locations in this book are real and well worth a visit. Change, however, is inevitable; businesses close and new ones open in their place. Thanks in advance to my readers for understanding that while most locations in this book as of the time of this writing are real, a few others are purely fictional.

TWO YEARS EARLIER
10:03 PST

Nicole Grant and everyone else sitting in the converted cargo container in Southern California knew that something had gone horribly wrong in Guangzhou, China. They'd all watched the spy drone's video feeds as fifty black-clad, SWAT-style Chinese operators carrying QCW-05 sub-machine guns had suddenly arrived in army trucks, surrounded the luxury five-story drinking club, and then stormed inside.

That was six minutes earlier. Right now Nicole's computer monitors showed a live night-vision feed taken from eleven miles up as their target, sixty-two year-old Wang Hongwei, one of the four Vice Premiers of the State Council of the People's Republic of China and the 7th ranked member of the Politburo Standing Committee of the Communist Party of China, was roughly manhandled into the back of a panel van at the rear of the club just off Shangxiajiu Pedestrian Street a little after 1 AM, Guangzhou time.

Wang was one of the most powerful politicians in all of China and the odds-on favorite to become the next president. As Grant sat in the drab stillness of the steel Conex box in a Pomona, California warehouse, it shocked her to watch as his mouth was roughly covered with duct tape. One of the most important men in China was being treated like some kind of street hoodlum. Of course, she'd learned over the last ten days as her team watched his every move and intercepted all of his communications that he was a corrupt, back-stabbing, rotten snake.

"They've put Wang into that panel van," said Grant over her communications link. "And the SWAT guys have his briefcase with the laptop inside."

On her own initiative, and without bothering to state it over the com-link, the slender fingers of Nicole's left hand danced upon her keyboard as her right hand manipulated a joystick which targeted a sensitive laser eavesdropping beam onto a window of the panel van. She exhaled audibly as the equipment began recording whatever was transpiring inside. She spoke perfect Mandarin, but didn't listen in live even though she thought the audio surveillance might provide good intelligence.

"They're not SWAT, they're soldiers from the Guangzhou Military Region Special Forces Unit," said Ron Hernandez, the person with the nebulous title of AIC—Agent in Charge—for the spy drone operation. His title could have been Main Honcho or Top Mucky-muck or Big Kahuna—rank and titles had meant nothing since the whole affair was so deep black, so far off-the-books that all personnel had even been discouraged from so much as having a drink together.

Not they they could do much socializing while confined to their individual RVs parked inside a gargantuan 50,000 square-foot warehouse in a Pomona industrial park. The same warehouse where the cargo container / drone control room sat. She figured Hernandez wasn't his real name since she herself had been assigned an alias.

Nicole Grant was a U.S. Air Force SIGINT, Signals Intelligence, analyst attached to the NSA, National Security Agency, and normally posted in Ft. Meade, Maryland. A Mandarin-speaking twenty-seven year-old Chinese specialist, she'd been responsible on this operation for tracking Wang's laptop. Since the briefcase was now in the van, she hadn't thought twice about the laser targeting.

All six personnel in the control room communicated via headset/boom mikes: Hernandez, the drone pilot, the sensor operator, Grant, and two other SIGINT technician/analysts like herself. All the analysts in the room were cross-trained and could do each other's jobs. After only three days of spying on vice premier Wang Hongwei, she and the other techies had discovered that Wang's personal hackers had managed to secretly crack the encryption used by the President of China.

Wang's laptop contained elegant software hacking suites allowing him to access encrypted phone calls, chat, e-mail, and instant messaging of the Chinese president, in an apparent attempt to solidify Wang's own political power base and increase his chances of being elected president in two years. Since Grant's team had compromised Wang's communications, they also had a doorway into the current Chinese president! Her team could listen in at will. Heady stuff.

But now Wang and his special laptop were in custody and no one in the control room had said much of anything. It was driving her nuts. Her normally pale skin had taken a more sallow pallor during the last few days of stressful pressure, abetted by her not being allowed to set foot outdoors. The lack of color made her appear fragile and her gangly physique seemed coiled, anxious to unwind but unable to.

"So, what's going on?" she asked, as she guided auburn hair away from her face and tucked it behind an ear.

"What's going on is that we need to pack up our toys and go home before we get caught with our hands in the cookie jar. Mission complete," came Hernandez's disembodied voice over her headset.

Grant blinked, looked up, and swiveled her head. *Mission complete?* She pushed more wayward strands of long, reddish-brown hair away from her green eyes flecked with hazel. Her forehead furrowed as she exchanged a questioning glance with the other techies sitting at workstations across from her in the cool confines of the cargo container, and they looked as confused as she did. She stretched out her long legs as far as she could and shifted uneasily in the supposedly ergonomic office swivel chair.

"Pilot, get the bird back to Udon Thani in one piece, please. I'm estimating wheels-down in Thailand at zero-one-forty-seven, local time," said Hernandez over the com-link.

"Roger that," responded the pilot.

For the last ten days one stealth spy drone had always been on station above Guangzhou while two other drones were either en-route, returning to base, or being maintained in a remote hangar at Udon Thani International Airport in northeast Thailand. With dual runways—one of them 10,000 feet-long—it had been easy for the team to use a front company and a good cover story to set up the secret operation at the airport / Royal Thai Air Force base that had essentially been built by the CIA in the 1960s in support of the Secret War that ran parallel to the Vietnam War.

The jet propelled, bat-winged RQ-180s resembled mini-B-2 bombers and were the most advanced and stealthy drones in the American arsenal. Housed in an old, secluded CIA hangar, they only took off or landed late at night on a stretch of macadam well away from any lights or prying eyes. The relatively close proximity of Udon Thani to Guangzhou meant the birds could stay over the target for over 24 hours at a time.

RQ-180s were usually flown by pilots of the U.S. Air Force's 30th Reconnaissance Squadron based at Creech Air Force Base north of Las Vegas. But the air force, which technically owned the three drones used in the current operation, was not involved. Nor, officially, was the CIA, which had often used stealth drones to track and kill terrorists or carry out secret spy missions over hostile territories.

"Taking up return-to-base heading now," said the pilot, who sat in a cushy leather chair in front of ten computer monitors mounted on electronics racks. He held one of the joysticks from his console as he punched in a new heading on a keypad. A sensor operator sat next to him in a quasi-pilot / co-pilot configuration of consoles and monitors that made their work area look exactly like what it was—a high-tech virtual cockpit.

It was all pretty "spooky" but since Grant's air force assignment was working for the NSA, even as a desk jockey analyst, well, that still made her a spook, didn't it?

Still, this operation was something else entirely. The NSA had se-cretly assigned her to be part of an "Omega Team." Omega Teams or "Cross Matrix" teams were specialized units formed from a con-vergence of private contractors, the military, and the IC, intelligence community. Distinct lines separating such disparate groups, and even chains-of-command became blurred when working as part of such a team. Grant assumed the other team members either came from NSA, the CIA SAD (Central Intelligence Agency Special Ac-tivities Division), JSOC (Joint Special Operations Command), or were private contractors from such companies as Quick Services LLC, ManTech, GK Sierra, R4, or a host of others. One thing that united them was that they were all Chinese speakers.

Grant craned her neck to look at Hernandez sitting behind his console on a slightly raised platform further back in the control room. She guessed him to be late thirties; a tall, muscular man, he possessed a confident intensity, and there was a... what should she call it? A *physicality* about him that most other armchair supervi-sors in the NSA lacked. She pegged him for a soldier, although his thick, wavy, dark-brown hair was too long for someone in the mili-tary. Deep worry lines creased his forehead and the intense gaze of his dark eyes was heavy with responsibility and concern. When he turned slightly and she saw him in profile, his strong chin, somewhat hooked nose, and ever present five-o'clock shadow imbued him with an aura of menace.

Hernandez spoke into a secure phone in hushed tones, turned away from the others, so Grant couldn't read his lips. She was an ex-cellent lip reader due to growing up in a hearing-impaired house-hold, although she'd kept that fact to herself.

With some trepidation she turned back to her computer moni-tor. The temperature was downright chilly in the cargo container for the sake of the electronics, but she'd broken out into a light sweat. For her entire life she had experienced clamminess when she got nervous. Even sometimes when she felt perfectly relaxed, her hands would be sweaty. Right now, feeling seriously uneasy, she had a good excuse to sweat. The whole crew had seen the raid as plain as day. Why would Hernandez announce mission complete as soon as the raid took place?

Was Wang Hongwei's arrest the goal of the mission? The Omega Team had the communications of the Chinese president compromised, so why terminate the operation now? She suspected some very secret something else was going on here—perhaps someone in Washington didn't want Wang Hongwei to become the next Chinese president when elections would be held two years from now—but felt frustrated that as a mere analyst, she didn't have a "need to know."

No wonder such elaborate measures had been taken to ensure mission security. All crew had been carefully vetted, but had still been forced to sign additional non-disclosure agreements, and were told in plain English not to even think about mentioning this operation to anyone, ever.

So, from the very beginning, Grant suspected something wasn't quite right with the Omega Team operation. It led her to take certain measures to cover her butt.

"Analysts, shut it all down," said Hernandez. "We're finished. Erase your hard drives. Every last file generated on this op."

She hardly believed her ears and stole a quick glance at the techs across from her, seeing they looked equally surprised. They had the Chinese president wired; why stop spying on him? The intelligence value had to be staggering.

Grant looked down to her keyboard. She was about to terminate the laser eavesdropping on the panel van containing Wang Hongwei, but hesitated. She knew Hernandez was fatigued—he supervised all three shifts and only slept when Wang Hongwei slept, and Wang usually took no more than four or five hours of sleep a day. Could

Hernandez be mistaken in terminating the op so abruptly? Surely someone would want to listen to what was taking place inside the van.

She was about to double-check the issue with him when the pilot's voice, shrill and excited, boomed over her headphones.

"I've lost control of the bird!"

Grant snapped her head toward the far end of the container where the pilot sat next to the sensor operator. They were toggling switches and pushing buttons on the consoles in front of and between them.

"Say again," said Hernandez over the com-link. She shot him a quick look. He stared at his computer monitors as he held the secure phone handset at arm's length.

"She's not responding to any commands! I've tried manual override. Not responding. Rebooting the control interface now."

"Is it still on a heading for Thailand?" asked Hernandez.

"Negative," said the sensor operator. The bird is now on a course for... Beijing."

"Prepare to engage self-destruct. Tell me when you're rebooted," said Hernandez calmly, in stark counterpoint to the pilot. "Analysts, if you haven't already done so, erase your data, now."

He's too relaxed, thought Grant. Could Hernandez be that cool of a customer? Everyone in the room was well aware of how an older model stealth spy drone had been lost over Iran a few years earlier, supposedly after Iranian hackers had taken control of the guidance system. She couldn't believe the same thing was happening now, on this sensitive Chinese mission. The engineers were supposed to have fixed the problem and made the ultra-secret drones hack-proof. And strangely, this was happening just when the operation had been declared mission complete.

She blinked her tired eyes, red from staring at computer monitors for eight hours a day, and focused. Without stopping the laser

eavesdropping on the van, she shut down all other programs and began erasing the files on her computers. But she had Darknet software running on an invisible, secure Internet connection she'd been
using for her own surfing, and for other reasons. She glanced up at
the other SIGINT analysts; they all wore a look of dread. Something
was very wrong here. Ten days over China and suddenly their target is apprehended in a massive raid, the mission is declared accom-
plished, and then they immediately lose control of the most sophisticated stealth drone America flew? She'd learned the hard way as an
intelligence analyst not to believe in coincidences.

"Reboot complete," said the pilot. "She's not responding, we
have no control!"

"Engage self-destruct," ordered Hernandez.

"Roger... engaged," said the sensor operator.

There was a pregnant pause, then the sensor operator said, "No
joy, repeat, no joy. She's in a controlled descent, still on a direct
course for Beijing."

The pilot slammed his balled-up fist down hard on the armrest of
his chair. "Damn those Chinese pricks! They're stealing our drone!"

Grant faced her computer monitors, but shifted her green and
hazel eyes toward Hernandez. She watched as he brought the secure
phone handset close to his mouth, and she very clearly read his lips as
he whispered into the phone, unheard by anyone in the room, "Objective effected. They've got it."

She gasped. *What in the hell is going on? Objective effected?
They've got it?* Grant reeled, her stomach instantly knotted. Her ana-
lytical mind strongly suspected, with some astonishment, that she'd
just taken part in a secret technology transfer, and that her Omega
Team had aided one faction of the Chinese government in a counter-
intelligence operation against another faction. Wang was supposed
to be taken into custody and then our most secret stealth drone
handed over. It was the only conclusion that made sense.

Although she wore a thick wool sweater, chills ran up her long, slender arms, while at the same time her hands were damp with sweat. Her initial suspicions that something stunk were being vindicated. The whole turn of events rankled her, since she spent most of her time in the employment of the United States Government fighting against a continuous onslaught of aggressive Chinese cyber spying that had stolen virtually every secret of any import from America's defense arsenals. Helping them, giving away our most secret stealth drone didn't make sense.

But then, the world had gone crazy some years ago. Even at age twenty-seven, Nicole Grant knew that.

Grant was a careful planner, loathe to make a decision without having first thought through all options and risks related to the act. But she felt she had to do something right now. She never allowed "instinct" to guide her, in fact she constantly fought against taking action based on impulse, but giving China the drone broke any number of federal laws, perhaps she was even a party to treason. Meaning all evidence should be preserved, such as the audio file.

Crap, there was no time to think! Perspiration formed on her forehead in the cold room. She had to take action, so her brain synapses fired and she opted to do something risky, something against orders and protocol but yet, she tried to convince herself, was still purely logical. And logic is what guided engineers like Nicole Grant. She canceled the laser eavesdropping on the panel van, encrypted the audio file, and then used the Darknet software that she had running to send the contents of whatever had been said inside that Chinese panel van to a secret place, off into cyberspace.

Almost immediately, she regretted it, because emotion, especially fear, usually trumped logic, and fear was right now wrapping its hands around her throat.

Oh my God, what have I done? What if this secret transfer has been sanctioned? What if they find out I sent the file... a file they didn't want saved? I've disobeyed direct orders on the most sensitive kind of operation involving State secrets of the highest order.

Grant's hands shook. For all of her adult life she'd struggled against spontaneity, and here with so much at stake, she'd just succumbed to it. Big trouble was coming, for sure. Sooner or later.

CHAPTER 1

T ODAY
    13:46

"Four hundred Hong Kong dollars," said the old lady in heavily accented English to Nicole Grant, who held up a fake Celine bag for close inspection on a glorious spring day for outdoor shopping. Yes, Hong Kong's famous mugginess was ever-present, making the humidity much higher than Phoenix, but a salty sea breeze occasionally wafted along Tung Choi Street in an area called the Ladies Market, gifting the shoppers with a pleasant caress.

Rich blue skies and puffy white clouds lolling overhead made for a picture postcard perfect afternoon. The shabbiness of the street market and rundown condition of this neighborhood of Kowloon called Mong Kok provided a stark contrast to Mother Nature's natural beauty.

Tung Choi Street closed every afternoon to vehicle traffic and stalls on both sides of the narrow street magically sprang to life to be quickly stocked with merchandise in a ceaseless pursuit of cash commerce. The stalls, constructed of steel poles, bungee cords and plastic tarps were assembled and disassembled more often than a Bedouin's tent.

Shoppers like Nicole had to muscle their way along the very center of the street, assaulted on all sides by towering racks of purses, tee-shirts, stuffed animals, blouses, sports jerseys, tapestries, and every gadget and gizmo known to man, in every size, color, and shape. Souvenirs, tchotchkes, cheap mementos, and plush toys abounded. The colorful displays livened what was otherwise just another dingy Hong Kong street lined by ratty, look-alike eight-story mixed-use buildings with each apartment having a terrace where laundry hung out to dry.

Still looking at the purse, she moved slightly so a shaft of sunlight illuminated the stitching. She'd seen a photo of one of the Kardashians with the bag, but liked it anyway. It was gorgeous, who wouldn't like it? She never needed a calculator and quickly did the math in her head. Compared to the price of a genuine Celine purse, $52 U.S. dollars seemed like a bargain. But her girlfriends back in Phoenix coached her to counter any price given by a street vendor by exactly fifty percent.

"Four hundred good price," said the old lady.

Grant smiled. She wore her auburn hair pulled back in a simple ponytail. Her relaxed face featured a light tan from recent time in the sun. She possessed a confidence common to successful business people, yet tempered by a genuine tendency to kindness. She didn't want to counter with an offer of only two hundred, especially to the older female seller. Negotiating over small money seemed silly, but just for the experience of it, she softly said, "Will you take three-fifty?"

The old lady smiled and said, "Okay, for you, three-fifty."

Hmm, she agreed too quickly. I could have gotten it cheaper. Still, she'd bartered and purchased what she wanted, so she felt a sense of achievement and satisfaction. She counted out exact change—a must for the serious negotiator, she had read—slung the new bag over her arm, then plunged onward for more shopping.

Her decision to include Hong Kong in the itinerary of her Asian vacation, her first overseas vacation ever, had not come lightly due to her involvement in the drone operation two years earlier. After the drone had been lost, she'd been a nervous wreck. Grant had bailed from the intelligence game almost immediately. Upon returning to Ft. Meade from the Omega Team fiasco, she'd requested a transfer out of NSA back to a regular air force posting.

She spent months on pins and needles, certain that her arrest was imminent. Questioned about the intelligence debacle in Top Secret Compartmentalized FBI and NSA investigations, she'd been asked only general questions. The whole episode had been an embarrassment and no one seemed to be looking for the truth. The investigators hadn't asked her about recording the audio file or sending it off into cyberspace, and she didn't mention what she'd seen Hernandez say into the secure phone.

Timing worked in her favor because shortly after the drone incident her re-enlistment came up. She opted to leave the air force and was mustered out with an honorable discharge. In short order she'd landed a plum position at Security-Tech Solutions, moved to Phoenix, and tried to put the nightmare behind her.

At Security-Tech she lost herself in the order, structure, and challenge of her position, which gave her lots of responsibility. It was perfect for an engineer like Grant. Two months into her new job—less than a year after that fateful night with the Omega Team in Pomona—her fitful sleep and anxiety faded away. She reached the conclusion she'd gotten off Scot-free.

While no blowback had befallen her personally, there was no denying she'd been party to some troubling, dark goings-on. So even though she was now a civilian with zero reason to believe that China might have some nefarious interest in her, she'd ruled out a visit to the Mainland. Hong Kong, on the other hand, while technically a part of China, still largely had its independence and freedoms and a Western-based rule of law that made her feel perfectly safe.

Anyway, why would the Chinese have a beef with her? They'd gotten what they wanted and she'd never revealed the audio file to anyone. And since all of the Omega Team members had used aliases, how could a foreign government even know her identity? Maybe Guangzhou was physically close to Hong Kong at only eighty miles away, but the drone op represented far off events to Grant that she chose not to dwell upon. Today, her only concerns in Hong Kong were related to shopping.

She checked her Timex watch with a scratched crystal, the same watch she'd worn since high school. It was almost two in the afternoon, so she allotted herself a little more time to look for bargains. Check that, she was looking for more cheap but authentic-looking designer knock-offs. Shopping in Hong Kong had stopped being a bargain years ago, as various guidebooks and magazine articles had informed her. Even the fakes were no great discount, considering what they sold for in the Asian enclaves of Los Angeles.

Slight guilt hounded her about buying counterfeit items since she would never download movies, music, or books without properly paying for them, but she'd promised some female co-workers at Security-Tech to bring back Hong Kong fakes for them, genuine Hong Kong fakes, they had joked, and she intended to deliver.

At first it had been strange going on vacation by herself, but her apprehension about traveling abroad alone had turned into a subdued feeling of triumph. She certainly didn't need a man with her, but a girlfriend would have been nice. Grant's adult life had been serious and regimented, mostly as a rebellion against her unorganized, impulsive father. She hadn't wanted to end up like him: a man with no pension, no retirement plan, no life insurance, but plenty of debt. So at age fifteen, she had put her nose to the grindstone and got into computers in a big way. Air force scholarships got her through college where she earned degrees in electrical engineering and computer science and excelled in Mandarin language classes. She then began serving her required stint in the air force, including six months at the Defense Language Institute Foreign Language Center to perfect her Mandarin.

At Security-Tech back in Phoenix she managed a staff of thirty. Her people were called pentesters or red teams or penetration specialists. Major banks, corporations, and institutions of all types hired pentesters to attack their computer systems—systems that should have been secure—and to breech them or to detect weaknesses, which sometimes meant gaining access to the systems' functionality and data. If problems were found, the pentesters figured out how to plug the holes and secure the systems from future attack.

With a continuing onslaught of cyber-attacks directed at business and industry, her team had a long waiting list of clients begging for their systems to be tested. So now, at the ripe old age of twenty-nine, Grant had a very good working knowledge of security systems, networking systems, hardware systems, and a general overview of most security suites being used by governments and private industry. She was on top of her game when she took this long-planned vacation to Tokyo, Seoul, and Hong Kong. Professionally, her life was in ultra-glide.

But this twenty-one day vacation already felt to Grant like a game changer, *personally*. She was now entertaining a radical concept: perhaps she was ready to go independent with her career and become a consultant. Her thinking had always been that kind of jump would happen after marriage; consulting would allow more flexibility to work or spend time at home as she grew a family. But she'd concluded she wasn't going to meet the man of her dreams while working at Security-Tech.

It was the story of her life: she was smart, funny, stable, and was a physically attractive package. Her mother constantly teased her about how much she resembled the Hollywood actress Katie Holmes, and pushed her to find her own "Tom Cruise." Yes, her nose was too big and when she grinned her cheeks resembled two ripe crabapples, but her smile could light up a room and her green / hazel eyes simply sparkled. At five-feet ten-inches she was on the rangy side, and had always felt somewhat awkward physically. That was one reason she tended to walk slowly, because she felt self-conscious about having a goofy walk.

But negatives aside, she was a perfectly cute package. So why was it that decent men had been a scarce commodity for most of her adult life? Okay, so her practical nature, engineer's mind, her need to plan out every hour of every day, and her Mensa-level IQ probably had something to do with it. She had given up on the concept of Mr. Right; she was now open to Mr. Almost Right.

Funny, a vacation was supposed to be a time when your could turn your brain off and just enjoy, but this trip had triggered constant examination of her life. Sure, she had gained financial security and stability by being very unlike her dad, but she hadn't gained happiness. She'd been thinking about happiness a lot, lately. People focused on wanting specific things, but how many people simply sought to achieve happiness? In whatever form it might present itself.

As an engineer, she wasn't even certain her thoughts on happiness were valid. She'd methodically gone from A to Z in her life, and wasn't Z supposed to result in those ephemeral concepts of fulfillment, satisfaction, happiness? From a career perspective she'd gotten to Z and all she had to show for it was Z. And a striking realization was that Z was not enough.

Maybe a big change was overdue.

At the next kiosk, crammed between DayGlo Disney backpacks and Star Wars posters she negotiated a little harder and got twenty-five percent off the purchase, an imitation Gucci bag that she dropped into a larger shopping bag. Some bootleg Michael Kors items at a stall just up the street caught her eye, so she casually ambled toward them. *If a career or some other change is coming, this is my chance to accessorize for it,* she thought, smiling.

• • • •

RON HERNANDEZ KNEW Hong Kong well, having spent months here tracking down and killing an Islamic terrorist bomber and his support network in an action that never saw the light of day. He felt comfortable here, and casually watched Nicole Grant amble amongst the crowds on Tung Choi Street through the viewfinder of his video camera. To anyone watching, he was just another tourist in shorts, tee-shirt and a khaki safari vest, wearing a fanny pack and backpack and shooting some jerky vacation footage on a balmy spring afternoon. No one could know thathisJapanese-made glasses wereconstructed of special light-reflecting and -absorbing materials whichdefeated facial recognition software, or that the video camera he held contained a suppressed .22 caliber semi-automatic loaded with sub-sonic ammunition.

Or that he was here to kill.

The video cam had what looked to be an elongated, foam-shrouded microphone extending from its front; that was the suppressor. The hidden pistol held five rounds and was rigged to fire whenever he pushed the red RECORD button. He could press the button and the camera / gun would silently shoot a lead bullet with enough velocity to penetrate a human skull, but not with enough velocity to exit said skull. The bullet would, however, bounce around inside the cranium performing terminal damage. A discreetly fired head shot, preferably aimed behind the ear, made a very small entry wound and no exit wound, hence, it was sometimes difficult for a first responder to even determine the victim had been shot. There was usually very little, if any, telltale blood visible.

Hernandez's dark brown hair was now longish and blond, courtesy of a wig, with a fake blond mustache to match. He hadn't seen Grant for two years, since the drone operation went down. And they had only worked together for ten days, so he doubted that she would recognize him even if he approached her from the front. Anyway, he didn't intend to approach from the front.

Cantonese pop music blasted from a stall selling CDs. The scent of fried noodles cooking in sesame oil rode the breeze for a moment, until a powerful incense aroma shooed it away. The incense came from a young female kiosk owner who'd just put out *cha siu* and fresh oranges as an offering to her ancestors on a tiny altar rigged on a pole. For a moment Hernandez watched the smoke carry her prayers aloft. He had his own prayers to say and he intoned them silently, hoping for healing for his family and for help with the Herculean task he'd taken on.

Grant appeared to be amazingly relaxed; she was clearly one very slick operator. Killing her wouldn't end his troubles, but it would be a step along the path. She had to be in Hong Kong for one reason, and one reason only, so he intended to foil that rendezvous with her Chinese masters. The busy street here was perfect for the hit, as it was filled with bustling locals and tourist crowds.

A sense of calmness washed over him just as it had in the old days. He took it as a sign to kill her right here, right now. Two rounds to the back of her head would do it. He closed in behind her, held up the camcorder with his right hand, and looked through the viewfinder.

She'd never know what hit her.

CHAPTER 2

13:58 When Nicole Grant suddenly spun around looking like she'd forgotten something, Ron Hernandez smoothly turned to the left, panning the camera as if he were recording the vibrant street scene. The video camera nicely hid his features as she crossed directly in front of him, then angled away. From his peripheral vision he saw that she'd returned to the old lady's stall where she'd bought the Celine bag. He felt certain she hadn't recognized him from the quick glimpse she got.

He didn't want to shoot her at the stall, so he looked through the viewfinder of the video camera as he waited for another chance. Through a gap in the kiosks, he noticed a very tall Chinese man in a lightweight black Polo jacket leaning against a building. The man swept the street with a glance and then spoke into his jacket sleeve. Curious, Hernandez zoomed in and clearly saw that the man wore some kind of earpiece—a communications unit.

A cold flash of suspicion caused Hernandez to regard the man more closely. The tall Chinese guy wore a jacket, but the print of a weapon was clearly visible.

It was a warm March day, but a shiver ran up Hernandez's arms. Was the man a Hong Kong gangster, a member of one of the local triads or tongs? Or an undercover cop? Hernandez had to be sure, he needed confirmation and he needed it *now,* so he casually lowered the video camera and then removed a tablet computer from the fanny pack he wore over his groin. As a Japanese tour group waded into the area snapping photos, he used his tablet to surreptitiously photograph the tall Chinese man, then logged onto a facial recognition database run by the CIA.

The match came up in seventeen seconds.

They're here. The Chinese wet team—an assassination team—was here.But were they after him? Or could they possibly be after Grant?

He might only have moments, so he regulated his breathing and worked to keep the adrenalin down, maintaining his cover by gawking about like a wowed tourist new to the city. He made his way toward a small walkway off Tung Choi Street thick with food carts and cheap electronic gizmos for sale. He bought a keychain gadget and pocketed it. While standing next to a teenage girl roasting sweet potatoes in a converted oil drum, he un-shouldered his backpack, reached in, and powered up two softball-sized drones. It only took thirty seconds to launch both of them into the narrow strip of airspace above the Ladies Market. Few Chinese in the hustle-bustle crowd paid him any attention; people probably thought the units were toys. And the locals were good at minding their own business.

He'd pulled up an app on his Samsung tablet computer and put the first drone into an automated low surveillance flight pattern, careful to avoid the maze of signage protruding from the buildings. He zoomed in on Grant and tapped her image, which told the drone to stay centered on her. Working quickly, he sent the other drone higher over the street for a more complete layout of the immediate surroundings. He shouldered the backpack but wore it so it rode on his chest, not his back, giving him easy access to its contents.

Screened by a throng of shoppers, he made an indirect path toward the tall Chinese guy in the black jacket, who had to be working with at least three other killers. The guy seemed oblivious to his presence, but that's exactly how a seasoned operator performing close surveillance would want to appear.

Hernandez needed to even the odds here on Tung Choi Street. After a few seconds an opening appeared in the crowd. He pressed RECORD twice on the camcorder / gun, double-tapping the tall Chinese behind his right ear from ten feet away. The muffled pops were lost in the tourist din, and he let the camcorder dangle from a shoulder strap looped around his neck. He moved forward with large strides and then pressed his body against the dead man to keep him from slumping to the street.

He reached under the Polo jacket and removed the man's pistol as he stole looks around the area, hoping no other member of the hit team had seen what just transpired. The gun was a Type 67 integrally silenced semi-automatic, meaning the suppressor was actually built-in to the design of the weapon. He dropped the gun into his open backpack and then pulled the tiny microphone from the guy's jacket sleeve and the radio transmitter from his pocket. Hernandez quickly checked for other pocket litter, and then walked off.

The dead man slowly slid down to the cement, but with no blood visible, he could just be another drunk or an exhausted worker.

While moving into the street flow of pedestrians Hernandez slumped, because even though Asians as a race were now much taller than at the close of WWII, at six-three he towered over many of the passersby. Breathing through an adrenalin rush, he caught sight of Grant with her back to him as she examined another knockoff purse. He scanned the crowd as he brought the just-purchased keychain gizmo from his pocket. The inexpensive device, usually bought by females, had a panic alarm, and he pressed the button for two seconds as he held the small microphone from the dead man against the keychain.

The sharp, shrill alarm caused a dozen people to glance his way, but more importantly, the loud tone was being sent over the dead man's comm-link. Hernandez caught sight of a well-dressed Chinese woman about thirty years-old who winced and pulled an earpiece from her ear. She wore a white silk blouse and had a red jacket draped over her right arm, possibly concealing a gun. Hernandez's eyes darted through the crowd and spotted a man of about forty in a brown shirt and wearing black-framed eyeglasses, rubbing his ear as if it hurt.

Only two? There has to be at least one more. Video from the second drone, the higher up one, might answer that question, but for right now, the lady in the white blouse was only about twenty feet from Grant. She was looking around as if trying to figure her next move and appeared hesitant to put the earpiece back into her ear. It wouldn't take her team long to figure out they'd lost a man, so he only had seconds to act.

But his certainty of only minutes earlier was now questionable. Yes, it was possible the Chinese were here to kill him. Or they might be Grant's protection detail, for if she were truly in bed with the Chinese, then providing her with security made sense. But now Hernandez wrestled with a third possibility: perhaps Grant was on the Chinese kill list too, just as he was. If so, they were about to wipe her.

He couldn't be sure why the hit team was here, but he wanted to kill as many of them as possible, so Hernandez hefted the tablet computer and spotted the Chinese female on the video feed. He entered commands and directed the lower drone to target her. This drone had a one-shot .22 caliber gun, with no sound suppressor.

The woman edged closer to Grant. Hernandez tapped the Chinese woman's image on the screen, then tapped the button to fire. But nothing happened. Damn, a misfire or some other malfunction!

The drone hovered no more than five feet in front of and about a foot above the woman in the white blouse. She couldn't help but see it, and stood frozen for a moment as she gawked at the device. He tapped the button again to fire just as the killer flung her red jacket at the miniature drone and knocked it to the ground. Some people stared, and others started to scatter, because the woman in the white blouse was holding a suppressed pistol.

Hernandez dropped the tablet into his pack. He could only think of one option: kill the woman and the man in the brown shirt.

He wanted justice and intended to fight for it to his last breath, and that meant killing as many of the guilty as possible.

The second, higher drone was not mounted with a gun. The Chinese woman lowered the pistol to her side to conceal it and slowly cut through the throngs and closed to about ten feet away from Grant. Again, Hernandez wasn't sure; were the Chinese guarding Grant, or about to terminate her?

Screw it! At the moment, it didn't matter. He had a chance to kill a killer and get a little street justice. And maybe he could do it without being seen. Hernandez grabbed the video camera. There were three rounds left in the hidden gun. He needed to make a head shot for a kill, but from this distance, even with a good shot, the bullet might not penetrate the skull due to the slow velocity of the sub-sonic ammo. This was a low percentage play but he decided to take it.

The Chinese woman kept the suppressed pistol to her side as she moved right behind Grant. He took aim through the viewfinder but couldn't get a clean shot, so he stepped forward, accidentally jostling a couple of tourists from Germany.

"*Schweinhund*!" snarled a bald, beefy German man, who gave him a shove. Hernandez took a stutter step away from the Germans, trying to get a clear shot, but bumped hard into two chunky middle-aged Russian women.

"ёб твою мать!" Go to hell, yelled one of the Russians, who reeked of vodka.

The slight ruckus caused the Chinese woman in the white blouse to turn in his direction. She registered a shocked look of recognition and then swung her pistol toward him. He aimed the camcorder, pressed the RECORD button, and a bullet soundlessly tore through her eye socket and into her brain. She reflexively held her hand to her eye as her knees wobbled and she stumbled backward. Even in the throes of death, with great determination she fired several rounds; the shots made the softest puffts, more quiet than popcorn popping.

Grant had already moved on, apparently unaware of the terminal drama unfolding all around her. The killer's bullets had torn harmlessly into a pile of cheap Dolce & Gabbana fakes from mainland China. No passersby screamed as the shooter collapsed to the ground, but they cut her a wide berth. Some people moved away, while others looked on curiously.

He lowered the camera / gun. The Chinese man in the brown shirt had disappeared, so Hernandez walked off as his hands shook. He worked to modulate his breathing and appear calm. Yes, in the last few years, he'd carried out scores of killings and pressed buttons that killed terrorists from thousands of miles away, but what just happened was dirty, up close, and personal.

Just like his killings in the old days had been.

Even though he'd taken out two assassins with lots of blood on their hands—killers who were on his personal "disposition matrix"—his kill list—he felt no relief or satisfaction. For if Ron Hernandez was to continue living and breathing, then there were many names remaining on that list that required his immediate attention.

With the crowd paying attention to the corpse, no one noticed as he reached down and retrieved the drone the female assassin had knocked out of the air with her jacket. He scanned the street, but didn't see Grant; she'd moved on. She'd been on his kill list, too, but as of right now she was the only one who had a question mark after her name.

He needed to act quickly to dope out her role, because if the Chinese killers hadn't already known of his presence in Hong Kong, they surely knew it now.

CHAPTER 3

14**:26** Hong Kong vistas of forest-green peaks, the blue waters of Victoria Harbor, and towering stainless steel-and-glass skylines were simply sublime; close up views of choked, dirty streets much less so. The part of Kowloon Nicole Grant currently navigated didn't have concrete canyons of skyscrapers, but the aging, eight-to-ten-story buildings lining the street radiated penetrating heat. Right now, the temperature felt like it had risen many degrees as she tried to keep pace with the pedestrians on Nathan Road, many of them barking sharp chords of Cantonese into their cell phones.

She navigated past an herb shop and the pungent, musky tang of the bitter, dried plants nearly took her breath away. She carried on, breaking into a small crowd reeking of perfume, cigarette smoke, and garlic. At a red light she found herself pressed against the steel guard rails that kept pedestrians from spilling out into street traffic. A soft, slow-paced series of clicks from a traffic light pole indicated "Don't Walk," so Nicole took the opportunity to refer to her print-out of Mong Kok Station as double-decker buses slugged past.

Although the station was only a couple of blocks from the Ladies Market, she'd already gotten lost once in Hong Kong when she wasn't paying close attention. When the clicking increased in volume and frequency, she looked up and saw that the traffic light had changed and the throngs began to surge across the street. Seeing an opening, she wedged herself forward and stepped into a street crossing painted with dizzying yellow markings. She maintained a brisk pace as she kept snatching looks for station entrance D2. Moist air scented with exhaust found her nostrils as a never-ceasing stream of walkers seemed to come at her from every direction, including above and below when one factored in stairs and escalators.

Tokyo and Seoul are also crowded, but the feeling was different. Seoul has wide boulevards, far more automobiles, and the crowds at places like COEX are thick but not intimidating. In Nicole's experience, Tokyo's masses behaved politely, even in kinetic Tokyo Station, where the pervading aromas were subdued and the soundscape not so glaringly invasive.

But the street hordes in Hong Kong were... well, Hong Kong is a very busy city that challenges one's sense of privacy and individual body space. Sensory overload of all five senses is a constant companion if you go anywhere, and sometimes even if you don't. As if to remind her of that, she could almost taste the onions as a draft of air from a fried dumpling shop enveloped her and the scent of vinegar and chili oil tickled her nose; an old Cantonese lady strategically pressed against Grant's arm in order to cut in front of her; pop music blared from a shop whose exterior was covered with so much signage it was hard to see what they sold inside. Sight, smell, sound, taste, touch—the street assault proceeded unrelenting. The only option was to keep moving if you didn't want to become part of the pavement.

It's a city that doesn't let much get in its way, she thought.

Hong Kong was Manhattan without the street hustles and petty mean-spiritedness, Hollywood but with straight answers and less phoniness, Vegas without the desperation. It was still full of British FILTH (Failed In London Try Hongkong), still retained a Far East exoticism, but functioned with precision and common sense. Its breathtaking panoramas (to call them mere "views" was a disservice) put San Francisco or Seattle to shame. It had the best Chinese food on the planet, period. Its grand hotels, with a staff-to-guest ratio approaching insanity, stood in a world-class by themselves. Hong Kong was historic and traditional, yet new and fresh, somehow constantly remodeling, rebuilding, and reinventing itself without losing its core identity. Even the iron fist of Beijing had not yet tamed Hong

Kong, although the mainland Chinese communist cadres were chipping away at freedoms and the democracy that Hongkongers held so dear.

There was a palpable sense that anything was possible here, that everyone was running around like they had a stick of dynamite shoved up their butt and if they didn't make a million dollars before dinner it would explode. Meaning, that in Hong Kong, you had to act fast; she picked up her pace, and even practiced making quick moves to cut off the approach of others, to keep them from getting in front of her as she snaked along toward a sign indicating D2.

• • • •

"THERE'S NOTHING TO worry about, Mom. I'm perfectly fine," said Nicole Grant as she looked at the Web cam on her 10" Samsung tablet. She'd propped the tablet in such a way that her mom would be able to take in the awesome sight of Victoria Harbor that beckoned though the large windows of her corner executive suite at the five-star Conrad Hong Kong in Pacific Place. They were video chatting and she used sign language as she spoke since her mother, Jan, had been voice and hearing impaired from birth. That's why Nicole was such a good lip reader.

With her dad having passed away, Jan now lived alone in a house Nicole had bought in Las Vegas as an investment. Vegas and Phoenix were close enough that she spent at least one, sometimes two weekends a month with Jan. Nicole was an only child so she understood that her mom was going to worry about her, regardless of her age, regardless of where she traveled to or who she went with. Worry was simply part of the equation in their relationship. The other part of the equation was that Jan meant the world to her. They were close and she truly loved and appreciated her mom. Except for some distant aunts, uncles and cousins who were essentially strangers, Jan was the only family she had.

"Could you at least tell the hotel people where you're going when you go out?" asked Jan, signing. "What if something happened? No one would have any idea where to start looking." Jan was one-quarter Cherokee and her thick brown hair fell past her shoulders. Her dark eyes looked worried.

"Mom, it's Hong Kong, not Baghdad. And in five more days I'll be back in Phoenix. The only thing you have to worry about is whether you'll like the Gucci purse I bought you today."

"Gucci?!"

"Well, it says 'Gucci,' and who are we to argue?"

They shared a smile.

"Have you met any nice guys on the trip?" signed Jan, with an inquisitive look.

"Nice guys aren't interested in me."

"You just haven't met the right one yet."

"I'm not sweating it, trust me," signed Nicole. "I don't need a man to define me or to make me whole. If I end up being a spinster, that's okay with me."

Jan scowled slightly, clearly not liking that idea. "Have you given any thought to my suggestion?"

"You mean getting a boob job?"

"Nicole! Your language!"

"Sorry, I meant breast implants. Don't feel bad that I inherited your flat chest. It's God's way to help me weed out the assholes," joked Nicole, signing.

Jan shook her head and smiled. "All I know is that I have a beautiful, intelligent daughter who will one day give me an awesome grandchild. The sooner the better. I bought a home pregnancy test at the dollar store yesterday. I'm mailing it to you."

Nicole rolled her eyes. "Love you, Mom. Same time tomorrow, okay?" She knew her mom was a night owl and that talking at midnight Las Vegas time was no problem for her. Jan would now go to sleep feeling a little better about her only child being in a far-away place all by herself.

Jan waved. "Bye-bye, and love."

"Love."

Grant turned off the app. Two short cream-colored sofas sat at right angles to each other at the corner of the living room area, with round glass tables between and in front of them. Behind the sofas, the windows beckoned. She crossed to the sofas, held up the tablet, snapped a panoramic photo of the Hong Kong Island skyline. The thousands of perfectly vertical skyscrapers racing heavenward looked like controlled explosions of concrete, glass, and steel, crowding every flat piece of earth between the glassy deep blue sea and the jagged green hills. Massive white and silver towers crowded right onto the lip of the land, erect and in seeming anticipation, like bathers standing on a beach waiting for the first person to jump in. Cruise ships looking as small as bathtub toys, junks, ferries, and pleasure craft skimmed the surface of Victoria Harbor as billowy clouds raced overhead with the speed of shoppers rushing a sale table on Li Yuen Street. Anticipation underscored everything in sight.

Grant took another photo, then immediately posted it to the Facebook page she used under an alias. Being serious about security, all of the information she provided to social media sites was bogus, and she never posted photos that showed her face. She smiled as she tagged the scenic photo: "Next time I'll get a room with a view!"

She sat on a sofa and logged into a special security app which presented her with a wide angle view of her hotel room. The clock radio on the round table between the sofas was a "spy cam" she traveled with. Grant knew that hotel room safes were not really 'safe.' Crooked hotel staff all over the world used master keys or override codes to plunder guests' valuables while they were out. It had happened to her once in Memphis. So she'd set up the secret video cam as a way to protect against such thefts. The device was motion-sens-

ing, and would ping her tablet computer whenever it was set off.
Grant watched the tablet screen and slowly moved the clock radio
until she had the exact view of the room she wanted.

A knock startled her. She hadn't asked for anything from the
hotel, so it had to be housekeeping. Grant crossed to the door and
opened it without looking through the peephole. A tall, bespectacled, blond-haired man in shorts and a khaki vest and carrying both a
fanny pack and backpack stepped in front of her. He looked vaguely
familiar. Brown eyes, broad shoulders and a jutting chin. She sensed
a quiet intensity and could almost feel an uneasiness coming from
inside him, even though he had the look of a hard man who could
take care of himself. He was good-looking in the genuinely rugged
way that soft, spoiled film stars try to look when they do an action
role. But his blond hair didn't look right somehow.

"Grant, it's been awhile."

"I'm sorry... have we met?" Her mind raced; did she know this
guy? Strangely, he maintained a neutral expression, like he wasn't
particularly happy to see her. She unconsciously tensed and gripped
the door a bit more tightly, closing it a few inches as she stood in
the opening. He had to be a hotel guest with an electronic key or he
wouldn't have been able to get to her floor.

"We worked together, remember?"

The voice! Pomona! The loss of the RQ-180! Hernandez! There
was no way she could hide the look of recognition—and fear—that
swept over her face. She couldn't think to speak, but stepped back as
she flung the door closed. Except it didn't close.

He lunged forward like a linebacker going after a star quarter-
back and pushed the heavy door open using his hands as battering
rams. The door flew open and caught her right arm, hurting it. She
spun around, but he charged into the room and quickly closed the
door behind him. She shot him a glance as she bolted toward the
desk in the living room. Her purse—and the pepper spray inside

it—was on the desk. So was a hotel phone. Scared beyond words, she made it to her purse and grabbed the pepper spray. As she fumbled to get the cap off, his large hand grabbed her wrist and squeezed.

He pressed behind her, against her back, so she slammed her left elbow into his ribs. Then again, as hard as she could. She struggled to twist free. Grant was no martial artist, but she'd taken a defensive tactics course for women. As he wrenched her right hand, causing her to drop the pepper spray, she lifted her left leg and drove her heel onto his left foot.

He grunted. She was about to scream, when he twisted her wrist into a painful compliance hold that caused her knees to buckle. Then he whispered into her ear, "This room might be bugged. So before we talk, we need to be on the safe side."

He paused, but kept her in the compliance hold. She decided to try and use her leg again, but he must have sensed this and pressed harder on her wrist. The pain flaring through her arm caused her to drop to her knees. As he stood over her exerting pressure on the wrist lock, she let out a small scream. Gritting her teeth, she looked up to find herself staring into the business end of a sound-suppressed Chinese-made semi-automatic handgun.

"Scream or make a move and you die," he whispered.

Breathe, remember to breathe. She fought panic, fought nausea creeping into her throat. Her mind raced as she took deep breaths, searching for an option as her eyes darted around the room.

"I'm going to let go," he said softly. "Try something, and I'll put a bullet in your brain. Then you'll never know why I came to talk. And believe me, at this point, I have nothing to lose by killing you."

Frightened out of her wits, she looked into his determined eyes. *My God, he's going to kill me because of what I did in Pomona on the drone operation!*

CHAPTER 4

15:15   Nicole Grant felt Ron Hernandez slowly ease his grasp and then release her. She tried to get a grip on the pure fear that vised like a clamp around her chest. Yes, she'd disobeyed orders during the drone op that he had supervised, but that was two years ago. Why was he in disguise? Why would he want to kill her? And what could she do right now to turn the tables on him? She worked to rub out the pain in her wrist, hand, and arm. He kept the gun leveled at her as he removed an electronic device from his backpack.

"White noise generator," he said.

She looked at the device as he placed it on the desk. The unit was used to mask a conversation in a room from listening devices. She'd seen them before and knew how easy it was to defeat the digital ones. A quick glance told her Hernandez was using an analog device, probably broadcasting a long loop of random white noise. The old technology was much harder to defeat. Thinking about technology and how it worked settled her a bit, grounded her into the form, structure, and safety of an engineer's reality, where life was ordered, cut and dried.

"This unit is good, but let's go into the bathroom to talk."

He gestured with his gun and backed away. She slowly stood up from the floor, mentally taking note of the fact that he hadn't noticed the clock radio was the type sold at "spy shops." *If you kill me, your face will be on every law enforcement watch list.*

He waved her forward with the gun, but the idea of going in there with him made her extra uneasy.

"Let's talk out here," she managed to say.

"Let's talk in the bathroom."

She shook her head. "No. Just shoot me. Shoot me right now. You try and drag me into the toilet and I will scream and bite and fight you to the end." She was finding her voice; at least she could get words out. Grant didn't think he would kill her. Maybe later, but not yet.

She watched his face closely as he seemed to weigh options. After a few seconds, he nodded. "Okay. Sit on the sofa."

She slowly moved to the sofa, furtively glancing around for something to use as a weapon. When she sat down, he pulled the upholstered chair away from the desk and turned it to face her.

He sat down heavily. He was a big, strapping fellow who somehow looked empty. Hollow. Like a man who wasn't even remotely in control of his destiny, not to mention the moment. As she stared at him she saw the fatigue, the dark circles under his eyes from lack of sleep. But talk about brooding intensity, Hernandez had it to spare.

Pomona. Udon Thani. Guangzhou. The repercussions of losing the RQ-180 drone over China had created an international incident that took months to die down and had put her through an emotional ringer. But that was two years ago. What could have happened to dredge up the past?

"You must be here about the drone op. I have honored my non-disclosure agreements. I've never said a word about the mission to anyone."

He looked at her like he saw right through her. "Really? You never did anything you weren't supposed to do?"

Crap, he knows about the audio file! And maybe about the other things, too.

• • • •

RON HERNANDEZ GLANCED out the windows and took in the view from Nicole Grant's hotel room. The beauty of the bay and low mountains usually fed his soul. But not today. Nothing about Hong Kong—one of his favorite cities on the planet—uplifted him today. He'd never felt this exhausted in his entire life. He hadn't slept for three days and carried a heavy burden of deep grief and painful guilt that was proving to be all-consuming. He'd barely escaped a hit team sent to kill him in D.C., had gone to ground, and had been on the run for ten days now. He sensed yet another adrenalin crash coming. Pulling an energy drink from the backpack, he downed it in a few gulps.

He was still alive, but had lost his life.

Hernandez closed his eyes for a moment and felt incredibly sad. He could kid himself, but his was a suicide mission. He'd fight until his last breath, but there was no reason to hope for survival. Not a defeatist attitude, just realistic. By coming to Hong Kong, he'd taken the fight to the enemy and that alone was a victory of sorts. He knew that any man unwilling to fight for what's right is already dead.

Grant stirred on the sofa, so he blinked his reddish eyes and looked her over. He hadn't remembered her being so pretty. About five-ten with nice legs and a firm butt. Her face was all soft contours and super-pale, impossibly creamy skin. And her eyes—green spotted with hazel. Hell, she looked like the kind of lady he'd enjoy cuddling up with, not that he thought he'd live long enough to ever cuddle with a woman again. As he studied her, he realized he hadn't remembered much about her at all, since he'd been so preoccupied during the drone operation. He put the gun on his lap. The next few minutes would determine whether he'd use it on her.

"Why are you here?" he asked.

"I'm the one who should be asking you that."

"Please answer the question."

"Who are you with? JSOC?CIA?"

He paused. "Christians in Action.Technically." Christians in Action, like the Company, or the Agency, was slang for the Central Intelligence Agency.

She furrowed her brow. "What does 'technically' mean?"

"It means if you're smart, you'll start answering questions instead of asking them."

She looked at him and took a breath. "I'm here on vacation, that's no secret. The Company doesn't need to send an operative to my room to ask me why I'm in Hong Kong."

"Kind of a coincidence, you being here right now," he said.

"Coincidence? I've been planning this trip for a year. I booked this room ten months ago. Check with the hotel if you don't believe me, I've made no secret about it. I didn't run here and go into hiding like Edward Snowden did, carrying four laptops full of classified information. I have no idea what coincidence you mean."

He hid his surprise. It'd be easy enough to confirm when she had booked the room. Regardless, it wasn't enough to prove her innocence. "Have you been in touch with any of the other people who worked the op out of Pomona?"

"I already told you that I've honored my non-disclosure—"

"Answer my question," he said sharply. "The non-disclosure forms you signed did not preclude you from having contact with the others. That's what I asked you. Have you had any contact?"

"No. None. Never," she said forcefully.

He watched as she wet her lips with her tongue. Her mouth was dry, she was nervous. There was a softness, a femininity about her that belied the toughness she'd shown him. It felt so much better to think about how Grant looked, than to think about what he might have to do.

"Hernandez, or whatever your name is. We lost the drone. That went public. Since the whole world knows there are no secrets from the American intelligence community, you must already know that I haven't been in touch with any of the others."

"People with your skill sets have ways to communicate that even the NSA geeks can't track. After all, you were an NSA geek," he said, matter-of-fact.

She lowered her head. He could see how scared she was, but that was too bad. "Look, Grant, you are your own lawyer in this little two-person kangaroo court. You might want to consider dropping the smart-mouth routine and make some forthcoming statements in an attempt to save your life."

"I'm sorry, but I'm scared." She paused, then, "Yes, I have skills, but I don't even know who the others were. I'd never met or worked with any of the other crew members before. I think you know that. I believe that was deliberate. I didn't fraternize with them because those were the orders. I mean, there were security cameras all over that warehouse we were in, so I just stayed in my own RV when I was off duty. Maybe you could check the videotape to confirm that, if it still exists. After the drone business, I got away from the NSA and all of that as fast as I could. My father always told me that the intelligence game was a dirty business."

"Your dad was right," he said, still not sure what to believe as he watched her closely. "Look, we don't have much time, but I have to search the room. Stay put on the sofa." He stood and dumped the contents of her purse onto the floor. He pocketed her cell phone and tablet computer and quickly examined the remaining items. He went through all the drawers and made a cursory search of the main room.

"Okay, into the bedroom," he said, gesturing with the gun.

"No, I said I would talk out here, and—"

Hernandez fired the pistol, putting a round into the sofa inches from her arm. The muffled gunshot wasn't loud enough to be heard outside the room, but Grant heard it loud and clear. She jumped with a start.

"We don't have time for this," he practically growled. "The next one goes into your heart. Your choice." He watched her swallow, then she slowly stood up on wobbly feet.

In the bedroom, Hernandez had her lie face down on the carpet as he searched the room. He found knockoff designer bags that had sticky notes attached: "Mom," "Grace," "Sandi," "Megan." He found similarly tagged inexpensive souvenirs from Japan and South Korea, and absolutely nothing incriminating. Her cell phone hadn't been used to make or receive any calls in Hong Kong, so he tossed it onto the bed. He checked her tablet computer and all of the photos she'd posted on her Facebook page. He frowned. No one traveling to make a secret rendezvous would post their location on Facebook, even if they used a social media alias. Her room looked like the room of a tourist on vacation.

"I'll be damned." He tossed her tablet on the bed next to her cell phone.

"No argument here," she said looking up at him defiantly.

"Answer one question honestly, then maybe we'll have a temporary truce. You used Darknet to send an audio file the night we lost the drone. What was it, where did it go?"

Her face fell. Not by much, but he saw it. If she denied it, he'd shoot her right now. "I'll explain that, but why is this just now coming up? Why wasn't I confronted with this before, or in the NSA investigation?"

"Because no one at Langley looked at the data very closely. The orders were to sweep it all under the rug. So I only figured out about a week ago that you'd done something very curious."

"Yes, I sent an audio file." She then explained how she had targeted the laser on the panel van to record the conversation inside, and how she'd sent it off. "You know how Darknet works. That audio file was broken into a thousand pieces and sent into the ether."

"Who has the key to retrieve the file?"

"Only me. I was trying to cover your butt. I thought it was important information that someone would want to listen to. You were on the phone, preoccupied."

"Your orders were to destroy everything." He pressed his lips together hard, biting back anger.

"I thought it was the right decision at the time," she said, meekly.

He exhaled, willing himself to calm down. His nerves were fried from lack of sleep so he had to work hard to control himself. "Did you listen to any of it, what you'd recorded?"

"No. I don't even know if the quality was any good. It might have been incomprehensible."

He knew the NSA was adept at filtering out non-verbal vibrations from such recordings and separating the wheat from the chaff. Grant was answering his questions, but she was holding back. Hiding something.

"That night as it went down, I was waiting to ask you about the audio file, to tell you what I'd been recording. But you were on the secure phone, meaning it was an important call, so I didn't interrupt you. Then when the pilot said he'd lost control of the drone, I kind of panicked and just sent it."

He digested her explanation with a neutral expression. "You retrieved that file?"

"No," she said emphatically. "I think you can imagine I was scared for my career. I didn't want to touch it. And you know how Darknet works. After about thirty days, if no one enters the key to request the file, all those thousands of pieces just kind of go away. Is that file I sent the reason you're here now?"

She was deflecting, and she was good at it. "Damn it, you disobeyed my orders."

"Yes, I did!" she snapped. "The orders of a traitor. You're the traitor, Hernandez, not me!" she practically shouted as her cheeks flushed and she drilled him with a contemptuous glare.

"Traitor?" He looked at her, taken aback by the accusation.

"I'm a lip reader. I saw what you said into the phone when the pilot confirmed the drone was in Chinese control. You said, 'Objective effected. They've got it.' The Chinese were supposed to get that drone. Wang Hongwei was supposed to get arrested. Your job was to see to it, right?"

"Traitor, huh?" His tone was not one of protest, but of resignation. Sadness clung to his words like stink on a rotting carcass. He thought back to the moment. Could Grant know what his true role had been? If she did, what should he do about it?

"So who is the guilty party here?" she demanded, as her hands shook. "Who should be getting a bullet in their brain?! The only thing I'm guilty of is running away from all of your dirty business."

He shook his head. "Well, you've got some balls, I'll say that. If I hadn't had a reason to kill you before, I do now," he said, leveling his pistol at her heart.

Grant looked like a terrified deer ready to bolt up from her prone position on the bedroom floor of her suite in the Conrad. It irritated the hell out of him that she thought he was a traitor, but the fact she believed that actually signaled her innocence. And if she were innocent, well, then he had a whole different set of problems.

After a moment, he lowered the gun and held up his hand. "I'm declaring a temporary truce. I need time to think." He stared off into space for several long seconds, and then pursed his lips. Grant had figured out what his mission had been on the drone operation, but that didn't worsen his already dire predicament. No, her knowledge of his true role didn't alter his disposition matrix. He'd kill her only if she was in bed with the Chinese, and that was now looking less likely.

"When did you leave on this trip... your departure from the States?"

"Seventeen days ago. One week in Japan, one week in Korea, and I've been here for three days. Check my passport, it's in the other room."

He didn't go for the passport, but retrieved her tablet computer from the bed and re-checked her Facebook page. He found her first posting from Japan—seventeen days ago. Grant had left on vacation before the killings in America had begun. That's why she was still alive, and that's why the hit team had been positioned on Tung Choi Street. She'd been the target today, not him.

"Damn, I almost wiped you on the street while you were shopping." He exhaled a sigh of relief. "For three reasons. Number one, the fact you'd secretly sent that audio file made you look like a spy—a mole for the Chinese is what I figured. Secondly, you're here in Hong Kong at Pacific Place the same time Zhao Yiren is here, also staying at Pacific Place. That's not the kind of coincidence I like."

Grant blanched. "Zhao Yiren is here!?"

"He's got a condo in the high rise across the way, right over there," said Hernandez, gesturing at the window. "With Wang Hongwei out of the picture, Zhao is a shoe-in to be elected president of China in two weeks."

She gawked out the window, obviously wracked with confusion. "But, what does that have to do with me? I've done nothing to—"

"The third reason is, you're still alive, which didn't make sense, unless you were working for Zhao." He stuck the gun in his waistband, and then offered his hand to help her up. "Sorry I had to put you though all of this. What say we go bust your mini-bar budget?"

She ignored his extended his hand and looked like she was about to burst into tears. She composed herself, stood up on her own, snatched her tablet from him and gathered her cell phone from the bed. She wouldn't look at him as she wiped at her eyes.

He felt bad for having put her through such a stressful ordeal and wanted to show her she had a lot to be grateful for. Beyond that, he needed to bring her up to speed if she was going to have a chance to live through this. "I've got something for you," he said, opening the drone surveillance video on his tablet computer and offering it to her. "It's a movie from your shopping trip today."

She turned away from him. "Not interested."

He grasped her shoulder and thrust the tablet into her hands. "You're going to watch this whether you want to or not. Because you need to understand." His eyes bore into her with an intensity that offered no compromise. He released his grip on her shoulder and moved toward the doorway, knowing there was a hotel phone in the bedroom and bathroom. He stopped at the door and turned to face her. Grant had become a different type of problem. He now felt a responsibility for her, but some mutual trust would make things a lot easier.

"Please watch the video. If you want to call the police or hotel security after you see it, all I ask is that you give me a five minute head start to get out of here."

She gave him a long hard look. "I want you to leave, so I'll watch your video. But then you get out," she said sharply.

Hernandez nodded and shuffled into the living room. He looked disassembled, like a Joan Miro painting where a person doesn't quite fit together right. He opened the mini-bar and took out two small bottles of Jack Daniels and a can of Coke. He poured bourbon and cola into a glass, used his index finger as a cocktail stir, and took a sip. He rubbed his eyes and then looked around the room, unhappily. Grant was a complication, but it felt good to save an innocent. And he needed some small victory right now to help him keep going. His thoughts drifted to his parents and his eyes misted. He immediately exiled these personal thoughts, shutting down all sentimental lines of thinking, an indulgence he couldn't afford. He glanced over to the windows.

Hong Kong.

He'd succeeded here before and he intended to do so again. A local man, his good friend Jaffir Khan was already assisting him. Probably not a good idea for Jaffir, but the man was loyal to the bone. With luck, and with Jaffir's technical assistance Hernandez hoped to land a big fish in the coming hours. In the meantime he'd attempt to contact William Snedeker once more. Maybe his old friend was somehow still alive. Hernandez checked his black-faced Suunto Core wristwatch, and that seemed to snap him alert. He threw back the rest of the drink.

"That woman with the red jacket was going to shoot me, wasn't she?" said Grant, in something of a bewildered daze as she moved into the main room from the bedroom while holding his tablet. "You saved my life."

He turned to face her. "Don't give me too much credit. It wasn't the original plan." He watched her closely now. If she fell apart and panicked, she'd be useless and he wouldn't be able to help her.

"You said the third reason you wanted to kill me was because I was still alive. Can you explain that?" She slowly moved into the room and sat on the sofa.

Good, she's thinking, she's engaged, trying to suss out the situation. "Oh, I almost forgot," he said, ignoring her question. "Don't talk to anybody who says they're from WikiLeaks. There are impostors floating around. There's a lot I still have to tell you."

"So tell me!" She sprung up from the sofa and crossed to face him. He saw that she'd gone from being scared to death he was going to kill her, to just being scared to death. Scared was okay, scared was normal.

He poured the other Jack Daniels and offered it to her. His mind raced as he calculated the rough draft of a course of action. "You don't trust me a hundred percent and I don't trust you a hundred percent, but we are in some deep kimchee, Grant. I can tell you that. Here, take a drink."

She accepted the glass, took a tentative sip, then coughed.

"Don't tell me," he said, "you're a non-drinker."

She shook her head. "Red wine."

"We'll have one together at the Marriott." He checked his watch again. "Meet me there at four. That's fifteen minutes from now. Disguise yourself. Put your essentials into one bag and bring it with you. Leave everything else."

He moved toward the door, then turned to her. "As a good faith gesture, and to generate a little trust between us, I'll tell you this: yes, my orders were to make sure China got that drone, and that Zhao Yiren got credit for stealing it. I hated like hell to do it, but I followed my orders. And that was the biggest mistake of my life." He saw the confusion written on her face. "Four o'clock, don't be late. I'll explain everything."

"Wait! Shouldn't we stay together?" she asked, in a tone verging on panic.

"We've got to move you to a safe place, but I have something to do right now and you can't tag along. The Chinese will come for you, so be out of here in five minutes. Three would be better. Here—" He fished out a stack of hundred-dollar bills from his backpack and pressed them into her hands. "Five thousand dollars of 'Just in Case' cash."

Hernandez checked the peephole. "Avoid the lobby. Make your way down to the shopping mall and then cross over to the Marriott Tower. There's a small wine bar off Q88. We'll meet there."

"Can't we call the U.S. Consulate and—"

"Oh, hell no. Don't even think about doing that. Don't talk with *anyone*. Don't answer the phone, don't open the door. Be out of here in three minutes, okay?"

"Okay." Grant nodded, but she didn't look okay, she looked ready to come unglued. Before he could take a step, she darted in front of him and blocked the door. They stood just inches apart and she took one of his hands in hers. "You're not leaving until you explain the third reason why you wanted to kill me. You said it was because I was still alive. What does that mean?"

He looked into her exotic green eyes, saw her intelligence, her steely determination. He decided on the spot he'd do everything he could to help her. After the briefest of moments, his countenance softened. He hadn't wanted to tell her this until later, but maybe there wouldn't be a 'later.'

"Everyone's dead but us," he said in a cottony whisper. "There were twenty personnel staying in that warehouse in Pomona. Myself, four security contractors, and three shifts of five crew members. In the last two weeks, the other eighteen died from poisonings, a carjacking, an 'accidental' fall, armed robbery, car accidents, a home invasion, a freak explosion, 'suicide', and outright murder." He reached into a pocket and handed her a USB flash drive. "All documented on this."

She swallowed, as if trying to take in the magnitude of his words. She hesitated, then took the flash drive.

"Why?"

"Because dead men tell no tales."

He watched her eyes flash as the heavy realization hit her. "Someone wanted to go public about the drone," she said in barely a whisper.

He nodded. "It wasn't me. But a couple of days ago, I did approach WikiLeaks in London to hedge my bets. So I've got good news and bad news. Good news is, I'm not going to kill you. I believe you're one of the good guys. The bad news is: the Chinese government and the United States government have sanctioned my assassination. And yours, too."

Nicole's mouth opened, but no words came out.

"Three minutes, Grant, because, trust me, they're coming for us."

CHAPTER 5

15:36 Seven million people call Hong Kong, Special Administrative Region, People's Republic of China, home. The city isn't choked with high-rises because they're fun to live and work in, but because there isn't enough land. So when the Hong Kong Convention and Exhibition Center decided to expand, there was no choice but to "create" land from Victoria Harbor. In four short years, the ever-busy Cantonese built an artificial island and completed the ultra-modern, light and airy expansion project. Now, the six-story Convention Center with breathtaking views of the water boasted five exhibition halls, two convention halls, theaters, and over 50 meeting rooms. Convention centers were, after all, about business, and the Hong Kong Chinese had sharply-honed skills in the fine art of generating cash.

Kate Rice, CEO of the hugely successful children's charity Kids First, also knew a little something about generating cash. Her charity's big annual fundraiser was being held in Hong Kong this year, and she and her staff utilized the Convention Center's ample facilities and amenities to their fullest. Rice saw herself as more business-woman than humanitarian, but kept Kids First focused on the basics: providing food, medicine, and shelter to at-risk children in at-risk places, mostly in the war-torn corners of the world.

A classically attractive, big-busted blue-eyed blonde in her late thirties, her straw-colored hair was pulled back into her trademark French braid. Rice filled out a designer business suit better than most. Her skirt hem was higher above the knees than many women her age, all the better to showcase her gorgeous legs. She knew all too well that her job was to get gobs of money handed to her, and sales, err, "donations" always went better with a little sexed-up interplay mixed in, charity or not.

She'd become something of a cult figure after YouTube videos surfaced of her shouting down warlords and even Islamic militants in order to get supply convoys through armed checkpoints or blockades and into camps housing children who'd fled the ravages of war, hunger, or worse. Her sex appeal and chutzpah sent Hollywood flocking to her door wanting to do a biopic. Corporate donors and sponsors had lined up, from Google and Sony and Huawei to Nokia and Daimler and PetroChina.

Kids First now had over 80 offices around the world in 60 countries. Operations expanded exponentially during the last few years. Over 10,000 attendees were expected for the conference, which featured celebrity guest speakers, documentary screenings, seminars, panels, and for Rice, lots of private meetings with heavy-hitter donors. Twenty kids who had essentially been saved thanks to efforts of Kids First would be hosting an Ice Cream Social later today, and there wouldn't be a dry eye or a closed wallet in the house. Over $100 million dollars was the conservative goal for the long weekend's take. The long weekend being Saturday through Tuesday.

This being Sunday, she was in the middle of the madness. If she could clone ten more Kate Rices, the event might be manageable. Three female assistants stood nearby, each holding multiple cell phones with calls on hold. She reached for a phone held by one of her assistants, but never got the phone.

Socorro Trujillo, a tall, twenty-something mix of Native-American and Hispanic stood erect in a well-tailored gray silk pantsuit as she thrust a business card into Rice's face. Slender but physically fit, she had a hooked nose that somehow added to her exotic beauty, like some kind of edgy, darkly sensual temptress. Trujillo's vibe was all business, and her black, soulless eyes suggested a latent menace.

Rice looked at the card and her mood darkened for a moment. She'd never met Trujillo before, but she knew who the business card belonged to.

"Where?" asked Rice.

"Grand Hyatt, same as you. He's waiting."

The Grand Hyatt and other hotels conveniently connected to the Convention Center via a spider web of overhead pedestrian walkways and passageways. For that matter, a person could practically walk across Hong Kong Island without ever having their feet touch the ground, not that it was any less crowded on the hundreds of overhead walkways.

Rice turned to the assistant holding the phone. "I'll be back in twenty minutes. Stall everything and everybody till I get back. If there's a crisis, attack, but never retreat," she said, smiling.

As she walked off with Trujillo, Rice's smile morphed into a scowl of frustration and her eyes betrayed a flicker of worry. *Damn. How hard can it be to kill two people?*

• • • •

THE AREA IN HONG KONG between Wan Chai and Central was previously the site of British military barracks and dockyards. It wasn't until the 1970s that the Brits turned the land over to the Hong Kong government, allowing the local Cantonese to do what they do so well: develop, build, and promote commerce. The area became known as Admiralty, and in the 1980s, Swire Group embarked on an ambitious project off Queensway near the High Court building to construct a massive, inter-connected, upscale complex with four sleek, architecturally distinct high-rise towers that featured shopping, dining and entertainment, office space, serviced apartments, and high-end hotels.

The tenant list for office space read like a who's who of global financial giants, investment houses, and professional services, with names like the World Bank, Deloitte, Moody's, Sotheby's, Baker and McKenzie, Daiwa, Northern Trust, CLSA, and Friends Provident among many others. Four hotels—incredibly, each one with a five-star rating—occupied gleaming high-rise towers. An ultra-fashion-able three-level shopping experience was the foundation that held Pacific Place together. This glamorous city-within-a-city was inter-connected both above and below ground.

The place oozed sophistication, and yet, two Chinese men who could never be accused of being cosmopolitan, sat in the back seat of a black Mercedes S-600 in the car park below the mall and plotted to bring to the gentile environs the kind of trouble Pacific Place had never seen.

Major General Ma Ju, Director of the much-feared Second De-partment, People's Liberation Army General Staff Department, nev-er did fill out a business suit very well, and he knew it. Even custom-fitted, expensive silk ones. Perhaps it was due to his poor posture and pot belly, which tended to rumple his look, whether standing or sitting. His medium-length dark brown hair was parted on one side, combed the same way since his youth, and he saw no reason to change. Like most Asian men, he used hair dye to cover the gray, but liver spots betrayed his sixty-four-year age. The wrinkles around his eyes tended to make him look like he was always squinting. Maybe he was.

He'd certainly seen enough during his rise to the top rank of Chi-nese military intelligence. The Second Department, which he ruled with an iron fist, sent highly trained undercover operatives overseas to overtly and covertly obtain military intelligence; Ma fielded excel-lent spies abroad. He was responsible for all of China's military at-taches worldwide; for a massive intelligence analysis bureaucracy; for a scientific directorate that included research and design; for the Bu-reau of Confidential Work, and importantly, the Bureau of Security, a unit that kept close watch on all of the other PLA general depart-ments and on members of the Central Military Commission. Gen-eral Ma stood at the top of a very impressive heap.

His career track wove inexorably with that of his old friend and former Beijing #4 High School and Peking University classmate, Vice Premier Zhao Yiren, the man poised to become the next president of China in a couple of weeks.

General Ma sat slouched in the backseat of his Mercedes listening to the report from MSS, Ministry of State Security, Director of Special Projects Tang Jie, the same bespectacled man in the brown shirt that Ron Hernandez had spotted on Tung Choi Street. Special Projects was a euphemism for assassination, and Zhao Yiren and General Ma had been using Director Tang in that capacity successfully for over fifteen years. But now, with so much riding on the outcome, something had gone wrong, and right here in their backyard. The situation made Ma squint a little tighter as he listened to Tang. The general was peeved, and he'd be damned if he'd let a screw-up ruin everything at this late stage of the game.

"We'll kill them both easily enough. They can't hide from us in Hong Kong," said Director Tang.

"Is the American woman in her room?" asked Ma, impatiently.

"Yes."

"Then kill her right now. Send people to her room, kill her, and remove all of her electronics."

Tang shifted a bit and tugged at his earlobe, displaying slight discomfort with the suggestion. "We could do that, but the hotel security video—"

"Have someone take care of that immediately in such a way that won't reflect back toward us."

"Very well," said Tang, in a way that suggested he didn't agree with the order. "The murder of an American tourist in a five-star hotel will become high-profile."

"Not any more than two dead agents on a tourist shopping street!"

"It will never become public knowledge that my two dead operators were Chinese agents," countered Tang, without rancor.

"You had better hope not," snapped General Ma.

Tang wasn't a military man and worked for MSS, so he wasn't technically under Ma's command. The arrangement had worked okay for years, but Ma now wished he'd used killers from the Second Department instead of Tang's people. Even during all of the killings in America, the director had begun showing too many signs of obstinacy.

"I have to contact Wheeler and Roberts to get their approval," said Tang.

"I'll take care of the CIA. I want our two targets dead. Now."

But Tang wasn't agreeing so easily. "The protocol is that the CIA has to approve before we kill an American. Those are my orders. An American team is to observe and document the kill, just as they did during the previous eighteen kills in America."

"I'm giving you new orders from Zhao himself! Shall I tell him you refuse to obey?"

Tang stared back blankly.

"Believe me," said Ma, "the American government wants these two dead just as much as we do. And you don't have to worry about collateral damage if you kill her in her hotel room. Now get going, I've got to finish with damage control over the mess you made in Kowloon." Ma looked away from Tang and turned his attention to a smartphone.

Tang was a thin forty-eight year-old with short salt-and-pepper hair, a long curved nose, eyeglasses, and full lips that seldom parted because he usually maintained a neutral expression. He was hard to read. Ma knew that whenever Tang yelled, pretending to lose his temper, it was a tactic; a tactic rarely used. The General could tell that Tang didn't like this turn of events, but that was just too bad.

Tang said nothing as he got out of the luxury sedan. General Ma pretended not to look, but he closely regarded the man who'd been Zhao's primary henchman for many years. Tang's earlobes looked like they'd been pinched off, and he had a habit of tugging on them as if trying to make them longer. A brutal killer since the age of sixteen, he moved like a cat as he walked a few steps toward an entrance to Pacific Place. Two of his men stood waiting just inside the glass doors and opened them for him. Tang hesitated and then pushed his glasses up on his nose as he turned to look back toward the Mercedes.

General Ma knew he was invisible behind the deeply tinted windows as Tang stared at him. And he knew without question he could no longer trust the man, which was a huge problem. Especially today. Today of all days.

• • • •

KATE RICE IMMEDIATELY calculated that Barry Bergman's Grand Hyatt suite had a 270 degree view of Hong Kong, while her suite only had a 180 degree view. The muted earth tones and clean lines of the interior design were possibly intended so as not to detract from the amazing vistas looking across the busy harbor toward Kowloon. She glanced over at Socorro Trujillo, Bergman's pretty assistant whom she pegged as a "full-service" aide, since a quick look into the bedroom had revealed rumpled sheets and two empty champagne glasses on the nightstand. Rice held little respect for a factotum like Bergman, even if he did have the president's trust.

"Still wasting the taxpayer's money, I see, Barry," said Rice, with a tone bordering on contempt. She'd shifted into offensive mode right off the bat, hoping to keep Bergman on his heels.

Barry Bergman, a paunchy, 55 year-old, was a Senior White House Security Adviser. A loyal hatchet man who always kept his mouth shut, he'd served a number of administrations and was known as a ruthless fixer who didn't mind getting his hands dirty.

His jowls shook like Jell-O as he munched from a plate of room service appetizers sitting atop the square coffee table. An oily sheen coated his face and his jaw seemed permanently set into a mask of displeasure. Bergman inclined his head toward the door and said, "Ms. Trujillo, could you leave us, please?"

Trujillo smiled an inscrutable smile and left the suite. As the door closed behind her, Barry stuffed a Cajun shrimp into his mouth. "We're not liking what we're hearing," he said as he chewed.

Rice leaned back against a mahogany desk and coolly regarded him. "Then listen to me and you'll like what you hear. Everything's under control. Two targets remain out of twenty. Now I know you didn't fly all the way to Hong Kong just to get sack time with your Mexican bitch. Nor did you come here to micromanage me, not that you could. So tell your boss we're almost there."

"The president is your boss, too," he said, ignoring the insults.

"This room has been swept?"

Barry nodded.

"Still, perhaps you shouldn't mention be invoking the president's name in this conversation. So here's where we're at as of thirty minutes ago. Grant and Hernandez are in the Pacific Place complex. Taking them out will be fairly straightforward. I'll admit its bad luck that they're here at the same time as me and Zhao Yiren, but that doesn't change anything. Grant was scheduled to be terminated in Phoenix, but the Chinese didn't realize she'd gone on vacation. So a decision was made to eliminate the rest of the US-based targets, and then wipe her while she was on holiday in Asia.

"As for Hernandez," continued Rice, now feeling firmly in control, "we all know that someone tipped him." She crossed to a service cart and poured herself a glass of expensive Bordeaux. "I've just learned that Hernandez' guardian angel is William Snedeker, a retired CIA officer. We've detained Snedeker at a secure location so we'll learn everything he knows shortly, but you should be focused on making sure everybody in D.C. keeps their mouths shut and not on second-guessing my actions in the field."

"It doesn't appear to me you're in the field, Agent Rice."

Rice knew Bergman's type only too well. He'd be the type of supervisor who would never give a kind word. You could perform well on a hundred missions and he wouldn't say a thing. But make one mistake and you'd never hear the end of it.

"I'm not an agent, I'm a CIA *officer,* Barry. Working under non-official cover. And after years of hard work, I'm about to deliver a golden goose. A CIA asset—*my asset*—will be elected president of China two weeks from now. Get something right for a change and focus on the positive."

"You don't appear to be fully involved in—"

"You want me to throw my cover down the toilet to go operational?" she snapped. "We have Chinese goons here for that.My instructions were to keep CIA involvement to an absolute minimum. Are you authorizing me to bring in Agency resources to hunt for and kill Hernandez and Grant?"

Bergman hesitated. "No, I'm not."

Rice nodded. "Then be reasonable in what you expect from me. I'm in the middle of hosting a frigging mega-conference. Zhao himself is one of the guests of honor at a private reception I'm hosting at the Shangri-La tonight. I'm so busy, I barely have time to use the toilet. Anyway, the Chinese don't need me or anyone else telling them how to kill people, they've been practicing for thousands of years."

"I'm well aware that it's the Chinese doing all of the dirty work, and that we have merely acted as observers, but I'm concerned that Hernandez and Grant are now working together," he said, nonplussed.

"Highly unlikely." Beeps signaling incoming text messages bombarded her smartphone. She took a healthy gulp of the red wine. "Unless they just formed an alliance."

"Open your eyes," said Bergman, wiping his greasy hands on a small napkin. "They're both at the same complex where Zhao has a condo, and they're here at the same time Zhao is present at that condo. That's not coincidence, sweetie. You'd better find out what Grant and Hernandez are up to."

"Call me sweetie again and I'll rip off your nose." Rice delivered the line in an offhand manner as she read through text messages, but her tone suggested she meant exactly what she said.

Bergman remained stoic. "That wouldn't be a good career move for you. *Officer* Rice."

They locked eyes. She could see he wasn't intimidated by her any more than she was intimidated by him. "Grant made her hotel reservation almost a year ago, but Zhao committed to come to the conference about three months ago. So, yes, it's a coincidence. But I agree that Hernandez is no coincidence. I suspect he knows Zhao's schedule and that he came here to kill him."

Bergman tapped his fingers together as he digested that tidbit. He belched, then, "So Hernandez knows the whole picture and this retired CIA guy Snedeker who helped Hernandez knows the whole picture. And Grant?"

"Yesterday I would have said 'no,' but like I said, they might have just teamed up. Hernandez could have figured out that she was the only other Omega Team member left alive. He must need her for something," said Rice.

"When I ask myself what role she could play for Hernandez, the answer is: to provide documentary proof and testimony. Two Omega Team members going to WikiLeaks, with each possibly having their own evidential input is much more powerful than a single whistle-blower."

"The WikiLeaks reporter in London was terminated." Rice slipped her phone back into her purse.

"I would have thought you'd be considering the bigger picture in that regard," said Bergman, selecting another shrimp with the practiced scrutiny of a diamond merchant choosing a stone.

Rice hated yielding initiative to Bergman, but she didn't understand what he was referring to. She wasn't about to ask him to elaborate, so she stepped closer and sat on the arm of a sofa. Her tan, perfectly proportioned legs angled toward him, like levers waiting to be thrown that were just out of his reach. She crossed her legs and the hem of her skirt rode dangerously high on her thighs. The undercurrent of her sexuality while appearing perfectly at ease, as if Bergman were inconsequential, was designed to nullify his advantage. She kept her gaze focused on a painting across the room, kept quiet, and kept a blank expression.

He ignored her legs and scowled. "You can't take WikiLeaks out of the picture by killing a reporter or two."

Prick. Just say what you want to say.

"Hernandez and Grant could simply e-mail what they have, they don't need some reporter as a middleman. We need to co-opt WikiLeaks itself."

Rice put her index finger to her mouth and chewed on the nail. It was a bad habit she indulged in when she got excited. "Maybe," she said, noncommittally. "What's the play?"

"Julian Assange," said Bergman, as if it were only too obvious. "Wanted by the Swedes and by us, he was given political asylum, but has been a virtual prisoner in the Ecuadoran embassy in London for years now. There's been some back-channel back-and-forth. The man wants his freedom back. I'm confident we can do some simple horse-trading with him and his organization."

"I thought he lost control of WikiLeaks."

"We don't think so. We'll ask them to forget about certain secrets and destroy all evidence."

"And we sort of unofficially lose interest in him."

"Something like that."

She uncrossed her legs. "That needs to fly yesterday. I mean right now."

Bergman nodded. "Now what about this computer of Grant's that the Chinese are so concerned about?"

"It was her home laptop back in Phoenix. The Chinese have it, she doesn't, so I'm not worried. Shoot-on-sight orders are out on both of them. They'll be dead within hours."

"Big talk is cheap. I'm looking for results."

Rice had heard enough. Time to take the initiative back. She stood and opened her purse. "From a big girl who walks her talk." She retrieved the smartphone. "Barry, I'm busy. Just eat your shrimp and leave the heavy lifting to me." She crossed toward the door, then stopped and turned back to him. "Better yet, go back to bed with your hooker assistant. I should have good news before you climax. Well, maybe not *that* fast."

She turned to leave, but before she got the door open, Bergman called out sharply. "Rice!" She stopped, but didn't face him. "Kids First is an excellent espionage platform, but questions have arisen regarding certain unsanctioned actions you have taken during your... 'quest' to have Zhao elected president Be advised: the president and I are in agreement that you are treading on very thin ice."

Rice flung open the door then slammed it closed behind her.

CHAPTER 6

15$^{:48}$ Fighting mightily to control the nervousness that washed over her like an unrelenting monsoon, Nicole Grant looked like a Muslim bag lady as she stepped onto the deeply padded carpeting of the hallway outside her room in the ultra-plush Conrad. She wore bone-colored silk slacks, a white linen blouse, and a pink headscarf covering her head like a *hijab*. She'd taken Ron Hernandez' warning seriously and had gathered up her essentials in under three minutes.

Today being Sunday, tens of thousands of Philippine and Indonesian *amahs*—a female employed to clean, cook, and look after children—had their day off, and clogged the streets in Hong Kong. Since the Indonesian *amahs* were mostly Muslim, Sunday meant a preponderance of *hijabs* could be seen all over town. Nicole had noticed that on her shopping excursion to Kowloon.

So she kept her head low toting her possessions in the new fake Celine bag she'd just bought, and she had countless other items stuffed into three shopping bags she carried. With clammy hands and tightness in her chest, she made her way to the end of the hallway and stepped through a door into the stairwell, knowing she had precious little time to get to the wine bar in the Marriott. She descended two levels, and then took an elevator down to the Lower Level where the Grand Ballroom and other meeting rooms were located. Just as she was breathing a bit easier, the elevator doors opened, shocking her with the sights and sounds of a massive gathering, predominantly male, predominantly attired in Savile Row three-piece suits, and predominantly displaying a lot of self-importance.

It all seemed so incongruous. She was running for her life but had just stumbled into a moneyed business reception hosted by Credit Suisse. Her displeasure faded quickly, since a packed hotel would make it harder for anyone to find her, much less do something to her. *Wait a second; Bill Clinton is in the hotel, staying in the Presidential Suite!* She'd heard about it when she checked in. Even though Clinton was a former president, he had a Secret Service detail. She began to feel silly hiding under the *hijab*. How could anyone hurt her in here? She was about to remove the headscarf when she noticed two Asian men in suits staring at her. She quickly looked away and swallowed hard. Had they recognized her? Were they staring because she looked out of place? Maybe they were reacting to the stereotype of a Muslim suicide bomber.

Nicole started breathing rapidly and broke out into a cold sweat. She forced herself to smile, and took a few steps to her right. She chanced a glance back to the two Asian men, and they were now shaking hands with several tall Caucasian men as they prepared to exchange business cards.

Nicole exhaled. She was being paranoid. But she then noticed a dome-like overhead security camera. Paranoid or not, better to err on the side of caution, so she put her head down and cut through the gathering of wolves toward a staff exit. After walking through a set of steel double-doors, her confidence grew, and she blazed a trail along cement-walled passageways, navigated a set of employee stairs, and then popped out through an employee entrance right onto the third floor of Pacific Place Mall.

The spacious mall never felt crowded like the sidewalks and MTR stations. No one invaded your body space or used sharp elbows to beat you to a ticket machine. Grant walked along at what felt like a casual pace toward the Marriott as the catchy rhythm of a World Beat tune played from hidden speakers. She suddenly felt exposed and naked, like some obvious fraud in the open spaces of the shopping mecca.

Were killers really after her? Could this all somehow be a cruel hoax, was she being punked by members of the intelligence community for some reason, maybe to re-recruit her? God only knew. Nicole felt angry, confused, and scared. She was slightly sick to her stomach with anxiety. She needed to check the flash drive Hernandez gave her, so she ran a fashion gauntlet, passing Chanel, Fendi, Celine, Gucci, Chloe, Lora Piana, Botega Veneta, a. testoni, and Salvatore Ferragamo, all selling the real deal at prices that were *tres cher*. Quite a switch from her earlier excursion this afternoon.

In a beautifully appointed ladies room rich with huge mirrors and blonde wood carved to create an undulating effect, she dumped the *hijab* into one of her shopping bags and donned a cotton mask, the kind commonly worn in public by Asians when they have a cold. She added a red St. Louis Cardinals baseball cap and in seconds was back out on the mall floor. An overhead sign indicated the entrance to the JW Marriott Hotel down a small corridor. With a sigh of slight relief, Nicole hurried along the corridor. No one appeared to be the least bit interested in her, unless she was being clocked by the security cameras.

Hernandez had said to meet in fifteen minutes, but she was running late. A glass of wine sounded like a pretty good idea, and if his flash drive contained what he said it did, she'd need more than one glass. A physical pang of fear suddenly gripped her; not only was her vacation in ruins, but her perhaps her life as well.

• • • •

THE SPECTACULAR MARRIOTT lobby opened downward toward The Lounge and upward toward dining options and the Q88 Wine Bar. A massive two-story glass curtain provided phenomenal views of the Hong Kong skyline, giving the impression that the entire lobby area, several stories above the traffic on Queensway, was floating in the sky. Often rooms with a lot of glass have a cool feel, but the lobby's golden color scheme lent warmth that felt inviting to Nicole and made her actually gawk for a few moments. At least that was the internal excuse she used as she paused to regulate her breathing and collect her thoughts.

But she couldn't shake the newfound anxiety that bordered on panic. She needed to speak with Hernandez and get more information. All problems have solutions and with his help she intended to find one. They needed a plan, a logical, coherent plan. Then they could fix things.

She'd already removed the baseball cap and cotton mask before entering the lobby, so she willed herself to get on with it and climbed the marble staircase. Within moments she found herself in Q88. It was a large wood-paneled room with glass and metal wall sconces, leather club chairs and banquettes. Two dozen patrons were quietly drinking as a combo on a small raised stage played mellow strains of a John Coltrane jazz standard.

It was four minutes past four o'clock and Hernandez wasn't present. The beautiful room didn't seem like the kind of place he'd choose for the serious talk they needed to have. Then she remembered he said "small" wine bar—this place was not small.

She spotted an entrance to Riedel Room @ Q88, and entered a darker, somewhat narrow and winding space. Polished hardwoods blended the look of traditional Chinese furniture with a modern feel. A couple sat in hushed conversation at a candlelit table, and a young woman slouched in a corner working on a tablet computer. Hernandez must be running late, thought Nicole.

A *sommelier*, not a bartender, tended the room. This intimate space was geared for serious wine drinkers or wine tastings and featured expensive Riedel stemware. It wasn't a place to just order a glass of wine, so Nicole splurged on a nice bottle of Bordeaux and asked for two glasses.

Until the age of twelve, Grant had been a military brat. While the family was stationed at Aviano Air Base in Italy, she'd gotten into the habit of drinking red wine, as most Italian children do. Her father was essentially fired by the air force—he wasn't allowed to re-en-list—and that's when the family moved to northern Nevada, where her dad promptly sank them into debt with pie-in-the-sky prospect-ing endeavors. How did she get from there to sitting in some rich man's wine cave in Hong Kong with killers on her tail?

The *sommelier* returned with the bottle of Bordeaux.

"May I sit in the private room? I'm expecting a friend."

"Yes, miss. The room isn't reserved, so you may have it."

Nicole moved into the tiny, swank space that could only hold about six people. The entire ceiling was a glowing light fixture of dan-gling crystals and featured banquette seating along three walls with a rectangular cocktail table in the center. She asked for the door to be left open since she didn't want to miss Hernandez, but she scrunched herself into a corner so she couldn't easily be seen by any passers-by. She connected her tablet computer to the free Marriott Wi-Fi, but used a VPN—virtual private network—to keep her Web surfing pri-vate.

After the serving ritual, Nicole sat alone. She tried to savor a few sips of the wine, but her taste buds weren't working. Probably from fear. She took a long quaff, hoping it would calm her down, and then retrieved the flash drive Hernandez had given her. She retrieved a vel-vet pouch from her fake Celine bag and dumped the contents: mi-cro- mini- and regular-sized SD cards, adapters, connectors, short ca-bles, memory sticks, SIM cards, batteries, an external power supply, and earbuds. She plugged the flash drive into an adapter which she then connected to her tablet.

The first file was titled: Berns, Frank David. She found a short dossier indicating Berns was a master sergeant in Task Force Orange, a super-secret military unit that operated under JSOC. He special-ized in communication intercepts often conducted in extremely haz-ardous conditions. He had a wife and two young children in Fort Belvoir, Virginia. A newspaper article indicated he died in a one-car crash seven days earlier on U.S. Route 1, just a few miles from his home. No use of alcohol or drugs was suspected as being the cause of the accident. He was thirty-one.

Tears came to Nicole's eyes and she bit her upper lip. She had seventeen more files to look at. She vaguely remembered Frank David Berns. He'd worked a different shift than her at the Pomona warehouse, so she only saw him briefly at shift changes. She remembered he'd always been smiling. And the people who'd killed him had almost killed her earlier this afternoon. She scanned the bar again; had they gotten Hernandez?

Grant fought her anxiousness and had gotten through five more files when her tablet computer pinged. It was the alarm from the motion-sensing clock-radio in her hotel room. Her hands trembled as she opened the security camera app. What she saw almost made her heart stop. Four armed Chinese, three men and a woman, were searching her room at the Conrad. How did they get in? Who were they?

Grant's stomach muscles tightened. If Hernandez hadn't gotten her out of the room, she'd be dead. Her head was spinning, but not from the wine. Should she call the front desk at the Conrad? Hong Kong police? Should she...?

God help me. Help me think. The files had been depressing. And sad.Unbelievably sad because each case was so much more than just the murder of a person, an innocent person, no less. It was the destruction of a family unit. Young children lost fathers. Mothers lost daughters. Wives lost husbands.

Where was Hernandez? Why couldn't they have just left her room together, why'd he have to run off like that? He'd told the truth, they were the only two left alive from the drone op team in Pomona. And here she was sitting with no disguise because she'd fooled herself into thinking she was safe.

"You look like you could use a drink."

Startled, Nicole looked up. It was the young woman who'd been sitting by herself, writing on a tablet computer with a stylus. An olive-skinned brunette with full lips, a slightly large nose, and who couldn't be a day over twenty-two, stood in the open doorway. Her wavy brown hair was pulled straight back from her face. Finely arched eyebrows tented big brown eyes that radiated youthful energy, confidence and intelligence. She wasn't smiling, but somehow her eyes made it seem that she was. Her accent sounded British, but her exotic looks suggested some other ethnicity.

Nicole was still reeling, but had to fake it. "I already have a drink, thanks," she said as she turned off the tablet screen.

"That's what I mean. You've got a nice bottle of red but you look totally stressed."

Nicole forced a smile but didn't say anything.

"I think I've been stood up," confessed the young woman, whose eyes darted to the second empty glass on the table next to Nicole's glass.

"My friend is running late," said Nicole in response to the unasked question.

"Then we have something in common. Two things, since we both like red wine."

It suddenly occurred to Nicole that sitting with the pretty young lady might not be a bad idea, since the killers wouldn't be looking for two females together. Years ago she'd read a few books on espionage and remembered that in the spy business it was known as having a "beard." Since it would draw attention to put the headscarf or ball cap back on, the only other disguise she had right now was this young woman.

"You're welcome to have a seat until my friend arrives," said Grant.

The girl sat down smiling. She lifted her glass, which was about a quarter full. "Well cheers, then. I'm Rena Musaad."

"Nicole—" Nicole quickly stopped herself, smiling. "Nicky. Nicky Johnson."

They clinked glasses and drank. Having just made the mistake of revealing her first name, Nicole decided her chat with Rena would be an exercise in the careful parsing of words. "You're too pretty to have been stood up. How long have you been waiting?" asked Nicole. Focusing on talking with Rena made her feel a bit better by getting her mind engaged in something other than abject fear. She quickly calculated that she'd wait for Hernandez until five o'clock. If he didn't show by then, she'd call her old boss Ernest Normann at NSA and enlist his help. There had to be a way out of this.

"Oh, I haven't been waiting long," said Rena, checking her watch. "About twenty-three hours now."

"What? You're joking."

"No, I'm not. I was supposed to meet a gentleman here yesterday. He's not answering my messages."

"Sorry. Not my business to ask," said Nicole.

"It's okay, I don't mind. It was a business meeting, not a romantic one."

Nicole nodded distractedly, working to keep up the patter. "So why keep waiting here?"

"Nowhere else to go."

"This is Hong Kong. There are lots of places to go," said Nicole.

"I'm trying to stay focused. It was an important meeting."

Nicole nodded even though she didn't understand. She suddenly felt a pang of suspicion about Miss Rena Musaad. "Your accent sounds British but you're so exotic-looking."

"Well, thank you."

"And Musaad is what, Middle-Eastern?" Nicole fidgeted and then absentmindedly wiped her sweaty hands on her slacks.

"Egyptian. I'm a Coptic Christian. Fortunately, my father sent me to boarding school in England when I was fourteen. I've been in London ever since. Cairo's not such a safe place to be these days."

Nicole nodded politely, trying to listen over the roar of thoughts that refused to die down inside her head. She'd keep chatting with the woman and establish a rapport. If Hernandez didn't show perhaps she could use Rena to help her get clear of Pacific Place.

"What about you? Here on business?" asked Rena.

"Um, yes. A few more meetings and then back to... St. Louis."

Rena smiled as she took in the sight of Nicole's SD cards, adapters, cables, and other accessories. "A Girl Scout were you? Looks like you're ready for anything."

"It's called life in the digital world. I travel with what I might need." Aware that Rena was watching, she tried to appear calm as she unplugged the adapter from her tablet and dropped it and Hernandez's thumb drive into her purse. "I saw you writing in longhand on your computer using a stylus."

"I'm a writer. Well, at least I'm working at it. I haven't gotten a by-line yet."

Nicole stiffened a bit. "You're a journalist?"

"That's my dream, but I work as a researcher."

Just as Nicole was forming a response, a soft knocking sound interrupted them. The *sommelier* entered the private room holding a smartphone.

"Excuse me, are either of you ladies Nicole Grant?"

Nicole failed to hide her surprise. Was that a question she should even answer in front of the Egyptian? She and Rena exchanged looks. "Why do you ask?" asked Nicole. "Is there a phone call?"

"No. A Mister Hernandez told me that if he wasn't here by five o'clock, to give this cell phone to Nicole Grant. And it's right now five o'clock."

"That's for me." Nicole reached out and grabbed the phone, sur-prising Rena. "Can you bring the check, please?" she asked hurriedly.

The *sommelier* nodded and walked off as Rena stared at Nicole in complete shock.

"You're waiting for Mister Hernandez? Ron Hernandez?" asked Rena, incredulously.

There was no hiding the fact that now it was Nicole's turn to be shocked. "I... don't know what you're talking about."

"The man who stood me up is Ron Hernandez!"

"I don't know any Ron Hernandez," said Nicole quickly.

"Your name isn't Johnson, you're Nicole Grant," insisted Rena, with a newly found sense of recognition.

Crap. Nicole wanted to run right out of the wine bar. Instead, she began gathering up her electronic accessories and putting them back into the velvet pouch. "No, my name's Nicky Johnson."

"No... I see it now... I recognize you from your dossier photo."

"Please leave me alone," snapped Nicole, who stood up and tossed the velvet pouch into her purse. Her hands shook as she searched inside for her wallet.

Rena stood and leaned in toward Nicole. "We have to talk."

"No, we don't." She found the bundle of cash Hernandez had giv-en her and peeled off two one-hundred-dollar bills. "Check please!" she called out nervously, but there was no sign of the *sommelier* or a waiter.

"I'm from WikiLeaks!" exclaimed Rena in a whisper.

Nicole's jaw almost dropped. What was it Hernandez had said? *Beware of imposters from WikiLeaks.* "If you're from WikiLeaks, then you're some anti-American misguided do-gooder revealing secrets that have been stolen and don't belong to you. Isn't that right?" Nicole tossed the money on the table—she wasn't going to wait for a check.

"Hernandez contacted me. Well, not me, but our London office. He sent files: dossiers and news clippings about a series of deaths he claims are linked to a super-secret U.S. government operation."

"I wouldn't know."

"Helen Bennet was supposed to meet him, but she had an accident and... died."

Nicole blanched. Another death from another "accident."

"No one else could come," continued Rena, urgently, "so I volunteered. I'm just an intern, but—"

"Excuse me," said Nicole as she moved to step around Rena.

"Don't you care about this kind of illegal behavior?"

"I care about living."

As Nicole tried to push past, Rena grabbed her arm. "I'm a Coptic Christian originally from Egypt. Do you know what that means? It means I know a lot about fear. From living in a majority Muslim country where our churches are burned down, we're discriminated against, beaten, raped, and murdered as a matter of course, all because we're not Muslims. As children, we learn to use sign language codes." Rena made a cross by putting her index finger over her thumb. "We try to show visiting Westerners that we're Christians, too. To find some solidarity."

"Sorry, you've made a mistake."

"But Westerns tourists could care less about our plight. They go to Egypt to see the Pyramids or the Sphinx and don't want to know about the truth of daily life."

"Let me go," said Nicole softly, not wanting to be obvious as she tried to pull herself free.

"I can see the fear on your face."

"You have no idea," said Nicole sharply.

"Really? You know about fear? Have you ever been stripped, beaten, gang-raped, and left for dead by a mob of men? Like I was at age fourteen?"

Nicole went still and tried to catch her breath.

"Do you know why no one else would come from London? Because they're afraid that Helen's death wasn't an accident. So I came, because someone has to be brave enough to look for the truth in this unfair world."

Nicole stood there reeling. *My God, what do I do?* Rena's words resonated with her, but...

"Maybe you won't help me, but I want to speak with Ron Hernandez."

Nicole clutched the smartphone given to her by the waiter. Where was he? Regardless of what was going on with Rena, Nicole had to get out of that wine bar.

"Look, I'm sorry for you, just like I'm sorry for myself. In my experience, the governments of the world aren't too concerned about what's legal or not. And as the Japanese say, 'The nail that sticks up gets hammered down.' So if you're as smart as you look, you'll take a taxi straight to the airport and fly back to London, *right now.*"

Nicole broke free. Rena thrust a business card at her. "Please, take this. My Hong Kong cell number."

Grant threw it into her purse and hurried out through the rear entrance of Riedel @ Q88, past some restrooms, toward a bank of elevators. She had never felt so alone in her life.

CHAPTER 7

17:03   The door slamming hard got everyone's attention. Major General Ma Ju looked royally peeved as he barged into the JW Marriott hotel suite. The collar of his expensive suit coat rode clumsily high on his back adding to his harried look of irritation. He cast a stern eye on the proceedings as several grim-faced members of the Second Department followed him into the room like bloodthirsty invaders of a conquering army.

MSS Director Tang stood up and met Ma's glare with his usual neutral expression. Tang had rented the one-bedroom suite and turned it into a makeshift CP, command post. Plainclothes MSS agents had ad hoc workstations with laptops and cell phones on every chair and table in the room, while others simply worked cross-legged sitting on the floor. All work stopped as men from the rival units eyed each other suspiciously.

As he tugged on an earlobe, Tang motioned for two of his men to move off the sofa, and then made a subtle gesture for Ma to join him there. Tang didn't fear Ma since Tang's unit was non-military and part of the Ministry of State Security. He didn't fear Ma, nor did he respect him and had never made a show of hiding how he felt about the general. But the situation right now was unlike any he'd ever had in his dealings with General Ma. Huge failures had taken place today. Tang knew that he needed to be careful, to protect himself and his team from possible unpleasant consequences in case events took an even worse turn.

After several uncomfortable moments, Ma crossed to the sofa and sat down. Then Tang sat down. "As you can see, there will be no more meetings in your limo. There's no time for that."

"Don't reproach me, Tang. Be careful how you speak to me," said Ma, practically hissing.

"Reproach you? I'm merely stating the obvious truth of our situation." Tang spoke matter-of-fact, cementing his refusal to be cowed by his rival.

Ma paused, as if he were trying to see to the heart of the matter. "You've allowed the Americans to escape, haven't you? So to hide your failure you go on the offensive against me," said General Ma.

"Allowed them to escape? Do you understand how large Pacific Place is?" Tang's slight incredulity stood in stark contrast to his normally even delivery. "There are dozens and dozens of entrances, exits, points of egress. You ordered me to only bring twenty people to Hong Kong. It would take at least two hundred agents, probably more, to seal Pacific Place. Tangspoke at normal volume, never betraying anger in his voice, but everyone in the room was hanging on every word. "I have operatives covering as many of the larger exits as possible. But Grant is not in her room and Hernandez's location is also unknown. Perhaps you should reconsider your orders to—"

General Ma slammed his fist hard onto the coffee table. He fixed Tang with a withering look. "I killed my first man with my bare hands when you were still a wet-behind-the-ears agent looking for your first bribe. And I've been doing the dirty work for Zhao and the highest political cadre since before your birth. Don't make me remind you again, that you would be well-advised to choose your words more carefully when speaking to me in front of our men, Director Tang."

For a long moment the two men stared daggers at each other, neither willing to break the gaze. Then Ma's aide Li Shan, a plain-faced woman in her forties, stepped forward and placed a bottle of Johnnie Walker Blue Label and two glasses on the table in front of the men. To Tang it seemed that she deliberately leaned in between them, using her body to break the staring contest. She poured two shots and handed the first to Tang, who reluctantly took the drink.

Ma took his glass and there was the most imperceptible nod between them as they tossed back the shots.

"So we must assume that Grant and Hernandez could be anywhere," said Ma. "What about security video?"

Tang hesitated, then put down his glass. "There is no centralized CCTV for Pacific Place. The mall itself has a camera system, but each store or hotel or restaurant has their own individual video security systems."

"So there are hundreds of individual CCTV systems?"

"Exactly. And this isn't Beijing. Flashing an ID from the Ministry of State Security in foreign-owned hotels doesn't get quick results. We even tried using fake Hong Kong police credentials, but management called police headquarters to confirm, so of course, we were denied."

"So you can't get surveillance video."

"I didn't say that," said Tang. "We have friends in the Hong Kong police and they're helping us. It's just not happening quickly. Some businesses cooperate, others do not. My hackers are working on getting us in the back way."

"Li Shan," said Ma to his aide. "Director Tang needs reinforcements. We have thousands of agents in Hong Kong. I've no doubt we can have two hundred operatives here in fifteen or twenty minutes. Make it happen so Pacific Place can be locked down."

Li Shan bowed and moved away.

"But it's quite possible that Hernandez and Grant have already fled the area," speculated Ma.

"Yes. They could be on the run, elsewhere in Hong Kong," said Tang. "I've quietly alerted our friends at the airport and other transportation hubs."

Ma nodded. "So we should 'unofficially' lock down the city. That might take an additional two hundred agents. I'll start making the necessary calls. Also, I'll send some of my people here to work closely with your staff. Hand in hand." General Ma stood up from the sofa. "The two Americans must not leave Hong Kong alive," he bellowed. Ma then made eye contact with each person in the room. "The future of every last one of us depends on that." General Ma let that hang in the air as he crossed to the door. "I want Hong Kong locked down and the Americans shot on sight!"

As the door closed behind General Ma and his entourage of Second Department muscle, Tang shook his head. This was the wrong mission for his team. They were a small, nimble group, designed to operate in the shadows. They were deft at studying a target, executing a kill, and then getting away undetected. Coordinating four hundred agents with shoot-on-sight orders in what could only be classified as a high-profile search was not his area of expertise and wasn't a smart strategy.

Tang shook his head with a feeling of impending doom. These were the wrong orders at the wrong place at the wrong time.

• • • •

AS HE BARRELED ALONG the Marriott's hallway, General Ma thought of his upcoming meeting with Zhao Yiren. He'd somehow have to spin the latest developments favorably. And he needed to start setting up Tang to take the fall, if necessary. His musings were disturbed as his aide Li Shan caught up to him and held out an attaché case.

"The American woman's laptop computer from her home in Phoenix just arrived here." She pulled the laptop partway out of the case to show Ma.

The general hesitated, not wanting to be distracted by the device; he had pressing matters to focus on. "Haven't we already 'imaged' the hard drive?"

"Yes. This laptop was initially sent to Guangzhou, where the hard drive was mirrored by members of the Fifty-seventh Research

Institute under the Seventh Bureau. They are at Sun Yat-sen University working non-stop to break Miss Grant's encryption."

General Ma was already well aware of this fact, since he had a secret relationship with one of the hackers in the 57th. "How much longer do they need?" he asked.

"I believe they're projecting success in a few hours, sir."

The hit team sent to kill Nicole Grant in Phoenix had been embarrassed to learn that Grant was away on vacation. But the laptop in her condo was suspicious. At that time, the identity of the original leaker was still unknown, and the Chinese had to assume it might be Grant. So their hackers took a look at her home computer and found something curious. A software program they couldn't open was pinging a request for information. What information? Where? Why was her laptop so heavily encrypted?

Earlier today, General Ma had learned that the original would-be leaker—the person who set in motion the murders of eighteen Americans and counting—had been one of the drone pilots who was now dead. Hernandez had only chosen to become a leaker in the last couple of days in an obvious attempt to save his life, after having been warned ten days earlier by William Snedeker, a retired CIA officer, that he was on a secret hit list. Snedeker was supposedly now in the hands of people working for Kate Rice who would conduct an "enhanced interrogation."

For Ma, that left the question of Grant's laptop. *Yes, we have the contents of her computer from her home in America, we just can't read it.*

"Perhaps Vice Premier Zhao would like to see the laptop, sir. A concrete example of achievement on a day when the news is not so good."

Li Shan had a point. He'd try to spin the computer to be a much more positive development than it really was. Li Shan was clever, and that's why he kept her ugly face around. He took the attaché case, but it felt heavy in his hand and he suddenly wondered if it was worth the trouble.

• • • •

THE SPRAWLING, ULTRA-modern East Campus of Sun Yat-sen University in Guangzhou occupied islands of flat land in the Pearl River Delta. The alluvial plain that comprised southern Guangzhou Province was bifurcated by vein-like, meandering waterways draining down into the South China Sea. The university campus was not as well known for its founder—Sun Yat-sen, a revolutionary who became the founding father of the Republic of China—as it was for Tianhe-2, the world's fastest supercomputer at 33.86 petaflops, housed in a clean-room environment in a special building just off the Pearl River.

Even though the supercomputer's use was intended for, among other things, "government security applications," General Ma had been unable to arrange for his team of computer experts from the 57th Research Institute, Seventh Bureau, Second General Staff Department of the PLA to gain access to Tianhe-2. He did manage to secure a much smaller, but still robust system of connected computers in the same building as Tianhe-2 for his team from the 57th to use in their attempt to break Nicole Grant's encryption.

Call them engineers, call them hackers, call them soldiers. Four of them—three men and a woman—sat in an eight meter-square room at individual workstations. They all wore jackets as the temperature was kept cold inside for the sake of the electronics. And, frustrating for the team, no smoking was allowed, nor could they pollute the room with snacks, tea, or even candy. Most of them would rather have stayed in Beijing where their status as hacking gods enabled them to do anything they pleased in the computer rooms.

The best of the bunch was Oi Lam, a diminutive twenty-five year-old who wore her hair cut fashionably short. She exuded confidence, had a naturally infectious smile, and wore trendy eyeglasses. Although she couldn't weigh more than one hundred pounds, her breasts were disproportionally large. Impossibly pale, she was smart, funny, and gave off an aura of innocence in spite of her very serious profession. She was an extremely attractive and well-turned out young Chinese female who didn't fit into the stereotype of a geeky hacker. Oi Lam looked over to the digital timer she'd set up as a countdown clock—a countdown to the breaking of Nicole Grant's encryption. It read: 04:19:12.

"Only four hours, nineteen minutes, twelve seconds to go," said Oi Lam, smiling. She clapped three times for good luck and to keep any bad spirits away who might otherwise cause her some problems. The American owner of the computer was clever, which made things more difficult for her.

Oi Lam badly wanted to crack the encryption and earn more praise from Major General Ma, head of all the Second Department, with whom she'd been having a secret affair. Well, for him it was an affair, for her it was a business opportunity. A superb actress, she knew how to make the older man feel special and she knew with certainty that he loved her. She had failed in her previous affairs to land a rich man, but men were weak and easy to manipulate. By capitalizing on the advice of her mother and aunties, she had every intention to succeed in landing General Ma.

Last night, during one of their brief secret phone calls, she'd told him the news: she was expecting his love child. He'd quickly rung off, and that had caused her endless worry. She now worked hard to hide her fears from her co-workers, none of whom knew about her pregnancy or affair with the general. Would Ma be happy or angry? Would he demand an abortion and break off the relationship? More importantly, would he financially support her and the child?

Early this morning she'd ducked out for a secret visit to a local clinic. Ultrasound had revealed the sex of her fetus. The next time she spoke to Ma, she'd give him the news. She thought it might make a difference in his reaction, but she couldn't be sure. This "accidental" pregnancy was anything but. It was a coldly calculated attempt to reel in a big fish and provide for her future.

She tried to focus on her work at hand and push her worries aside, but she couldn't; she knew full well that this gambit might backfire. General Ma might dump her, throw her out of the 57th, or worse. Oi Lam put on a good front, but she was worried sick.

CHAPTER 8

(Pacific Place, Hong Kong)

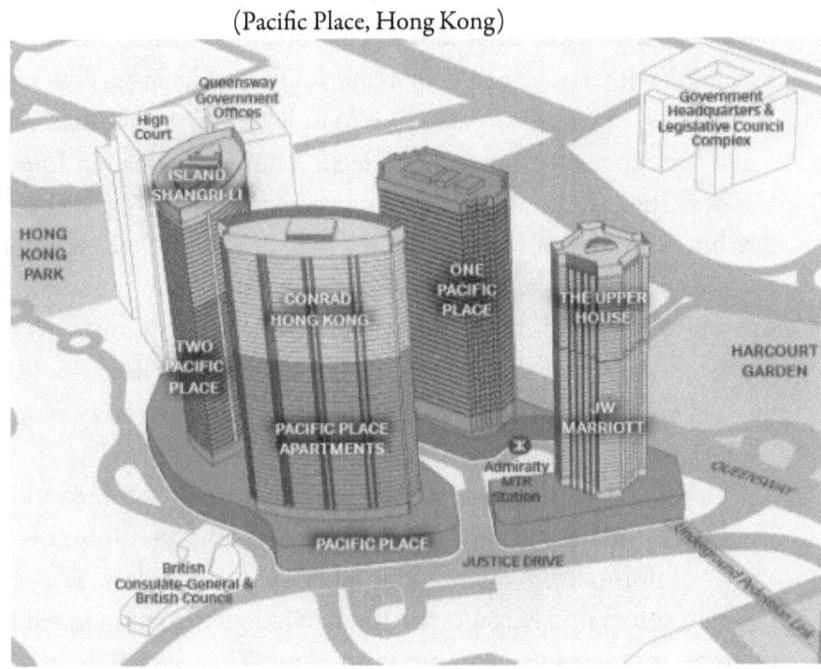

17 :05

A small crowd milled around the bank of elevators off the Marriott's lobby as Nicole Grant hurried away from the wine bar's rear entrance. Shaken to her core, her insides were being squeezed with rising panic that she fought to keep in check. The WikiLeaks reporter—a person Hernandez didn't trust—had recognized her. And someone named Helen Bennet was dead in London. Grant wished she could hit the rewind button and go back to yesterday, but wishing wouldn't change the mess she found herself in today. Hernandez hadn't shown up, but the cell phone from the sommelier was burning a hole in her pocket. She wanted to examine its contents, but to do that she had to get someplace safe. Where would that be? Where does one hide from the two largest superpowers on the planet?

Grant slowed her pace as she eyed the hotel front desk and the glass-walled main entrance area where tranquil piped-in music cast a spell of normalcy. A smiling doorman opened the door as a young bellman rolled in a luggage cart for arriving guests who looked happy to be entering such glamorous environs. Taxis sat idling just outside the doors, not more than forty yards from where she now stood. Beyond the taxis stood the other three towers of Pacific Place—the Conrad tower, the Island Shangri-La tower, and the office tower of One Pacific Place. The pricey high-rises now loomed like guard towers and Pacific Place itself felt like a sophisticated prison. Nicole wanted out right this second, sensing some terrible reality flooding in all around her, a killer tsunami rising slowly, without obvious malevolence, but with inexorable power hell-bent on exacting a terrible toll.

Forty yards to freedom! If she could just make it through the gilded doors and onto the plaza where fresh air and the scent of hibiscus and Frangipani awaited. The portals, so tantalizingly close, beckoned like the sirens tempting Odysseus with their irresistible songs and enchanting calls. All she had to do was take that first step, and then another after it. Fortune favored the bold and the temptation was too great, so even with no disguise she took a deep breath and decided to make for the front entrance. Grant mustered-up her best look of confidence, took a long stride forward... then froze in her tracks.

Two hard-looking Asian men stood just off the entrance way, holding 8×10 photographs. They kept shifting their eyes from the photos to people entering and leaving the hotel. Nicole knew with certainty that her photograph was somewhere on those 8 X 10s. She spun around and walked back toward Riedel Room @ Q88. No escape, not yet. Crap-on-a-stick but she was angry with herself for succumbing to the allure of an easy way out. She steeled herself with the understanding that she needed her "A" game if she were to survive. She strode toward the wine bar, but before she got there she made a hard right through a set of double doors that said STAFF ONLY.

Servers gave her confused looks, but she just smiled and kept saying, "Excuse me."

She ducked down a plain-looking hallway with closed doors on either side. She was about to turn around when she spotted what she was looking for—a stairway—at the end of the hall. She broke into a run, and then entered the stairway. She rifled through one of her shopping bags, retrieved the baseball cap and cotton mask, and put them back on.

After what seemed like a couple of flights down, she left the stairwell and pushed out through an emergency exit into a service corridor, a passageway behind the retail shops of the mall. She cut right, forced open a heavy set of double fire doors and spilled out onto the second floor of the mall right next to Prada.

She tried to orient her location, but was too nervous, so she found the Pacific Place pamphlet she'd tucked into her purse earlier. She scanned the second floor map, then walked quickly to her left. A large enclosed pedestrian walkway called the Sky Bridge led from Pacific Place all the way across Queensway to the United Centre or the Admiralty MTR station. If she could get to the station, she'd blend in. Hong Kong might be an Asian city, but hundreds of thousands of Caucasians lived, worked and visited here. She could melt into the masses and get someplace far from immediate danger until she could come up with a plan. A lifelong careful planner, not having a plan was the absolute worst position to be in.

She saw the Sky Bridge just past a down escalator. The walkway was all glass and shiny stainless steel. And wide. Five or six cars could easily fit in there side-by-side. Just after five o'clock on a Sunday afternoon meant the crowds weren't too thick, and that made it easy to spot a Chinese man and a woman standing equally spaced apart across the opening to the walkway. They were more discreet with the 8 X10s, but they had them.

Grant took a stutter step trying to decide which way to go, when the female spotter seemed to look right at her in a way that melted her confidence. So she stepped to her left and took the escalator down to the first floor, doing her best to appear bored.

More watchers stood near the ground level entrances, forcing Grant to walk to her right, doing her best window-shopper impression as she struggled to hold herself together. At least in the wine bar, she'd had a modicum or privacy, but now, she stood out in the open. *A plan, I need a plan!*And a new disguise. The ball cap and cotton mask had to be wearing thin by now, especially to anyone watching the security cameras. So she caught another escalator—the place had dozens of them—to Level One. She browsed storefronts and this time she wasn't pretending. The window display at Kate Spade stopped her in her tracks. She saw exactly what she needed and strode into the shop toward the lone clerk.

"I like those wigs. How much are they?" Nicole asked, her anxiety now overshadowed by a flinty determination.

She stood near the cash register and eyed several racks of merchandise. The clothing line this season featured attention-getting bright colors, but there was also a selection of black cocktail dresses. The wigs she referred to graced eight different mannequins—five in the display windows and three elsewhere in the shop. The wigs were either blond or black but otherwise identical: short, straight hair in a blunt block cut that curtained both sides of the face as it curved in toward the corners of the mouth, so the cheeks were covered by hair all the way below the jawline. The bangs fell down to the eyebrows and met large dark sunglasses that masked the eyes. The wigs and eyeglasses were a look she'd seen in other shop windows and was a perfect disguise for super-trendy Hong Kong.

"The wigs are for display, they're not for sale," said the store manager, a short-haired Hongkonger about forty, wearing bright red lipstick.

Nicole pressed her lips together and turned away from the woman. She quickly grabbed a couple of items from racks and then returned to the counter. "I'll take this black dress, this blouse, this sailor's cap, a pair of the sunglasses, and two wigs. One black hair, one blond."

"The sunglasses and wigs aren't for sale, but I can help you with the other things."

A week ago Nicole would have taken no for an answer. But a week ago she wasn't on a hit list in Hong Kong, a city where making money was the primary religion. "You're the only employee here right now?"

"Yes, I'm the manager."

"Well, you have eight wigs on display here and I only want two. I'll pay one thousand U.S. dollars for both of them. To *you*, not to the shop. And I'll give you two hundred for the sunglasses. *To you*. I'm sure you could go out tonight and buy new wigs and sunglasses to replace what I want. And you'll pay a lot less than twelve hundred

American dollars. Meaning you'd get to keep all that extra money. When you come to work tomorrow, you just replace what I'm going to buy right now. The money for the dress, blouse, and cap you put into the register."

She had the manager's attention. But the woman wasn't biting, yet. "I could get into trouble for that. Lose my job."

"No one will know except you and me," said Nicole, pulling the money Hernandez had given her from her purse. "Here's your cash right here." She counted out $1200. "But let's make it a lucky thirteen hundred U.S. dollars." She topped off the stack with another C-note, and then built a new stack of hundreds. "And here's the money for the other purchases, with a little extra thrown in as a tip for your help."

The manager looked around and outside the shop to see if she was being watched. She pursed her lips as if trying to make a decision. "Make it a lucky fifteen hundred."

"No. Thirteen hundred, plus the tip, and that's only if you give me the tube of red lipstick you're using. You're going to throw that in as a gift to me." Grant smiled inwardly; her reticence to negotiate hard in a Hong Kong business deal had vanished.

The manager hesitated for a moment as she looked at the mounds of cash. She reached into her purse for a tube of lipstick and handed it to Nicole. "Deal."

Nicole took the lipstick, scooped up her purchases, and darted into a changing room. The transformation only took moments. The black wig radically narrowed Nicole's slightly round face, and the sunglasses hid most of the rest of it. She topped the wig with the inside-out red and blue sailor's cap that matched the new blouse. The LBD, or little black dress, was a just-in-case purchase—just in case she needed another disguise, probably to be used with the blond wig.

As she regarded herself in the mirror in the changing room, she felt a jolt of hope, if not confidence; she had a solid disguise. She re-

arranged her belongings in the shopping bags, threw open the changing room curtain, and strode out of the shop without looking back at
the manager.

Almost immediately she turned a few heads as she strolled
through the mall. With her fear momentarily at bay, a plan had
wormed its way into her consciousness. She'd go to the Island
Shangri-La hotel, walk out the main entrance, and take a taxi. There
couldn't be *that* many people looking for her—there were too many
ways in and out of Pacific Place, and why would they be looking for
her in the Shangri-La? It seemed reasonable, so she picked up her
pace.

But thoughts of Hernandez's cell phone invaded her consciousness with a raw urgency. She knew it held more bad news. Still, news
equaled information, and she desperately craved more information.
So she stepped onto an up escalator toward Level Two, fished out
the phone, turned it on and examined the contents. No numbers
saved to the contact list, no call log entries, no texts, no downloaded
files, no text files... but then, there it was. A single video saved in the
gallery.

Her stomach churned as she plugged in earbuds and tapped the
play icon. The screen showed... sheet metal? She heard an engine,
traffic noise. Okay, it was inside a vehicle, maybe a van. Driving, but
the view was dim. He must have recorded the video with the phone
lying flat, so she was seeing the inside roof of a van.

She got off the escalator and pretended to window shop as she
moved deeper into the mall, before riveting her eyes back onto the
phone screen.

"I can only imagine that you're even more scared than you were
when I left your hotel room." It was Hernandez's voice, but the cell
phone video view of the van roof didn't change. "I didn't show up at
the wine bar with some plan that would save the day and give you
hope. The truth is, I don't have any hope to give. After all my years

working in Special Operations and then for the Company, I know exactly what I'm up against. The only real hope I have is that I can kill Zhao and spoil everyone's party. So the question for you becomes, 'What to do now?' If you want to stay alive, that is."

Nicole's knees buckled slightly. Her breathing quickened. She glanced around to see if she was being watched.

"If I were you I'd get to the harbor and hire a boat with enough fuel to reach the Philippines. If you make it—a big if—then what? It's not like you have enough cash to start a new life. Sometimes running isn't so easy.

"I don't have any answers for you. Our government gave Zhao Yiren that drone to help him become the next president of China. He's America's guy, he's in our pocket, and they can't let anything screw with that. So you and me and a bunch of other folks have to die. It's a simple, easy decision for a D.C. suit sitting behind a desk to make.

"Anyway, for what it's worth, I'm very sorry." There was a long pause, then, "If you're watching this video, that means I didn't show up at the bar, and that probably means I'm dead."

Grant stopped in her tracks and almost dropped the phone. She retched, gasped for breath, and touched the glass pane of a display window at Jean Paul Gaultier for support. *No! It can't be. This can't be happening!*

Her head was spinning. After a few moments, she started to walk. She had to keep moving, had to appear normal. Follow the plan. Stick to the plan! She looked around, not remembering which floor she was on.

Okay, she needed to get to Level Three. Concentrate. Level Three, one floor up. There was an escalator up ahead. Get to the Shangri-La, get a taxi, and get out of Pacific Place. Stick to the plan. Her hands shook as she willed herself to take another step.

CHAPTER 9

17$^{:12}$ Zhao Yiren, one of four vice premiers of the People's Republic of China, was two weeks away from becoming the next Chinese president when the National People's Congress held their elections in Beijing. As such, he now traveled with a significant entourage and his movements were closely scrutinized. He was officially in town to attend the Kids First charity fundraiser. Kids First had gone into several earthquake-ravaged Chinese cities and lent enormous help rescuing children from collapsed schools, all the while giving credit to local officials to make the efforts go more smoothly. There was goodwill between the Chinese government and Kids First.

While in town for the charity event, Zhao also filled his time with business meetings, like the one he currently hosted in his Pacific Place condo. Officially, there were no condos at Pacific Place, only furnished apartments. But when your family is worth billions and you're the son of one of the "Nine Elders" of the Communist Party and have been a privileged "Princeling" for most of your adult life, well, you can make things happen that mere mortals can't. Princelings like Zhao were the children of senior communist officials who've had everything handed to them on a silver platter through nepotism and cronyism.

Being a princeling, Zhao had been coming to Hong Kong long before the changeover in 1997 when the Chinese took back control of the territory from the British. He'd bought his condo in the Island Shangri-La tower before the tower had been built. A few select others had done the same. Hotel rooms occupied the upper floors while offices and condos were mixed in on the lower floors.

So this was an official trip, as all of his overseas trips now had to be. His staff of twenty stayed in various rooms throughout the hotel. Four bodyguards were posted inside the huge condo and two out in the hallway, while six others were off duty. Whenever he went out in public, an additional six Chinese security agents supplemented his private security detail. This visit would generate Zhao some good PR back on the Mainland, since he traveled with a PR secretary and a personal photographer.

Unofficially, though, Zhao came to Hong Kong for sex. That was one reason his bedroom area was completely soundproofed. Years ago he'd become addicted to "riding the white horse." He'd become obsessed with having sex with Caucasian women. He was the opposite of all the Western men who went to the Far East looking for Asian girlfriends. There was one Western woman in particular who'd long ago become his primary Hong Kong gal pal.

But now, it was time for business, and so Zhao Yiren and Conner Green sat in the condo's library on comfortable cushioned chairs with floor-to-ceiling glass windows providing the usual stupendous view. A superstar Canadian architect, Green reigned as the most in-demand architect in the world. His attachment to a project meant guaranteed funding, positive press and a lot of cachet. The Canadian had been about to commit to a two-year project in France, but Zhao was determined to steal him away from the French. Green simply needed a bit of wooing, and that's what this meeting was about.

Conner Green had a slender build, narrow face, gray eyes and long silver hair tied back in a ponytail. A perfectly tailored herring-bone suit by Canali looked dashing on him. A blatant egotist, he thought so highly of himself that he was actually making Zhao work to bring him into the fold—as if the overly generous money offer alone wouldn't do it. Green had spent many minutes expressing his concerns about Hong Kong's future, as if he feared the militant Chinese military was going to swoop in and ruin everything.

Zhao thought Green was beyond naive. The truth was, he didn't need Green to help raise money—money wasn't a problem for the Chinese. He just wanted the man's brand name attached to his project—well, it was his girlfriend's project. His secret girlfriend. Zhao could care less if Green actually designed the building, as long as he could legally say he did. So as big as Green's ego was, Zhao trumped him.

And while Green possessed a playboy reputation and cut a sharp figure, Zhao loomed larger than life. The Chinese politico stood six-two and spoke with a clear, deep voice that simply resonated. Dark, brooding eyes seemed to draw people in on unspoken secrets. Thick black hair was always perfectly coiffed. His nose was a little too fat, his ears a bit too large, but that was all overshadowed by that thing called machismo.

For Zhao Yiren simply dripped masculinity, oozing a smooth charisma reminiscent of film star Robert Mitchum, especially with his deep voice and the mannerisms he used when smoking a cigarette. Zhao was simply "cool," and how could a politician be cool?

A cursory look at the last several Chinese presidents made it clear that they didn't get elected based upon their Q Score or sex appeal. They could pass for technocrats, bureaucrats, or mobsters, but would be lucky to get elected dog-catcher if looks-obsessed America had anything to say about it. Even raffish Hong Kong box office king Andy Lau was quoted as saying that Zhao was like an Asian Lee Marvin, and that he had studied him for one of his tough guy roles. That kind of compliment can't be bought.

There certainly was nothing metrosexual about Zhao. Just watching him light a cigarette or tie his tie and you knew he was a man's man, a rich guy maybe, but he could probably change a flat or handle a sledgehammer or breakdown a 9mm in the dark. Smart, cagey, and wary, he knew how to play to the huddled masses even though he was a cozy insider.

Coming from a politically powerful family that in 1966 had been labeled "revisionist," Zhao had been imprisoned and tortured as a teenager during Chairman Mao Zedong's Cultural Revolution—a ten-year spasm of violence, chaos, and upheaval that killed at least 45 million Chinese, all to purge Mao's political enemies and solidify his power base. Zhao's mother and sister died in a "re-education" camp, and while he never forgave Mao, he later studied the way Mao wielded raw power to neutralize his competition.

When his family eventually returned to prominence, Zhao became a true princeling. Anyone who saw the scars all over his hands and arms from the burns his female captors branded him with knew he had actually lived that Cultural Revolution horror. The scars helped establish his *bona fides,* and made him appeal to the common man. They also functioned as a daily reminder, spurring him to climb the ladder of Chinese political power into the same pantheon Mao Zedong himself haunted. Once his power consolidated, massive payback would be brought to bear upon countless families and institutions indelibly etched into Zhao's mind.

On the surface, Zhao would bring something to the Chinese presidency it had never had: celebrity. Genuine celebrity, that is. Below the surface lurked something else entirely.

And although Zhao came off as suave and sophisticated, film star Andy Lau had it right: Zhao was a tough guy. The dirty little secret was that he'd not only ordered men and women killed, but he'd killed them with his own hands. Many years ago Zhao had been reunited with his Cultural Revolution oppressors. The event was secretly held in a warehouse late at night and Zhao used a white-hot poker to maim and then kill his female torturers, one at a time. He wasn't the least bit squeamish about the gruesome work.

Early in his career, Zhao had shot others in cold blood: people who stole from him, cheated him, or plotted against him. He'd earned the respect of henchmen like General Ma because he hadn't been afraid to get his hands sullied. But even Ma didn't completely understand the fire in Zhao's belly for revenge, flamed by his vivid memories of the starvation and degradation he'd endured at the hands of Mao's Red Guards. "Getting even" with the top cadre and beating them at their own game was the driving force in Zhao's life. He had little interest for his wife and children and seldom saw them. They were simply necessary accoutrement for his rise to the top and his quest for comeuppance.

As a young princeling life had been simple. Now, he found himself locked in a cutthroat race for the mantle of Chinese Supreme Leader. The complexity and level of treachery he currently dealt with was mind-boggling. He'd even chanced using the help of the Americans two years earlier to ensnare his chief rival, Wang Hongwei. The risks he now ran were huge, and maybe that was the reason his drinking had increased so greatly.

Regardless, as much as he'd prefer to be focusing on the finishing touches to sewing up the presidency, he instead turned to the spoiled superstar architect sitting across from him in his private library.

"Conner, many people were worried that the Hong Kong economy would dive after the change-over in 1997, but, on the contrary, Hong Kong boomed," said Zhao, who then took a healthy gulp of champagne.

"Why was that?" asked Green, as if he were trying to make the simple question sound incisive.

"Chinese immigration began allowing Mainlanders with money to come and visit, and there were lots of them. Hotel demand skyrocketed, and so did the price for a room. A hundred-dollar hotel room became three-hundred. Restaurant and shopping centers did great business, and that created employment and wage increases."

Zhao put down his empty champagne flute and stood. "Care for a cigar?" He crossed to a standing humidor made of elegantly patterned burl wood.

"I don't smoke," said Green, a little smugly, as if not smoking were a badge of honor. "It's bad for your health."

"I have acupuncturists and doctors for my health," said Zhao smiling. He knew Green didn't smoke cigarettes or cigars, but loved to puff on Thai sticks and pack his nose with Peruvian flake cocaine. What a politically correct hypocrite. Zhao selected a rare Gurkha Black Dragon cigar that cost over $1000 USD. He expertly cut the tip, used a wooden match to "toast" the cigar, and then lit up, savoring the first puff. "Smoking cigars is very relaxing. Why don't the doctors ever mention that?" he asked.

Green didn't respond.

"Anyway," said Zhao, looking out toward the Bank of China building that very intentionally dominated the skyline with an artful menace, "Hong Kong has come to rely on China, and the Chinese want to continue spending their new wealth here. Mainland Chinese in Tsim Sha Tsui used to be easy to spot—they weren't dressed as fashionably as Hong Kong people, but carried lots of shopping bags, like Julia Roberts in *Pretty Woman*."

"Yes, that's true," said Green as he chuckled.

"But now that Mainlanders have earned all of this new wealth for some years, it's harder to tell the difference between them and Hong Kong people. The Chinese have become more cosmopolitan, but forget about Shanghai, because Hong Kong," he gestured with his cigar to the city below, "has become the most prized shopping mall in all of China."

"Yes, but the PLA has come to town," interjected Green. "That's a very clear and vivid—some would say threatening—difference from the old days."

"The soldiers stay in their barracks," said Zhao, holding his hands out palms up. "There's no marching around like the drunken Russians do in Red Square. Sure, the British troops left and the power now rests with China, but we want to maintain the status quo here. And we have for many years."

"I'd like to be sure about that before I committed to a two year project. Hong Kong has a very large and active democracy movement that rankles the Beijing leadership, as you well know. And China's military is causing all sorts of trouble these days—with Vietnam, the Philippines, Japan, Taiwan, the Americans... claiming sovereignty over the entire South China Sea."

Unbelievable; Green was lecturing him about China's foreign policy.

"Hong Kong's biggest worry regarding the Mainland is that there won't be enough designer bags for the local *tai tais,* the rich Hong Kong ladies, to buy! Wealthy Chinese were coming to Hong Kong and buying twenty or thirty bags at a time. Real bags, not fake ones. So all the famous brand name shops had to put some limit—only three bags per customer—or something like that. China has done nothing but pump even more wealth into Hong Kong," he said emphatically. "There is nothing to worry about."

Zhao crossed back toward his chair and loomed over the architect. "I'm going to be the next president of China, and I'm not looking for a fight with the West or our Asian neighbors. Trust me. Hong Kong is simply too valuable to tinker with. It's a cash cow, a money-making machine! It's a major tourist destination, the number one financial center in Asia, and a gateway for trade. And I'm going to keep it that way."

Zhao was lying, of course. Hong Kong was no longer as important to Beijing as it had been fifteen years earlier; China was simply too wealthy now. Hong Kong was going to lose its autonomy, lose its freedoms, and lose its special status. This was inevitable. It was the open secret that most people didn't want to discuss. The process of chiseling away at Hong Kong's freedoms was proceeding, slowly but surely, and as president, Zhao had no intention of changing that. Hong Kong would be made an example of for the rest of China, to keep the entire population in line. Beijing could have it no other way. They would *never* tolerate freedom of the press, free-dom of religion, freedom of speech, freedom of assembly, freedom to dissent and protest, freedom to have as many children as you liked, freedom to use the Internet without strict censorship—all freedoms Hongkongers now enjoyed but Mainlanders didn't.

"You sound sincere," said Green.

Finally. Green had been acting like they were drafting a peace treaty, not a simple business deal. Time to deliver the "champagne close."

"I am sincere." Zhao refilled both of their flutes with champagne, sat back down and placed his cigar in a crystal ashtray. He indeed was sincere; a sincere liar.

"We're in the Pacific Century, Conner. I guarantee that you'll do very well riding the Chinese wave. I'll introduce you to a few impor-tant colleagues tonight at the charity reception. It will be no trouble arranging financing in the billions of dollars for your most cherished designs to reach fruition."

"That sounds delightful."

Zhao raised his champagne flute in a toast.

"To our first Hong Kong project together."

Green paused for a moment, and then clinked his crystal flute with Zhao's. "To our deal."

As they drank, an aide magically appeared with several copies of a contract and a golden, $50,000 USD Mount Blanc fountain pen.

"It's the same document your lawyer sent yesterday, sir," Zhao's aide said to Green.

"Lovely pen," said Green, as he signed the contracts. "May I keep it for good luck?"

Greedy bastard. Zhao was already picking up the tab for Green's several thousand dollar-a-night Shangri-La suite, exactly one floor above the condo where they now sat. "It's my pleasure to gift it to you, Conner," said Zhao, hiding his displeasure behind a smile and already calculating how he'd cheat the Canadian out of a hundred thousand American dollars as payment for the pen.

• • • •

THE ARRIVAL OF GENERAL Ma Ju provided a nice excuse for shunting Conner Green out the door. Ma was a close childhood friend, a trusted associate, and enjoyed *carte blanche* in terms of dropping in on Zhao Yiren at all hours. But since the issues they tended to discuss were of the most sensitive nature, they always spoke alone in a sitting area off the master bedroom that was swept for surveillance devices twice a day. The General had an extensive brief to give Zhao and had begun with the worst news first, that Grant and Hernandez were still at large.

"Are you sure that one of them is the leaker?"

"I found out this morning that the original leaker is already dead," said Ma, slouched in an upholstered chair. "It was one of the drone pilots. Documents in his home showed he wanted the American president impeached for committing treason, since giving China the drone was an illegal technology transfer of highly sensitive equipment. But the pilot had no proof, only the experience of his personal involvement."

"Why did he wait two years to act?" asked Zhao.

"He had a breakdown due to burnout, and became embittered with his government. This happens to some of the American drone pilots who are overworked."

"And Hernandez?"

"Ten days ago, four days after the operation to eliminate the Omega Team members began, Hernandez's father-in-law warned him he was about to be killed."

"His father-in-law?" Zhao sounded somewhat incredulous.

"Kate Rice failed to mention that to us, but, yes, his former father-in-law, William Snedeker is a retired deputy director of the

CIA's National Clandestine Service. A man who obviously still maintains top-level relationships in Washington."

"How did Snedeker find out?"

"Rice's people are waterboarding him to answer that," said General Ma. "Also troubling is that the file she provided to us on Hernandez didn't indicate this family connection, nor did it provide details of his background and training as a covert operator."

"So Hernandez is our biggest concern."

"I'd say so. As you know, he contacted WikiLeaks in London a few days ago."

Zhao nodded. "Does he have any proof?"

"Unknown," said Ma.

"And WikiLeaks?"

"We eliminated their reporter in London, the person Hernandez contacted. But someone else was sent to Hong Kong in the dead woman's place. We should have a name any time, and we'll neutralize this person by the end of the day." General Ma felt good. The briefing was going well. Zhao was asking the right questions and not bitching too much.

"Hernandez must have something. WikiLeaks would want documentary evidence." Zhao was still nursing the exorbitantly priced cigar and took a long puff.

"If he has evidence, that's another serious breech from the American side. They can't seem to keep their house in order. Perhaps you should bring this up with Rice and demand they take strong action."

Zhao nodded. "As I think about it, Hernandez doesn't need hard proof. He can simply make a video claiming American spies helped me destroy Wang Hongwei and gave me the drone's navigational control code so I could steal it. He could say the death of all the crew members was my attempt to silence them after one of them tried to go public. In other words, all he needs to do is speak the truth. If

WikiLeaks promoted that, it would infect Chinese media, and my many powerful enemies would feast on my carcass."

"If any accusations surfaced after you are elected president, you'd survive. Especially if the accusations came from a known American spy and assassin."

"I'm not so sure," countered Zhao.

"There's a chance you'd become a hero. We have carefully documented all of the intelligence you've gathered over the years from your CIA friend. I have no doubt we can 'sell' you as having been a deep cover spy for China, wringing secrets from your CIA lover, all done in service to the Motherland. This, in fact, is true."

Zhao nodded, seeming to evaluate the statement. "That's correct, but don't forget our hackers supposedly took control of the American drone. That event helped leverage me to where I am now—the threshold of the Chinese presidency. But I've never presented evidence of how exactly we got the drone and haven't revealed which of our hackers was responsible."

"There's an assumption at the Fifty-seventhResearch Institute that the best hacker, Oi Lam, hacked the drone. I must confess I fed fuel to the rumor."

"Arrange for this hacker to have a terrible accident. Handle this personally, perhaps tomorrow."

Ma blanched. "That would be... a pity. She's our best." Ma didn't dare tell Zhao that Oi Lam was pregnant with his love child.

"We have tens of thousands of good hackers. She can be replaced."

Ma squirmed in his chair and his face drained of color. "She's been my lover for more than a year."

The two men locked gazes. Ma felt the intensity of his longtime friend's stare boring in, probing for evidence of weakness or lack of resolve. Finally Zhao looked away, took another puff, and exhaled, watching as the bluish smoke curled upward and rolled in on itself. He studied the smoke as if searching for some revelation.

"I'm well aware that you have many lovers, old bull. In many Chinese cities. This lover of yours, Oi Lam, can become a national hero in death." Zhao watched as the last of the cigar smoke sank downward toward the floor and dissipated. Finally he turned back to Ma with fire in his eyes. "Make sure her apartment burns, or maybe create an explosion from leaky propane gas. That way we can claim the proof of her hacking was lost with her." Zhao's tone made clear this wasn't a suggestion, but an order.

Ma worked to maintain a blank expression and immediately replied, "I'll see to it." Showing any hesitation would have caused Zhao to become suspicious and look into the matter himself. And that would ruin everything.

"Now what about the American woman, Grant?"

"I have her laptop right here." Ma silently exhaled, relieved that the subject had changed. Putting Oi Lam out of his mind for now, he reached into the attaché case given to him by Li Shan and pulled out a thin HP laptop. "This is more good news. We've already copied the hard drive and our hackers tell me they'll break the encryption in a few hours. We have no reason to believe Grant possessed damaging information, but if she did, we'll have it soon."

General Ma set the laptop on the floor, leaning it against the attaché case next to his chair.

"Sounds like there are a lot of loose ends that need to be tied up in the next few hours," said Zhao, darkly. "Make sure they get done, old friend. We all have too much to lose."

CHAPTER 10

17$^{:37}$ General Ma remained alone in the alcove off the master bedroom in Zhao Yiren's condo using a secure phone to make numerous calls to Hong Kong authorities, seeking their low key, unofficial help in locking down the territory—Hong Kong was designated a SAR, Special Administrative Region, a semi-autonomous territory within the sovereignty of China, yet not a part of Mainland China. Any kind of official order to arrest or detain Hernandez and Grant would inevitably lead to questions being asked in Beijing.

Zhao's staff members here in the condo would not disturb General Ma, nor would they enter the master bedroom unless summoned. Ma's role was duel, for right now his friend of over forty years was having a sexual tryst with a Western woman, and that kind of thing needed to be kept secret. Especially considering who this woman was. So staff assumed that Zhao and Ma were still in their meeting. General Ma had played the same role dozens of times and didn't mind that Zhao had descended down a tiny, secret staircase to another condo two floors below. He knew it would be a "quickie" because there were more meetings scheduled and a charity reception to attend later this evening.

Ma was focused on urgent matters as he waited for Zhao to reappear, and completely forgot about Nicole Grant's laptop leaning against the attaché case that was out of his sight on the floor, tilted against his chair.

• • • •

KATE RICE LAY SPREAD-eagle on the conference table in the condo owned by Trans-National Corporation, two floors below Zhao Yiren's condo in the Island Shangri-La tower, and immediately below Zhao himself as he became more urgent in thrusting home his point. She didn't have to fake the orgasm since he had always made her come with great pleasure. Yes, there was exaggeration to vocalizing the sexual release, but the climaxes were real indeed.

Trans-National was a dummy corporation with two locations in Hong Kong and was about thirteen shell companies removed from the Central Intelligence Agency. Rice always wore a wig and disguise when she came here. And a business suit. And black panties and bra, which always got ripped from her body early in the encounter.

The CIA shrinks had explained to her why Zhao wanted her dressed in a certain way, and why he ripped off her undergarments and yanked her hair and squeezed her nipples so hard they bruised. She no longer cared about his subconscious need to debase powerful women. Their dalliances were coming to an end, with a new blue-eyed blonde handler already in place in Beijing who was ten years younger and trained to please.

Rice had first "turned" Zhao almost eleven years ago. He'd begun providing classified information to her almost immediately. In the last four years, when it became clear that a CIA asset had a shot at becoming the president of China, Kate Rice's star rose as high as any NOCs star had ever risen in the agency's history. Convincing the American president to give Zhao the RQ-180 drone in order to cement his rise to the top hadn't been an easy sell. But ultimately, the idea of having a pro-Western friend of America who held the keys to the Chinese kingdom and was willing to share them with Langley was a shot that had to be taken. If Zhao became president, it was reasoned, war would be averted and untold lives saved.

Rice didn't even feel terribly bad about all the recently murdered Americans who'd been on the drone op. The leakers or would-be leakers among them clearly deserved to die. As for the others, well, they'd willingly chosen a risky profession, she told herself, and sometimes the piper came calling. She reasoned they had to be sacrificed in order to avoid a much more horrible future. She gave no thought at all to the devastation caused to the innocent families.

At age thirty-eight, Rice was a sixteen-year CIA veteran and had spent the last fourteen years undercover in the National Clandestine Service. She personally founded the charity, with CIA backing, as an espionage platform in Asia. She'd immediately known it had to be a children's foundation. Gaunt, hollow-eyed, lice-covered eight-year-olds made for the kind of ad copy that kept donations flowing and would grow the espionage tentacles of the organization.

To help expand Kids First and by extension increase her stature within the CIA, Rice had taken it upon herself to sleep with prime ministers, heads of state, diplomats and bureaucrats. And having sex in the most exclusive hotel suites or the most luxurious villas with titans of commerce or world leaders was a validation of sorts that got her juices flowing. The charity's Asia success was so spectacu-lar—Rice was a natural at recruiting agents and setting up productive spy nets—that the Agency allowed her to expand into Africa, South and Central America, and countries of the former Soviet block.

As the CEO of Kids First she earned a cool million a year, and the Agency let her keep it. She'd become so valuable to the CIA they made a special deal with her; if she stayed undercover with the chari-ty for one more year, they'd induct her into the SIS, the Senior Intel-ligence Service, a cadre of veteran CIA officers who were considered to be the cream of the crop. Being promoted into the ranks of SIS was exactly the kind of recognition and acknowledgment Rice se-cretly craved. She was already being promoted and given career-track advancement that would have been hers had she been progressing normally—transferring to different positions and assignments—in the clandestine service.

Zhao's ascent to the Chinese presidency would be her crowning glory in one helluva spy career in service to her country, and was the kind of grandiose achievement that Rice felt she deserved. Except she wasn't doing it for the United States, wasn't acting out of patriotism. Nor was she running a children's charity because she loved kids. She didn't dislike kids, she simply had no feeling for them one way or the other.

Bad things happened to kids all the time, just as bad things had happened to her when she was a teenager in middle school. She'd been a fetching fifteen-year-old when her parents were killed in a car accident; the fallout destroyed Rice emotionally. The only "help" she got was to be placed into a series of foster homes where she'd invariably been sexually abused. She managed to survive three years of that, until at age eighteen she took on the world on her own terms. The pain-filled emotional wounds that had never entirely gone away filled her with a general distrust of people and made her emotionally independent. She became adept at covering up her true feelings and hiding behind false fronts. Ironically, her traumas made for a useful skill set within the clandestine service.

A shrink in private practice had told her she was a socially skilled extreme narcissist who was good at changing into various roles as events demanded. Rice rejected the diagnosis. It was true that no one was close to her and never had been—at least not since the emotional traumas that befell her in middle school. It was also true that she was haughty and had a sense of entitlement, but so what? And yes, she was so success-driven, she only kept people around who had something to offer. When someone was no longer useful, they were deleted from her life. She considered it a recipe for winning.

But a narcissist? Rice continually told herself—and many of her CIA colleagues agreed—that she was simply a hard-charging, Type-A overachiever.

Washington D.C., after all, was a sewer filled with sell-outs looking out for Number One. Why should she be any different? So, yes, she was doing it all in service to herself and she'd damn sure do anything to get Zhao into the Chinese presidency, because his ascension guaranteed hers. As she thought about that, she climaxed.

• • • •

WITH THE SEXUAL TRYST finished, Zhao Yiren had retreated back up the secret stairway to his own condo. Kate Rice showered and rinsed off the exudate of their lovemaking, watching as his semen circled the drain. Hopefully for the last time. She dried off, entered the master bedroom, and looked into a full-length mirror. Zhao had taken to calling her *pangzi*—fatty. Yes, she was carrying some extra weight, but maybe only ten pounds more than when they'd met over a decade ago. She put on weight easily now and tried to make up for it with dieting and exercise, but it just kept getting harder to stay slim.

She also knew not to stay too late at a party. She was ready to turn Zhao over to the new handler, scale back her work in the field, and accept light duty once she was inducted into SIS. She fully intended to keep running Kids First for no other reason than the adoration it afforded her and the million bucks a year she pocketed.

Rice accepted just how ruthless and amoral she was. What Barry Bergman had hinted at was correct; there was blood on her hands from unsanctioned kills, but if it meant the difference between winning and losing, there would be more. She'd figure a way to finesse things. But that didn't make her evil, did it? It just made her—willing to go the extra mile to make sure her operations, righteous operations, succeeded.

Yes, she was ready to come in from the cold. As long as she went out on top. And that's what worried her right now. It was as if Hernandez and Grant were some kind of monkey wrenches thrown into her smoothly oiled machine at the worst possible moment.

CHAPTER 11

$17^{:38}$ The small hallway off Level Three of Pacific Place that led to the Island Shangri-La was just up ahead, right where Nicole Grant's pamphlet map said it would be. She was still reeling internally from the upheavals of the last few hours and from Hernandez's cell phone video informing her that she was on her own and needed to make a run for it. Still, each step she'd taken since viewing the video had made her a bit more physically composed. She was trying to stay focused on her plan: get to the Shangri-La lobby, make her way outside to the taxi stand, and head for Central Station.

She gained confidence as she walked. The wig and sunglasses from Kate Spade made her reflections in the shop windows unrecognizable. In fact, with the black wig and super dark glasses, she could pass for an Asian. As she neared the turn leading to the hotel, her confidence got tweaked when she noted from her peripheral vision a man in a sport jacket angling toward her. He was holding an 8 X 10 photograph.

Nicole's heart raced and her chest tightened, but she didn't miss a stride. She forced herself to reach into her fake Celine bag, retrieve her cell phone, and hold it to her ear. "*Wei?*" she said loud enough for the man to hear. She launched into a fake one-way conversation in flawless Beijing-accented Mandarin about how great the shopping was.

The man eyed her closely from about six feet away. She turned away from him, into the hallway, and kept chatting as she walked toward the doorway at the end of the short hall. She listened in between her words. With great dread, she heard his footsteps, following her. *Is it my shopping bags? Crap, I've changed my disguises, but I'm carrying the same three shopping bags since I left my room at the Marriott! Maybe they have me on video with all the bags.*

Her body went clammy, her mouth dry, her stomach queasy. She hated herself for being so frightened, but she did have slightly better control over her movements than she had earlier when she'd first gotten scared. Maybe she was getting used to it. She was almost to the door but the footsteps behind her grew louder and more frequent.

She reached out for the push bar with her trembling hand that was holding the three shopping bags, when the man's hand suddenly thrust forward...

...and opened the door for her.

She managed to give him a glance. He was smiling. She somehow smiled back, gave a slight nod, and walked through the door with no footsteps following. After a few steps into the swank hotel, she allowed herself to take a breath. She'd made it to the Shangri-La.

Nicole spotted a ladies room. She ducked inside, rushed into a stall, and promptly threw up. She looked at her trusty old Timex and allotted two minutes to pull herself back together. At the sink, she washed her hands and quickly ditched two of the shopping bags and their contents, including the ball cap, headscarf, and cotton mask, into a trash bin.

Back outside she took a couple of deep breaths, and the first thing she heard were strains of soft jazz. As she moved forward into the Shangri-La's lobby, she saw it lacked the Marriott's openness and sense of space, but was tastefully elegant. To her right was a wide marble staircase carpeted in green and gold and abutting a stone wall displaying museum quality paintings and oriental tapestries. Above her, gigantic chandeliers, like waterfalls of crystal, hung down from octagonal recesses gilded in gold. Across the room, a trio of classically uniformed bellmen stood at attention next to the main entrance where a highly-polished black Rolls-Royce Phantom sat parked just beyond the tall glass doors.

With a sense of relief she saw taxis idling outside. Portraying a sense that she belonged in this rarefied atmosphere, and wanting to get this over with, Nicole moved across the white marble floor in the direction of the doorways. But she didn't get far.

A phalanx of Asian security men wearing earpiece comm-links suddenly emerged from the elevator area and bifurcated the lobby. One of them drilled Nicole with his eyes and held his hands out for her to stop. At first, she thought she was being detained, then realized this must be some kind of security detail for a big-wig. As she stood there, however, she drew the stares of other security men.

Was it because she looked good, or was it something else? Grant didn't feel like waiting for the answer. Just a few feet to her left was the Lobby Lounge. It was fairly full of well-heeled patrons enjoying cocktails. A quartet played the *bossa nova* background music she'd first heard a few moments earlier.

As if she knew them, Nicole impulsively waved toward a table where two older ladies were sitting, then stepped away from the security blockade and moved into the Lobby Lounge. A hostess sat her immediately next to the two women, whom Nicole quickly sized up as well-off Hong Kong *tai tais*, or married ladies of a certain age, getting sloshed.

"Do we know you, darling?" asked Vivian Chu, the one in a pale green silk blazer, speaking English with a crisp, although slightly slurred from alcohol, British accent.

The accent made Nicole think. She'd spent years living in Italy when her father was stationed at Aviano. She spoke fluent Italian and could mimic a northeastern Italian accent. Feeling the need to remain hidden, she instantly morphed into an alternate identity.

"Sorry, I was mistaken. But you're both lovely and it's my loss that we're not friends," purred Nicole, sounding authentically Italian.

"Then let's become friends, at least for the next hour or so, if not longer," said Vivian. "You're Italian, perfectly gorgeous, and I should introduce you to my grandson, except he's a complete cad and I already like you far too much to foist him upon you."

They all three shared a laugh at that. Nicole ordered an espresso and they introduced themselves, with Nicole calling herself Ariana Faccioli, the name of a childhood friend. Nicole noticed the eyes of several security men lingering on her, so she casually checked her cell phone as a way to mask her nervousness.

"Why does the hotel have so many police? Is there some problem?" asked Nicole.

Eleanor Chow, the second *tai tai* heavy with diamonds, leaned forward conspiratorially. "Security, darling.For the Prime Minister of Malaysia or some other boob."

"Eleanor, the Malaysian PM is indeed staying here, but he's trumped by a Chinese princeling, Zhao Chow, or something like that. He has more security than the Sultan of Brunei. My husband says he'll be the next President of China, poor chap."

"Do you mean Zhao Yiren?" asked Nicole, remembering that Hernandez had said the man had a condo here at Pacific Place.

"Yes, that's the fellow. He's a bit long in the tooth, but is actually quite... magnetic," said Vivian, as if she were sharing a bedroom secret.

Magnetic isn't the word Nicole would have chosen. Despicable?Vile?Murderous? To think that he was about to walk past made her blood run cold.

"Yes, yes, Zhao will be at the reception tonight," said Eleanor, fingering her diamond necklace, "I could introduce you to him if you'd like, but didn't you know that Prince Harry is in town? Staying at the Peninsula, of course."

"He's so dashing, why aren't we drinking there?" asked Vivian. "But I did notice that Conner Green is staying here."

"Who's that?" asked Nicole, not really interested but wanting to stay in the conversation. She glanced to the musicians as they segued into a rendition of the Brazilian classic "*Corcovado*."

"I'd venture to say he's the most famous architect in the world," said Vivian. "Perhaps a bit old for you, but he's quite wealthy. He has long silver hair in a ponytail so you can't miss him. He dresses impeccably."

"Conner Green is friends with Zhao," said Eleanor conspiratorially. "My friend spotted them together late last night in a club at the Ritz-Carlton. They are both quite the lady killers, so watch out."

"They'll both be at the Kids First reception tonight. If you're coming, we can introduce you to whomever you'd like to meet."

"Perhaps I'll see you there," said Nicole, noncommittally.

The conversation drifted. Since more security men appeared, Nicole sat tight. As the *tai tais* leaned in close to gossip with each other, Nicole used her tablet computer to make some notes regarding her immediate future. A simple list wasn't exactly a strategy, but it was a start.

1. Call Ernest Normann.
2. Taxi to Lan Kwai Fong.
3. Walk to Central Station.
3. Train to Kowloon side.
4. Avoid taxis, use crowds, walk to a hotel.

Grant understood that she couldn't use her passport or any other ID for anything. Getting a hotel room was questionable, unless she could find a real dump that didn't require a passport. Nor could she use credit or debit cards. She'd have to stick with Hernandez's cash.

She tapped the tablet screen, reconsidering. This was nothing more than a short-term escape plan. Fine for right now, but in the larger scheme of things she needed *solutions*. As an engineer and penetration tester Nicole not only discovered a system's weaknesses, she proffered solutions to patch the problems. That meant becoming proactive and engaged. Running away wouldn't render any kind of permanent fix.

She looked up to see a short, swarthy-looking VIP escorted out of the hotel by the security detail. That had to be the Malaysian prime minister. The coast was clear for her to leave, but Nicole hesitated. She'd call Ernest Normann right now from the Lobby Lounge, then pay the check, move to a safer location, and strategize how to attack the problem. Every problem has a solution and she was highly motivated to find one.

She attached an earbud/microphone combination to her cell phone, found Earnest Normann's name in her CONTACT LIST, and called. She was using the Hong Kong SIM card in the phone for the first time and had paid cash for it, so it wasn't connected to her name in any way. She calculated that it was about 7 AM East Coast time on Sunday morning. On the eighth ring, a man's voice, obviously stirred from sleep answered gruffly, "Normann."

Nicole whisperedwith her mouth close to the small microphone. "I used to work for you. My code phrase was Spike Vector."

There was a terribly long pause at the other end of the line. Ernest Normann had been a fatherly boss and had made it clear to Nicole that if she ever got into trouble to call him and use that phrase. As she waited for a response, she wondered if he'd forgotten. Just as she was about to ask if he was still there, he said, "Are you on a secure line?"

Her heart sank. "No, but—"

"Don't call back until you get to one." The line went dead.

Secure line? She was fresh out of those. Crap. The rest of her list had suddenly become meaningless. There was now only one To Do item: find a secure phone. As she sat there pondering that, she saw something that made her practically jump out of her skin.

CHAPTER 12

17:53 Ron Hernandez sat above the Shangri-La's lobby at the grand piano at the top of the marble staircase, playing a muted, passable homage to Papo Lucca's version of *Bambeando*. The song brought back a flood of sweet childhood memories and for a moment filled the gaping hole that had been ripped open in his heart when he'd heard the horrible news. A bittersweet smile formed on his lips, and then quickly melted into a frown of sorrow. He glanced down to check his watch, then focused on the keyboard as his father had taught him.

His parents had immersed their children in Latin Jazz from a young age, particularly *Salsa, Pachanga, Cha cha cha*, and *Guaracha*. Hernandez had fond memories of watching them dance to a mambo beat in the basement of their Texas home when he was a kid. His mom got him to learn to dance when he was just a boy, and he tried to mimic his hero, the legendary flutist and bandleader Johnny Pacheco, who quite simply had the smoothest moves ever. But Hernandez didn't study the flute, he studied the piano. His younger brother Willie had been outgoing, a little on the chunky side, and always smiling as he learned to play congas while hamming it up, pretending he was Tito Puente. They'd had a lot of fun as kids dancing and playing music, even though they were just amateurs.

A mix of Spanish, Dominican and French bloodlines, Hernandez had come a long way from growing up lower-middle-class in Fort Worth. At the moment, he looked downright snazzy, dressed in an expensive light brown suit. A brown briefcase sat upright atop the piano on the Shangri-La mezzanine. A tablet computer instead of sheet music was in front of him. He wore the facial recognition-defeating eyeglasses and a salt-and-pepper toupee with matching goatee.

Hernandez knew that his dad back in Fort Worth would laugh if he could see his eldest son right now. But his parents weren't laughing much these days. His dad had been a lowly janitor in a high-rise when Ron was born. By the time he was a teenager, his father had opened his own janitorial service and was struggling with business challenges. They were far from poor, but Hernandez joined the army to help ease some of the family's financial burden. He never intended for it to become a career, but the military gave him a college education and appealed to his sense of order.

Because Hernandez was driven to excel, early on he attended the U.S. Army Ranger School and fought overseas as a member of the 75th Ranger Regiment. As he made rank he gravitated to intelligence and graduated from the army's intelligence center in Fort Huachuca, Arizona, becoming an officer along the way. Amongst other units, he served with the 513th Military Intelligence Brigade in support of challenging CENTCOM operations in the Middle East. He was eventually drawn to return to special operations and survived the rigorous selection process to be accepted into 5th Special Forces Group. He didn't become a Green Beret until his late twenties, making him an old man in his outfit, even though many Delta operators are in their thirties or forties. Hernandez had six overseas deployments by the time the CIA's SAD—Special Activities Division—heavily recruited him. He left military service and joined the Company, swiftly becoming one of the more elite covert paramilitary operators working for SAD's Ground Branch. Long bloody years of stressful, intensely dangerous assignments took a heavy toll. Hernandez had become physically exhausted, emotionally spent, and the endless deployments had cost him his marriage. In spite of the personal costs he felt deeply committed to protecting his country. So he came in from the field and went to work in the CTC, Counter Terrorism Center, the CIA unit that oversaw their drone operations and had over 2000 personnel. He'd spent the last two years on drone ops, mostly working as a supervisor on agency teams that located, identified, and terminated BGs—Bad Guys—in the Middle East and South Asia.

The burnout from endless drone operations was a different kind of animal. Waxing BGs up close while deployed in the field, on the ground, was one thing. But when tracking an individual for days or weeks while building a video dossier, operators like Hernandez got to know the target intimately. He watched them leave their house to go to work, knew when they would stop for tea. He watched targets make love to their wife on the roof of a mud hut, watched them relieve themselves in a field. He saw the poverty, and he sometimes also saw the utter evil of what they did.

And Hernandez had done it all from the air-conditioned comfort of a mock cock-pit at a U.S. military base on American soil, working nine-to-five. It was a bizarre way to conduct a war, he thought. What had at first seemed like a low stress posting turned out to be psychologically challenging, because when he ordered the button pushed that sent a Hellfire missile to execute the kill, he was terminating someone he'd gotten to know a little bit. And strangely, that was harder to do than to just shoot a BG in the back of the head in the dark of night in an unfriendly place.

And now, here he was, a highly trained elite operator more at home in the hardscrabble killing fields of the Third World, sitting in the glamorous Island Shangri-La Hong Kong preparing for yet another kill, this one not quite up close, but not so far away, either.

The placement of the piano, right at the edge of the glass rail on the mezzanine overlooking the front entrance, was perfect. One of Zhao's security pukes stood only thirty feet away, covering the high ground for when his boss emerged from the elevator and headed for the Rolls parked outside. Hernandez knew Zhao was being driven to a dinner meeting and would return to the Shangri-La later for a children's charity reception. Regardless, he intended to wipe him now, as soon as he crossed below. And Hernandez, sitting with his back to his target, couldn't have looked any less threatening.

Even the briefcase didn't look threatening. Snugly held inside was a specially-rigged .40 caliber suppressed pistol, canted for an overhead shot. Thin brown vinyl matching the brown leather covered the hole where the bullet would exit. After he fired, Hernandez would place a new vinyl sticky strip over the exposed hole. The pistol was loaded with custom-made "chemically enhanced" ammunition that would insure every shot was a kill shot. Special optics aligned with the barrel provided a video feed to his tablet, meaning he could aim the weapon by watching the tablet screen and by slightly panning or tilting the briefcase using only one hand, while he played piano with the other. The bottom of the briefcase was specially weighted to help mitigate recoil. The remote switch to fire the weapon was on the floor, next to the three piano pedals, so he only had to step on it to shoot. He'd designed this with the help of his old friend Jaffir, who was right now waiting in a box truck somewhere in the parking lot.

Hernandez glanced at his watch. Any minute now. He could tell by the body language of the plainclothes security man that some pronouncement had just come over the guy's comm-link. Zhao was on the move. When the moment came to fire, he'd play *allegro* so that even the guard nearby wouldn't hear the shot.

There was a slim chance he might even get out alive. Even if he didn't, this assassination would collect a blood debt owed to the Hernandez family. He stared at the tablet and subtly moved the briefcase so it sighted on the most likely kill zone. He was incredibly focused, playing piano while at the same time aiming the weapon, when a hand touched his shoulder, causing him to butcher a slew of musical notes as his whole body jerked.

The security man looked over toward the musical miscue as Nicole Grant leaned down and kissed Hernandez on his cheek like an old friend. "It was your walk," she whispered. "I recognized it when you approached the piano."

Somewhat stunned, Hernandez looked at the dark-haired beauty who slid in next to him on the piano stool. *Grant? Damn, she's learning fast.* He couldn't see her eyes through the dark glasses, but saw her turn slightly toward his briefcase.

"Zhao is about to walk through the lobby below us, and here you are playing the piano with a briefcase I've never seen before."

"Get the hell out of here," he said, and he meant it.

"No," she said firmly and without hesitation. Grant glanced at the nearby security man and smiled. She appeared centered and focused. "Why did you blow off our meeting at the wine bar?"

"Sorry, but that was unavoidable. You got the cell phone?"

"Yes, and it appears you're anything but dead."

"This isn't the time," he said, almost growling.

"I know a better way to beat them than to kill people in a hotel lobby."

"Then you've got about five seconds to make your case."

"I've kept the audio file alive on the Darknet," she said quickly. "The digital key is on my laptop at home. We can use the key to request the file on Darknet, and that gives us the recording, exposing Zhao and proving he was complicit with American intelligence."

Hernandez almost blanched. He quickly calculated the potential value of such a file, if it indeed existed. "You said you didn't listen to the audio file."

"I lied. As the op went down I didn't listen, but a week later I did. It's incriminating, dangerous information and that's why I've kept it alive on the Darknet."

"Doesn't sound like something you would do," he said, suddenly doubting her.

"It's true. Remember, a file sent to the Darknet is only good for maybe a month if no one uses the key to request it. Pieces of the file sort of drop off and the file becomes corrupted. So I wrote an insanely encrypted script that requests the file from the Darknet. It throws out a random request every few days, but doesn't actually download anything. The data is received, then deleted. My program was designed to keep the audio file fresh, because the Darknet systems see that the data was requested."

Hernandez's eyes drilled her, trying to fathom whether she was telling the truth.

"We can get the audio file. If we go public with what you have and what I have—"

"Going public isn't so easy. The American mainstream press won't touch this."

"Probably not, because they're part of the establishment. But WikiLeaks will."

"I already told you to forget about—"

"I met the WikiLeaks researcher who was sent here to replace the dead woman."

"What dead woman?" said Hernandez, apprehensively.

"Helen something. Bennet, I think. You were supposed to meet her, right? She had an accident in London. And we know all about deaths from accidents, don't we?"

"Yes, we do." His mind flicked to a bad memory for a moment. He glanced at Grant. She'd collected some good intelligence in a very short period of time.

"Anyway, there's a brave, very determined young lady named Rena Musaad who's been hanging out in the wine bar since she got here, hoping to meet with you."

Hernandez considered the situation. "I was supposed to meet Bennet there yesterday, but she didn't show. That girl Rena introduced herself, but I pretended I was a Brazilian tourist." So the young woman he'd avoided meeting with in the bar really was from WikiLeaks, thought Hernandez. Interesting. But that didn't change the fact that he'd gone to a lot of trouble and expense to set up this hit in the Shangri-La. It wasn't every day you get a clear shot at a soon-to-be world leader. And he had other very good reasons for wanting to personally kill Zhao. "There's going to be pandemonium here in a second. Head down to the mall, then take the escalator up to Hong Kong Park. I'll meet you at the statue."

"Get me someplace that has a secure phone and T-3 Internet speed. We can get the whole cancer, not just one piece of it," she said quietly.

He was silent for a moment. "I have a personal investment in killing Zhao," he said with a deadly quiet.

"An investment?"

"Why do you think I came to Hong Kong? I didn't come for you; I learned you were here after I arrived. I came here to kill Zhao. I came for this very moment that you're trying to spoil."

Nicole blinked. "Well I have a selfish, personal investment, too. It's called wanting to stay alive."

"I didn't come for myself, I came for my brother. They killed my brother!" he whispered, struggling to reign in his rage. "My younger brother Willie was part of the security detail in Pomona. He 'fell' in front of a train at Foggy Bottom Metro Station in D.C. ten days ago. The security video conveniently wasn't working that day." Ron Hernandez had a very strong emotional investment in shooting Zhao Yiren dead right damn now.

Grant sat there looking flabbergasted. "Your brother?" She lowered her head as if she was having a hard time taking everything in. "I'm... so sorry. I can't imagine how you must feel."

"No, you can't. Now move out," he practically hissed.

She hesitated. "I will if you tell me that killing Zhao will bring your brother back," she said unflinchingly.

Hernandez fought a wave of emotion as he worked hard to focus on playing the song. He'd already lost the sight picture on his tablet of the kill zone.

"If you want revenge, be smart about it," she insisted.

"I'm about to waste the Chinese bastard behind it all. Give me a little credit for being smart."

"It's not just Zhao we want," said Nicole, practically pleading. "We want the actual killers. We want the American co-conspirators. Every last bureaucrat or politician who signed off on this travesty.And there's something else I want." She took off the sunglasses as her eyes moistened. "I want to live. I want to see my mom again. I want to get married and have children and grow old with my husband. I want you and me to walk out of here together and figure this out. But I know that if you do what you came here to do, it'll be over for me, for you."

Hernandez glanced at her. "It's already over for me, Grant. Willie was in Pomona because of me, I talked him into taking the security job so we could spend some time together. How can I ever face his wife, his little kids? He'd dead because of me. I destroyed my own family."

She hung her head. "I'm so terribly sorry. Do what you have to do, but I'm staying, I have nowhere to go."

Hernandez briefly closed his sorrowful eyes. He looked empty, like a man torn fifty different ways. What had been so certain mere moments ago was now questionable. And once again it was due to Grant. Then, from the corner of his eye, he saw Zhao's entourage enter the lobby below. It was now or never, he still had time. He reacquired the sight picture and watched on screen as Zhao entered the kill zone. Zhao paused to shake someone's hand—he had the Chinese leader in the crosshairs of the video gun sight. He eased his foot off the piano pedal and placed it above the remote firing switch on the floor.

He shot a look at Grant; she wasn't going anywhere. Damn it all to hell. Whacking Zhao had seemed like the best move he could make. The bastard certainly had it coming. And it would rob the gutless wonders on the U.S. side who had approved of this nasty business of their prize. They'd be complicit in the deaths of almost twenty Americans, for nothing. Net gain: zero; technology loss: substantial; human cost: incalculable. Not that he thought the sleazeballs would lose a night's sleep over it.

But now... what if she was right? What if they could make everyone pay?

Hernandez took a deep breath and let out a long exhale...

...but he just watched the tablet screen as Zhao exited the hotel unharmed. The nearby security man bounded down the stairs without giving him a second look.

Hernandez turned off the tablet and stopped playing. He lowered his head and stayed silent for a full minute as he tried to clear his thoughts, tried to see his next step. Willie was a former Marine, and when things were difficult, he'd often spouted the mantra "Improvise, adapt, and overcome." The motto now flooded Hernandez with a sense of purpose.

Improvise. Adapt. Overcome.

He cast a quick look at Grant. She didn't say anything, she just sat with him.

Finally, he reached down and carefully retrieved the remote firing switch from the floor. "There's a CIA front company in One Pacific Place, the high rise just across the way," he said, his voice finding strength. "It's a field office and has everything you need. I used it when I operated out of Hong Kong five years ago." He checked his black-faced Suunto watch. "Our timing is good, if they've kept the same schedule."

"You want to break into a CIA facility?" she asked.

"Do I want to? No. But if we ring the buzzer, I don't think they'll open the door."

CHAPTER 13

18:10   As evidence that not all Hongkongers got around on foot or via the Metro, the above-ground streets and underground parking levels were choked with vehicle traffic at Pacific Place. Couples on dates, young people headed for the movies, families stopping in for dinner, local shoppers, and out-of-town hotel guests coming and going kept the complex, which was open until midnight, busy in a city that always seemed to be fully engaged. A large outdoor wedding was about to take place on the plaza between the Marriott tower and the One Pacific Place tower and just off the curving road that connected all four towers.

With the tension of the Shangri-La lobby behind her, Grant relaxed a little. She thought they fit in perfectly as she and Hernandez skirted the wedding crowd. She let him lead her toward a green and white sign indicating a stairway that threaded down into the bowels of Pacific Place. She'd felt tremendous relief that Hernandez refrained from shooting Zhao, and linking up with him had given her a huge jolt of renewed hope. She felt horrible that his brother had been murdered and knew Hernandez was saddled with guilt over the death. But right now she wanted some answers.

"You haven't explained why you stood me up."

"Jaffir and I had a problem with the gun in this briefcase I'm holding."

The temperature cooled as they descended a damp concrete stairwell, and she digested the fact that he'd abandoned her in order to prepare for a kill. "Who's Jaffir?"

"You'll meet him in a minute. We worked together in Pakistan."

"What kind of work?"

The look he gave her suggested it wasn't her business to ask, but he answered, anyway. "Jaffir graduated from Caltech. He got his cit-

135

izenship and spent ten years working for the Company in the Technical Services Division."

"Technical Services?"

"They provide gear, gadgets, documents, and weapons to officers in the field." He tapped his eyeglasses. "Like these glasses I wear that defeat facial recognition software.Anyway, Jaffir resigned to escape the Langley bureaucracy and went independent. In Pakistan we contracted with him as a facilitator, procurer, engineer, forger, make-up artist, burglar, and gunsmith. He's also a demo man, gourmet, poet and is trained as a combat medic. Plus he's not a bad singer. And that's the super-short description. The guy is brilliant. As a field operative, I can tell you he provides the best support I've ever seen, by a long shot. Every American and many Western spooks operating in Islamabad used Jaffir."

Hernandez opened a steel door and they entered an underground parking lot on Level LG1 below One Pacific Place, not far from a service elevator. Dozens of trucks and vans making deliveries or providing maintenance or repair services to clients in the tower sat parked all around. Hernandez scanned the area then motioned her forward.

"So what happened?" she asked, quietly.

"ISI, Inter-Services Intelligence in Pakistan is heavily infiltrated with Islamists sympathetic to the Taliban or Al-Qaeda. And with America-haters.They learned what Jaffir was doing and targeted him for death. Our government turned its back on him because helping him would have angered certain factions of the Pakistan government. Anyway, I got him and his family out and set them up here in Hong Kong. So now he performs the same kind of services to Western and other friendly intelligence agencies on a freelance basis. For instance, he'll have a Canadian passport for you, driver's license, working credit cards and so on in a few more hours."

"But... you left me to fend for myself."

"You think I abandoned you?" He locked his eyes onto hers. "You took my cell phone from the *sommelier*. So we used the phone to track you. We even had Jaffir's daughters following you for a while. They enjoyed the window shopping."

Nicole didn't like the fact she'd been so easily manipulated, and flashed him a challenging look. She'd practically had a meltdown, but he'd just been toying with her.

"Look, it was something of a test," he said. "I needed to know what you would do, how you'd react to being on your own. You passed with flying colors."

Before she could respond he turned away and walked off through the parking lot, threading amongst all the trucks. He seemed to be avoiding security cameras mounted on the cement walls.

"I could have walked right into the hands of the Chinese," she said sharply, as she caught up to him.

"But you didn't. And it's not just the Chinese we're avoiding. We need to learn who the Americans are in this little game. That's part of the reason why we're busting our way in to the Dragon's Lair."

Nicole wasn't placated by his explanations and pursed her lips unhappily. He stopped next to a DHL delivery van and cut her a look. "Grant, you're the one who wanted to work together. And since there's no time for pouting, let me paraphrase General Patton: 'Lead me, follow me, or get the hell out of my way.'"

Her eyes narrowed. She didn't like being dressed down so brusquely. Yes, she desperately needed him, but she also needed a level playing field. After a moment, she locked him with her hazel-flecked green eyes into a stern gaze. "I'm going to amend the general's directive: I won't lead or follow you, but I'll walk side-by-side. Agreed?"

He regarded her for a moment. "Sure you can keep up?" He set off with long strides, snaking his way through a maze of trucks. She scrambled to stay next to him.

"I'm assuming this Agency field office we're going to has redundant biometric security controls." She wanted him to understand that she had plenty to contribute. In fact, she felt a strong need to prove her worth to their newly formed partnership. "Facial recognition, iris scan, and finger vein scan."

"Forget facial recognition, you can defeat it with something as simple as cell phone video of a person with access, so the Company stopped using it. To get in we're looking at a smart card, iris scan, and finger vein scan. Plus an armed guard just inside the door. Unknown if there will be additional personnel present."

"Iris scans can be spoofed, but there is no way to defeat a finger vein scanner unless I can intercept the signal from the scanner itself."

"The scanner will be hard-wired, so you can rule that out," he said.

"Then I could try hacking into the command center, but that would take—"

"Way too much time. So we have to defeat the finger vein scanner."

"There's no way I'm aware of to do that. You can't just cut off someone's finger and use it like you could with a fingerprint scanner."

"There's a way," he insisted. "But it will take an extra twenty minutes that we don't have, because, believe me, our shelf life here at Pacific Place might expire any second."

Almost as if on cue, a truck door slammed from about twenty yards off to their right. They stopped in their tracks andsilently watched as a uniformed repairman wheeled a hand dolly loaded with plastic tubs toward the elevators.

She'd been holding her breath, so she let out a long exhale, then regarded him with a penetrating stare. "Two years ago, I thought you were a desk jockey. A middle management burnout case. I felt sorry for you."

He looked at her but said nothing.

"How do you know how to kill people with mini-drones or to defeat finger vein scans? How did you know Zhao would be leaving the Shangri-La at exactly the right time? A gun in a camcorder, a gun in a briefcase. Who are you really?"

He didn't answer, justmotioned for her to follow. They stopped behind a white Isuzu reefer truck from which they still had a good view of approaching vehicles.

"Hernandez," she said, with an edge to her voice. "I don't care if you *are* some super spook or assassin who's been to hell and back. No more games, no more tests. Shoot straight with me, or I'll take my chances alone."

He looked at her for a long moment. "Fair enough."

Hernandez rapped twice, paused, and then knocked three more times in quick succession on the back door of the box truck. The door opened almost immediately. Jaffir Kahn, a tall, rail thin, forty-year-old Pakistani-American stood there in a perfectly tailored single-breasted Brooks Brothers suit and tie. He flashed a toothy, sincere smile as he pushed up the wire-rimmed glasses on his large nose. His dark brown skin was wrinkle-free, and nicely styled thick black hair made him look like some kind of pampered executive.

"Miss Grant, it's a pleasure to meet you. Please, can you quickly step in to my laboratory?" Jaffir's Pakistani accent was greatly softened by almost fifteen years of living in the States. He held out his hand; his fingers were long and graceful like they belonged to an artist.

Cool air escaping from the refrigerated truck enveloped her as she masked her surprise at his proper appearance. He didn't look like some kind of spook support geek.Not knowing why, she took an instant liking to Jaffir, so she took his hand and climbed up into the inner sanctum of the box truck.

"I'll be back in a few minutes," said Hernandez, standing on the pavement as he started to close the door behind Nicole.

She flashed him a look. "Don't be late this time."

• • • •

SINCE NEITHER THE *sommelier* nor any waitstaff had seen her confrontation with Nicole Grant, Rena Musaad simply took over the table in the private area of Riedel Room @ Q88, and took over the bottle of Bordeaux, too. And she had Grant's $200 to pay for it.

Rena composed a detailed, encrypted message to the London WikiLeaks office, insisting she was on to something BIG. She requested they provide funding to pay for at least two more nights in Hong Kong. She'd already confirmed Grant was a hotel guest and had called her room, but there was no answer.

Ron Hernandez was the key. So she went back to work, using the Internet to do what she did best: dig deep down for information, forgotten facts, and secrets that sometimes stood right out in the open.

• • • •

SPECIAL PROJECTS DIRECTOR Tang Jie stood surrounded by the entire MSS team in the CP at the Marriott. Tang intently watched security video from both the Marriott and the Conrad that his hackers had finally obtained. Footage from the Conrad showed what looked like a Muslim woman holding three shopping bags as she got into an elevator two floors below Nicole Grant's floor at 15:51. Footage from the Marriott clearly showed Nicole Grant at 16:03 holding a purse and the same three shopping bags as she crossed through the Marriott lobby and entered the Q88 wine bar.

Tang glanced around making sure that neither General Ma's aide Li Shan nor any other officers from the Second Department were within earshot, as MSS team members pressed in closer.

"Our main problem remains, that we have access to very little of the CCTV footage here at Pacific Place. But from what we do have, we pieced together the following. Grant left her room just before four o'clock disguised as a Muslim with three shopping bags and a purse. She must have taken the stairs down two floors, and then took an elevator," said Tang, filling in the gaps of events that the video didn't show. "She gets rid of her disguise somewhere as she walked to the Marriott, but she kept the three shopping bags. Put out the description to all agents. Have the rovers show photos to clerks in all the shops, waitresses in the cafes. Key on the three shopping bags. Make sure you get the colors correct of the clothing. And find out what she was doing at the wine bar."

"And if we see her?" asked one of the men.

"Close surveillance until we can make a clean snatch."

"Ma's orders are shoot-on-sight," said Tang's aide Choi, a sharp-eyed thirty-five year-old man with a round face.

"Forget about that, or we'll be shooting every *amah* in Hong Kong," said Tang, softly, so only his MSS agents could hear. "And somebody check to see if Grant or Hernandez has any old friends or contacts here. Perhaps they've reached out for help."

• • • •

THE DIGITAL COUNTDOWN clock in the computer room at Sun Yat-sen University in Guangzhou read: 03:01:37. It was a median estimate. Oi Lam's team might break the encrypted files from Nicole Grant's laptop computer a bit sooner or a bit later, but the Chinese hacker's estimates in the past had always been accurate. She'd finally been able to push aside the fears regarding her pregnancy and lose herself in the technical puzzle of how Grant constructed a program that caused the laptop to randomly, but frequently, send out requests for information. What information? What was so precious that this data was continually being requested, but not downloaded?

Oi Lam sat lost in deep thought when her cell phone rang. She recognized the caller ID and her stomach muscles tensed. "*Wei*?" She didn't put the phone on speaker so at least his end of the conversation was masked from her co-workers.

"I trust you are well and the university is giving your team all it needs," said Ma.

"Yes, everything's fine." She wanted to say more, but the room was too quiet, her co-workers could hear. She had to speak in some kind of code to give him the results of the ultrasound check she had this morning. "We are all here working hard and on schedule," she said, sounding formal.

"Good. Tomorrow morning, you, and you alone must return to Beijing for a special assignment. Someone will contact you with the arrangements."

She paused, surprised, wondering if this would be a real work assignment or an assignation of a different type. "Yes sir. Where shall I report?"

"Return to your apartment. You'll be contacted there with further instructions. And don't mention this to anyone, this is a secret assignment. You'll have to tell your comrades something, so say you're being evaluated for a possible transfer to another unit."

"Yes, sir. Oh, and General, do you recall the special test you wanted me to research?" She paused, waiting to see if he understood her code for the ultrasound test.

"It's a girl, right?" asked Ma, unenthused. He already had five daughters, with four different women, but no sons.

"No sir, just the opposite. But the situation is quite normal."

There was a long pause, and then Ma stammered, "We'll talk later."

The General rang off. Oi Lam struggled to hide her fears. Why hadn't he responded positively? Every Chinese father wants to have a son, first and foremost, whether they admit it or not. And since Ma didn't have any male heirs, Oi Lam had gambled by getting pregnant while she was supposed to be on the pill. Being pregnant with a girl would have guaranteed her nothing except the end of her relationship with Ma. If the ultrasound this morning had revealed a girl, she would have aborted.

She'd spent a year carrying on with the man, carefully shunning his gifts of cash and gold jewelry in an effort not to appear greedy. Her cultivated lack of interest in his money was crafted to win a much larger prize. After a year during which he'd made no substantial effort to secure her financial future, she made her move by taking the pregnancy route. The research she'd done had convinced her that having a boy would make all the difference to him. So why did he hang up? She frowned. She'd give Ma one month. If he didn't step forward with massive financial assistance and an ironclad commitment by then, she'd abort the boy and claim she miscarried. That scenario would leave her with nothing to show for her year spent with the general except for the breast implants he'd paid for. But she could use those breasts and her youth to land another big fish; she already had two candidates in her sights, men who she simply thought of as "wallets."

• • • •

GENERAL MA SAT ALONE in his parked Mercedes where he'd gone to make the call to Oi Lam. He didn't bother masking his exhilaration. A son! He long ago gave up hope of producing a male offspring. He loved all of his daughters, but in China, the cold truth was that boys were more highly favored than girls.

A son! What a blessing! Zhao's order to kill Oi Lam had just become terribly problematic. He'd been given a definitive, direct order from the soon-to-be president of China to kill Oi Lam. Ma swore silently to himself. If he disobeyed Zhao he'd get a bullet to the back of his head, yet how could he obey? He needed to think of something, and fast, because there was now no way in hell he'd let anything happen to Oi Lam.

• • • •

CENTRAL SERVICES WAS the name of the cleaning company that had cleaned the CIA front company at Pacific Place five years ago when Ron Hernandez spent over a month working out of the facility as he and a small team tracked down and assassinated a Muslim terrorist and his support cell hiding out in a Kowloon tenement. He remembered the company name because he often found himself present at 18:30 when the cleaner arrived. The man was a CIA subcontractor who held a SECRET clearance. Sensitive facilities needed their toilets scrubbed, too, and the spooks themselves aren't going to do it. Hernandez and the man named Ping had joked about it.

But that was five years ago. Hernandez was in the system then and used a magnetic keycard, a fingerprint scan, and facial recognition to gain access. All old technology that had been replaced. Mr. Ping was going to have to explain a few of the current security details, whether he wanted to or not.

Two minutes later, a Central Services van pulled into a dimly lit slot near the service elevator. The uniformed Asian driver came around to open the back doors and was jumped from behind by Hernandez and put into a bar arm choke hold. He choked the driver unconscious, opened the back door and laid the body inside face down. He was about to climb in, when he got a look at the face. It wasn't Mr. Ping.

An Asian female lay unconscious on the floor of the van. Hernandez frowned. How in hell was he going to impersonate an Asian female?

CHAPTER 14

18 :52

Trans-National Corporation took up the entire 23rd floor of One Pacific Place. After stepping out of one of the eight elevator cars, a visitor had only one choice, and that was to approach the secure front entrance to the suite of offices. A push-to-talk intercom was positioned above a smart card reader next to the door. Tasteful couches and coffee tables comprised a small waiting area. Multiple security cameras covered the entire space, including the elevator bank.

Nicole Grant wore the black wig and sunglasses as she used her left hand to wave the smart card taken from the Central Services cleaning lady over the card reader. The real cleaning lady was bound and gagged in her van down in the parking structure. The cleaning uniform was a little small on Nicole, so Jaffir had made some quick alterations. All she appeared to be carrying was a new mop head in her right hand.

And then there was the Smith & Wesson Governor, a large, six-shot revolver that chambered .410 shotshell rounds, the smallest shotgun round, that she had stashed in a nylon shoulder bag. Each .410 cartridge in the pistol was less-than-lethal and contained rubber buckshot, since Nicole had refused to carry a gun that would kill someone.

In addition to providing Nicole with the gun, Jaffir had attached a Taser Axon wearable camera to her belt, so he was watching a video feed of her progress from his box truck/work lab. Hernandez was watching the feed, too, on his tablet computer while standing in the stairwell on the 22nd floor, exactly one floor below Nicole.

Mr. Ping, the janitor Hernandez had known, retired from Central Services and forty-seven year old Rose Chin, who'd been very cooperative once she regained consciousness, had taken his place a year ago. Chin cleaned Trans-National five days a week, so there was no way that the hulking figure of Ron Hernandez could have impersonated her. And there wasn't even time to think about it, there was only Nicole's insistence that she would take point on getting them into the super secure office.

Half the people in Hong Kong walked the streets with earbuds in their ears, and Nicole also now wore a pair. But she wasn't listening to classic rock or a best-selling audio book; she was in radio contact with Jaffir and Hernandez. *What am I doing, what the hell was I thinking?* Nicole kept her head down as her chest muscles tightened. She had experience testing physical security at companies that hired her as a penetration tester, and so had deluded herself into thinking that impersonating Rose Chin wouldn't be much different. But really, this was all about trying to prove her worth to Hernandez. She'd let herself fall into competition with the man, and now she felt like a fool.

Just as she was about to chicken out, a buzzer buzzed—the smart card had worked—so she forced herself to open the heavy door using her left hand and stepped into a small anteroom that held no furniture. She focused on the biometric scanners recessed into the wall as the outer door clicked closed and locked behind her, sealing her into a kind of no-man's-land and infusing her with a sense of dread.

· · · ·

HERNANDEZ SHOOK HIS head. Special operators like himself generally oozed confidence and instilled it in others, but as he looked at the video feed of Grant approaching the biometric scanners, he had a bad feeling. Unless she froze, she'd pass the iris scan. But Jaffir had confided that the finger vein scan was a fifty-fifty shot.

It had only taken Jaffir minutes to photograph Rose Chin's eyes and generate the contact lens that Nicole now wore. Then he'd scanned Chin's right index finger with his own finger vein scanner and fed the data into a computer. Special software created a 3D digital model of Chin's finger, including the veins, and that digitized information was sent to a 3D printer that was only 12" X 12" in size. Jaffir could manufacture solid objects of any shape with the printer, using materials of his choosing. Hobbyists could buy such printers for as little as $200 and with the right software do exactly what Jaffir could do.

As the clone of Rose Chin's finger had begun taking shape, the computer directed an additive process of construction—successive layers of resin and other material were "printed." So as the printer manufactured the faux finger it incorporated the system of "veins" below what became the "skin." The skin was created from a translucent resin compound while the veins were printed from a slightly metallic material.

Hernandez and Jaffir knew the CIA's vein scanners utilized an infrared camera to read a thermal image of the tip of the finger, so using an amputated digit to spoof the system wouldn't work, due to blood/heat loss. Years earlier, Jaffir had solved this problem by connecting a tiny microprocessor powered by a single CR2325 coin-type battery to the metallic material of the printed vein system. The microprocessor provided the correct amount of heat to fool the infra-red capacity of a vein scanner. Amazingly, it had taken only nine minutes to print the finger that Nicole Grant now had protruding from the fringes of the mop head, with her right hand concealed below. Hernandez knew that Jaffir had previously cloned many fingers and even palms to successfully get past vein scanners, but typically such work took several painstaking hours. Tonight was so rushed, Jaffir had confided to the veteran field agent that using the finger was a crap shoot.

Time was so tight and Grant had been so insistent, that, short of aborting, there simply hadn't been another option. So here he stood, one floor below the action, watching on video as the amateur Nicole Grant disappeared into the bowels of the beast. He fully expected he'd have to come running at any moment and pull off some kind of rescue—he had a small quantity of C-4 plastic explosive stashed in his pocket—but how to blow the exterior door safely with Grant standing just on the other side?

• • • •

NICOLE GRANT LEANED forward and pressed her eye socket against the padding of the iris scanner. She trembled because she knew she was on CCTV being watched by armed security on the other side of the door. And she was locked up tight in the ante-room—anyone leaving had to be buzzed out by security or they weren't going anywhere. Just as she'd broken out into a cold sweat, a recorded, monotone female voice said, "Thank you, Rose Chin."

Okay, so she passed the iris scan.

Now came the tricky part. While trying not to be conspicuous about it, she kept her head angled away from the CCTV camera as she extended her hidden right hand toward the finger vein scanner. She maneuvered the fake finger into the glass trough and waited. Hopefully, it wouldn't look odd on camera that she was holding the mop head as she scanned the finger.

Nicole stood there and unconsciously released a large exhale as she waited. But nothing happened. She gently moved the finger in the scanning trough. Still nothing. Her clammy hand tightened its grip of the fake finger.

• • • •

AN AFRICAN-AMERICAN security guard sat at the reception console of the CIA field office that masqueraded as a real estate de-velopment company at One Pacific Place. Due to his expanding belly he always took off his heavy duty belt to feel more comfortable. The stiff black leather duty belt held gear like a Glock 21 in a Bianchi holster, handcuffs, pepper spray, collapsible steel baton, folding knife, and a radio telephone that connected with the communications room at CIA station in the U.S. Consulate on 26 Garden Road. The guard only removed the belt if no one was present. Like right now. He'd have plenty of time to put it back on if one of the CIA spooks showed up.

The spooks came and went, but all he had to do was buzz them out. There were other small duties: communication checks, alarm checks, and he had to make rounds every two hours.

Four security monitors were mounted below the reception counter. Each monitor showed four different camera views. A small console allowed an operator to switch camera views, zoom, pan, or tilt. There were 34 cameras total in the facility, but only the 16 most important ones were displayed on the four monitors in front of the guard.

Right now one of those camera views showed the Asian cleaning lady who came every day at this time standing in the anteroom with her finger on the vein scanner. He'd already glanced at her when a soft chiming alarm alerted him to someone approaching the exterior door out in the hallway. He hadn't bothered to look up from the TV show streaming on his laptop, but he heard her enter the anteroom and then heard the computerized voice say "Thank you, Rose Chin," when she'd done her iris scan. She'd be entering the reception area any second, but there was no need to put on his duty belt for the cleaning lady. He had the sign-in sheet right in front of him ready for her to sign.

He laughed at an off-color joke, but then glanced back at the CCTV monitor. WTF? Get your ass in here girl, I'm busy! Irritated, he moved his left hand to the camera control console, selected Camera Three, and grabbed the joystick.

• • • •

WORKING HARD TO TAKE silent deep breaths, Nicole Grant continued to move the fake finger slightly, and then waited, hoping the scan would read it. So far it hadn't. The battery-powered microprocessor was safely in her pants pocket. She wondered if somehow the connection had come loose. How could she check it without raising suspicion?

A voice suddenly came through her earbuds. "Miss Grant, keep shifting the position of the finger," said Jaffir, gently.

"Rose, what's going on?" camethe guard's voice over the PA speaker in the anteroom. Nicole hadn't seen a microphone, but didn't want to reply, anyway.

Then Hernandez's voice came through the earbuds. "You have to answer the guard. Don't sweat it if you don't see a microphone, it's probably hidden. I know you only speak Mandarin, not Cantonese, and I know they sound different, but you have to fake it. You heard Rose talk in the van. Try to fake her voice and say, *Gāozuŏ lā,* like you're irritated."

Nicole looked desperate, so it was a good thing she wasn't looking at the CCTV camera. "*Gāozuŏ lā,*" she said, trying to sound impatient.

"*Sik bak guo,*" said Hernandez in her earbuds, like you're frustrated it's not working."

"*Sik bak guo,*" repeated Nicole.

She knew it would look weird on camera, but she moved her left hand under the mop head and felt the wire connecting into the fake finger. The connection felt loose, so she pressed the wire into the soft, resin compound comprising the finger, then placed it again into the scanner.

Nothing happened. Fighting panic, Nicole removed the finger from the scanner and then placed it in one more time.

"Thank you, Rose Chin," said the monotone female voice. The inner door clicked open, startling Nicole.

"Nicole, put your hand in your shoulder bag and find the gun. Then walk straight through that door with your head down," said Hernandez. I'm coming your way right now."

But before she made a move, the inner door suddenly flung open...revealing the guard standing there as a quizzical look swept over his face.

"Who the hell are you?" he asked.

Nicole stood flat-footed, trying to think of something to say.

"Nicole, the gun," boomed Hernandez's voice in the earbuds. "I'll be there in thirty seconds."

She reached into the shoulder bag and started fumbling around. The look on the guard's face suggested he knew something wasn't kosher. He grabbed the door.

"Move forward, dammit! Get in there!" shouted Hernandez over the earbuds.

The guard flung the door trying to close it, but Nicole lurched forward at the last second and put her shoulder into it, and then stumbled into the room almost falling down.

The man reached for his gun, but it wasn't there. He wasn't wearing his duty belt. His eyes went wide as Nicole raised the big black pistol with the extra-long cylinder that fired shotgun shells. He backpedaled as she pointed the gun at him. But she didn't fire and couldn't hold the heavy gun steady with just one hand.

He backed away further and then turned and ran for the reception desk.

"Grant, I'm at the front door. Take a deep breath and pull the trigger," boomed Hernandez's voice through the earbuds. "If you don't shoot that son-of-a-bitch with the rubber pellets, he'll shoot you with lead and you'll be dead."

Fighting fear that weighed down her feet like anchor chains dropped into a troubled sea, she shuffled toward the reception counter. Shooting another human being was simply the last thing she

ever wanted to have to do. Even with rubber pellets. Waves of nausea wracked her and she felt like she existed in a bubble of perception
where everything slowed down. She watched with detachment as the
guard stumbled while rounding the corner of the reception console,
angling toward his duty station and gun.

"Stop," she managed to utter, closing the distance between them.

He didn't. He bounced off of a cabinet, his eyes wide as saucers,
and staggered toward his desk chair. His gun, radio, the whole duty
belt were wedged into an open drawer.

"Stop or I'll shoot." She spoke louder this time, but without
any kind of convincing authority behind the words. She sounded
drugged.

"Hold the gun with both hands," said Hernandez in the earbuds.
"Don't jerk the pull, just squeeze."

She steadied her aim by grasping the pistol butt with her left
hand for additional support. Nicole stood less than six feet from the
man. He lunged for his pistol and pulled it free from his duty belt.
Oh God, he's going to shoot me. Their eyes met as he raised his weapon.
Grant bit down hard on her lip and yelled, "Don't!"

A loud report boomed like a cannon in the reception area.

The pistol wavered in Grant's hands as she lost strength. Breath
rushed from her chest as she tried to focus. She blinked, and saw the
guard fall backward. His head slammed hard into a solid wooden
cabinet. He crumpled to the floor, barely conscious. The impact of
rubber buckshot from a .410 shotshell fired at close range could be
fatal, but Hernandez had assured her the guard would be wearing a
bulletproof vest. She stared down at the prone man and saw no sign
of bleeding. Thank heaven for small favors.

"Get behind the counter and buzz me in." Hernandez's calm
voice sounded in her earbuds.

She stood rooted in place, her eyes closed in silent thanks.

"Grant, there might be others," he warned.

She snapped out of her stupor and ran behind the reception counter, suddenly free of all fear. The sick feeling evaporated, the altered perception vanished. Hyper-alert, she retrieved the guard's gun from the floor and then plopped into the desk chair. Being intimately familiar with physical security systems it only took a moment to find the door switch. She saw Hernandez on camera standing just outside the exterior door and she buzzed him in through both doors.

She pushed aside the laptop playing a TV show, and checked the sign-in sheet to see if anyone else was present. She quickly cycled through the camera views to double-check that they were alone. As Hernandez came running up, she looked at him and indicated the sign-in sheet.

"The sign-in sheet says we're alone and I don't see anyone else on the cameras." She looked at him with a straight face and said, "What took you so long?"

Before Hernandez could respond, a soft chiming alarm sounded. Grant checked the CCTV monitors and her eyes went wide.

"Two people approaching the front door, holding smart cards!"

CHAPTER 15

18:55 CIA contract agents Chuck Wheeler and Gail Roberts stepped out of the elevator on the 23rd floor of One Pacific Place. Wearing slacks and a dress shirt, Wheeler had an oiled-canvas shoulder bag slung over his shoulder. A man with a reputation for doing the dirtiest jobs and doing them well, Wheeler had a sour taste in his mouth and felt grouchy. The fluorescent overhead lighting reflected off his waxed, bald head in a dull blueish glow. A man who constantly updated his situational awareness, his dark eyes flicked back and forth, like balls bouncing around inside a *pachinko* machine. His friendly acquaintances—he didn't have any real friends—who didn't know his true job, kidded him about his constant eye movement and gave him nicknames like Bouncy and Pinball. Wheeler always smiled at the monikers. Being alert had kept him alive, and he intended to live long and prosper.

At fifty-three, he was short but maintained tremendous upper body strength through rigorous daily workouts. He never wore clothing that revealed his muscular build, and his wire-rimmed glasses made him look like a schoolteacher. Hence, opponents usually underestimated him.

"Still no answer?" he asked.

"No answer," said Roberts, his red-haired partner, as she terminated the call on her cell phone. She was a big-boned thirty-seven year-old from Colorado, dressed for success in a black Fendi business suit. Freckles splayed out over her pale white skin from her nose to the middle of her cheeks like too much red pepper on mashed potatoes. Blue eyes ringed with crimson and droopy eyelids suggested she was running a deficit in the sleep column. Her cover as VP of software development for a Silicon Valley firm fit her well. She had the kind of cool detachment that many woman in powerful positions have. She moved with complete confidence giving a sense that she was accustomed to giving orders, not taking them. Wheeler's partnership with her was always a balancing act between two strong personalities who would never admit the other had been right.

"Trust me, we're being played," he said. "Rice won't take our calls, and Ma tells us to check in for new orders? What, we're working for PLA military intelligence now? A commie general tells us what to do?"

"Not out here in the hallway," she quietly admonished.

"This hallway is clean," said Wheeler, brushing off her concern as his eyes darted about. "The Company owns the whole floor."

"Rice is busy with the charity thing. So she didn't pick up," said Roberts, sounding like she was making an excuse.

"Bullcrap. I've seen this kind of thing before. They're in crisis mode. They've pushed us aside. There won't be any more consulting with us, we won't be witnessing and recording any more kills. The Chinese are going to whack Grant and Hernandez as soon as they find them, wherever that might be. You saw all those new goons posted in the mall and in the Marriott."

They moved through the small waiting area, both holding smart cards as they approached the front door.

"I don't really care if the Chinese are cutting us out. That's on them, not on us. And this thing needs to end tonight."

Wheeler and Roberts didn't particularly like each other, and the nature of what they'd witnessed over the last two weeks—the murders of eighteen Americans—didn't help their moods any. They'd both seen some of the ugliest business the Agency had been involved in during the last fifteen years, but in a sick kind of way, the last two weeks had been the icing on the cake. Wheeler knew she wanted this job to end. More than that, she wanted a change. Roberts would never share her true desires or motivations with him, but Wheeler sensed she was looking to do something other than contract work.

"It would be nice to wrap it up tonight," said Wheeler, "but Hernandez is long gone. He's too smart to stick around Pacific Place."

"We both watched him take out two of Tang's killers on Tung Choi Street this afternoon, before they could kill Grant," she said pointedly. "His file indicated he was a middle management type, but we saw a very talented solo assassin at work, didn't we?"

Wheeler suddenly understood why she was anxious for the operation to finish. "So you're thinking Hernandez is here to kill the killers. And you think he might also want to get anyone else connected to the murders, including you and me."

She nodded. "Somebody tipped him, that's why he went to ground. So he knows more about this whole business than we do, which wouldn't be hard, since we don't know why our employer wanted twenty American citizens eliminated.It's possible Hernandez might even know our identities."

Wheeler paused, thinking. He wasn't about to admit he agreed with her. "Be nice if we had his real file. Then we'd know what he's all about." If Hernandez wanted to exact vengeance on anyone connected to the whole ugly affair, so what? Let him try. The chances of him living to the end of the week were slim to none.

"The writing on the wall suggests our services are no longer required. They'll probably send us out on a red eye flight, so I'm going to pack my gear right now," she said.

"Until we hear from Rice, we're not going anywhere. But sure, pack your gear, and don't forget to upload your video." Wheeler was an old school gentleman, even with someone he didn't particularly care for, like Roberts, so he swiped his smart card in front of the sensor, the lock buzzed, and then he opened the door letting her go in first.

"What's that?" she said, stepping into the anteroom.

The mop head Nicole Grant had used when she held the fake finger lay on the floor. The finger itself was partially visible under the cloth fringes. The connecting wire had been pulled free from the microprocessor, and that wire was clearly visible.

"Looks like the cleaning lady dropped something," said Wheeler, squinting.

The outer door clicked closed and locked behind them. Roberts then looked into the iris scanner. "Thank you, Gail Roberts," was the computerized response.

As Wheeler looked more closely he noticed the wire which ran under the mop head. *What's up with that?* He bent down for a better look.

Roberts slid her index finger into the scanning trough. "Thank you, Gail Roberts." The door clicked unlocked and Roberts pushed through just as he spotted the index finger.

"Roberts, wait!"

Still squatting, Wheeler reached for the .45 caliber Kimber Super Carry Ultra HD pistol in his shoulder holster when...

"Pull a gun and I blow her head off."

Wheeler looked up to see a tall man standing in the inner doorway with a Chinese Type 67 integrally silenced pistol against the side of Robert's head. The man's appearance was completely different from earlier this afternoon, but Wheeler could see it was Ron Hernandez.

What the hell!? Had Hernandez known he and Roberts were coming in tonight? How could he? And how would he have known about this field station? They'd been shown a file on the man, but now there was no doubt it had been grossly incomplete. And if he busted in to this CIA field station then he was definitely here in Hong Kong to kill anyone involved with the deaths of the eighteen Americans. If Hernandez knew that he and Roberts were part of the operation, they were as good as dead unless he pulled his weapon and took his chances in a shootout.

"What makes you think I give a damn about her?" asked Wheeler, evenly, as his eyes zipped from Hernandez's face, to the suppressed pistol, to the back of Robert's head.

Wheeler calculated that he could get his weapon out of the holster at about the same time Hernandez could shift his aim and shoot at him. But if he went for his gun and Hernandez shot Roberts first, he'd have time to kill Hernandez, for sure.

"That's cute," said Roberts, who stood in the doorway with her back to Wheeler, "but there are two of them. And the girl has a cannon pointed at my chest."

Wheeler could care less if Roberts was killed, but he was not about to be taken prisoner. Just as he made the decision to go for his gun...Hernandez pivoted and fired.

Wheeler pulled the Kimber free from his holster just as a bullet whizzed past his ear.

"Don't!" said Hernandez sharply. He stepped forward, closing the distance between them.

The physical dominance of Hernandez towering over him was not lost on Wheeler. The Kimber was in his hand, out of his jacket, but wasn't pointing at anyone. But Hernandez's gun, now only five feet away, was quite definitely pointed at him.

"The first one wasn't supposed to hit you. This one will. Right between the eyes."

Wheeler believed it. He didn't want to be taken prisoner, but at least the capture would be recorded on camera and no one could fault him. And being taken prisoner was much preferable to being shot on the floor. He had a backup gun in an ankle holster. The smart play was to surrender now and look for an opening later.

"If you so much as twitch, I'll kill you," said Hernandez. "Very slowly, release your grip and let the gun fall to the floor."

Wheeler closed his eyes. This contract had become a Grade-A goat rope. He dropped his gun.

• • • •

NICOLE GRANT SAT IN a small room in the CIA field office. Looking deflated, she eased the handset of the secure phone back into its substantial cradle. She felt like she'd been gut-punched. Ernest Normann hadn't answered her call. Why? He always answered. At any hour. He knew she might be calling back, knew she was in deep trouble, but he didn't answer. She'd just gone to extreme lengths to get to a secure phone, but he hadn't answered. He'd been a father figure as well as a boss, and she hadn't anticipated being dumped by a father figure.

She stood up looking dejected, then hurried into the hallway and rushed back to the guard post behind the reception counter. She had tasks running on different computers there and needed to get hands-on. She had no choice but to put the disappointment about Normann's refusal to take her call out of her mind for now.

She turned to the guard's laptop. Scant minutes earlier she'd hacked into a Hong Kong government Website to get the blueprints of Pacific Place. Those blueprints were now downloaded onto a USB flash drive. Nicole removed the drive from the guard's laptop and used adapters to connect it to her tablet computer. It took only seconds to move the blueprints onto the tablet.

Next, she turned her attention to the desktop PC at the security post, where she had Darknet and a few hacking programs running. Before attempting the phone call to Normann, she'd hacked into the security systems of Pacific Place and the Conrad, Shangri-La, and Upper House hotels. She'd spotted other hackers doing exactly the same thing and had traced them to the Marriott. She then took downmost of the major CCTV systems in Pacific Place. Facial recognition software was useless without the CCTV feeds, so she felt a sense of accomplishment. Still, the hackers—she assumed they were Chinese—had locked her out of the Marriott security system.

She assumed the other hackers had "seen" her, just as she'd seen them. Neither she nor they had bothered to use many proxy servers, meaning they were in as much of a hurry as she was, meaning she was probably up against Chinese government hackers working in the field in direct assistance to the killers after her and Hernandez.

Nicole picked up her tablet computer. Using commercially available software, she attempted to remotely access her home laptop at her condo in Phoenix. This was a simple procedure that she'd performed countless times, but right now, now of all times, she couldn't gain access. A pop-up window stated that her laptop was "Offline." Had there been a power outage or some kind of mishap? Her home laptop was offline, and that made no sense.

A look of confusion skewed her normally attractive features. With that laptop offline, she couldn't access the secret keys stored inside. Without those keys, she couldn't retrieve the files she'd stored on the Darknet. Without those files—she had lied to Hernandez, there were many more than just the one audio file—she had no documentary evidence to use as leverage to save her and Hernandez's lives. More than one file and more than one key. Yes, she'd lied to him and would have to explain everything soon.

More pressing was the question of how long had her laptop been offline? During the two-plus weeks of her vacation, no alarms had come in from the elaborate security system that protected her Phoenix condo. So what happened? She turned back to the duty station PC, connected to a super-fast fiber-optic Internet connection, and logged in to her home alarm/CCTV system. She had six interior cameras, and it only took a moment to see that something wasn't right. Her condo had been ransacked! She brought up the view of her home office. Her desk was a mess, the laptop gone.

Since her condo alarms were sophisticated, the skill of the in-truders who broke in had to have been high. They'd gotten past all of her systems without alerting her. The killers after her now must have first gone looking for her in Phoenix. Approaching footsteps inter-rupted her speculation and she reached for the heavy pistol in front of her.

"Whoa, cowgirl. I'm a friendly," said Hernandez as he came around and joined her behind the counter. He had Wheeler's oiled-canvas shoulder bag in hand. She sheepishly put the gun down.

"Guess I'm still nervous."

"You should be. Anyway, I've got the guard and the two agents secured but I need to ask them some more questions. Obviously, we need to get out of here quickly. How much more time do you need?"

She thought about it. There was a lot she hadn't yet explained to him. "A few more minutes. But there's a problem."

He seemed to brace himself. "Let's hear it."

She explained how her place had been burglarized and the laptop was missing. "I guess they broke in because they were going to kill me in Phoenix."

"That's a safe bet. But without that laptop, we have no key. And without the key we're screwed?"

"Yes, but I was just about to track it."

"Your laptop has a tracking device?" he asked, somewhat sur-prised.

"All of my electronics do. Either a software app or physical mi-cro-module with a dedicated lithium battery. I programmed it so that GPS determines the position every ten seconds, giving me a ten-week operational window before the battery dies."

"Spare me the technical specs. You can track your laptop right now?"

She nodded and opened up software called KCS on her tablet. "I use software tracking apps for my phones, but for my laptops and some other devices I install a tiny GPS micro-module tracker made by a German company."

"So your computer doesn't need to be turned on?"

"No, but it has to be within range of a cell tower or Wi-Fi signal for the GPS function to work."

"Why do you have such elaborate security on your electronics?"

Nicole felt a little defensive. As an engineer, she was used to being mocked for her cautious ways. "Do you think it's obsessive? I mean, I'm in the security business. I even use a steel stylus to scratch an identification number onto the plastic cases of all my devices."

"Why?"

"If my units are stolen and the police should recover them, they'll enter the ID number into a database. I'll be identified as the owner and get my stuff back."

"Grant... I know that engineers are 'different,' but your boyfriends must hate you."

"What boyfriends?"

"Exactly."

Hernandez opened Wheeler's shoulder bag. He removed a pair of Bushnell binoculars with digital video recording capability, and was about to show them to her when...

"My God, it's here!"

He shot her a look. "What? Your laptop is in this office?"

"Practically. It's in Hong Kong. Right here in Pacific Place. I'll have to match up the elevation coordinates with the correct floor, but it's at Two Pacific Place."

Curious, Hernandez moved in close to look at the screen. "That's the Island Shangri-La tower. Where Zhao has a condo."

"If it's in his condo, we have to break in and get it," she stated emphatically.

"Out of the question—the place is crawling with security," he said, with finality. "You said your laptop was offline. Does that mean it's turned off or does it mean there's no Internet signal?"

"That's unclear. If you're asking me if we can access my laptop remotely, the answer is 'maybe.' But not from here. We'll need to get a lot closer."

"Okay, we'll talk about that later. Just hurry up and finish what you're doing." His hand moved down to Wheeler's shoulder bag. "One more thing." He removed the binoculars and a small camcorder. "Download the video from these two units. Make a physical copy and send encrypted copies off into cyberspace."

She reached out and took the devices. "What's on them?"

"The killings of eighteen Americans. I just watched how my brother was murdered," he said. Nicole could see he was struggling not to choke up. "The assassin was the same man I saw today wearing a brown shirt on Tung Choi Street."

She looked at him plaintively, but had no words.

"It's more evidence for us, but we still need that audio file of yours." He turned away quickly and hurried back down the hallway.

Nicole watched him go. She bit her lip and a deep sadness washed over her. Who were they kidding? How could they hope to survive? How could she and Ron Hernandez defeat the military/intelligence apparatus of two superpowers whose operatives make movies of the innocent civilians they killed?

Nicole had just risked her life to break into a federal facility—a CIA field office, no less—and had come up with zero. No Ernest Normann and no home laptop.

So much for her plans.

CHAPTER 16

19:09 Wheeler sat on the floor, hands and feet duct-taped. Hernandez had watched enough of the video from the Bushnell binoculars and camcorder to understand what the two CIA contractor's roles had been in the killings. He still felt furious from having seen the video of the thin, fortyish, bespectacled Chinese man push his brother onto the tracks of a metro train at Foggy Bottom Station in Washington, D.C. The same man in the brown shirt from earlier today. So far, Hernandez had compartmentalized the emotion as he interrogated Wheeler. He needed to keep that rage in check.

"I had a nice chat with your partner in the next room. So you guys are quality control, huh? Make sure the job gets done right with the least amount of muss and fuss." He wanted Wheeler thinking that Roberts had talked. She hadn't.

Wheeler remained silent. He hadn't spoken since surrendering in the anteroom.

Hernandez had their weapons, cell phones, computers—all of their gear—since this room functioned as their workspace just as a room across the hall had done so when Hernandez worked out of this field office five years ago.

Hernandez had found the call log on Roberts' phone with recent calls to RICE, MA, and TANG. "So who do you report to? Rice, Ma, Tang, or all three?"

Wheeler stayed silent. "I'm Ron Hernandez, by the way. And you are...?" As Wheeler gave him a hard look, he used his tablet computer to snap a photograph and then logged into a CIA database using a password provided to him by his father-in-law William Snedeker, the man who'd warned him ten days ago to go underground. In moments he had his answer. "You, sir, are Charles "Chuck" Wheeler, CIA contractor par excellence, it seems." He scanned Wheeler's dossier. "Quite a few impressive kills in here."

He aimed the suppressed Chinese pistol at Wheeler, then swung the gun up and shot out the overhead camera. "The microphone, as you probably know, is right here." He crossed to a picture frame on the wall and removed a small listening device from behind the frame, then crushed it under his shoe. "So now the CIA won't have a record of what we discuss," said Hernandez, who had his own hidden unit recording everything.

"Did it not occur to you or your partner that there's evidence linking you to all of the murders? You flew on airplanes, rented cars, stayed in hotels. Maybe you used phony names, but you can both be ID'd. You were present in every city when the killings took place. Present at or very near every crime scene. So that's Plan B on how to deal with you, if they need fall guys." He paused. "But understand, you'd be a fall guy in death. First they kill you, then information emerges suggesting you two went rogue and started killing former co-workers, something like that."

A trace of concern spread across Wheeler's face.

"But I doubt it will come to that because of Genghis Khan's funeral."

"What?" asked Wheeler, with his eyebrows furrowed.

Good. Wheeler had spoken. "Genghis Khan's funeral. Soldiers killed the entire funeral procession of about eight hundred people to keep the treasure-laden burial site secret. But not long after the soldiers left, they themselves were ambushed and all were massacred. And then later, the second group was also wiped out, to the man, insuring that no one left alive knew where the great Khan was buried."

"Yeah, well, we're not in Mongolia and this is the twenty-first century."

Hernandez laughed. "You and your partner were dead the moment you took the assignment. You're no rookie, how could you not have seen that? Maybe your ego got in the way and you started believing your own PR, like you're too valuable an asset to the Agency."

"I've successfully completed every assignment I was ever given. The reward is not a bullet in the head."

"Except I'm sure you're off the books here. This isn't an official Company op. Think about it, Wheeler, how could Zhao let you live, knowing what you know? In fact," he held up Roberts' cell phone again, "I'll bet Zhao will have Rice, Ma, and Tang killed, too. It's the only way to secure his presidency. Anyone who knows much of anything will be erased."

"I know squat!" protested Wheeler. "Our job was to document some killings, to make sure they were designed to avoid collateral damage. Period. No questions asked. Langley wouldn't have approved this if the targets weren't bad guys who deserved to die."

"Except, like I said, you're off the books. Do you really think this op was approved by the lawyers on the seventh floor at CIA headquarters?"

Lost in thought, Wheeler's eyes drifted downward.

"Since you know squat, let me clue you in." Hernandez launched into a brief explanation of the drone operation over Guangzhou run out of Pomona, and how elements of the U.S. government had aided Zhao Yiren, a CIA asset, in his bid to become the next Chinese president. "We gave him America's most sophisticated spy drone and we gave him his chief rival, Wang Hongwei, on a platter. And now, in less than two weeks, he'll becomethe Chinese president. So Zhao and the secret cabal in D.C. that's supporting him can't let a whistleblower ruin things by going public with the truth.

"Get the picture now? Does it sound like I deserve to die, to use your words? Does Grant? Or the eighteen others—did they deserve it?" Hernandez paused, and then looked at Wheeler. "Do you deserve to die, just so Zhao doesn't have to worry about being outed?"

"You could be lying through your teeth."

"You know I'm not lying, you just haven't admitted it yet." Hernandez held up a flash drive for Wheeler to see, then placed it on a table. "The person who warned me that I was about to be killed got his hands on the recordings of some private conversations. It won't stand up in court, but you might recognize a voice or two. When this goes public—and it will—along with your video that I now have, where will that leave *you*?"

Wheeler looked long and hard at Hernandez. "Let's say I believe you. How are you going to help me?"

"Answer my questions and I can get you out of Hong Kong alive."

"And if I don't?" asked Wheeler.

"If I thought you were complicit in the killings, I'd off you right now. But I believe you were just QC and didn't know the truth of the matter. If we don't make a deal, your handler and the Chinese will deal with you. Know what I mean?"

A scowl of frustration spread across Chuck Wheeler's face. "I don't like my choices."

"Welcome to my world."

Wheeler looked up at Hernandez and regarded him carefully. "I don't trust you, but I guess you're my best shot. What do you want to know?"

"Tell me about Grant's computer. The one taken from her condo in Phoenix."

Wheeler hesitated, then, "Tang took it."

"Tang?"

"Director Tang. A chief in the Chinese Ministry of State Security. He runs the wet team that did all the kills."

"Tang and his people killed all eighteen Americans?"

Wheeler nodded.

Hernandez suddenly got a gut-hunch. "What color shirt was he wearing today? Was he on the street when they were going to whack Grant?"

"Yeah, he was there. Roberts and I watched the whole thing go down from a pedestrian overpass about a block away. Tang is a thin guy with glasses; I think he was wearing a brown shirt."

So the man who killed Willie was a director in the MSS named Tang. Hernandez hid the fact he was thrilled to get this information. "Okay, so where did Tang take the laptop?" This was a good test question since Hernandez already knew the answer.

Wheeler shrugged. "They got real curious about that computer. Something it was doing. They used the word 'pinging.' And it was heavily encrypted. They were desperate to know all about it. Why was that?"

"Because they thought Grant might be a whistleblower with damaging evidence. Evidence they would need to seize or vacuum up if it had been sent elsewhere."

"Well, I heard somebody say the laptop was going to the Fifty-seventh Institute. I remember fifty-seven because of Heinz ketchup—fifty-seven varieties. I figured that was in China, but I don't know who or what the Fifty-seventh is."

"Okay, so far so good. So who's your control? Somebody named Rice?"

Before Wheeler could answer, the door flung open revealing a wild-eyed Nicole Grant holding the big S&W Governor handgun. "Eight men at the door, trying to get in!"

"Caucasian?"

"Asian," she replied.

Hernandez scooped up all the gear belonging to the two CIA contractors into a backpack and slung it over his shoulder. He pocketed Roberts' cell phone, but placed Wheeler's phone next to the flash drive on the table. He coolly looked at the CIA contractor sitting on the floor. Given a little more time, he might have turned the man into an ally. "We have more to talk about, Wheeler. But a deal's a deal. I'll be in touch," he said, indicating the phone, then he hurried out the door wondering what in the hell had gone wrong now.

• • • •

NICOLE GRANT'S HAND shook slightly as she put the big pistol back into the nylon shoulder bag while Hernandez studied the CCTV camera view of the group of Asian men outside the exterior door of Trans-National Corporation. A couple of the men were talking on cell phones while others were trying to force open the door. Grant had things she needed to tell her partner, but it didn't look like this was the time.

"Mainland Chinese intelligence agents is my guess. They don't look like Hong Kong police and they're not CIA."

"So the Agency still doesn't know we're in here?" she asked.

"I doubt seriously that these thugs know they're trying to jimmy the door to a CIA field station. But I'm guessing Christians in Action will find out damn quick." He gave Grant a serious look. "What could you have done to tip off the Chinese?"

Her eyes briefly rolled up as she thought about that. "Well, I hacked the security systems of the hotels and mall here at Pacific Place. Others were hacking in at the same time," she admitted.

"Others?" he asked.

"I... they must have been Chinese agents. Chinese government hackers." Embarrassment washed over her. She felt horrible that she'd screwed up so badly by not thinking to tell him earlier.

"So the people who want to kill us traced our location via the Internet based on what you were doing, correct?"

"I was rushed, so I only set up a couple of proxies, so yes, that's probably what happened."

"Well that was pretty stupid," he said sharply. "We went to a lot of trouble to get in here, and I'm not done with what I need to do."

She blushed a deep red. "But I've taken down most of the CCTV security video in the entire complex. They'll have a much harder time finding us now."

"They're right outside the damn door! They don't need CCTV to find us, you sent them an electronic invitation. They've had enough time to flood in dozens of agents. So nice work, but now we have to run. Grab everything and follow me." He turned and jogged off down the hall.

"I shut down the command system. No one can get through that door," she called out, trying to put a positive spin on the situation. He didn't look back or say anything else. She flashed angry—angry at herself—then took off running after him.

She ran flat out. He'd fished out a cell phone and made a call just as she caught up with him at a set of heavy steel double-doors that led to the service elevators.

"Jaffir, any BGs down there?"

Hernandez's phone was on speaker, so Nicole clearly heard Jaffir say, "Negative, but security is searching every vehicle leaving Pacific Place."

"Understood. Standby for now, but give me a heads-up if the status changes down there." He closed the phone, and then looked at her. "They're tightening the noose."

Hernandez slid open a massive door lock bolt and disengaged other locks on the steel double-doors.

"I'm sorry I screwed up. But if you open those doors, an alarm will go off at CIA station in the consulate," she warned.

"We don't have a choice. The Chinese probably have people on the stairs, so we have to take our chances with the service elevators." He drew his two pistols, gave her a look, and then kicked the door open, ready to fire. The small foyer for the two service elevators was empty, so he stepped in holding the silenced pistol and Wheeler's Kimber—one gun in each hand. He gestured with his head as he took up a shooting position and she pressed the down button. It only took a moment for a service elevator to arrive.

Hernandez stood ready to fire, but the car was empty. They hurried in and he pressed the button for LG1. "If this car stops at any floor other than LG1, we could have a problem."

She nodded as the elevator doors closed.

"I'm trying to give you a hint to pull your damn gun, Grant," he said, irritated. "Like you should have pulled it when I opened the steel doors, and like you should have pulled it while we waited for the elevator to arrive. You want to be my partner, then back me the hell up." Nicole saw that Hernandez wasn't trying to hide it, he was royally steamed.

She blushed again as she reached into the nylon shoulder bag and retrieved the heavy handgun she'd shot the guard with. They stood on opposite sides of the elevator doors, guns out and ready as the car silently, slowly descended.

"What else haven't you told me?" he asked accusingly.

Her eyes met his and she quickly explained to him about her old NSA boss Ernest Normann and how he didn't answer her call using the secure phone.

"I asked you not to contact anyone."

"Your cell phone video message said you were dead, so any agreements we had were null and void," she retorted. He'd put her on the defensive but she had no intention of staying that way. "I called Normann just before I saw you at the Shangri-La. He told me to call back on a secure line."

"His phone was probably monitored. Most likely he's been waxed."

"No, don't say that. Don't even joke about that." Her words rushed out like they'd been swept away on a tide of fear. She couldn't face the notion that her call might have led to his death. Too much anguish pressed on her chest as it was, and the idea that call could have...

"We'll talk about it later. What else?"

Crap, how did he know there was more?

"I hacked a local government computer and stole the blueprints for Pacific Place."

"Good. What else?"

She hesitated. This was the big revelation. Was it wise to tell him now, while they were both holding firearms? Screw it. "An admission. I was a spy for Normann, for the NSA, during the drone op. We stole everything. It got sent to NSA, and I personally saved hundreds of files on the Darknet to cover my ass. Not just the one file I've told you about."

She felt a sense of relief at have blurted out the secrets she'd been holding back from him, but her relief was tempered by the sight of Hernandez's face flushing with anger. She imagined white-hot rage rising in his throat.*He's thinking that I'm nothing more than a spy, a mole, and that I've betrayed him.* All afternoon she'd been playing the innocent, but Nicole knew she was guilty as hell. She'd lied to him several times. First about not having listened to the audio file of Vice Premier Wang Hongwei in the van, and now this. She had no idea how Hernandez would react to these revelations.

"So my laptop in Phoenix was pinging dozens of requests every day to the Darknet to keep all of those files fresh in cyber-space—that's what got the attention of the Chinese."

She watched as fury seemed to well-up inside him, but he didn't say a word.

"You probably want me to take a long walk on a short pier. You might even be wondering if you can trust me. That's up to you, but I swear I've got no more surprises. No more secrets. You know everything I know. So I hope you can be professional and put aside your anger, because we need to create a plan to remotely access my laptop."

He frosted her with an icy stare, then leveled his weapons as the elevator car arrived at LG1. Nicole also aimed her gun as the doors opened... but no one was there. They hurried out of the lift and he led her to a steel door. "Since you crashed so much CCTV video, use the blueprints you stole to lead us someplace safe," he said, pulling open the door that led into a concrete passageway.

"But isn't Jaffir waiting for us?"

"Forget about Jaffir. You and I need to have a private conversation," he said coldly.

Her heart sank. The tenuous trust she'd had with Hernandez lay in tatters like trash strewn in a dirty gutter

19$^{:23}$ MSS Director Tang's command post in the Marriott buzzed with electrified activity. Tang hid his impatience as he held a cell phone to his side while getting a briefing from his aide, Choi. Events were quickening, but not in a smooth fashion, and that frustrated him to no end. His hackers had identified an adversary hacker operating from an office at One Pacific Place. Whoever it was had crashed most of the CCTV systems in the entire complex. So Tang had dispatched his men and got lucky; a security guard identified Hernandez from one of the 8 X10s. The American had been seen loitering in the building. So Tang had felt confident in assuming that Hernandez and Grant were operating out of a company called Trans-National on the 23rd floor.

The problem lay in Tang's lack of manpower. Having to co-ordinate with the Second Department through Ma's aide Li Shan slowed everything down. It was also a recipe for confusion and screw-ups.

"Two more things," said Choi, continuing his briefing. "Nicole Grant had a long conversation with a female at the Marriott wine bar. We have this woman under close surveillance. She's British and might be the WikiLeaks replacement."

"Find out if she is. And the second thing?" asked Tang as he tugged at an earlobe.

"Six of General Ma's men just gained access to Trans-National Corporation at One Pacific Place through a service elevator entrance. They are right now inside the offices."

"So our MSS agents are still outside the front door. Ma's people have the stairwells covered and have just now entered through service elevators?"

"Yes, that's right, sir."

"Send six more of Ma's men in using the service elevators."

Tang turned away from Choi and brought the cell phone up to his ear. "Sorry to keep you waiting, General Ma, but at this moment we can't yet confirm that Grant or Hernandez are present in that office. But your men are now inside and will begin searching at any moment."

"Tell my men to shoot them on sight," came General Ma's voice from the cell phone.

• • • •

NICOLE GRANT FELT RON Hernandez drill her with a hard stare. She'd used the blueprints uploaded into her tablet computer to lead them deep into the inner workings of Pacific Place. They now stood in a large cement-walled room full of gargantuan HVAC—heating, ventilating, and air-conditioning—equipment, standing in broken rows like some kind of medieval maze of steel. Wide, six-foot high, battleship gray metal cabinets housed scrubbers that used massive filters to clean the air. Oversized air handlers conditioned and circulated the air, while giant dehumidifiers drained large amounts of water from Hong Kong's muggy atmosphere. Segments of the floor were made up of steel plates. Individual plates could be lifted for access to crawlspaces below the room. Duct work, steel conduit, and all kinds of cabling running on horizontal and vertical cable trays laced the room into a large industrial knot of efficient, humming machinery.

Grant thought Hernandez looked completely out of place standing there in his three-piece suit. He'd picked the lock to get them inside, but she could tell he didn't like being in this room. She was keenly aware he hadn't spoken to her since right after they'd left the elevator. She stood next to him fumbling with her tablet and suspected he now trusted her as far as he could throw a brick.

Nicole had gotten rid of the Central Services uniform shirt. She had the nylon shoulder bag she'd used as part of her cleaning lady disguise draped over a black pullover top, and still wore the clunky polyester uniform pants, black wig and sunglasses. The relentless sound of blowers and fans and pumps and other equipment provided a kind of Machine Age techno soundtrack to the unfolding drama between the two fugitives, like a baseline of tension.

"I don't like it here," he said, scowling as he looked around.

"Why? We have a strong, locked door. We can take some time and work up a plan to—"

"There's only one way in and one way out. If the bad guys start doing room-to-room searches and walk through that door, we're screwed."

"I was under the impression we were pretty much screwed, period."

"I don't know about you, but I'm no quitter," he snapped. "That's why you're going to answer some questions. Beginning with, are you still with NSA or some other agency?"

"No, I'm not." It was unnerving trying to hold his accusatory gaze. She looked to her tablet, to the blueprints of the building.

"Why did you lie to me?"

She hesitated, and then reluctantly looked up. "I'm still wrestling with the reasons."

He wasn't amused. "Answer my question."

"I was afraid, okay?" she blurted out. "I'm ashamed to admit it, but I was scared out of my wits. Considering my job and background, I should have better control over my emotions, my behavior, my fear. But you forced your way into my room, manhandled me, shot a bullet next to my arm, threatened to kill me, and then showed me video of an assassination squad assigned to end my life. So maybe I had good reasons to be frightened." She looked away, avoiding his gaze. "I guess I'm not as tough as I thought I was, as tough as I'd like to be, and that bothers the hell out of me. Anyway, fear can be irrational, but fear was only part of why I lied."

He watched her for several seconds. "What's the other part?"

She let out a long exhale. "I guess I'm facing up to the fact that I'm devious. I've become... dishonest. And it's not a particularly nice trait, is it?"

He crossed his arms. "That depends on intention."

"As a penetration tester, I have to think like hackers, thieves, criminals, think of how they might break into a system. I even go to physical locations and do risk assessment. How could I gain access to a building, break into the server room? How could I infect an unsuspecting employee's computer with spyware? So my intention is pure—I'm working to protect a client. But I wonder if by spending so much time thinking like a criminal—"

"You wonder if it's changed you for the worse," he said.

Considering his background, maybe he could relate, maybe he could understand what she was getting at. She looked at him through her dark glasses. "The reason I lied about not having listened to the audio file of Wang Hongwei in the back of the panel van was self-preservation. At the time, I thought you might kill me if I confessed to knowing what had been recorded. But since you already knew I'd sent a file to the Darknet, I admitted it."

"So you committed a sin of omission by not telling me about all of the other files. Or mentioning the fact you were a mole for the NSA."

"Yes. I was gaming you. Even after I'd come to trust you, I still held back the truth."

He nodded, seeming to digest her words. "Not too long ago, you told me that if I didn't shoot straight with you, you'd take your chances alone. But you're the one who hasn't been shooting straight with me."

Her mouth opened slightly. She started to say something, and then stopped. Then she simply said, "I'm sorry."

He finally broke his gaze and looked around at the machinery. "I'm going to find Jaffir. Your new passport and credit cards should be ready. I'll text you, tell you where I've hidden them." He turned and walked toward the door.

"Wait!" She wet her lips, took a breath and right there and then, in a flash of absolute certainty and clarity, made peace with her death. Her mother Jan would eventually recover from the news, if it came to that. Jan was so strong and brave. If Hernandez walked out that door, so be it. She'd do her best on her own, and that was all she could do. She pulled off the oversized sunglasses and stuck them into the shoulder bag. She realized almost immediately that it was an unconscious gesture that she was ready to come clean. "I want to tell you what I did for the NSA."

He checked the time on his Suunto watch. "Make it fast."

She took a breath, and then sat on the floor with her back against the cool cement wall. She placed her tablet computer on the steel floor next to her. It looked odd since he was wearing a three-piece suit, but Hernandez sat on the floor in front of her.

"The very first day of the op, acting under orders from Ernest Normann, I used a flash drive to infect the computers in Pomona with invasive, invisible, fast-loading software developed by the geniuses at Fort Meade. That software caused all of the data generated by the Omega Team to be sent to NSA. The data was piggybacking on the carrier signal going to Langley."

Hernandez nodded. "Clever." He crossed his arms, as if waiting in judgment to hear the rest.

"Normann had told me he wanted to know what the hell that super-secret Omega Team was up to. I felt uncomfortable spying on fellow Americans. But those were my orders, so I carried them out, even though I've never been trained as a field agent."

He nodded.

"But I'm a careful person and I like redundancy."

"So you also started sending the same data to the Darknet?"

"No. I altered the NSA's software so that everything that was sent to NSA was also sent to me. To a secure server I controlled. That last night of the operation you terminated the carrier signal before the audio file I'd recorded could be sent to my server. So that audio file of Wang Hongwei was the sole file I sent directly from Pomona to the Darknet—it was the only way to preserve it."

"Not like an engineer to do something so risky."

She nodded. "It was an impulsive decision that I've regretted ever since."

"What did that audio file contain?"

"Zhao Yiren was inside that panel van, waiting for the soldiers to bring in Wang Hongwei and Wang's special laptop."

Hernandez raised his eyebrows slightly. "I knew the mission was to help Zhao, but I didn't know he was inside the van."

Her eyes unfocused a bit as she recalled the details. "Zhao was gloating. He told Wang that instead of becoming the next president of China, Wang would become an inmate in a Chinese prison for the next thirty years. He threatened to have Wang's entire family killed if he didn't reveal information about secret bank accounts in the Caribbean. Wang was giving up bank names and account numbers all the way up until I stopped recording."

"So Zhao Yiren stole all of Wang Hongwei's dirty money. If the political elders in Beijing heard that tape they'd put him in front of a firing squad." Hernandez pursed his lips. "You're telling me you have that audio file, plus you kept copies of data generated on the drone operation?"

"Yes. A few months after it all went down, I sent the files on my secret server to the Darknet, and have kept them alive ever since. Like I said, I'm devious. Logically, the risk was *not* to keep copies of everything. I was being careful because something wasn't right with that Omega Team operation. Subsequent events would seem to confirm that." She looked at him straight on.

"Grant, you're full of it."

Nicole felt her face flush. Here she was letting her guard down, being honest with him and he was calling her a liar.

"You're not devious, you were cautious," he said, with a slight smile.

She blanched, and her anger evaporated into the ozone-rich air of the HVAC room. "You think so?" She watched as his countenance softened into something approaching neutrality. She absentmindedly wiped her clammy hands on her pants. "Can you answer a question for me? I understand that I'm alive thanks to you. But how is it that *you're* alive?"

He paused, as if considering how to answer. "I was warned by a highly placed contact. Someone who knew about the operation from the beginning."

"I didn't think many people knew about it."

"Giving the drone to the Chinese two years ago had to have been a deep black covert action program approved by the president. So maybe a dozen people knew. Not a huge number, but more than a few. This cover-up they're now doing with the killings is the kind of off-the-books operation that would be highly compartmentalized with only a handful of people in the loop. But what's the old saying by Benjamin Franklin? 'Three can keep a secret if two of them are dead.'"

"The person who warned you. Are they—?"

"Dead?"

He looked away, but his eyes betrayed intense worry. Nicole could tell that the person who'd helped him was someone special. He'd already lost his brother and now maybe someone else important to him. It hit home to her because she was worried sick that the

Chinese or even the Agency might grab Jan in Las Vegas to use as bait against her.

"Maybe he's dead. I'm not sure. Something is wrong, but I don't know what," said Hernandez, as if trying to swallow the emotion underlying the words.

There was nothing she could say, so she reached into the shoulder bag and handed him a business card. "Rena, the WikiLeaks girl, asked me to give this to you. I think you should talk to her."

He took the card and then looked at Nicole. "For the sake of argument, let's say we can go public. The first possibility is that we'll be ignored and nothing will happen except a stronger effort to find and kill us. The second possibility is the government will respond, meaning you and I would be demonized in the press. It's called the politics of personal destruction, and they're good at it. What we'd see is a huge cover-up, with a fall guy or two thrown in for the establishment mainstream media to devour."

"So why contact WikiLeaks in London? Wasn't it to try and save your life?"

He smiled a sad smile. "My goal since my brother's murder was to kill Zhao and anyone else responsible. But I've been living on borrowed time. WikiLeaks was a backup plan. If I died before I could get revenge, I thought maybe WikiLeaks going public would result in the Chinese government itself killing Zhao and some of the others."

He checked his watch, rubbed tired eyes, and wearily stood up. "Considering the video we got from those two contract agents," he said, "you hold some good evidence. But it's not enough. Your drone op files are the clincher that might make a difference for you. So I hope you can get the files back."

Crap, he was leaving, ending their tenuous partnership. She fought back freeze-dried panic. Her eyes told it all and she didn't care. She wanted to stay with Hernandez, but before she could say anything, they were startled by the sound of the door handle jiggling and then a key entering the door lock. Someone was about to enter.

• • • •

A PANEL VAN BACKED up to within five feet of a service elevator on Level LG1 and deposited eight hyped-up members of the Consulate General of the United States, Hong Kong and Macau, Special Response Team. Tension hung over them like a low thundercloud as the men crowded into the large elevator and armed themselves with HK 7A1 sub-machine guns and HK 416 assault rifles from two duffel bags. The team included members of Diplomatic Security Service, the U.S. Marines, the DEA, and the CIA, and all wore body armor that identified them as federal agents. Identified them to readers of English, that is.

They came in hot because the command security system was down, CCTV coverage was down, the guard on duty had not made a scheduled communications check and wasn't answering the desk phone or his cell phone, and the alarm on the double doors that led to the service elevators had been tripped. A building security officer on routine patrol had reported a group of men acting suspiciously on the 23rd floor, and two CIA subcontractors known to be using the facility were not answering their secure phones. A consensus quickly emerged that the field station had been breached, and after the Benghazi debacle, the Feds put in place protocols to act decisively in such instances.

When the service elevator doors opened on the 23rd floor, the first thing the SRT shooters saw were two Chinese men holding handguns.

"Drop your weapons!"

The two shocked Chinese men didn't understand English and couldn't fathom why these *gwailos* were pointing weapons at them. The West didn't run Hong Kong anymore, China did, damn it. The two men standing in the open doorway were Chinese soldiers in civilian clothes on loan tonight to General Ma and the Second Department. The soldiers resented Westerners and weren't about to be pushed around by these white faces stepping out of the elevator car.

"*Nǐ shì shuí*?!" asked the taller Chinese soldier, angrily. Who are you?! As the man spoke, he gestured with his gun hand. The movement of his gun barrel caused the nervous Americans to open fire.

The popping sounds of automatic weapons erupted from the elevator and the two Chinese men were riddled with dozens of high-capacity rounds, dropping them onto the hallway floor. The consulate SRT team stacked into the small service foyer that, unknown to them, Hernandez and Grant had exited through some minutes earlier. Two marines pulled the dead Chinese from the hallway into the foyer. When one of the marines chanced a look down the hallway, he was shot in the head. A nine-minute gun battle ensued between the SRT team and the remaining ten Chinese PLA soldiers in plainclothes from the Hong Kong Garrison. General Ma's aide Li Shan hadn't been able to conjure up enough intelligence agents on short notice, so she had taken it upon herself to enlist help from the army garrison located only minutes away. Her decision to use soldiers, and not covert operators, resulted in a bloodbath.

CHAPTER 18

19 :37 Kate Rice looked absolutely ravishing in a cleavage-revealing LBD—Little Black Dress. But her skin tone turned several different colors during the walk from the Shangri-La's Island Ballroom to an elevator, and then to the condo secretly owned by the CIA two floors below Zhao Yiren's condo. At least it looked like her skin tone changed to Socorro Trujillo, Barry Bergman's sharp young aide who had been delivering a whispered brief of the debacle at the CIA field station as she escorted Rice.

Trujillo, watching through her cold black eyes, had secretly enjoyed seeing Rice go bright red right off the bat when she told her she was being summoned to an emergency meeting, meaning she had to leave the frenzy of last-minute preparation for the Kids First charity reception in the hands of her assistants. Rice's reddish glow continued as anger mounted from hearing gory details of the situation at Trans-National. Trujillo then thought she turned slightly green at hearing the figures of dead and wounded—three Americans dead, four wounded; seven Chinese dead, three wounded. This was a potential catastrophe of epic proportions.

Finally, as Rice bit a fingernail, she looked a little yellowish or maybe just very pale. Probably something to do with fear. Trujillo knew Rice was something of a legend, so it was difficult to imagine her afraid of anything. But she looked quite shaken. Scared, even. Trujillo looked down her hawk-like nose at the older woman whom she regarded as a dinosaur living off her reputation. She took a measure of delight in having given Rice a briefing which made her so uncomfortable.

They paused at the door to the CIA owned condo. "On another front, I've confirmed that Rena Musaad, a British citizen from London staying at the Marriott works for WikiLeaks. She had a meeting with Nicole Grant in a wine bar at there."

Rice looked distracted, but nodded. "Okay, thanks."

"Barry asked me to tell you that your Chinese friends should have already terminated the Musaad woman, and he's disappointed in how sloppy things have become."

Rice flashed angry, then spun away from Trujillo, who smirked.

• • • •

KATE RICE ENTERED THE condo alone, swallowed, and tightened her stomach muscles as her mind raced. Unless there was another bombshell waiting, she could contain the fallout from the gunfight at One Pacific Place. There would be hell to pay, but the mission of getting Zhao elected to the Chinese presidency could still go forth.

She bit a fingernail, took a deep breath and psyched herself up. She'd held hundreds of meetings with kings, presidents, generals, CEOs, gangsters, prime ministers, tribal elders, dictators, and the filthy rich. Nervousness didn't factor into it, it was all about leverage and timing. She was short on leverage and the timing was problematic, so she'd have to bluff her way through. She crossed through two rooms and then stopped at a closed door. Her demeanor had shifted; she now looked and felt totally in control as she knocked twice, then opened the door.

The chilly conference room was dim thanks to navy blue velvet blackout curtains that blocked out every hint of natural light. A thick, smoky haze, the kind of miasma more common to a crowded opium den, hung in the air. Plush celadon-hued, sound-absorbing carpeting blanketed the floor. An oil painting of the Kowloon docks from when the British ruled the seas in the 1800s hung on a bone-colored wall. Rice noted all of these details in a microsecond as she hid the shock racing through her body from seeing Senior White

House Security Adviser Barry Bergman sitting at one end of the long teak table and Vice Premier of the People's Republic of China Zhao Yiren at the other. *So Bergman and Zhao have been talking to each other behind my back.*

She instinctively knew Bergman wanted to drive a wedge between her and Zhao. Had he succeeded? Director of the PLA's Second Department Major General Ma Ju, and Ministry of State Security Special Projects Director Tang Jie sat smoking on one side of the dark polished table, meaning Rice had one side to herself. Bergman was sending her a message with this seating arrangement—she was on her own, isolated, positioned to take the fall for any failure. This knowledge only strengthened her resolve to succeed and rub Bergman's nose in the stink of it all.

Rice sat down. Although she hated Bergman, she understood that he and Zhao were the senior people at the meeting, so she waited. Protocol called for one of them to speak first. The fireworks would start soon enough.

"Thank you for joining us, Miss Rice," said Zhao, taking a sip from a coffee cup as he made eye contact. By the look in his eyes, she knew there was something other than coffee in the cup.

"Sorry we had to pull you from your party," said Bergman.

Rice ignored Bergman's slight. Since the ice had been broken, she was free to speak. "Do the Hong Kong authorities know what happened at Trans-National?" she asked, directing the question to no one in particular.

"No," said Director Tang.

"Then I don't see that we have a problem—"

"You don't see a problem!?" said Bergman, cutting her off.

"A problem that we can't handle," she finished. "The American side will cover up the American deaths and evacuate the wounded from Hong Kong without this leaking out. I assume the Chinese can do likewise."

"With some difficulty, yes," said Ma.

Rice locked her eyes onto Ma's. "General Ma, why was an attempt made to execute Grant and Hernandez without informing us?"

"Director Tang is the person overseeing the—"

"Don't try and put this disaster off on me," interrupted Tang with quiet assertiveness. He held up a digital tape recorder. "I recorded you, General, in your Mercedes, ordering me to kill Hernandez and Grant and to *not* inform the Americans. And I have a recording of you issuing shoot-on-sight orders—an unfortunate order since your men couldn't tell the difference between Nicole Grant and the Mona Lisa. You also ordered Pacific Place to be locked down, but the men you sent to assist me have been manhandling VIP guests in five-star hotels, and those guests have filed complaints with the police and with their embassies. And it was your bumbling men who entered the CIA field station and got into this gunfight. So please, point your finger at the Second Department, not at the MSS," said Tang, evenly, maintaining his ever-present neutral expression.

General Ma sat there steaming, but he couldn't deny any of it. "We're not in America anymore, this is China. Informing the CIA and waiting for their approval could have meant failure, since time was so short," said Ma, glaring at Rice.

"It would seem failure resulted, anyway," she retorted. "And let me remind you we're in Hong Kong, Special Administrative Region, not mainland China. But even if we were in downtown Beijing, you should have honored the agreement. Then Wheeler and Roberts would have stopped you from sending men into a CIA facility and creating a bloodbath."

Ma scowled, but said nothing. He looked more rumpled than ever. Zhao looked thoughtful but said nothing.

"Miss Rice, how is it that Hernandez and Grant were able to access that CIA office?" asked Tang."Their dossiers which you provided don't indicate the kind of skills required to do such a thing."

"The dossiers given to you were incomplete for national security reasons. Regardless, whether you were hitting a CIA facility or a fried chicken stand, our agreement mandates that before termination occurs, first, we approve of the plan. Second, we witness and document the act." Her tone was firm, but not impolite. She looked to Zhao; he met her gaze, but said nothing as he tapped his index finger on his chin.

"My desire was to act quickly to put out a small fire before it became big," replied General Ma.

"Unfortunately, it appears as if gasoline has been poured onto the fire. Has it occurred to you General, that Hernandez and Grant might be here to kill Vice Premier Zhao?"

By the look on Ma's face, it hadn't occurred to him.

"Do you really think I'm in danger, Miss Rice?" asked Zhao. The deep richness of his voice and the authority it carried seemed to penetrate her skin.

"Without question." Now she was getting somewhere. She'd worked the facts to her advantage and was now playing upon Zhao's fear. Rice pulled her gaze away from him and lasered it onto Ma. "Perhaps, General, you could spare some of your men to supplement the vice premier's security detail. That would be more productive than having them grope foreign diplomats in hotel lobbies."

This was not turning out to be a good meeting for General Ma. "It would be even more productive if you Americans had honored your agreements and prevented certain Omega Team members from going to the press! So yes, I acted in haste, to save my old friend," said Ma, defiantly, as he gestured to Zhao. "And I would do it again."

"Then how about allowing me to bring in American agents to help locate Grant and Hernandez?"

"Absolutely not!" said Ma. This is a Chinese operation. The few-er Americans involved the better."

Bergman shifted a little uneasily in his chair. Rice, however, leaned further over the table toward Ma and held his fiery gaze. "I understand your sentiments, General, but I'm looking for positive re-sults."

Zhao made a point of loudly setting down his coffee mug to get everyone's attention. "What have been the results of the water-boarding?" he asked, lighting a cigarette, then exhaling smoke that curled upward into the serpentine fog that hung over the table like a shroud of concealment. "Hernandez's father-in-law, the retired CIA man Snedeker should have been questioned by now. How did he find out about our operation, and who else in Washington now knows what we've been doing?"

Some of the color drained from Rice's face. She had hoped the Chinese wouldn't make the family connection between Hernandez and Snedeker, since she'd redacted that information from the dossier she'd provided to them.

"Vice Premier Zhao, when I have the results of the interrogation, I'll pass them on immediately." Rice began to suspect that something had indeed shifted. Zhao was putting her on the spot in front of others, and he'd never before done that. *My God, he's in league with Bergman, now.*

"Waterboarding?" asked Bergman as he fixed Rice with a pene-trating stare.

"I informed you earlier today that Snedeker was about to be in-terrogated," said Rice, trying not to sound defensive. "We have to plug any leaks and plug them immediately." Rice looked at Bergman and knew he must be livid, since the president was vehemently op-posed to waterboarding, regardless of any extenuating circum-stances. However, since the president's own ass was on the line, she doubted Bergman would make an issue of it.

"How can Vice Premier Zhao hope to gain the Chinese presidency when so many Americans can't keep their mouths shut?" asked General Ma.

Time to go more directly on the offensive. She wanted Ma off balance. "Was it Americans who botched the assassination on Tung Choi Street earlier today? Was it Americans who allowed Nicole Grant to meet with a WikiLeaks reporter in a bar at the Marriott, in spite of Chinese assurances that there would be no WikiLeaks presence here in Hong Kong?"

"Gentlemen, and Miss Rice, we shouldn't lose sight of what our goal is," said Bergman, the cagey politico dripping words like honey. "We want to help the Chinese people by having a moderate reformer in high office. A lot of sacrifices have been made in that regard. And some mistakes, too. But gentlemen, since Miss Rice guarantees that we can still achieve our goal, then let's deal with these recent unfortunate developments quickly, put our differences aside, and move forward."

Zhao nodded.

Rice made a mental note that Bergman had just claimed she could guarantee success. She now held no doubt that this meeting was about setting up some scapegoats, and Zhao was in on it. She was already on the way out, being replaced by a new handler, so he didn't need her anymore.

"Are Hernandez and Grant still in the complex?" asked Zhao.

"We believe they are," said Tang, "even though I have no doubt they could have escaped. Meaning they *want* to be here. So I agree with Miss Rice that we should adjust our manpower to provide you with more protection, sir."

"I'll arrange for a helicopter to be made available. I strongly urge you to return to Beijing immediately," said Ma, looking at Zhao.

"If I leave in a rush without attending the charity function, eyebrows would be raised. But just to be safe, have my jet and a helicopter made ready and make up a good excuse to explain a sudden departure." Zhao took another deep drag, savoring the tobacco smoke as it penetrated his lungs. "As I think about it, why can't we simply evacuate Pacific Place and then conduct a thorough search for the two Americans?"

"The Hong Kong authorities would be in charge of such an operation, and we would need to publicly state a legitimate reason to evacuate that could not be connected to our true mission," said Tang.

"I would caution against an evacuation," said General Ma. "This complex is full of dignitaries, diplomats and luminaries. There are literally thousands of wealthy, influential people here, thousands of tourists and local shoppers, and thousands of Hong Kong workers. We'd have a chaotic, public relations disaster. Hong Kong investigators and the press would be everywhere, and," Ma turned to face Zhao, "your enemies in Beijing would hear of this instantly and start sniffing around. There is also no guarantee that an evacuation would expose Hernandez and Grant."

Rice watched Zhao carefully; he looked unhappy with Ma's remarks.

"I would urge you General Ma, Director Tang, to revert to the kind of elegant use of your men that you exhibited in the United States," said Bergman. "Finesse is called for right now. The president continues to support Vice Premier Zhao one hundred percent, but the slaughter in our field office is of tremendous concern to him." Bergman leaned forward with his elbows on the conference table and riveted General Ma, and then Director Tang with dagger-like stares. As he did so he casually touched the oversized, boxy red secure phone on the table in front of him, as a not- so-subtle reminder of his close connection with the U.S. president. "Actually, he's quite angry with the amount of incompetence that has been on display. Terminate your targets tonight, gentlemen. Otherwise, the president feels that a new direction of leadership is called for." Bergman looked directly at Zhao. "Do you agree, Vice Premier Zhao?"

Zhao shifted his gaze from Tang, to Ma, to Rice. A chill ran down her arms and she was shocked to hear him say, "Yes, I agree. End this tonight!"

Rice almost shuddered. Ten thousand successes instantly forgotten due to one failure. And it wasn't even her failure. She'd be relegated to collateral damage. There was one way to turn this around and that was by stopping the hemorrhaging. Drastic, decisive steps had to be taken to end the leaks and seal the ship. She wouldn't delegate these actions; she'd do what had to be done. Back on the East Coast she'd order Snedeker killed as soon as he broke, which should be any time now.

Rice quickly shifted her eyes to each man as a freezing silence held sway. A sense of brittle malevolence had entered the meeting. Rice felt it, and she was sure her Chinese counterparts did too. She knew with absolute certainty that she and Ma and Tang would be wiped if things went south.

19 :42
Rows of quietly humming equipment stood between Ron Hernandez and Nicole Grant and the entry door to the HVAC room, but he was certain he'd heard a key going into the door lock. Gesturing for Grant to be still, he crawled a few feet to one of the steel floor plates checker-boarding the floor. He put his fingers into a hole the size of a golf ball and strained as he lifted the heavy plate from its slot. He motioned for Grant to quickly get down into the dark crawlspace below the floor.

They both heard the door open as Chinese voices and footsteps entered the room.

She snaked her way into the tight space brimming with cable and conduit. As soon as she was in he followed, trying not to step on her. He was about to lower the plate when he saw her mouth the words, "My tablet!"

He glanced over and saw her tablet computer on the floor where they'd been sitting. But whoever was coming was right now on the other side of the nearest equipment cabinets. No time for the computer, he squatted down, and since she hadn't crawled out of the way, had to stretch out horizontally right on top of her as he noiselessly lowered the steel plate.

The crawlspace was very dark, but not completely black, since light filtered in through small holes in the steel that were there so workers could do what Hernandez had just done, namely, insert a few fingers and lift up. But Hernandez quickly realized there was too much light entering the crawlspace. He hadn't lowered the steel plate perfectly back into its slots! One corner was sticking up slightly.

In sex it would be called the Missionary position, and their faces were just inches apart. Just as he took his hands from the panel, something slammed the steel with a vibrating blow. Nicole blanched and clutched Hernandez, pulling them closer. What was that? Had they been spotted? He eased the Kimber from his jacket pocket. He moved his free hand toward the panel, when...

"Don't even think about stealing that tablet computer," said a Chinese man speaking in Mandarin.

The steel plate vibrated again. *They're walking on it.* Hernandez peered through the small hole and saw two Chinese—one tall, one skinny—standing just a few feet away.

"Nice tablet. Why would it be here?" asked the skinny guy as he bent over and picked it up.

"Probably belongs to one of the maintenance people. Is it turned on?"

The skinny one tapped the screen. The program running the blueprints Grant had illegally downloaded came on.

"See? Those are engineering blueprints. Put it back," said the tall man.

Hernandez let out a silent exhale. Good thing it was blueprints that came up and not Grant's Facebook page.

"No, I want it. Engineers in Hong Kong make good money, soldiers like us make spit. The poorest Hong Kong people make more than us. And don't get me started about the rich, big-nosed *lao wai*, the foreigners from America and Europe who walk around like they are special. Anyway, the engineer who owns this tablet can afford to lose it."

Nicole touched Hernandez to get his attention. She shook her head and mouthed the word, "No!"

Hernandez felt it wasn't worth the risk to confront the two men, so he looked at Grant and shook his head. If the man took her computer, so be it.

"Don't be stupid," said the tall man. "When it gets reported missing, the finger will point to us since we are the ones who searched this room. Now put it down!"

The skinny soldier hesitated—he really wanted the device. He shrugged and reluctantly put the tablet back on the floor. As they started to walk out, the skinny soldier stubbed his toe on the corner of the steel plate protruding slightly above the slot where Hernandez had failed to fit it. The man nearly tripped.

"*Wo kao*!" he cursed. Well screw me! He looked down at the steel plate that was slightly off-kilter.

Hernandez had twisted his head for a view through one of the small holes, and was looking right up into the man's face. He turned away and pressed himself down further on top of Nicole Grant. She gently locked her arms around him, as if in a lover's embrace.

"Come on, we have to finish quickly," called out the tall man, who was already moving away.

"Why couldn't we have just stayed in the barracks? Why couldn't they have found someone else to do their scut work?"

Grant and Hernandez lay there, entwined in the crawlspace, listening, as the footsteps faded and the door slammed closed. He lifted his head slightly and looked into her eyes. Her lush gaze was soft and inviting. Neither of them made any effort to move or shift their intimate position. The men were gone, the coast was clear. They could get up now. Instead, she inched her head toward him, seeming to offer her full lips. He hesitated, sorely tempted, but turned away and eased off of her as he pushed up on the steel plate and moved it aside. He climbed up to the floor, extended a hand, and helped her out.

"Get your computer," he said as lowered the large plate back into its slot. "We need a change of clothes."

She snatched up her tablet. He felt her eyes on him and gave her a glance. She looked flushed, but showed absolutely no embarrassment. The brief intimacy had felt perfectly natural, even considering the dire straits they were in. That seemed odd, but he put it out of his mind.

"If we're going to change clothes, does that mean we're still partners?"

He avoided her gaze and brushed himself off. "Do you have a plan to remotely access your laptop?"

"Yes."

He glanced at his watch, and then met her eyes. He fought back a powerful feeling of lust toward Nicole Grant. It was common to sexually bond with a female partner after having survived stressful, life-threatening conditions together, but for both of their sakes he had to keep that kind of distraction at bay. "Let's run your plan by Jaffir. If he signs off on it, I'll give you one more shot."

• • • •

KATE RICE AND GAIL Roberts sat at right angles on comfortable upholstered chairs in the sitting area off the bedroom in the CIA condo at the Shangri-La hotel tower. Floor-to-ceiling windows revealed the soft glow of millions of lights as Hong Kong's nighttime skyline beckoned, presenting an alternate universe of exotic temptation. But the only temptation Rice felt was to get this over with and head back to her charity bash. A large purse sat on her lap and she kept reaching inside for cosmetics as she touched up her makeup.

After the emergency meeting in the conference room had broken up, Rice had summoned Wheeler and Roberts to the CIA safe house / condo. Wheeler currently sat cooling his heels in the conference room.

During the last ten years, Rice had worked with Roberts on certain CIA operations that required additional staffing. She'd also used Roberts on a job that was completely off the agency's radar. It turned out to be a bloody, brutal affair, but Roberts had performed well. They'd shared meals and drinks several times and had built up an "old girl network" sort of trust between them.

"I know it wasn't good that Wheeler and I got captured at the CIA field office, but how can we be blamed?" asked Roberts, cutting right to the chase.

She knows me well enough not to waste my time, thought Rice. Good.

"Have you seen the video of what happened?" asked Roberts.

"There is no video. Grant sabotaged the system."

"Video would exonerate us. As soon as the inner door opened I had two guns pointed at me. Hernandez and Grant were waiting for us. How did they know where to find us? Who blew our cover?"

"All I know is that Hernandez worked here years ago."

Roberts nodded slowly. "The file you gave us indicated he was a desk jockey. It was a sanitized file, wasn't it?"

"Yes," said Rice, powdering her left cheek. "You and Wheeler weren't cleared to know everything."

Roberts hesitated, choosing her words carefully. "Optimally, any hit team should have all pertinent facts about a target before engaging it."

Rice smiled. Roberts was worried about her ass. "Yes, that's always optimal. And I should have beefed up security at the field office because Hernandez once worked there, but I didn't. I'm too distracted with the ten million things I'm doing right now. I take full responsibility for that. Trust me, the timing on all this sucks. I have no beef with how you and Wheeler performed, but I have some questions. What did Hernandez tell you?"

Roberts tried to hide it, but she tensed up. "He mostly asked questions."

"He figured out what you and Wheeler were doing?"

"It wasn't hard. He took our electronics with the video of all eighteen killings, plus the video of the attempt on Grant today. How did they get in there, anyway?"

"The guard could tell us, but his head was blown off when he got caught in a crossfire. Anyway, did Hernandez expound on why the U.S. and China have sanctioned the killings of Americans? That it was all about putting Zhao Yiren in office?" She opened a lipstick and began a touch-up job.

"He did. But I don't really care and it's none of my business."

"Do you think Wheeler has told anyone about what you two have been doing?"

"Wheeler?" She seemed surprised by the question. "We're both pros who know how to keep quiet. You can depend on us."

Rice simply nodded.

"So turn me lose. I'd like to kill both of them myself."

Rice put the lipstick away, closed her compact and put it in her purse. "No, you and Wheeler will be sent out shortly." Rice smiled as she fumbled for something in her purse. "Documenting all those deaths didn't bother you?"

"If some Americans have to die in order for the CIA to have the president of China as one of their assets, then maybe that's a fair trade."

"Glad you feel that way," said Rice as she calmly pumped three bullets from a suppressed Boberg XR9-L hidden in her large purse into Gail Roberts' chest. The shots weren't completely silent, but Rice had heard louder belches.

Roberts had only the briefest moment to display utter shock, batted her eyes, and died sitting in the chair.

· · · ·

CHUCK WHEELER SAT ON the edge of the teak conference room table smoking a cigarette and holding a smartphone. The gray-ish stale pallor of second-hand smoke still stubbornly floated aloft, aided by his long drags on a Marlboro. He watched closely as Kate Rice strode into the still room and closed the door behind her. When he caught her eye he smirked and theatrically pressed the phone's SEND button.

"Perfect timing, I just transferred the money," said Wheeler.

"What money?"

"Money to an escrow account. Were you smiling when you killed her?"

Rice blanched. "What are you talking about?"

She put her purse on the conference table, but before she could reach inside, Wheeler pulled his back-up gun, a Glock 26, from his ankle holster. He leveled the subcompact semi-auto at her. "I'm talking about Roberts is worm food and you will be too if you don't slowly hold your hands out where I can see them and step away from the bag." Wheeler had his game face on and closed the distance between himself and his control agent.

He contemptuously flicked the cigarette onto the carpeting. "See, Roberts and I never liked each other, but we knew how to work together as a team. So she's wearing a transmitter that I've been listening to, and I'm wearing one that she would have been listening to, if you had talked to me first. I heard the three shots."

Wheeler shook his head with disdain as he regarded her. He'd served his country well for decades, but, hells bells, his whole career had devolved to serving under Rice, a traitorous murderer of innocents. And she was an Agency golden girl, no less. He should have seen this coming. No, he should have retired last year. Not that he hadn't already taken certain steps to cover his butt. He had plenty of money stashed and multiple identities set up in several Southeast Asian countries. Christ, he even had a wife and young kids in Vietnam that no one knew about.

As he closed in toward her, he motioned with the gun. "Go stand by the window."

A sour look crossed her face. He could tell that her mind was in gear, but Rice backed away near a window where she stood facing him. He pulled a blue latex glove onto his left hand while still keeping the Glock pointed at her chest.

"I don't have any problem with killing you right now, but Langley would frown on it, even though they all joke behind your back about how you're just a two-bit, dye-job blonde douche bag who would sleep with the Polish army if it could get you somewhere."

Her look hardened but she didn't speak. He reached with his free left hand into her purse and brought out her suppressed Boberg, holding it by the butt end. He sniffed it. "Just been fired. For what it's worth, I'm impressed you have the balls to pull the trigger yourself." He dropped the gun back into her bag. "Anyway, I'd rather not kill you because, so far, I haven't done anything wrong. I've just followed orders."

"We can work a deal, you and me."

"Oh, we're going to, but shut the hell up unless I ask you a question." He lasered her with killer eyes. "Now where was I? Oh yeah, maybe you think you own Langley, and you're running this super-secret off-the-books op, but I've been making a ton of calls since the SRT boys cut me loose in the field office. Calls to people all over the IC. High-ups, some of them close friends. You are in deep trouble, lady. You have no idea how many people know about this huge mess you've created."

She didn't react. Her gaze stayed even, her breathing normal, her face a blank page. Wheeler admired her poise. He'd have to be careful; she was slippery as a snake.

"You think I'm bluffing, but then again, you have to consider that I'm telling the truth. Trust me, I have you dead to rights."

"You always were smarter than Roberts."

"Obviously." He lowered the gun but kept it pointed in her general direction. "Let's don't speak of the dead, but of the soon-to-be-dead—Grant and Hernandez. My position would greatly improve if they die before the night is out. It would provide an element of clo-sure and help settle things down."

He watched as she started to speak, and then stopped herself.

"I can set up a meet with Hernandez," he offered. "He put his number in my cell phone. He thinks I'm scared you're going to whack me, and offered me a way out of Hong Kong in return for some in-side scoop on what you've been up to."

Wheeler stopped and ran his eyes up and down her voluptuous figure. Some guys really went for women like her, but she simply wasn't his type. "Just so we're clear, if something happens to me... any-thing. Sickness, accident, whatever. If I suddenly become terminally unhealthy, I've put out an irreversible contract on your head. If I die, you die within seventy-two hours. Additionally, my death will result in the release of videos to the press and key people in D.C. You know, the killings of Americans on U.S. soil, all to put Zhao in power. And baby, I don't bluff. It's a done deal." He looked to her. She'd remained completely composed, cool as a cucumber; he had to give her that. "Questions?"

"Do Grant and Hernandez know my identity?"

He thought about it, and then gave her a non-answer. "I'll find out for you."

She smiled, as if humoring him. "Wheeler, it doesn't matter how many friends you have in high places or how many video copies you make. The Chinese are in disarray, Washington is panicking. If we don't kill Grant and Hernandez tonight, then you, me, Ma and Tang... we're all dead. That message, in so many words, was delivered less than an hour ago by Barry Bergmanand by Zhao himself."

Wheeler's gut hunch told him she was telling the truth. And if the powers that be were going to kill Rice and the others, they sure as hell would come after him, too. As he thought about that, she boldly stepped forward toward him. He leveled his sidearm and stepped to the side, away from her. "Easy, Blondie."

She stopped, and without taking her eyes from him, slowly reached over toward her purse and grabbed it by the strap. "Meet me downstairs in the Island Ballroom in an hour. I have an idea that might save both of our asses."

She casually picked up the purse and started to walk out. "Rice!" She stopped and turned to look at him. "I gave the contract on you to the Wo Shing Wo. Feel free to check."

"Hong Kong gangsters are the least of my worries," she said, and then walked out.

CHAPTER 20

19$^{:53}$ Jaffir Khan had moved his white Isuzu box truck from beneath One Pacific Place to a truck parking area several levels below the Conrad Hotel tower. After meeting with Grant and Hernandez, Khan had set out on some vital errands leaving the two Americans alone in his air-conditioned, soundproof, cramped truck/lab to prepare for their attempt to retrieve her laptop. Metal cabinets holding weapons and ammunition, electronics and communications gear, burglary tools, theatrical stage makeup and prosthetics, forgery equipment, clothing, a sewing machine, and first aid supplies filled the walls of the sixteen-foot long cargo area. Miniature power tools crowded a multipurpose work bench. Grant felt the juxtaposition of all this gear with the soft rendition of a Beethoven piano sonata wafting from hidden speakers was a bit surreal. But then, her whole life had become surreal ever since Hernandez showed up.

She'd put on the blonde wig, and right now sat in a folding chair leaning over a fold-down table as she looked into a small mirror and prepared to put blue contact lens into her green eyes. She'd already reclaimed her fake Celine bag, and had changed into the little black dress from Kate Spade. She'd noticed Hernandez had a hard time keeping his eyes off of her as she'd done so.

Hernandez now wore a charcoal-colored light wool suit and sported a different wig—this one longish and gray. He sat next to Grant and shared the mirror as he applied spirit gum to a fake salt-and-pepper goatee.

"I want to ask your advice. I'm worried about my mom. When she doesn't hear from me, she'll freak out. And I'm worried that they might... hurt her." She turned to look at him, worry lines creasing her face.

"When were you supposed to call?"

"Tomorrow afternoon"

Hernandez tamped down the fake goatee onto his chin. "I might be able to arrange some protection for her. I've already done that for my parents. What about your father?"

"He passed away a long time ago." She got the first contact in and then blinked several times.

"Sorry to hear that. Was he an engineer like you?"

"Exactly the opposite," she smiled. "He was so unorganized. Something must have happened to him while he was in the air force in Italy. I think it was some perceived injustice when he was passed over for promotion. Dad started talking about how everything was rigged. So he got discharged and we all moved to Nevada where he became a prospector."

"What's wrong with that?" Hernandez selected a mustache that matched the goatee from a tray of fake hair pieces.

"He didn't have any kind of business model. He'd act on a hunch or a feeling and even started using dowsing rods to try and find a strike. He prayed to Native American spirits to help locate a vein of turquoise or something like that. As a teenager I rebelled against him. I planned out my future and knew it related to computers and technology. From the age of fifteen on I gave him nothing but grief about how he'd ruined his life and was just a failure."

"Ouch."

"Yeah, ouch," she said. "We argued about everything, and since I was an only child and up until then had been his best friend... well, he lost his best friend. After I left for college his health started to decline. He died while I was away at school." She looked into the mirror and then got the second lens in.

"So you never had a chance to reconcile with him."

She blinked and looked at Hernandez in complete shock with his having spoken the words so bluntly, and for having summarized the issue so succinctly. She'd long been in denial, and there it was, all laid out. Her mouth was slightly open, but she had no words.

She considered the one failure of her life to be her relationship with her father. The guilt and pain she carried from her behavior—she'd treated him with undisguised contempt and scorn—cut her deep when she allowed herself to revisit the memories. By the time she'd hit her early twenties, her matured attitudes resulted in her becoming best friends with Jan. She'd begun speaking to her father in prayer, asking forgiveness for being such a jerk, but the process didn't expunge her guilt. Initially, her father's death had seemed like a remote event, but for the last several years, his absence felt like a chronic open wound that could never heal.

Hernandez poured a glass of water. "Planning is imperative in most lines of work. But you and I didn't make plans to run for our lives. We're operating on the fly, making things up as we go along. Kind of like what your dad did when he was looking for turquoise or the pot of gold at the end of the rainbow to support his family."

He handed her the water and she absentmindedly took a sip. Nicole didn't know what to think right now, much less say. A realization was dawning on her that felt like a crack in her foundation.

"So I need you thinking on your feet," he said as he added spirit gum to the back of the mustache. "Sometimes, ditching the plan is the only way to stay alive."

She sat there dumbfounded. The last thing Nicole ever imagined was to become more like her father. But as she thought about it, the fact she had acted on instinct, impulsively sending that audio file of Wang Hongwei inside that panel van, that spontaneous act was the very thing that just might save her and Hernandez.

"Think of it as dancing," he said, probably mistaking her introspection for confusion. "Was your dad a good dancer?"

"Yes," she managed to say.

He carefully pressed the mustache onto his upper lip and patted it down. "Once you know the basic steps, there's a lot of room for improvisation or adding your own style as you get in tune with the beat and the rhythm."

"I never learned how to dance. I have two left feet."

"Your dad didn't teach you?"

She looked away. "I wouldn't let him."

"You never had a teacher. You can dance, you just don't know it yet."

A different realization crept into Nicole's thinking as they sat in silence. Technology—computers and science and all that she'd immersed herself in as a counterpoint to her father—wasn't enough to save her. Quite the opposite, she needed to become more like her dad. She had to learn how to dance.

A tear rolled down her cheek and she bit her lower lip, trying not to completely lose it. "My mom is hearing and speech impaired. That's why I know how to lip read. My dad used to joke that he married her because he knew he'd never have to listen to any nagging." More tears erupted from her eyes and she could barely get words out. "But he chose to marry a handicapped person because he had a huge heart and was full of love."

She wept openly. Hernandez handed her a tissue. Still seated in the box truck, they leaned into each other and held on tight.

• • • •

DIRECTOR TANG HURRIED into the CP in the Marriott hotel suite that his team shared with Li Shan and other members of the PLA's Second Department. Abject worry vised Tang's chest, but he kept his concerns hidden. He needed some kind of victory—a positive—that he could report to Zhao. If he couldn't feed the tiger, the beast would turn on him.

Tang's senior aide Choi looked anxious and crossed quickly to his boss. "Sir, Hong Kong police have flooded Pacific Place. There are at least a hundred uniformed officers in the mall, the hotels—"

"So I just saw." Tang had gotten a dose of hard reality in the emergency meeting with Zhao, Ma, Bergman, and Rice. He'd decided to make some changes, but the invasion of police complicated things. "Did you get my text about the WikiLeaks reporter?"

"Yes, she's still in the wine bar, under surveillance," said Choi.

"Good. Where is Chang?"

"Here, sir."

Chang stood five-ten, weighed 185 pounds and kept her thick black hair cut severely short, like a man's. Powerful thighs and a well-developed upper body spoke of hours in the gym every day. At age thirty-two, her round face featured a fat flat nose, and soulless dark eyes. It was a challenge to determine this was a "she" not a "he." In Asia they're called toms, or tomboys, and are often hardcore lesbians who dress and do their best to project masculinity. Tang had met plenty of toms all over China. Some of them were pretty, but no one could ever accuse Chang of being anything approaching good-looking. Or cute. Or even average. She was butt-ugly and made for an ugly man when she cross-dressed, which was all the time. Her looks didn't matter to Tang. She was smart, strong as a water buffalo, great with a blade, and specialized in quiet kills. She'd killed dozens, either with knives or with her large powerful hands.

"Director Tang, I have learned that Hernandez has an old friend in Hong Kong. Jaffir Khan, a Pakistani-American who is former CIA," said Chang.

"Good work, but let someone else track down this Khan person. Right now I need you to take three people and terminate the WikiLeaks woman. Do it without being discovered. And get rid of the body, get it out of Pacific Place." Chang nodded and started off, but Tang held her by the arm. "Chang, I was just humiliated in front of the Americans because of our failures." Tang spoke softly, so no one else could hear. "And General Ma is looking to blame everything on the Ministry and not himself or the Second Department. So please accomplish this mission without any problems." He slowly released the muscular woman.

"Yes, Director Tang." Chang bowed slightly, and then hurried off.

Tang motioned for Choi to move closer, and spoke softly, barely above a whisper. "Assign twenty good men to Zhao's security detail. And pull out all of the soldiers from the PLA garrison. They are not suited for this kind of work."

"Yes sir."

"Listen up, everyone!" called out Tang, addressing the room, including Li Shan and members of the Second Department. "There is a chance that our targets have remained in Pacific Place because they intend to kill Zhao Yiren."

Startled looks and murmurs rippled through the room.

"So let's tweak our thinking accordingly. In five minutes, I want some new suggestions about how to find and kill Nicole Grant and Ron Hernandez."

• • • •

USING OBSCURE WALKWAYS and stairways it only took minutes for Grant and Hernandez to reach the main elevator bank on a lower floor of the Island Shangri-La tower. Completely composed now and looking like some kind of hip power couple, they fit right into the moneyed atmosphere of the hotel. They entered an elevator car alone and he pushed the button for the floor directly above Zhao's condo. If everything went smoothly they should be able to get within Wi-Fi range of her laptop, download the keys, and retrieve the files she'd hidden on the Darknet. He hoped like hell she could pull it off. Grant's strategy of getting the evidence, he now admitted to himself, was a better plan than simply killing Zhao and anyone else connected to the whole stinking mess. Let the Chinese kill him.

"If this doesn't work, we'll need to get inside Zhao's condo to get my laptop."

"I wasn't kidding when I said to forget that idea, so remind me of how your gizmos will work."

She brought out her tablet computer from the fake Celine bag. "Once we get close to the computer, I'll send out a clone of my home Wi-Fi signal. It's an old trick used by us geeks for years now."

"So your laptop will automatically log on to the Internet using the signal you broadcast."

She nodded. "My tablet here is connected to the Internet via the cell phone system and is acting as a Wi-Fi hotspot. If I can spoof my laptop and it logs on, I can download all of the keys we need for the Darknet files onto this tablet."

"How long will that take?"

"A few minutes, once the laptop logs on."

The elevator doors opened and they stepped into a luxurious hotel hallway decorated with Chinese tapestries in green and gold accents. Hernandez checked the altimeter reading on his watch. "The elevation is good," he said. "We should be about fifteen feet higher than the laptop, if your tracking coordinates are correct."

Grant had several programs running on her tablet, and she checked the KCS tracking software. "To the right," she said. Their feet sank into ultra-plush carpeting as they slowly walked past hotel room doors.

About halfway down the hall, she stopped. "It's somewhere on the floor below us, about forty feet northwest of where I'm standing," she said.

"You're broadcasting the Wi-Fi signal? And it's strong enough?"

She nodded, and then scowled. "But the laptop's not logging on."

Hernandez continued down the hallway for a few steps as he pulled out his cell phone. "So it's not in sleep mode, it's been shut down?"

"Actually, because of certain software I installed, even if it's shut down there's a way I could take control of that laptop as long as there was power," she said, looking up from her tablet. "Meaning the battery's dead and it's not plugged in."

He looked up to face her. "In that case we're back to square one, because—" Before he could complete the thought, they both heard the sound of a deadbolt sliding open on the hotel room door that was practically in front of her. Hernandez spun clear and pressed himself flat against the wall, but Grant stood rooted to the spot as the hotel door swung open.

"Well, what have we here," said a male voice in a way that sounded lascivious. Hernandez couldn't see the man from his position against the wall, but he must be drinking in the sight of Nicole's attractive figure in front of him: blue eyes, creamy pale skin, trendy blond hair, and a perfectly proportioned figure in a form-fitting dress.

Grant looked shocked as she appeared to remember something. "You're Conner Green!" she softly exclaimed, instantly shifting into an Italian accent as she stepped toward the man and into the doorway,

"Go Green," he said, as if reciting a slogan. "And you are?"

"Ariana Faccioli... your biggest fan."

"Well, in that case, please come in." Hernandez saw the man's hand reach out to take Nicole's hand as she strolled into the suite.

As the door closed, Hernandez remained flattened against the wall, not quite believing what just happened. He'd earlier been lecturing her about needing to think on her feet. Either she took his words to heart or he could have saved his breath because she handled that situation like a pro. But who is Conner Green? And Grant had called herself Ariana Faccioli. So what the hell was he supposed to do now? He waited for a few seconds, and then brought out his own tablet computer as he silently retraced his steps back toward the elevator. He brought up StartPage, his preferred search engine, and entered CONNER GREEN.

Less than an hour earlier he'd been thinking about dumping Grant. It now appeared she'd beaten him to the punch.

CHAPTER 21

20$^{:27}$ Two beige, floral-print sofas set at a right angle faced a wall of glass. The visual splendor of the Hong Kong skyline at night—a sparkling exotic universe that dazzled with possibilities—looked close enough to touch yet remained opaquely out of reach. A bottle of *Veuve Clicquot* sat in a stainless steel ice bucket on a drinks cart next to the large rectangular coffee table. A twenty-five year-old sexed-up Asian beauty remained seated on one sofa. Grant wondered if the woman was a high-priced escort, then admonished herself for such thinking. Conner Green led Ariana Faccioli nee Nicole Grant to sit next to him on the other sofa. She steeled herself, managing her nerves much better than earlier today as she flashed on the *tai tais*, Vivian and Eleanor, who'd said that Zhao and Green were friends, and that they'd both be at the charity reception tonight. Maybe Green could get her into Zhao's condo.

"Tiffany, this is Ariana. Ariana, Tiffany. Tiffany is... an entertainer."

"*Buonasera*," said Nicole, as her butterflies melted away and she eased into the role of a mysterious Italian beauty. *Entertainer, my ass, she's a hooker.*

Tiffany forced a smile, perhaps sensing unwanted competition or complications, and arched her back slightly, the better to showcase her ample fake bosoms.

"Champagne?"

"Perfect," said Nicole.

As he poured her a glass he asked, "How did you get my room number?"

"But I didn't, darling."

"Come on. You must have known this was my room." He handed her the glass. "Cheers." They all clinked glasses and took a sip.

"No, I was in the hall speaking on my phone. Sorry, but I get lost easily. I got off on the wrong floor."

He seemed to be having a hard time believing it. "You didn't give a large tip to a front desk clerk to get my room number?"

Wow, the ego of the guy; a weakness to be exploited. "I would gladly have done such a thing, if I'd only thought of it!"

They laughed. Tiffany forced another smile.

"And why did you open the door?" asked Nicole.

"I heard voices outside."

"Yes, I was talking to my friend on speaker. I feel this is simply a beautiful coincidence and I'm so happy to meet you, but if you think I somehow planned this, then I should leave," she said, putting down her champagne and trying to sound serious. Leaving was the last thing she wanted to do.

"Nonsense. You're staying."

"To be truthful, I thought I might meet you tonight at the charity reception. Not in your room for drinks!" Nicole said, laughing.

He smiled and raised his glass: "To beautiful coincidences."

They toasted, this time leaving Tiffany out of it. Green had had a few and was loose, but not drunk. Tiffany looked stone cold sober.

"What brings you to Hong Kong?" he asked.

"Mostly pleasure, but a tiny bit of business," she said without thinking. *Crap, I need a background story!* Her mind raced back to her many childhood friends in Italy.

"What kind of business?"

Her eyes fell on the glass of champagne. "My family has a small winery, but we have no sales in China." Wineries were a dime a dozen in Italy. It was a safe cover.

"Faccioli," he said thinking. "I believe I've had your wines." He paused for effect. "I might be able to help you with that."

Nicole's heart suddenly beat a bit faster. "Really?"

"I have excellent *guanxi*—influential relationships—with powerful Chinese figures." He took a healthy sip of champagne.

She'd wanted to steer the conversation in a certain direction, and Green was unconsciously helping her cause.

"Are your friends in the government? Because to gain a foothold in the Chinese market, I would need—"

"I have very good friends at the highest levels of the Chinese government," he said, mildly miffed, as if she were questioning the level of his contacts.

"Forgive me, I'm sure you must. You're a superstar. Chinese officials are probably begging you to design signature structures for them."

"You're right about that," he said, smiling. He then turned to the sexy Chinese girl. "Tiffany, my love, I've been ignoring you. Come sit next to me." He patted the sofa. Tiffany smiled and it almost looked genuine. She moved over and sat very close to him.

"I'm making a short speech at the reception tonight, Ariana. Boring, but I promised I'd say a few words to help them raise money. Care to come?" he asked.

"I'd love to hear you speak," purred Nicole.

"Excellent," he said, smiling."Nothing like entering a party with a beautiful lady on each arm."

Nicole's mouth felt dry, from anticipation. Green was taking her to the party, but hadn't offered to introduce her to Zhao. Meaning she'd have to find Zhao herself. She brought out her tablet computer from her purse. "I'll just text my friend to cancel." But instead of texting, Nicole used the LINE messaging application to send Hernandez the audio file she'd been recording of everything that had been said since she'd entered Conner Green's suite.

• • • •

RENA MUSAAD HAD YIELDED the private room in the wine bar to a party of four and returned to the table she'd had before joining Nicole Grant. The couples in the private room had already polished off two bottles of Chilean Shiraz, while Rena still nursed the bottle of Bordeaux left over from her run-in with Grant. London had responded to her breathless message: they would not be sending more money to extend her stay. This obviously meant they didn't believe that she was on to something. The cost of remaining for even one extra day was beyond Rena's means, so she had little choice but to make her midnight departure on British Airways. Meaning it was time to go to her room, pack, and get a taxi.

The *sommelier* entered and was heading her way when she signaled to him. He placed a black leather bill presenter in front of her which she assumed contained the guest check. But when she opened it she saw a note:

"I PAID YOUR CHECK. I HEAR YOU WANT TO TALK TO ME. GO TO THE LOBBY AND ASK A HOTEL STAFF MEMBER TO ACCOMPANY YOU TO THE JW BALL-ROOM. I'LL FIND YOU THERE. R.H."

Rena sat up straight with a jolt of shock and worked to contain her excitement. As she was about to leave, with failure knocking on her door, Ron Hernandez had contacted her! She might get the story after all. She quickly gathered up her things and left using the same route Grant had used some hours earlier. She glanced all around the busy lobby area. She found a young female staff member whose job was to provide basic assistance, mostly directions, to guests. The staffer immediately agreed to accompany Rena to the JW Ballroom. They got into an elevator car with a twenty-something Chinese couple. After a brief ride, they all got out of the car and the young staffer pointed Rena in the direction of the ballroom.

• • • •

WILLIAM SNEDEKER WAS still not responding to any of the emergency contact protocols he and Ron Hernandez had established. Meaning they'd gotten to him and possibly killed him. Snedeker had been Hernandez's father-in-law during his five-year marriage. Hernandez was the son Snedeker never had, and the men remained close friends. They'd often gone hunting and fishing together, and either smoked and cooked what they'd killed or donated the meat to homeless shelters. They spent long hours talking philosophy, politics, and world history. Hernandez had taught his father-in-law how to make Dominican-style *longaniza*, as well as the joys of eating *mofongo* with an ice-cold Presidente beer.

Snedeker had had a lot to teach, too, since his title was Deputy Director of the National Clandestine Service. He provided wisdom regarding tradecraft and acted as an unofficial sounding board, adviser, and mentor. Now retired and widowed, Snedeker's daughter—Hernandez's ex-wife—had remarried and moved to California. The old spook was left all alone, but Hernandez visited frequently, especially during the last three years when he'd joined the CTC and held a 9-5 job just outside D.C.

It had been William Snedeker who, ten days earlier, had smuggled him out of A-Town Bar and Grill, Hernandez's favorite stop for a happy hour drink and free appetizers in Arlington. Chinese killers had been literally waiting in cars outside on North Fairfax Drive. It was Snedeker who'd given him the news that Willie had been murdered earlier that day. Hernandez had practically gone to pieces as they'd driven out to Snedeker's cabin in rural Virginia. Later that night, his father-in-law gave him cash, multiple access codes to multiple CIA databases, weapons and other gear, since going home had been out of the question. It was still out of the question.

Would his death be the only way this nightmare would end? Losing both sons would destroy his parents, and that angered him as much as anything else. He'd called in favors and spent money to provide for a private security cordon around his mom and dad at all times. He wished there was something he could do for Snedeker, a man who'd gone operational at age 77 while carrying an oxygen bottle in a special pack on his back. He'd done it to save Ron's life. The old man almost never left his house anymore, and the doctors had given him less than a year to live.

Snedeker refused to say how he found out that all the Omega Team members from the drone operation were being killed. "It's better if you don't know so it can't be tortured out of you," was the sobering excuse he'd given him that last night they'd spent together. "I'm going to blow the lid off of this one myself, and I don't care who goes down with the ship," were the last words Snedeker had spoken before a humbled Hernandez had disappeared into a chilly Virginia night.

Right now, Hernandez sat in the foyer adjacent to the JW Ballroom in the Marriott hotel, once again wearing the eyeglasses featuring special textures that defeated the best facial recognition software. His heart felt heavy. First his brother, now maybe his father-in-law. Except for his dad, Hernandez had lost the two men in the world closest to him. He owed it to both men and to the families of all the dead, to make amends.

A large wedding reception in the ballroom had ended earlier. Cleanup of the stemware, silverware, and china was complete, but since the ballroom wasn't booked to be used for the next few days, the on-duty staff had not yet broken down the elaborate red-themed decorations for the Chinese-style wedding. The hotel staff was busy with other doings on the other side of the elevator bank, so the decorations wouldn't come down until the morning.

The ballroom wedding reception had been a major soiree, and the foyer here was extensively decorated. Red bunting draped the walls and crisscrossed parts of the ceiling while dozens of tall, fat red candles like the kind found at Taoist temples sat in clusters throughout the entrance hall. Eight large individual red draperies hung from the ceiling, each one bunched and tied with red ribbons and forming a sort of flowing colonnade of crimson that seductively led into the ballroom as if one were entering a forbidden inner sanctum sanctorum for induction into a great mystery.

Hernandez sat with his back against a marble wall of the now dim foyer, his straight-back chair covered in shiny red silk. He sat behind three long tables placed end-to-end, also draped in red silk. The tables had probably been used for guests to sign the guest book and to drop off gifts. He caught sight of his reflection in his dark cell phone screen. The silver ponytail and glasses made him appear different than he'd ever looked in his life, but he was anxious to ditch the itchy wig. He was about to scratch the back of his neck when shards of sharp laughter from the far off salon rooms down the hall sliced the quiet. He looked and listened for something sinister. Nothing.

As he sat waiting, he used one of the access codes given to him by Snedeker to confirm the identities of Rice, Ma, and Tang. By cross-referencing his searches with Zhao Yiren, he came up with Major General Ma Ju, Director of the Second Department, People's Liberation Army General Staff Department—China's top military spook. After reading the general's CIA dossier, he decided this was the guy whose phone number was in Roberts' cell. Ditto for Director of Special Projects Tang Jie of the Ministry of State Security. Both men were heavy hitters and their careers intertwined with Zhao.

Rice was the unknown quantity. Dozens of people named Rice populated the CIA personnel database. He puzzled over the type of agent who would be Wheeler and Roberts control on such a sensitive, bloody op, but came up with too many variables. Maybe this Rice person wasn't even CIA or maybe Rice was a *nom de guerre*. The easy way to find out would be to call.

But he wasn't ready to do that.

He'd listened to the audio file Grant had sent him of her conversation in Conner Green's hotel suite. Amazingly, she'd soon be attending the big charity function at the Shangri-La and seemed likely to meet Zhao. A logical play would be to get into Zhao's condo using some kind of ruse, but could she really do that? She must have some kind of plan—she always did. Whatever it was, he didn't want to see her get hurt. Yes, she'd lied to him, had spied on his op, was clumsy in the field, didn't take orders well, but... he kind of liked her.

Grant was making her own play alone, so in the meantime, he'd take steps to increase their odds of surviving. Which is why his gun hand rested inside his backpack as he waited for Rena Musaad.

And whoever was following her.

• • • •

AS RENA MUSAAD ENTERED the foyer area just to the east of the elevator bank, a chill went up her arms. Dim lighting cast long shadows from hanging bunting and giant candles. Except for the decorations, the hall in front of her stood eerily empty. The dramatic red ornamentation took on symbolic malice to her in the faint light and she suddenly felt uneasy. Was Hernandez waiting behind one of the billowy red drape shapes?

She forced herself to keep walking. It made sense, after all, that the man was lying low. Being careful.

Unless, it wasn't Hernandez who sent her the note, but instead, some killer looking to scratch another WikiLeaks reporter. Rena flashed on Nicole Grant's earlier admonishment: "If you're as smart as you look, you'll take a taxi straight to the airport and fly back to London *right now.*" Her gut tightened, her throat constricted, and she felt pressure in her chest. These were panic symptoms and she'd felt them before, had surrendered to them. But she was older now, determined, and hopefully smarter. She took a few deep breaths and consciously fought back the fear.

Still, Rena was wondering just how smart it was to be down here alone, when she caught movement from the corner of her eye. She turned and saw a pony-tailed gentlemen sitting behind a long row of red-draped tables. He dramatically held a finger to his lips and motioned her to keep walking down the hallway. Was that Hernandez?

She was about to speak up, when he emphatically gestured for her to be silent and to keep moving through the pillars of red draperies and into the ballroom. She saw him silently drop down below the line of sight of the tables, hidden by the red bunting. Shivers ran up her arms. She felt the danger in the air and knew without a doubt she faced big trouble right here and right now. She swallowed hard, remembering walking down narrow dark stone passageways alone in Cairo when she was a teen. She'd lived through that, and she hoped to live through this. So she whispered a nearly silent prayer as she melted away into the sea of red cloth.

CHAPTER 22

20 :29

The 400-person reception in the Island Ballroom of the Island Shangri-La Hong Kong was due to officially begin soon. Meaning that Kate Rice had been running around like a force of nature making last-minute split-second decisions, mediating disputes, berating staffers over mistakes, and sometimes holding hands with the offended.

The black-tie event tonight was an exclusive, invitation-only private adjunct to the Kids First charity conference over at the Convention Center, and was designed for the richest donors to have adult fun. Titled "Bet on Us," the reception featured a tasteful casino theme that prevailed throughout the hall. Roulette, pai gow poker, pan 9, blackjack, craps, and other tables with games of chance were salted throughout the ballroom, the whole shebang decorated with silver and gold accents. All guests would be given 100 HKD worth of chips and be encouraged to have at it.

Rice had intended to do some serious schmoozing with six potential mega-donors tonight, but that was now unlikely thanks to that prick Chuck Wheeler. She'd confirmed that he had a contract out on her with the Wo Shing Wo that would become active should he be killed. Then she spent time making arrangements for how to use Wheeler to get to Hernandez. She expected Wheeler to show up any minute, but events had taken such a sudden turn for the worse she might have to go operational herself. What bad timing.

Almost as if on cue, Rice looked up from an easy chair and saw Wheeler standing in the entrance to the partitioned-off area of the ballroom that served as her private lounge, with plush chairs and sofas and a full bar set-up. Wheeler's eyes darted around the room, taking in the layout. He didn't look impressed and pulled out his cell phone.

"Hernandez hasn't called. Whatever you got, I hope it's smart, because I can't be wired, I can't have a tracker—no electronics of any kind. He's too good to miss anything like that. And tailing me won't work either. He'd spot it."

Rice held up a pack of Marlboros and a stainless steel Zippo lighter. "You smoke, right?"

"Occasionally."

"Tonight is one of those occasions. Nothing special about the pack of cigarettes, but when you meet Hernandez, light up. The Zippo works, but when you use it, it sends out your GPS coordinates, and then shuts off. Use it again, same thing."

"So it's passive unless I light it?"

"Correct. If he checks you for electronics, it won't register as anything but a dumb lighter."

He nodded and took the lighter and cigarettes.

"I've mobilized a dozen very dependable contract agents. Not Americans and not CIA. They're your back-up, but not for close surveillance. Use the cigarette lighter and they'll be there in minutes."

"Theoretically," he said, skeptically.

"I'm also swapping out your phone." She held up a cell phone that resembled his. "Put your SIM card in here. That way I can listen in on the conversation and track you. Even if he checked, there's no way he could know this was anything except a regular phone."

"Chances are he'll have me dump my phone and pick up a different one along the way."

She shrugged. "If you dump it, you dump it. You'll still have the Zippo." She apprised him carefully. Wheeler oozed confidence, but he wasn't cocksure. The man was a total pro and had Hernandez's scent. Without taking her eyes off him, she slid a thick, plain manila folder across the table toward him. "Hernandez's personnel file. I didn't want the Chinese to know everything, but it's all here for you, unredacted."

He nodded.

She was surprised that he didn't reach for the file. "Tell me about the kill plan."

"I have a couple of discreet weapons. If I get close to him, I can kill him."

"You sure as hell better. Last thing: you have to wear a vest." Rice reached into a gym bag and brought out a bulletproof vest.

"I don't need or want a vest," said Wheeler, emphatically. "It's going to get physical. A heavy, cumbersome vest is the last thing I need to be wearing in a fight."

"It's probably some kind of lawyer nonsense designed to absolve the Agency of negligence in case Hernandez shoots you dead. If you don't wear the vest, my orders are to have you escorted to the airport and fly you to D.C. right now. I'll deal with Hernandez and Grant myself if I have to."

Rice watched him carefully. *He should have killed me in the conference room when he had the chance.* But he was cautious, and smart. Smart, but not brilliant, not a big, strategic thinker. Yes, he could be counted on for your garden variety wet work—he'd killed low-level terrorist assets, mid-range Iranian agents, and highly-trained North Korean operators who were hard targets. Wheeler acted either alone or with a team. He'd performed black bag jobs, surveillance, intelligence collection, and support roles. A competent jack-of-a-trades.

But he remained a contract player only. Maybe she hadn't personally killed as often as Wheeler, and didn't have his extensive field experience, but she'd founded and built a multimillion dollar organization from the ground up, all as an espionage platform. She ran with the jet set, Wheeler haunted open-air bars full of bitter, drunken expats in Southeast Asia. He was an expendable pawn used in the endless grand games of people like her. After all, a human life was the cheapest commodity on planet Earth.

"All right, I'll wear the vest," he said, reaching for the file that contained the secrets of Ron Hernandez.

• • • •

ZHAO YIREN'S PRIVATE jet and a helicopter were made ready for an estimated 11:00PM departure. He was back in his Pacific Place condo, sitting in the library where he'd always been comfortable, but tonight he felt troubled and wasn't sure he'd ever be relaxed in Hong Kong again. For the first time in his adult life he pondered a future without Ma Ju. The General right now sat across from him in an overstuffed leather chair engrossed in his smartphone. Zhao selected a cigarette from the box of Huang He Lou 1916 smokes on the table next to him and lit it with a solid gold Dunhill lighter.

Unlike General Ma, Director Tang was easily replaceable, and in fact, his replacement had already been chosen. The fact Tang had lasted more than fifteen years was perhaps poor judgment on Zhao's part. But unlike Tang, Ma had been his great friend since they were teenagers together. Over forty years had passed since they'd become blood brothers. How could he dare replace General Ma?

But he must dare. The three pinnacles of power in modern China were within his reach! Zhao was poised to be elected General Secretary of the Communist Party of China, Chairman of the CPC Central Military Commission, and President of the People's Republic of China at the next CPC National Party Congress in a mere two weeks. He'd grasp the brass rings of power and forever rehabilitate his family name. Those factions and institutions which had so wronged his family would be held accountable, one way or another, in his Great Reckoning, a dream living and breathing inside of him since his teenage days as a torture victim.

Nothing must stop him, so General Ma would have an accident, a terrible, tragic accident. As head of Chinese military intelligence, his death would be seriously investigated, so the hit would have to be done right. And he had just the man to do it: Chief Lin, the head of his personal security detail.

Zhao looked up at his old friend Ma and they exchanged slight smiles. He felt a rush of exhilaration from the decision to get rid of old baggage no longer needed.

• • • •

GENERAL MA SMILED AT Zhao Yiren. Ma had minutes earlier seen to the addition of the twenty men sent over to beef up the vice premier's security detail. There was no way Zhao could be feeling good about the way things were going, but he hadn't complained. And that troubled Ma, because he was a complainer and whiner. The rich and powerful usually are. He knew his old friend very well, knew he was up to something, crafting plans in his mind.

Ma covertly arranged for his *own* helicopter to be prepped for flying and had it standing by at the Peninsula over in Kowloon, the only hotel in Hong Kong with a helipad, a leftover regulation from those damn British who ran the territory for one hundred years. The general wanted to put distance between himself and any more failures. Better if he went to Guangzhou to see Oi Lam. He'd have to secure her safety and the safety of the boy she carried in her belly. His son! Zhao himself had ordered her death, but Ma would not allow that to happen.

So screw Zhao, he would never harm Oi Lam. He was chief of the Second Department, one of the most powerful positions in all of the Chinese military, he could do pretty much as he pleased. He'd already made arrangements to provide Oi Lam with an authentic Singaporean passport. He might put her on a plane out of Guangzhou tonight. So he closed his phone and took a healthy sip of Remy Martin Louis XIII Black Pearl Limited Edition cognac and considered the situation.

What was Zhao up to? He'd already ordered Tang to be murdered if the Americans weren't killed tonight. Would he, could he, was he amoral enough to order the death of his oldest, most loyal friend, too? Ma put himself in Zhao's place, and could not rule it out.

But General Ma had no intentions of dying anytime soon. Suddenly, with the clarity of spring water from the Yuecheng Mountains, he concluded he must confront Zhao and negotiate a detente guaranteed by the knowledge of mutually assured destruction should either man attempt a first strike. Yes, the time was almost here. So he needed to do a few things, sooner rather than later.

CHAPTER 23

20 :36

Hernandez crouched under the table and watched through a narrow slit in the red silk as Rena Musaad disappeared into the unoccupied JW Ballroom in the Marriott. He'd earlier spotted a Chinese surveillance team watching her in the wine bar when he'd given the *sommelier* the note for Rena. He had five rounds left in the suppressed handgun, the gun he'd taken away from the tall man on Tung Choi Street this afternoon. Was it this afternoon? It seemed like an eternity ago. Five cartridges should be enough.

He regulated his breathing to counter the rising anticipation of imminent violence. There was no escaping the jittery feelings when one waited in ambush, but he remained in control. The breathing helped, as did the many years of training and experience under his belt. The only sound in the foyer was of distant, muffled laughter coming from the other salon rooms. The space was completely still, until...movement. Shadows entered his field of vision.

A casually-dressed young Chinese couple—the surveillance team he'd spotted earlier—appeared as silently as ghosts drifting through a wall. They stepped soundlessly on rubber-soled shoes into the foyer with the sureness and confidence of professional assassins, which was exactly what they were. And a skilled killer is finely attuned to danger; perhaps they sensed it, too. The couple exchanged the slightest of nods and both pulled suppressed automatics from under their jackets.

Hernandez unconsciously bit his lip. These two weren't just doing surveillance; they were a wet team here to wipe Musaad. They'd simply been waiting for her to leave the wine bar. Damn, not good.

The tall woman with a hooked nose like a bird of prey suspiciously eyed the row of draped tables as she crept past, just feet from where Hernandez lay in wait. Her muscular male partner angled toward the ballroom's lavishly festooned entryway. Hernandez couldn't afford to let him get too far.

"*Bie dong! Fangxia ni de wuqi!*" yelled Hernandez.Don't move! Drop your weapons!

The man and woman both spun toward the long tables that together ran over thirty feet long. The woman, hesitated, seemingly unsure of where to shoot. She fired twice into the bunting, the shots from her suppressed pistol sounding like two short coughs. Before she could fire a third time, two muffled shots spoke an answer and she fell to the floor.

Her companion fired four times—puft puft puft puft—into the red bunting draping the front of the tables, then tuck-and-rolled to his left. It took the man a couple of seconds to regain his balance and his sight picture, then he squeezed off two more shots as he cut toward the far end of the tables in a flanking maneuver.

As he leveled his weapon to take aim, two slugs tore into his chest. The Chinese man looked utterly shocked, and then collapsed at the end of the row of tables.

Hernandez stepped forward from the corner of the marble wall, just feet from where he'd been hiding under the table. He'd scrambled into the new position when the killer had performed his tuck and roll. He shook his head, silently berating himself for having called out the warning to the killers. They had already pulled their guns and had come to kill Musaad, so he should have just shot them down like rabid dogs. They certainly hadn't given any of their American victims a chance to surrender.

He tucked the gun away and hurried forward. It only took seconds to pull the dead man under one of the tables hidden from sight by the bunting. The female was a little farther away and left a blood trail as he dragged her body over to join her dead partner.

"You must be Ron Hernandez."

Startled, he swung the gun around. Rena Musaad looked remark-ably composed as she stood next to one of the hanging draperies. Then she saw the blood on the floor and color drained from her face. "Oh my... I thought you'd just... knocked them out or something."

"I did—permanently. Do me a favor and pull down one of those drapes and wipe up this blood before somebody sees it."

"Um, shouldn't we call the police instead of hiding the bodies?" she asked, sounding nervous.

He squatted next to the corpses and checked their pockets. "Not if you want to keep living." He stashed the dead man's gun into his pocket and then glanced up at her—she now looked ashen. "These two were killers, Ms. Musaad. The drapes.Do it now, please," he said, a bit sharply.

She snapped alert and yanked on the drapery closest to her. Within moments, she'd wiped up the blood and they'd stashed the bloody drapes under the table with the stiffs. Rena looked slightly green around the gills as they stood up together. "I saw them in the wine bar not long ago."

"They followed you." Hernandez noticed the female's gun still on the floor. He quickly bent down to retrieve it, and then placed it into Musaad's purse. "Keep this for now."

"I'd rather not, Mister Hernandez." She looked down into her purse but didn't seem to want to touch the gun. "This isn't how I usu-ally begin an interview. I'm sorry I feel a bit off, but you've just now killed two people."

"Two assassins," he countered. "More will be coming, so I suggest we get out of here right now and—" He stopped as a sound ap-proached from down the hall. Footsteps and something else.

He touched the gun inside his jacket but didn't pull it out. They exchanged a glance. He could read on her face that she understood danger was approaching. "Kiss me," she said. "But keep one eye open please." She didn't wait for a response, just stepped forward, wrapped her arms around him and kissed him, so her back was exposed to whoever was coming.

He squinted through both eyes as two male hotel staff members hurried into the foyer with a rolling cart. The taller, stocky one had an androgynous look; the guy pushing the cart had a buzz cut and thick lips for an Asian. The staffers seemed to be in a hurry and only gave the couple a casual glance.

Just as they were about to pass and enter the ballroom, the buzz cut staffer who'd been pushing the cart, pulled a large knife with an eight-inch blade. He lunged toward Rena and began an upward thrust.

With no time to think, Hernandez jerked Rena to his left, tripping her with an extended left leg and sending her to the floor. He crossed his forearms into an "X" at the same time he shot his hips back to move his belly away from the approaching razor-sharp steel. His crossed arms stopped the momentum of the attacker's hand just in time.

Hernandez instantly slid his top arm up to the man's elbow and sharply pulled the joint toward him. The fat-lipped killer was now off balance with Hernandez in complete control of his right arm. Hernandez wrenched the arm, forcing the man to bend over as the knife was now pointed directly at the killer's back.

He forced the long blade into the assassin's back, pulled it out and then in rapid succession stuck the man four more times, twisting the knife each time to slice up his innards. He pushed him to the floor, now holding the moaning man's knife. The whole sequence had only taken seconds.

Rena let out a small gasp, having watched the bloodletting from just a few feet away. "Rena, get back!" he yelled, stepping between her and the second killer, who was on the move.

A fast mental count told him he had one round left in the Chinese semi-auto inside his jacket. The silenced pistol he'd just put into his pocket had been fired four times and held an unknown number of rounds. The gun from the dead Chinese woman was in Rena's purse, a few feet away on the floor. Hernandez preferred shooting to slicing and dicing and wanted to go for a handgun, but this unusual-looking killer was lightning quick and coming right at him.

Rena was just able to fast-crawl away, leaving her purse behind, before the stocky assassin attacked, holding a wide, fixed-blade hunting knife with a gutting hook at the tip. If you stabbed someone in the lower abdomen, you could jerk the knife upward, hook the intestines, and pull the guts right out of the body. Hernandez spun away from a thrust just in time.

The two adversaries locked eyes and Hernandez realized he was fighting a woman, a tomboy, not that it gave him any advantage. This muscle-bound lady knew what she was doing. She'd just lost three partners, so there was bloodlust in her menacing gaze. She stood with slightly bent knees, holding the knife in her right hand.

"Mister Hernandez, I am Chang. I have come to kill you and the lady."

"Funny, that's what your three friends thought."

Chang's nostrils flared and she barred her teeth. Good. Make her angry, emotional. Help her to make a mistake. Hernandez was an okay knife fighter, but was better at defense than offense, so he completely surprised Chang by tossing the knife. "Rena!" he called out to the beautiful Egyptian. The blade skittered across the floor and she scrambled to pick it up. He wanted her to at least have a chance in case he wasn't the last man standing.

Hernandez held his hands up, palms facing his adversary. He wasn't surrendering, this was a defensive posture. He stood slightly bent over, keeping his hips further back from the vertical plane of his arms. With Rena now scampering further away, Hernandez quickly moved to his left, into the middle of the entryway and away from the tables.

Chang lunged with a straight thrust toward Hernandez's midsection, making no secret of the fact she wanted to gut him and finish things quickly. He reacted to the thrust by pivoting his body as he shot his left arm forward and then swept it outward, pushing Chang's arm and knife away from him, while at the same time moving his right hand to her right shoulder. His body was now leaning forward at almost forty-five degrees as he used his right arm to leverage weight down upon her shoulder, forcing the tomboy's head further down.

He would have preferred to have a grip on her knife. He straightened up into a solid stance as he vised his right hand around the back of Chang's neck, all the while keeping her knife arm away from his torso with the continued use of his left arm block.

· · · ·

CHANG BEGAN TO PUMMEL Hernandez's midsection with her most powerful left jabs—she had good upper body strength—while still twisting her right wrist, trying to slash the man wherever she could. He was strong, maybe the toughest target she'd ever had to face. He now stood straight, knees slightly bent. She held a greatly inferior position, bent over almost to seventy degrees, her feet spread too wide apart. Not good. She needed a dramatic move, and reached with her left hand to grab his testicles. She would squeeze them to meat mush if she could reach them.

Hernandez anticipated and twisted his hips away, so Chang came up empty. Angry and frustrated, she was now bent over at fully ninety degrees as the American smashed his right knee hard into her chin, cracking several teeth and causing her to bite off a small slice of her tongue. She refused to cry out. She'd taken worse beatings. Beatings and rapes by her uncles when she was a young teen. Her abuse had always come at the hands of a man and so she took great pleasure in venting her boiling rage by killing men all over the world in service to her government. But it was really in service to her venomous desire for vengeance. Suddenly another knee slammed into her face, breaking her nose, which spurted blood. She turned away from the third blow but felt Hernandez gaining control of her right arm, her knife hand arm.

Blood gushed from her nose and mouth and dripped to the floor. She knew she looked bad, so he might underestimate her resolve. She had a backup knife, and needed it now, because he had control of her left arm and guided her manlike body with the leverage on her neck.

She reached the small automatic folder in her left pants pocket and the blade sprung open like a horse leaping out of the starting gate. Just as the big man sent her flying into the marble wall, she managed to stab him hard and deep in the left thigh, hoping she hit a blood pathway.

• • • •

HERNANDEZ DIDN'T LET go even though Chang had stuck him good. He wanted to end this, but the tough Chinese tomboy was a tenacious fighter and wasn't about to quit. She tried to stick him again but he moved his hips away from her reach. He still hadn't been able to get her to drop the big knife but continued using her left arm to control her movement. He wrenched her arm even higher and wedged her against the wall as his right hand found her left hand which held the smaller blade.

She was incredibly strong, and they fought for control of both knives.

It was a death dance, their upper bodies locked together as they took turns kneeing each other in the groin and vying for position as they spun around. They knocked over meter-high heavy red candles that must have weighed fifty pounds each. Red drapes hanging from the ceiling got caught up in their bloody ballet and entwined them both. Only nineteen seconds had elapsed since the battle with

Chang began, and it was still anybody's fight as their arms twisted into odd configurations as they combined instinct and training to gain advantage.

Hernandez then jerked hard on her right arm as he shot out his hip and pivoted, sure that this would drop the Chinese killer to the floor. But it didn't. Chang stayed on her feet in a wide stance, and although she was half bent over, her left hand was now free again, so she slashed with the small shank toward his legs.

Chang had a free hand again, but so did Hernandez, who now had both of his hands on her right wrist. He jerked and she screamed as the unmistakable sound of her wrist breaking filled the foyer. The menacing gutting knife she'd been holding like some kind of mystical object fell to the floor as she dropped onto her side, legs akimbo.

Standing over her now, he wrenched her arm, breaking it with a series of sickening cracks. Chang screamed and lashed out weakly with the small folder, but couldn't reach flesh. The tomboy was going to fight to her last breath and Hernandez understood and respected that he was fighting a true warrior.

He stomped his right foot onto her left arm so she couldn't use the small blade. He dropped down and slammed his right elbow into her face. As hard as he could, again and again, until the Chinese killer's visage was nothing but blood and meat. He then delivered a blow that crushed her windpipe.

Thirty-seven seconds had elapsed since the fight had begun. Panting to catch his breath, feeling gloriously alive, Hernandez remained stooped over the dead body and could have stayed there for a long time even though pain from the stab wound and the other blows had found his consciousness.

He looked down at her grotesque form and felt no compassion. Four more killers scratched, for Willie. Six counting the two on Tung Choi Street. But the blood justice didn't make him feel better at all. Willie was dead and nothing would change that. His family was forever ripped asunder. How could they ever have another family bar-beque without Willie the master griller? What would their Christ-mas reunions be like without the young man who sang carols in a red Santa hat as he made mulled wine for the adults and hot chocolate with marshmallows for his young kids? The life of every party, a cata-lyst for good clean fun, Willie had been an irresistible force of nature that bound the family together, like the strongest magnet.

Ron still couldn't accept that his brother was gone forever. He knew he could kill every Chinese dirtbag from here to Dalian, and Willie would still be dead. Some wounds simply cannot heal. Grant was right. Killing wasn't the answer. The maggots responsible for the whole travesty needed to be exposed to the light of truth. If only they could somehow pull it off. Just as he began to feel woozy, a soft hand gently touched his shoulder.

"Mister Hernandez, thank you... but perhaps we should leave."

CHAPTER 24

21 :00

They were lined up waiting to get in when the doors opened exactly at nine. Funny how the promise of an open bar and free gambling chips can instill a sense of punctuality in the high and mighty. The rich want something for nothing just as much as everybody else.Vivian Chu and Eleanor Chow were some of the first through the door. The two *tai tais* Nicole had met in the Lobby Lounge were already well into their cups, but the old ladies headed straight for one of the many bar stations in the ballroom.

At least three hundred guests had already poured in when Conner Green escorted Nicole Grant and Tiffany the hooker into the entryway, which contained two X-ray scanners and uniformed Hong Kong police wielding handheld metal detectors for thorough security checks. Guest IDs were carefully matched against an invitation list, but since Green was one of the speakers tonight, he had *carte blanche* to bring in uninvited guests. A row of sharp-eyed security men assigned to the individual protection details for dignitaries from various countries stood by closely eyeing everyone who entered. Grant hoped Hernandez was okay. She felt slightly... what was the term? Cut lose? How good it would feel if he were here to back her up. She'd impulsively run with the scenario of somehow scamming her way into Zhao Yiren's condo, but now realized the scenario didn't include a role for Hernandez to play, so she shouldn't be blaming him for his absence. When she had a chance, she'd get another IM off to him.

Conner Green stood just feet away, ignoring her and Tiffany as he air-kissed and glad-handed with some of the ultra-wealthy. She and Tiffany were arm candy, only to be summoned when needed, so she wandered away in a stream of passing party-goers.

A waiter held up a tray of champagne and she took one to use as a prop. She scanned the room, hoping to spot Zhao. He wasn't at any of the gambling tables. Bill Clinton leaned against a roulette table vigorously chatting up a gorgeous young Chinese woman. Prince Harry was easy to spot since a cluster of females surrounded him wherever he went. Nicole noticed a couple of Hollywood stars lounging at a high table with the Executive Chairman of Google, Eric Schmidt. Jeff Bezos from Amazon was here, Elon Musk, Larry Ellison. Crap, this was a heady crowd. Nicole had to stay centered or she'd become nervous.

The tai tais, Vivian and Eleanor. I need to find the tai tais. But Nicole didn't need an introduction to Conner Green as they had earlier offered; she needed an introduction to a Chinese Princeling.

• • • •

KATE RICE HELD A WIRELESS microphone and scanned the crowdas she prepared to approach the podium. The rich, famous, and powerful in attendance were present due to her efforts and hard work. Her sweat had built Kids First from nothing into a world class charity. A sense of satisfaction and physical exhilaration washed away her fears, and anointed her with a renewed sense of grace. In spite of the present problems, look at what she'd created: a shimmering facade of philanthropy cloaking a ruthlessly efficient intelligence apparatus. She was too important to be terminated by Bergman or Zhao. She had a plan in motion with Wheeler and had every reason to believe it would work. She smiled as she glided up to the podium, reveling in the ovation that greeted her.

"Tonight is all about you," said Rice as the applause died down. "You, our biggest donors, our greatest fans, our hardest workers. All of you here tonight make up the heart and soul of Kids First. I'm so deeply grateful that good people put their money where their mouth is and step forward to help. Grateful that good people bring hope where none exists. Grateful that good people bring light to blackness, bring healing to the sick, shelter to the homeless, and food to the hungry children of this cruel world."

Tears rolled down the perfectly made-up cheeks of Kate Rice. What a performance! She'd choked up just enough so it could be heard in her voice, but not enough to interrupt the rhythm of the speech. The cameras and big screen monitors set up around the room had caught the tears, and number of guests got caught up in the emotion as well.

"I pledge to you that Kids First will stay focused and do what needs to be done—rules be damned, regulations be damned, danger be damned! We will do what must be done, what governments or other aid organizations can't do, or won't do. That's what makes Kids First different, and makes you the heroes. You are the heroes, not me. You are my heroes, and I love you all."

Rice turned and made a gesture to a hotel staffer.

"I'd like to propose a toast."

Dozens of staff held pre-poured flutes of expensive French champagne on serving trays. It only took moments for everyone in the hall to get a glass of the bubbly. Rice smiled, nodding acknowledgment to some in the crowd as she waited to make the toast. Suddenly her eyes riveted on Zhao standing close to a pretty young blonde she didn't recognize. Two Hong Kong *tai tais* Rice knew were standing with them. Was it jealously she felt... or suspicion?

Rice plastered a smile on her face and held her flute of champagne high into the air. She paused, taking in the sight as hundreds of glasses in the crowd were likewise lofted, following her lead and deepening her sense of satisfaction and power. "To the children... and those who love them!"

Cheers and shouts erupted as four hundred people took a drink together. The band launched into a spirited rendition of Donna Summers, *She Works Hard for the Money*. She waved to the throngs, checked to make sure the microphone was off, then handed it to an assistantwho had been waiting on the edge of the bandstand. "Find out who the blonde bitch is with Zhao Yiren... and get a close-up photo."

• • • •

PACIFIC PLACE HAD FOUR five-star hotels and Ron Hernandez had asked Jaffir Kahn to rent a suite in the artful luxury hotel above the Marriott called Upper House. Working out of his Isuzu box truck had become risky, and more space was needed than the truck could provide. Unwitting bellboys had schlepped up a veritable arsenal of goodies in luggage Jaffir had hastily purchased.

Pressing a handkerchief firmly over his thigh wound, Hernandez limped slightly as he led Rena Musaad into the 2000 square-foot, two-bedroom suite that featured clean lines, cool elegance, and bespoke furniture. He tossed the room key onto a counter that held a wine fridge and an espresso machine. Following suit, she put her purse on the counter, and gingerly removed the silenced handgun and the knife.

"Make yourself at home," he said, easing off his suit jacket. He draped it over a high stool and then reached for a bottle of Crown Royal while continuing to press the handkerchief against his leg. Beads of perspiration dappled his forehead. The stab wound probably wasn't serious, but the adrenalin rush from having killed the four Chinese in the life-or-death confrontation still coursed through his body.

Rena eyed the fancy digs. "A tad bit nicer than my basement room in London," she said dryly. "I see you have wine, and since I'm a nervous wreck I could use some, but... shouldn't you call a doctor? I mean, you've been stabbed."

"Jaffir?!" Hernandez called out. "You here?"

"Coming!" said Jaffir from oneof the bedrooms.

"Rena, you can't mention Jaffir, either in your reporting or in private conversation. And that goes for his family, if you meet them. You can't create a composite of him. You can't reveal you ever entered this hotel. Agreed?"

"Agreed."

Jaffir hurried into the room holding a large first aid kit.

"Jaffir Kahn, Rena Musaad. Rena, Jaffir."

"A pleasure to meet you, Miss Musaad, even though the circumstances are not ideal." The thin Pakistani-American bowed slightly as he shook her hand.

"Nice to meet you as well. Is there some way I can help?"

"Absolutely," said Jaffir. He handed her latex gloves and put the first aid kit on a chair. "Ron, let's do it in here on the dining table. The light is better."

Hernandez nodded and then glanced over to the table where bath towels had already been spread out on top. He took a long quaff directly from the bottle of Crown and leaned against the edge of the heavy wooden dining table as Jaffir pulled on latex gloves. "Splendid. Could you please remove Ron's shoes, Miss Musaad?"

"Only if you call me Rena," she smiled. She stooped down and started untying his shoe laces.

Jaffir shined a penlight into Hernandez's eyes, then checked his pulse. "Any other injuries?"

Hernandez shook his head no, then looked to Rena. "Sorry you had to see all that killing downstairs."

"I've seen killing before, and it's always so... sobering. It reminds me how precious life is. And how quickly it can be taken away." She got one shoe off and went to work on the other.

"Now that you've seen with your own eyes just how serious this all is, are you still interested in getting the story?"

"Yes, of course!"

Hernandez watched her carefully. She'd spoken too quickly, without thinking. He could tell she was upset by the violence and trying to hide her feelings.

"Rena," said Jaffir. "Please look away while our patient 'drops trou.' Not that there's much to see. And give me your handkerchief, Ron, I can see it needs dry cleaning."

Hernandez smiled as he dumped his sat phone and the contents of his pockets onto the table. Jaffir often inserted levity into serious situations as a way to put everyone more at ease. Taking a compress—in this case, a handkerchief—off a wound, especially your own wound, always came with fear attached. Will blood suddenly spurt? Will there be some other problem? So even though he was smiling, Hernandez felt a tickle of dread as he took pressure off the wound and removed the makeshift compress.

Jaffir took the bloody handkerchief and Hernandez unhooked his belt and dropped his blood-stained slacks. He grunted from pain as he stepped out of them. "Ron, move the toes on your left foot, then rotate the foot itself," said Jaffir, watching closely. He followed the instructions as they watched. "Bend your knee."

"Everything feels okay," said Hernandez, bending his knee.

"Okay, let's get you on the table."

Jaffir and Rena helped him lie back on top of the table. The bleeding had stopped, but his upper thigh was caked with dried blood. Jaffir quickly cut away a section of Hernandez's boxer shorts, and then used large swabs to clear away the blood.

"Not enough blood present for it to have cut a major pathway, and since there's no evidence of nerve or tendon damage, it looks like this is your lucky day," said Jaffir.

"Antibiotic ointment?" Rena asked Jaffir, as she held up a tube of the stuff.

"No, grab a bottle of water out of the fridge, please. Then we'll use the saline solution."

Hernandez lifted his head slightly to watch as Jaffir closely examined the cut. Rena fetched the plastic bottle of drinking water and Jaffir began to irrigate the wound. Hernandez shifted his gaze to Musaad.

"Rena, I want to make sure you're clear about the danger you face. You haven't really done anything yet and they almost killed you. You need to understand we're talking about your life."

"My life?" She looked confused.

Jaffir emptied the last of the water into the puncture wound. Rena leaned in and repositioned a towel to absorb the overflow as Jaffir then tore open a half-liter pouch of saline solution and now poured that into the wound.

"The four Chinese I just sent to hell were following you, not me. They certainly wanted to murder me, too, but that was a kill team sent to eliminate you, and they weren't going to bother making it look like an accident, like they did with Helen Bennett in London."

"They wanted to kill *me?!* That's not possible... is it?" Hernandez saw her cool facade slip a bit. More than a bit. "Perhaps they were following me to get to you," she countered.

Jaffir tossed aside the empty saline pouch. "Sorry to interrupt, but I'm only going to give you a couple of stitches. Basically, this wound should be left open for now. You can get it properly sutured up in a week or so if there's no infection."

Hernandez propped himself up on an elbow, took another hit of whiskey, and then offered the bottle to her. "You may want one too, Rena, because I have to tell you, the first two Chinese pulled their guns before they even saw me. And didn't you hear what the last killer said? 'Mister Hernandez, I am Chang. I have come to kill you and the lady.'"

"Oh," said Rena, as a shocked realization seemed to seep into her consciousness. "I thought he was referring to Nicole Grant."

Rena took the whiskey bottle, but didn't drink. She appeared sobered by this turn of events. "I should contact the London office right away."

"That might not be a good idea."

"Ron. I'm in a lot of trouble, is what you've told me. Life or death trouble." Rena locked her deadly serious eyes with his. She put a hand on the counter as if unconsciously stabilizing herself. "So why can't I call my office?" Rena was a tough young lady, but right now looked utterly lost.

"How did the Chinese find out about you? Have you told any-one other than Nicole Grant you're from WikiLeaks?" he asked.

She paused for a moment as her eyes rolled upward, as if she were double-checking her memory. "No."

He grunted, due to Jaffir's stitching. "They took out Helen Bennett, so they had killers on the ground in London. They knew she was in touch with me. How did they know that? Are the Chinese intercepting WikiLeaks' encrypted communications? Are the London offices bugged? Maybe they have someone on the inside, on their payroll."

"An inside man."

"Or woman. Who has now given them *your* name." Hernandez grimaced as Jaffir made another hole in his skin and pulled the needle through.

Rena poured herself a shot of whiskey and took a drink. She was doing a good job of trying not to look scared. "Can you help me get back to London?"

"Short term, I think you'd be safe at the British consulate here in Hong Kong."

"It's right next door to Pacific Place. We can walk there in minutes," said Jaffir, looking up at her from his handiwork.

"But we haven't had the barest of interviews yet," protested Rena. "I can't—"

"Jaffir will give you a couple of memory sticks as soon as he finishes with me and you two can be on your way."

"Thank you, but..."

"It's all on the memory sticks. Damning documentation. The longer you stay with us, the more danger you're in," said Hernandez, insistently. "You saw what happened. The hit was meant for you, Rena."

She swallowed hard. Before she could respond, a chiming sound came from her purse on the counter. "That's an encrypted message from the office in London." She seemed almost happy to have the distraction. She took a step, then stopped and looked to Hernandez for permission.

"Go ahead and read it," he said.

She removed her tablet computer and read the message. She didn't bother to disguise her shock. Disbelieving, she read the message again. She looked over to Hernandez and Jaffir.

"What is it?"

"A confidential message from my best friend in the London office. A decision has been made amongst the executives. They want me to scoop up all of your evidence. But it doesn't matter what proof you might have. WikiLeaks isn't going to touch this story."

Hernandez and Jaffir exchanged serious looks.

"Somebody got to WikiLeaks," said Hernandez, pondering just what kind of threats or dirty dealing it would take to co-opt that activist organization. "I hadn't counted on that."

"I still want the story. I have an idea for a strategy," said Rena, with a cold certainty. She met Jaffir's eyes, then Hernandez's.

Hernandez looked at her, impressed. In the last few minutes she'd learned she had a bulls eye on her back and that her employer was selling her down the river. But instead of falling apart or shifting into a run away and hide mentality due to the shocking news, Rena was energized. She was choosing "fight" over "flight."

With determination, she crossed to the table and reached into the first aid kit. "I can get the story picked up by Middle East press outlets, and some of the European and Asian outlets. We'll go on YouTube and do a social media push."

Jaffir tied off the last stitch, and then Rena then applied a sterile bandage over the wound. Jaffir patted Hernandez on the shoulder. "Finished, boss. You're golden."

Hernandez sat up and swung his legs over the side of the table.

Rena looked him in the eyes. "There are ways to get the truth out."

He reached out and gently touched her arm. "I'll help you however I can." He eased off the table, fished his encrypted sat phone from his shirt pocket and turned it on. The cell beeped with incoming messages. All from Chuck Wheeler. With Grant tied up at the fundraiser and with WikiLeaks out of the picture, it was time to start seriously hunting the hunters.

CHAPTER 25

21 :42

Perhaps it was because they were drunk. Vivian Chu and Eleanor Chow had taken Nicole Grant's hand, told her they liked her much better as a blonde, and then practically dragged her across the ballroom, where Vivian unceremoniously elbowed aside two Chinese security men in cheap black suits and pushed their way right up to Zhao Yiren.

Zhao had waved off the security detail and spoke with Nicole and the *tai tais* in perfect English. His graciousness and charm didn't seem forced as he quizzed her closely about her background and why she was in Hong Kong. There wasn't a hint of recognition as to her true identity.

That had happened about fifteen minutes earlier, before the speech from the charity's CEO, which Zhao had literally ignored. He kept checking his watch, but his demeanor was too cool to seem concerned with the time.

Grant had also kept her cool in spite of her usual clamminess. Focusing on the role she played kept her nervousness at bay. Nervous, no; excited, yes. Zhao had paid close attention to her and touched her arm several times in a manner that unquestionably suggested interest.

As soon as Vivian and Eleanor finally wandered off, Zhao gently took Nicole by the arm and smoothly guided her toward the exit. "What did you say your family name was? Faccioli?" he asked.

"Yes. Our winery isn't grand, but our wines are very nice. Perhaps I can send you a few boxes," said Nicole with a lilting Venetian accent.

"Italy is so beautiful. It's a shame we can't get on a plane and go visit."

"But we can!" she laughed. "Please come and be my guest," she said, smiling coquettishly.

"I wish I could," he said smiling. "I have a condo upstairs. We should go discuss the business of bringing your wines to China. And then we should discuss pleasure."

I'm going to get into his condo. A tingling feeling raced through her arms. Was it anticipation, or a warning? "Why not?" she said, masking with her smile the feeling of being very much alone.

· · · ·

CHUCK WHEELER SELECTED a piece of Crab Rangoon and popped it into his mouth with a satisfying crunch. The buffet table in the Songshan Room on Level Five, just down the hall from the raging Kids First function in the Island Ballroom, was loaded with gourmet appetizers and high-end liquor. Wheeler casually grazed from the spread as if he didn't have a care in the world. He suspected the room had been intended to use for intimate side meetings with high-rollers, but here he was, stinking it up. He had the bulletproof vest on under a dress shirt. When not stuffing food into his mouth he twirled an eight-inch-long non-metallic spike that he could hide up his sleeve. Metal detectors wouldn't pick it up.His darting eyes cut a quick glance at Kate Rice who paced on the other side of the small room as she bit her fingernails. He knew his cool demeanor was irritating her, and that was swell.

"Why the hell hasn't Hernandez called you back?" carped Rice, checking her watch.

"I'll call him again, if you insist," said Wheeler, spooning *foie gras* onto a toast point, "but I've left two messages. It's better if I don't seem too anxious."

"You're supposedly running scared, so it doesn't matter how many messages you leave," she countered. "We're running out of time, call him again." She stopped pacing and readied her cell, preparing to eavesdrop on the call.

But before Wheeler could dial, his cell phone rang. He looked over to Rice, who nodded. "Go ahead," he said into the phone.

"Where are you?" came Hernandez's voice.

Rice pressed her cell closer to her ear as she exchanged a quick look with Wheeler.

"I'm safe for now—let's leave it at that," said Wheeler, doing a good job to sound nervous. "Which is more than I can say for my partner—the redhead. My control pumped three slugs into her chest while I was in the next room. And that's what I'll get if they find me. I want to meet, and I mean right now."

"Who's your control?" asked Hernandez.

"No, no. No names, no info. Not until we have a deal. You sell me on a plan—show me specifics—to get my butt safely out of here, and I'll sing the *Hallelujah Chorus* for you."

There was a pause on Hernandez's end. "I'll send you a text in thirty minutes."

• • • •

THE BUSINESS PART OF their conversation about allowing her family's wines to be imported duty-free into China lasted only as long as it took Nicole Grant and Zhao Yiren to duck out of the reception in the Island Ballroom and ride the elevator up to his condo. He apologized for the heavy security presence and wrote it off as a sign of the times. Having now spent the last twenty minutes with him, she realized the *tai tais* had been right—the man dripped *machismo*.

Manly or not, Zhao was drunk. He concealed it well, but Grant picked up some of the telltale signs: glassy eyes, occasional slurred speech, and diminished motor coordination. The Chinese were legendary drinkers—it was a matter of great pride—and she hoped he was a happy drunk. As they rode the elevator she used the excuse of needing a breath mint to root around in her purse and surreptitiously check her tablet computer. The KCS tracking site indicating the location of her laptop was up and running. She then minimized the tracking page.

When they entered his condo it was crowded with more security people. "It looks like a bodyguard convention in here," he cracked.

"You must be terribly important," she teased.

"Think about it," he said slurring his words slightly. "It's like being in prison."

"But such a nice prison," she said, looking around the handsomely furnished condo, much of it with an Art Deco and Machine Age design theme. A tall, muscular Chinese man in his early thirties approached them.

"Good evening, sir."

"Ariana, this is Security Chief Lin, head of my personal protection detail." As soon as he made the introduction, Zhao took a cell call and faced away from the security check.

"Nice to meet you Chief Lin." The man looked like a stone killer to Grant. Under his fake smile hid the cold face of a butcher. She actually felt a shiver as he came near. A three-inch scar ran across his chin, and his nose had been broken so many times it would never look right again. His black eyes were a dead pool of muted hate. She instantly disliked him, an uncommon reaction for her.

"I'm sorry, miss, but would you be offended if I looked into your bag?"

It sounded like a request on the surface, but it wasn't, it was an order. "Perhaps embarrassed, but not offended," she said, offering her fake Celine bag. She forced herself to keep smiling, even though she worried that if he kept her electronics, then this was all for nothing.

After what seemed like an eternity of going through her things, he held up the tablet. He turned it over in his large hands whose knuckles bore many scars. He tapped the screen, bringing it to life, and was presented with the unlock pattern. Surely he wouldn't ask her to unlock the device.

"Would you mind unlocking this for me?" he asked without smiling. An unfriendly arrogance permeated his demeanor.

Nicole blinked. She felt like she was about to come unglued. She hadn't imagined the contents of her tablet would be checked by security. It would only take them seconds to learn it belonged to Nicole Grant, the woman they wanted to kill. After everything she'd been through today, to just waltz in and announce who she really was, via her tablet, well, could she have made it any easier for them? She could only think to somehow make light of the situation. "Do you need to send an e-mail?" she joked.

He held the tablet tightly and looked at her more closely, as if trying to see something under her surface. "No, I just have to check."

He was pushing. That's the kind of man he was, someone who pushed others around. She wouldn't let him do it to her. "Chief Lin, you have confirmed I have a functioning tablet. If you want to examine the contents, my *private* information, I have to say 'no.'" She said it firmly, without a smile. She looked to Zhao and tapped him on the shoulder. He turned to her and ended the cell call. "Perhaps it was a mistake to come up here, darling," she said to Zhao.

She reached for her purse, but Lin held on to it. "I will hold your purse for you, miss."

"No you won't, I'll be leaving now." Grant flashed a challenging look.

Impatient, Zhao came to the rescue, looking irritated. "Thank you Chief Lin, that will be all."

Lin bowed slightly, returned the tablet to her purse, and handed the bag back to her. His thin smile made her skin crawl.

"Forgive them, my security people are on edge. Want to escape with me?" whispered Zhao, as he led her across the room, deeper into the condo.

"To where?" said Grant, trying to shift back into a relaxed, flirtatious state. Inside, she felt like a dishrag that had just been wrung out.

"A quiet place in the back with a full bar. We'll be able to talk privately there."

"Could you give me a quick tour first? I love your interior design."

Zhao hid his impatience, but Nicole had her own agenda, she needed to find her laptop. "There's not that much to see," he protested.

She let him lead and kept her fake Celine bag on the side away from him so she could sneak peeks at her tablet screen checking the location arrow indicator. After looking into a few rooms they entered the huge soundproofed master bedroom area. She stole a glance into her purse. *My laptop is in this room!* She barely noticed as Zhao closed and locked the bedroom door behind them.

"Such a wonderful flat. Do you spend much time here?" she asked as her eyes flitted around the room, searching.

"Not as much as I'd like. Champagne?" He crossed to the sitting area where he'd earlier sat with General Ma.

"Only if you'll join me," she said. She followed him and then almost lost her breath as she neared two antique French lounge chairs facing each other. Her laptop leaned against an attaché case sitting on the floor next to one of the chairs.

He moved to the small bar with his back to her.

She quickly sat down. She had two options to power up her laptop, both supplied by Jaffir: a standard power cord, or an external battery pack. The battery pack could only provide power to her laptop for a short time, so Nicole glanced around for an electrical outlet to use with the power cord.

"Champagne is one of my bad habits," said Zhao, selecting two clean champagne flutes from a shelf.

"Champagne is a good habit," she said, keeping the conversation going as she scanned the area for a three-holed British-style electrical socket. Crap, she didn't see a socket and couldn't very well get on her hands and knees to go looking for one. So she retrieved the external battery pack from her purse.

But then Zhao turned around with a huge smile and looked at her. "You're right, it's a good habit." He winked, then turned back to his task.

Good thing he was drunk. From a distance a battery pack could be mistaken for a cell phone, but he didn't seem to notice it one way or the other. A loud pop startled her as the cork shot into the air and hit the ceiling, but then she leaned over and plugged the battery pack into her laptop. She tucked it out of sight between the computer and the attaché case and then sat up just as he turned around holding two glasses of bubbly.

Her heart raced, her throat constricted, but she forced a smile, reached out to take the champagne and managed to say, "*Grazie.*"

"To smart, funny, sexy, beautiful blondes." They clinked glasses.

"But darling, what if I wasn't a real blonde?"

"Then I'd say you were the same as most of the other 'blondes' I've known." Zhao stood there and burst out laughing.

His laughter put her immediately at ease. Okay, he's a happy drunk. With a rakish swagger he drained his entire glass, then reached out, took her hand and pulled gently so she stood up. Using an unforced smoothness he swept her into his arms and they kissed. She went along with his passion, at least for now. All she needed was a minute or two on her tablet computer and she could download the Holy Grail—the keys for the files hidden on the Darknet.She broke off the kiss and pushed slightly away, grabbing her purse. "I have to freshen up. I'll be right back."

She pressed her fingers to his lips. He bit them playfully. A happy, horny drunk, she thought, correcting herself. As she started to move away, he grabbed her and threw her onto the bed. He was all over her and strong as a bull. She was at a loss for what to do.

The foreplay was hot and heavy when she rolled on top of him. Her purse was above his head on the pillows, out of his sight. Without thinking, she sensuously rubbed her body over his. She snaked one hand into her purse and removed her tablet computer. The battery pack she'd connected to her laptop was designed to charge smaller electronic devices, not big units like hers, and might only provide ten minutes of power. Meaning she had to act fast.

She fought her own arousal—maybe from the danger of it all?—and focused on enabling her tablet as a Wi-Fi hotspot. She was terribly nervous, but somehow, calm. What a marked change from earlier this afternoon! Zhao lay relatively still as she kissed his cheek and tongued his ear.

She'd prefer to get out now, before the sexual thing went too far. She'd make an excuse, and leave. Take the elevator up one floor to safety and get the files remotely. But all of that could easily take ten minutes, and by then, the battery pack might be exhausted, putting her right back to square one.

And since the Chinese had imaged her laptop, what if they'd broken her encryption? What if they had the digital keys and were right now requesting her files from the Darknet? What if the race to the Darknet files was still on? That meant she had no time to waste.

She sneaked a look at the tablet. Her laptop had finished booting up and had recognized the phony Wi-Fi signal. She had access! There was no choice but to go for it, right here, right now. It would only take a few minutes, and a few minutes was all she had.

CHAPTER 26

22^{:09}

22 :09   Kate Rice approached the Songshan Room holding the red Nikon Coolpix camera and a black cable that her assistant had just given to her. The camera held photos of the blondethat Zhao had left the party with. She was irritated only because he'd done it at her very own event, so it was like a slap in the face. In spite of that, she felt like a large weight had been removed from her shoulders, because she'd just turned the entire charity event over to the assistant. Rice had walked away from her own party.

Her obsessive need to control her creation had blinded her to the larger picture. That asshole Berry Bergman had been right; she needed to be in the field, giving 100 percent to any issue that would interfere with Zhao's ascendance. Hernandez was on a baited hook; Israeli, South African and German freelance agents she'd secretly hired were standing by all over Hong Kong to eliminate him once and for all, since the Chinese seemed incapable of doing the job themselves. Only a couple of minefields remained to be maneuvered through tonight, and then she could relax.

Unfortunately, she'd just learned that the waterboarding of William Snedeker back in the States had produced no intelligence of any value, but had sent him into a seizure. He was barely alive and in a coma. Meaning she had no idea whom he might have told about her operation, nor did she know who had alerted him to it.

And that whanker Chuck Wheeler was in the room she was about to enter, eating her food, acting like king of the hill. He wouldn't live to see the morning, but right now he held the upper hand.

Additionally, she'd just sent freelancers to track down someone named Jaffir Khan, a local friend of Hernandez and a likely candidate to be lending support. She just wished she'd made the connection sooner. So there were both negative and positive last minute developments, typical to the closing of huge deal, the deal being putting Zhao into the supreme seat of Chinese power. Looking back with a bluntly honest appraisal, Rice admitted to herself she'd made a number of key errors, but the mistakes would stop, starting now.

She entered the Songshan Room and crossed to Wheeler. Before she said a word, he handed her the cell phone. "This text just came," he said.

Rice looked at the screen. "GO TO THE POOL AT THE CONRAD IN PACIFIC PLACE. LOOK UNDER THE TOWELS ON THE COUNTER."

She checked her watch. "Good, he's early. Do us all a favor and go kill that SOB."

As soon as Wheeler was out the door, she made a cell call to an Israeli operative. "The pool at the Conrad." She ended the call and took a sip of her drink, then put it down, remembering the Nikon camera. She connected it to her smartphone using the black cable and found the photo of the blonde who left with Zhao. Then she logged-in to a CIA database.

• • • •

ZHAO YIREN LAY ON THE bed with his eyes closed as Nicole Grant lay on top of him. His hands were under her black cocktail dress and he was grasping her buttocks.

This man will be the next president of China, she thought. A corrupt, amoral man who wanted her dead, who had ordered the murder of eighteen Americans, the man who would probably give almost anything to find her right now and put a bullet in her head. And here she was, reduced to serious sexual foreplay with him, something she never engaged in lightly, to say the least. But if she was going to win, to survive, she needed to become a different person.

Fighting to stay focused, she looked up at her tablet leaning against a pillow just above his head. She gently moved her right hand to open the software which allowed her to control her laptop remotely. In only fourteen seconds she'd downloaded the digital keys from her laptop to her tablet. But there were nine of them. Nine digital keys! It would take a number of minutes to make nine individual requests to the Darknet to obtain the drone op files.

What am I doing! Am I crazy!

Nicole felt panic rising in her chest. She could get up and run right out of the condo. But then she remembered Hernandez's dead brother. Was someone going to hold the guilty accountable, or not? She logged onto the Darknet and started submitting the requests, asking for the highly sensitive files to be sent to simple e-mail accounts, as Zhao tried to slip his fingers inside her panties.

• • • •

THE RECTANGULAR OUTDOOR pool was on a lower floor of the Conrad. A dozen burgundy-colored chaise lounges lined each of the long sides, while six enclosed cabanas stood at the far end. Ten or so guests, including children, were either swimming or relaxing poolside as Chuck Wheeler stopped at the counter that had a stack of towels resting on top. Trees and shrubbery surrounded the pool on all four sides, creating an incongruous effect since the pool area was nestled in the concrete canyons of Pacific Place and dwarfed by steel-and-glass high-rise towers.

Thousands of glowing lights softened the black sky. Muted, submerged lighting made the pool seductively inviting. Wheeler smiled. Hernandez could be watching him from countless vantage points—terraces, overlooks, patios, balconies, office or hotel windows, rooftops, or even using video cams. But sooner or later tonight, they'd come face-to-face. He took a deep breath of the moist, salt-tinged, slightly cool night air and felt invigorated. Having to kill

Hernandez was unfortunate, but there wasn't much choice. Going on the run from the CIA would eventually result in his being gunned down, just as Roberts had been earlier today. So he reached under the stack of towels and found a two-way radio. Talk about low-tech. He pushed the talk button. "It's me." He released the button and waited.

After a few seconds, Ron Hernandez's voice came through loud and clear. "Don't take anything out of your pockets. Jump into the pool. Swim to the other end. Go into the second cabana from the right."

Wheeler smiled, walked over to the end of the pool and jumped in.

• • • •

KATE RICE SPOKE INTO an encrypted satellite phone as she stood pacing in front of the makeshift bar in the Songshan Room. She had two devices on the table in front of her: a smartphone connected to a red Nikon Coolpix camera via a small cable, and an orange-colored remote bomb detonator switch that used the cell phone network.

"What do you mean he disappeared into a cabana?" asked Rice into the sat phone.

"He picked up a two-way radio, said something, jumped into the pool fully clothed, swam to the other end, got out, and went into the cabana. That was two minutes ago," said the male voice with a thick South African accent.

Rice furrowed her brow as she bit a fingernail. "Where are you now?"

"Behind some trees at the edge of the pool."

"So the Zippo lighter GPS tracker is useless?"

"Yes."

A rage surged from inside Rice and flowed into her head. Her cheeks flushed deep crimson and her lips formed into a snarl of malice. "What about the bomb mechanism? Is that worthless, too?" she asked sharply, as the anger poured out.

"It's supposed to be waterproof."

"Supposed to be?" she mimicked acidly. Rice held the phone to her side as she took a deep breath and struggled to keep her emotions under control. She had Pacific Place surrounded by a dozen freelance operatives waiting to pick up Wheeler's tail. When he met with Hernandez, they would both be killed. But everything had been set to pick up Wheeler as soon as he left Pacific Place. If they couldn't track him then her plan was in the toilet, and maybe her life, too. "Is it waterproof or not?" demanded Rice.

"Are you suggesting I should have personally tested it?!" snapped the man, over the sat phone. "Was I supposed to have blown up something underwater in the miniscule amount of time you gave me to rig up a bomb in a bulletproof vest?"

"Don't get smart with me!"

"Screw you, Rice. My loyalty to you is exactly zero. I'm hearing whispers on the street that you're going down. And I'm not going with you," said the voice with a quiet intensity and a hint of malevolence.

She was on the verge of losing control of her mercenaries when she needed them most. "Look, forget about the bomb. It was a backup plan which I now realize was a bad idea. I'm tripling your fee, okay? Does that up your loyalty quotient? Can you stay in the trees and make your way to that cabana? Maybe check the rear, see if you can hear something."

Rice switched the phone to speaker and set it down so she could rub her temples. It was never easy to win the big prize. The world was mostly made up of failures and quitters. The meek, the little people with small dreams.The wannabees who never had a clue. Navigating to the top of the top took cunning, courage, perseverance and ruthlessness. She had them all in spades, but it didn't make the fight easier, it was still a bruising battle with no prisoners taken, no quarter given. The closer to the top of the mountain, the more treacherous the terrain. The damage control for this action in Hong Kong was going to be something. She absentmindedly bit at her nails as she waited for the man to report.

"I'm in the cabana," said the voice over the speakerphone. "The back was slit open. Wheeler's shoes, his clothes, the vest, the phone and lighter are all on the floor. But he's gone, there's no one here."

Rice's jaw went slack. They'd lost Chuck Wheeler before he'd even left Pacific Place! She flung her drink into the array of liquor bottles on the buffet table creating a shower of crystal shards and a spray of alcohol that spewed forth like a poisonous hiss. Why was everything suddenly falling apart in Hong Kong?

"Rice, advise," said the man.

The sound of the South African's voice jolted her. "Did you say Wheeler left the bulletproof vest in there, too?" she asked.

"Affirmative. The swimming pool is almost at ground level with all the vehicle traffic. Wheeler must have dropped down to the driveway. He can't be far. Do you want me to look, or not?"

Rice's attention was drawn to her smartphone which beeped very softly. "Standby," she said. The CIA database had a match on the blonde in the photo with Zhao taken a short time ago. Rice picked up the smartphone and then blinked out of pure shock. She was staring at an NSA identification photo of Nicole Grant.

Suddenly, Rice's world was spinning around her. She reached out with one hand and held onto the table. Everything was topsy-turvy; everything seemed to be coming unglued. Years and years of hard work, planning, sacrifice, and her own personal debasement had gone into reaching this point, where she was less than two weeks away from installing an asset, *her asset*, as the president of all of China! Her feat would be the greatest espionage achievement in modern times, sealing her place of honor, granting her respect, acceptance, adulation. She was simply too close to fail now.

She flashed on something Zhao had said in the emergency meeting. He wanted to know why Pacific Place couldn't be evacuated. General Ma said it would take a real event, a quasi-catastrophe to make that happen and pull it off without getting caught. A spark reappeared in her eyes: the vest. Perhaps there was still a way to net them all.

With the cell phone firmly in one hand, she grabbed the orange bomb detonator with her other hand.

• • • •

DOZENS OF CANDLES CAST a warm golden glow in the outdoor area called The Lawn on the 6th floor of the boutique hotel known as Upper House. About fifteen well-heeled trendoids had been sipping crafted cocktails and making muted small talk as Ron Hernandez, wearing khaki slacks and a navy blue sport coat, had shuffled his way across the open space toward a high hedge. He was favoring the leg, but the limp was barely noticeable. Jaffir had provided antibiotics and Naproxen, relegating the stab wound to nuisance status.

Minutes earlier, Hernandez had gazed down through an opening in the hedge onto the swimming pool of the Conrad Hotel, just across the way. He'd used Wheeler's own binoculars to watch the man as he worked to swim the length of the pool while fully clothed and wearing shoes. Any trackers or electronic bugs Wheeler had been carrying were now worthless. The smart assumption was that Wheeler was bait for a trap, so Hernandez hoped to trap some of the trappers and then beat the truth out of whomever he captured.

Hernandez had noted that Wheeler was in damn good physical condition for a guy in his fifties; he'd have to keep that in mind. He'd watched as Wheeler climbed out of the shallow end, and then he lost sight of him as he ducked into the cabana where written instructions awaited.

That was all some minutes earlier. Right now, Hernandez had the Bushnell binoculars recording video of what he was observing. Wheeler sat placidly on the outdoor patio of Domani on the ground level of One Pacific Place. He wore the outfit Hernandez had stashed in the cabana: black sweat suit, black baseball cap, black sneakers, dark sunglasses. Hernandez had also left a cheap cell phone which Wheeler held in his hand.

Casually panning the binoculars back to the Conrad pool, Hernandez saw a man move through the trees, approach the cabana from the back, and enter. He kept watching for about a minute, but the man still hadn't emerged. Hernandez was about to pan back to Wheeler and give him a call, when...

...An explosion ripped the very fabric of the night. The cabana, all of the cabanas simply disappeared. So did the twenty-four chaise lounges and the guests, including children, who'd been in the water or lounging poolside.

Since he was trained to kill and observe death through an optic sight or a drone video camera feed, he didn't lower the field glasses but instinctively zoomed out. Hernandez saw water and blood rise like a fountain of death, a massacre conjured by the devil himself. Trees and shrubs summer-salted in all directions and slammed into vehicles on the drive below the pool that connected the four towers, causing multiple traffic accidents. Debris and body parts flew across the drive and tore into the wedding party on the outdoor plaza just across the way, cutting down dozens of guests where they stood.

The entire pool area then collapsed in a massive cloud of concrete dust and twisted rebar onto the level below as if falling through a chasm straight into hell. The man in the cabana had been vaporized.

Hernandez's mind desperately tried to compute what had just happened when the delayed explosive sound and percussive blast force hit him like a punch to his solar plexus. It was only then that he lowered the binoculars, allowing himself a moment of shock. He immediately raised them to his eyes again and found Wheeler, on his feet now next to his cafe table, staring at the carnage. Hernandez zoomed in; Wheeler looked shocked, panicked even, and then started to walk away.

Hernandez lowered the binoculars, ashen, trying to comprehend the ramifications of this heinous act of carnage. He hoped Grant was safe, wherever she was. Then screams of horror and cries from the wounded punctuated the devastation like an aria of death.

He pulled out his phone but wasn't sure who to call.

What kind of people would do this? Innocent men, women, and children had just been blown to pieces. Children! Was the explosion an accident, a mistake? Had the CIA intentionally killed their operative? If it was intentional, then how in the world could he hope to defeat an enemy willing to destroy anything and everything that stood in the way? Hernandez felt sick to his stomach.

Screw Grant and her frigging files! If he'd ignored her and had just killed Zhao when he had the chance, this wouldn't have happened. Those people would still be enjoying their holiday on a beautiful spring night.

If he hadn't brought Wheeler to that cabana, those people, those kids would still be... Jesus, sweet Jesus. Hernandez wasn't responsible for the dead and wounded, but was connected to their fate in a way that would make for more nightmares and guilt in a life that already had plenty, starting with his dead brother Willie. His brother would still be alive if he hadn't... Ron Hernandez stood there for several moments fighting emotional riptides that threatened to tear him apart.

He'd seen enough of death, but apparently death hadn't seen enough of him.

Time to go back to the original plan and just kill every one of these pieces of human garbage he could find. Every single one: American or Chinese or whatever. And there was no way in hell he'd let Grant or anyone else stop him this time.

CHAPTER 27

22$^{:32}$ Chuck Wheeler walked at a normal pace toward The Petit Cafe at the base of Two Pacific Place tower. The long outdoor escalator just beyond it would take him up to Hong Kong Park. Panic-stricken cafe patrons stood holding each other and making cell phone calls. The really smart ones were paying their checks so they could get the hell out. A pall of smoke blowing in from the bomb site sent some into coughing fits. The normally welcome sea breeze had become a pariah, the bearer of bad tidings carrying plaintive moans, horrific screams, acrid-smelling fumes, and the stink of death.

For once, Wheeler didn't feel superior to by-standers at a crime scene. He didn't scare easily, but he was shakento his very core. He didn't think Hernandez had anything to do with the bomb, he knew it was Rice, but all bets were off now. He was going to ground. He needed cash, which would be his first chore tonight, after activating the contract to assassinate Kate Rice. He'd pay for a boat to Hainan Island, and then make his way to Vietnam.

The cell phone rang. The one Hernandez had left for him in the cabana. His head swiveled as he checked for threats, and then took the call. It was a good reminder to throw away the phone, and fast.

"So that was meant for me?!" Hernandez's voice was low, barely above a whisper, but he sounded livid. "You saw the people at the pool. Innocents.Kids. You waxed one of your own men."

Wheeler struggled to maintain a neutral demeanor as he skirted a group of on-lookers. The customers at Petit Cafe were now leaving *en-masse*, perhaps unconsciously fleeing from the sounds of approaching sirens which filled the terror-stricken night.

"I had nothing to do with that. They must have rigged the bullet-proof vest." Wheeler spoke softly so no one could hear. And he didn't want to say the word "bomb" on an unsecured line.

"Keep talking," said Hernandez, as if trying to reign in his anger.

"I had guns to my head," he lied. "They forced me to call you and set up a meet. I wasn't lying about my partner, the redhead—they whacked her inside a safehouse in the Shangri-La tower."

"Go on."

"They gave me a cigarette lighter. Lighting it would activate a GPS tracker so a snatch team could grab you. I also had to wear the vest. Supposedly because they thought you might cap me. I didn't want to wear it, but then I figured it might be a good idea. But I'll bet you anything the ceramic plates weren't ceramic and that the whole damn thing was full of you-know-what." Wheeler looked up as he stepped on the long escalator that would carry him out of Pacific Place and into Hong Kong Park. "They were going to take out both of us. Two birds with one stone."

"So why wait until you took it off?"

Wheeler turned and looked out upon the unfolding havoc. "No idea. They've created pandemonium and panic, so maybe they wanted that. But I swear, that bitch is history."

"Who? Who's your control?"

"Kate Rice. Her cover is CEO of Kids First charity. They're having a huge conference this weekend over at the Convention Center. Right now there's a party in the Shangri-La ballroom. Rice was in the Songshan room at the Shangri-La less than twenty minutes ago."

The line went dead. Wheeler tossed the phone from the rising outdoor escalator. Hernandez hadn't held up his part of the bargain to provide some means to get out of town, but the whole meet had been a ruse to kill him, so Wheeler couldn't really complain. He'd wanted to erase Hernandez and Grant, but as he stepped off the escalator and into the park, he decided to root for them, instead.

• • • •

A CHEER WENT UP IN the computer room in another part of the building that housed Tianhe-2 at Sun Yat-sen University in Guangzhou, China. Oi Lam had just announced to the group of hackers from the 57th Research Institute that the encryption used on the American woman's laptop had been broken. The timing was only seventeen minutes off from her estimate on the digital countdown clock, which was now zeroed out.

The programs and files from the computer were quickly divided up between the hackers to speed the process of understanding what had been going on and what information was contained therein. All of the hackers could read, write, and speak English at a very high level.

Oi Lam shunted aside all thoughts of her pregnancy and whether General Ma was going to be financially generous or not. That would become clear soon enough. Her pulse quickened as she concentrated on examining a group of Grant's files. After opening a file named JETA, she found nine letter and number configurations. Code?Keys?Bank accounts? Now that the puzzle box had been opened, the challenge was to put the pieces together.

"It's the Darknet!" exclaimed Oi Lam. "I suspect the American wrote this software program herself. It has been randomly submitting keys daily to the Darknet to obtain files, but never downloading them.Quickly, let's submit these keys and download the files."

· · · ·

NICOLE FELT THE MOVEMENT and anticipated the roll of Zhao's body, so she reached up and just managed to stash her tablet computer back into the fake Celine bag. She'd broken out into a sweat, but not from sexual heat. She was scared silly that at any second the future president of China, the man who wanted her deader than a doornail, would realize what she was up to. He was straddling her now and pulled her dress up to her shoulders. With one incredibly strong jerk he tore her bra open revealing her small but pert breasts. The same thing then happened to her panties. Penetration was moments away unless she fought or unless...

"Please, let me wash for you, first," said Nicole tenderly, as she held his face. "I have to take out the tampon. I want to be clean for you, not dirty."

This last remark stopped Zhao cold. She hoped the idea that she had a dirty tampon inside her might turn him right off.

"Please do it quickly," he said, and drunkenly moved off of her.

Grabbing her dress and purse she hurried into the bathroom, where she closed and locked the door. She used a towel to mop beads of sweat from her forehead as she took deep breaths. The breathing exercise helped calm her but didn't change the fact she had only minutes to act. She stood naked at the vanity and checked her tablet. The files documenting the secret drone operation were downloading! She reached over and turned the tap water on strong as a masking sound. She took another deep breath as she opened the audio file of Wang Hongwei and Zhao Yiren in the panel van, which had finished downloading.

No! NO!

The file was corrupted. It was incomplete. She checked another file; same result. She'd kept the files alive on the Darknet but they wouldn't be of any help in this defective condition. Nicole closed her eyes and exhaled. She refused to accept this had all been for nothing, but felt like a fighter who'd been fighting valiantly against a stronger opponent and had now been knocked down with such force that maybe she wouldn't be standing up again. She listlessly pulled on her dress. Perhaps the problem was that the files simply couldn't be kept whole after two years on the Darknet. She wasn't sure.

A pounding on the door jolted her back to the reality of her tenuous situation. "Ariana, I have a plane to catch tonight," said Zhao, sounding drunk and insistent.

"Just two more minutes, darling. You'll be happy you waited," said Nicole, shocked at how easily she now shifted into a persona created out of thin air. Two minutes to come up with an escape plan, because now it was time to run.

• • • •

EVEN THOUGH HE KNEW Zhao should be disturbed due to the window-rattling explosion next door, General Ma had kept Chief Lin and the security team from entering the master bedroom. Ma knew his old friend was having a tryst with the blond girl and there would be hell to pay if he were interrupted, bombing or no bombing. The general stood at one of the windows, craning his neck to take in the devastation at the outdoor pool of the Conrad Hotel tower just next door.

Ma had just learned that additional bomb threats had been called in and that the Hong Kong police had just launched a mandatory evacuation of all of Pacific Place.

Had Zhao Yiren secretly arranged this? Zhao had advocated an evacuation of the facility just a few hours earlier, and now it was happening. Ma crossed to the closed master bedroom door. An evacuation meant he had to risk the ire of the man and interrupt. Even if, as he suspected, Zhao was behind it all.

• • • •

DIRECTOR TANG COULD barely hear himself think. His thrown-together CP at the JW Marriott buzzed at an extra high frequency with incoming reports of the bombing at the Conrad—an explosion that they had heard and strongly felt in this very room. In addition to himself and his aide Choi, four people in the room worked for him at the MSS. The other ten personnel in the room were military intelligence members of the Second Department.

Tang and Choi stood together in the open door to the bathroom where they spoke quietly, in semi-privacy.

"I have very bad news. We've found our people. All four are dead," said Choi, his drawn face now taking on an almost greyish pallor. "Two shot, two stabbed."

Tang couldn't believe it. "Chang is dead?"

Choi nodded. "All four bodies are hidden under tables next to the ballroom downstairs."

Tang fumed inside, but his face remained neutral. "And the Wik-iLeaks reporter?"

"We've lost her."

"*Ai ya.*" Tang rolled his eyes skyward as if looking for divine guidance from the spirits of deceased Taoist masters to whom he sometimes prayed. He blinked several times and started tugging his ear as he thought. He had now lost six members of his twenty-person team in Hong Kong. All six of them had been involved in the killings in America. Could Hernandez have known that? Was he exacting retribution?

To lose six people out of twenty was a staggering loss percentage, almost one-third of his team. And his people had not only failed to find and kill Hernandez and Grant, but had now failed to kill a lone woman reporter. It must have been Hernandez who'd killed his people, but it didn't matter. This failure would not be tolerated. That chunky bastard General Ma would have him shot, absent some dramatic reversal of fortune in the next few hours. Tang faced a grim fate, but he didn't want his remaining people to also suffer.

He performed a quick mental calculation, and then fixed Choi with a stare. "Including you and me, there are fourteen of us left from MSS. Six in this hotel suite and eight elsewhere. Have our people in this room begin to quietly slip away."

"And the eight already outside?"

"Set up the CP across the street, but don't tell Ma's people. I should have pulled us out hours ago. Our job is not to be police who perform dragnets. We are assassins who operate in the shadows. And if we don't kill the Americans tonight..." Tang left the words hanging in the air. He vowed to himself that, if at all possible, he would personally seek revenge upon the killer of his six people, meaning he wanted to personally exterminate Ron Hernandez.

• • • •

PANDEMONIUM RULED IN the Marriott's lobby. As soon as police had announced the evacuation, guests already spooked from the explosion at the Conrad's pool bolted without paying their checks from Flint Grill and Bar, Man Ho, Marriott's Cafe, and Dolce 88. The elevators and stairwells were now depositing scores of panicked guests into the lobby who weren't sure what to do or where to go, overwhelming Marriott security and uniformed Hong Kong police. There weren't enough taxis, and the driveways inside Pacific Place were jammed bumper-to-bumper with vehicles, anyway. The Marriott's front entrance had devolved into fist fights and shoving matches. General Ma's security men and the 8 X10s they held were simply pushed aside.

Into that maelstrom stepped Rena Musaad wearing a black *burka*, accompanied by Jaffir Kahn and his two teenage daughters, also hidden under *burkas*, as they hurried out of a stairwell. When Rena caught sight of herself in a large mirror the irony of her situation hit her like a ton of metaphorical bricks. She'd grown up hating Muslims, had been viciously abused by Muslims, and went out of her way to avoid having any contact with Muslims. But right now a Muslim family risked their own lives to get her to safety. Furthermore, it was a black *burka*, a garment that evoked strong negative emotions in the non-Islamic world, a garment that to many represented the oppression of women, that spoke of things dark and impenetrable and unknowing, it was a *burka* that shielded her from the eyes of her would-be killers.

Rena said a silent prayer to God and expressed thanks for this unlikely divine intervention that was not only saving her, but teaching her a valuable lesson. "I'll work hard to get the story out," said Rena quietly to Jaffir. "But I'd rather stay until we can resolve a few items."

"The situation is resolving itself, it's called a mandatory evacuation," said Jaffir, holding onto Rena and his daughters as they pushed into the crowd.

"Do you really believe there are more bombs?" she asked in a whisper.

"It's a moot point. You'll be safe at the British consulate. You're not safe here."

"Where are we going, papa?" asked Jaffir's eldest daughter.

"The single elevator over there! We can take it down to the shopping mall," he said, trying to pull them free of the crush. The four of them made it to the single elevator which was being ignored in the hysteria, since most everyone saw the large front doors and naturally headed in that direction.

"I wish you success, Rena." The elevator arrived and Jaffir pushed them all inside. "Because I think you might hold the key to saving Ron and Nicole's lives."

The weight of Jaffir's remark almost caused Rena's knees to buckle, just as the elevator doors closed, sealing them inside.

CHAPTER 28

22:41 The normally sedate lobby of the Island Shangri-La buzzed with a genteel but still quite tense evacuation as police guided concerned VIP guests toward the main exit. Ron Hernandez wormed his way inside through a side entrance, decisively cut through the crowd, and pushed through a stairway door. He flew down the empty stairwell. There may be an emergency evacuation in progress, but God forbid the rich and famous would have to walk up a flight of stairs to escape. He shot out through a steel door and into a human wall of 400 well-dressed, half-drunk party-goers outside the ballroom who were all trying to get into one elevator car at the same time.

Hernandez sliced through the crowd and followed signs to the Songshan Room. As he ran down the hallway, he pulled of the long gray ponytail wig and tossed it aside. In seconds he was at the door and burst in. The room stood empty. He eyed the food and drink set-up, and then spotted a red Nikon Coolpix camera at the makeshift bar. He crossed to the table and checked the camera. A cable was still attached, as if someone had been uploading photos to another device. Hernandez pressed the power button. The view that appeared on the camera screen was a shot of Nicole Grant standing with Zhao Yiren.

• • • •

THE HACKERS FROM THE 57th Research Institute working temporarily at Sun Yat-sen University in Guangzhou looked sullen. Oi Lam wore a lightweight pink jacket zipped all the way up and rubbed her arms, trying to stay warm in the sterile, chilly room. The group had been practically chained to their workstations for days now and no one would mistake them for being fresh.

Oi Lam looked at the others. "Is anyone getting anything?"

They all wearily shook their heads.

"Could we have used the wrong keys?" she asked, as she took off her glasses and rubbed her eyes.

None of the other hackers said anything. They were spoiled by their past successes. Inevitably, when they'd targeted a particular Website or foreign corporation or government entity, they had succeeded. They'd planted sophisticated worms, Trojans, malware, spyware, and viruses. Some of their hacks remained undiscovered and still yielded top secret data. Oi Lam was particularly adept at targeting American government employees with what appeared to be personal emails from friends, so that when an unsuspecting worker clicked on a link in one of her specially crafted missives, the computer would be instantly infected. But here in Guangzhou they were coming up empty.

"They should have given us Tianhe-2," said Oi Lam.

• • • •

AFTER SLIPPING INTO her LBD and smoothing down some of the wrinkles, Nicole Grant looked into the large bathroom mirror gilded in faux gold. She took a deep breath and exhaled slowly. A plan had taken shape in her mind, but if thegambit didn't work, she'd simply try to leave. Considering how drunk he was, she might be able to avoid him altogether and simply sneak out unseen.

She quietly eased open the bathroom door and listened. No one stirred. Slow steps took her silently into the darkened master bedroom, but where was Zhao? Maybe he'd passed out. The closed door was to her left and she padded towards it. She mentally recreated the route she'd take to get back to the front room where Chief Lin waited. She'd almost reached the bedroom door, when a fast blur of movement appeared in her peripheral vision, and then a hand grabbed her.

A cry escaped her lips as Zhao yanked her toward the bed with his left hand, and then slapped her with his right hand so hard her wig flew off. She cried out as his rough hands dragged her across the floor toward the windows.

"Definitely not a blond!" he said drunkenly. He pushed her against a low dresser as he lifted her dress.

"Darling, there's too much blood," she managed to say, as a trace of blood spilled from the corner of her mouth where he'd hit her.

"Blood I don't mind!" he said as he squeezed her breasts hard and twisted her nipples, causing her to cry out. She whimpered as he slapped her hard again and tightened his vise-like grip. She'd dropped her purse and looked for something to hit him with as he lowered his pants. He pushed her legs apart and moved in closerlike some kind of crazed bull in heat.

She felt his bare member pressing against her loins, seeking entrance. She reached in to squeeze his testicles, when she looked up and saw the wall behind the small bar slide open. A blond woman about forty, backlit by the harsh glow of bright light in a concrete stairwell, burst into the room.

"Do you have any idea who you're screwing with?!" yelled Kate Rice, making a beeline toward Zhao and Grant.

He awkwardly pushed away from Grant and turned to face Rice as he pulled up his pants.

"I'll screw with anyone I want!" he bellowed with a powerful rage. He moved fast toward his CIA handler. "Who gave you permission to come in here?!" Before she could respond, he lashed out with a hard right that caught her square on the jawand sent her crashing into the small table that separated the two French antique lounge chairs.

Grant didn't wait for an invitation. She jumped off the dresser, scooped up her fake Celine bag from the floor and bolted through the open entryway through which the blonde had just come.

• • • •

GENERAL MA STOOD DIRECTLY outside the closed door to Zhao's master bedroom suite. He'd heard muffled shouts and so he unlocked and threw open the door, immediately realizing something was very wrong. He hurried into the shadowy room and saw Zhao yank Rice up from the floor and load up like he was ready to deliver a right hook to her bleeding face.

"Stop!" yelled Ma, rushing forward and grabbing Zhao's right arm. "What are you doing? A bomb went off at the hotel next door!"

Zhao was drunk, but cognizant enough to understand there was a problem. He shifted away from rage to a more sobered anger. "I thought it was a sonic boom."

"No, it was a bomb. We have a bad situation," insisted Ma.

"You don't have a bad situation, you have an opportunity, provided by me!" howled Rice, straightening up. Blood dripped from her nose and the corner of her mouth. She looked sharply at Zhao. "You wanted an evacuation of Pacific Place, I provided it. I blew the bomb! I called in the bomb threats! Now maybe your people could do a simple thing and find Hernandez." She spat out the words with vile contempt.

General Ma couldn't hide his shock at hearing her admission. Zhao himself looked stunned. Rice stepped up to the vice premier, almost nose-to-nose. "As for Nicole Grant, she just ran out of this room, down those stairs!" Rice pointed toward the open entryway. "The blond bitch from the party you brought up here to bang was Nicole Grant in disguise."

"What?!" exclaimed Ma.

"That can't be true," said Zhao.

Rice barked orders to Ma. "Get some men and get after her. And can you at least seal this one hotel and catch her?" she asked, scathingly.

Ma yelled loudly for security back-up as he pulled his pistol and cell phone and ran into the entryway. Several seconds later, four agents stormed into the room and Zhao pointed them to follow Ma down the stairs Grant had just taken.

Two more security men entered the room and stood by, unsure of what was going on. Zhao staggered a little, looked at Rice and softly said, "I'm sorry."

One of her teeth had been knocked loose when he hit her, so she reached into her mouth, pulled it free and flicked it into his face, spattering blood on him.

The security goons pulled their guns and sighted on Rice, but Zhao yelled, "No! Leave us!" He motioned angrily for them to go. The men backed out of the room.

"Why did she come up here, can you answer that?" she asked, rubbing her sore jaw where he'd smacked her. Rice scanned the room and her eyes quickly settled on the laptop leaning against the lounge chair. "You don't own a computer, you don't even know how to turn one on."

As she bent down to pick up the laptop, she saw it was connected to the external power charger. "What the hell is this?"

"General Ma brought that computer here this afternoon. It belongs to—"

"Nicole Grant." Rice smoldered with rage. "The woman we've been trying to kill suckered you into bringing her up here so she could get her files! Files that will most likely destroy you. And me!" Rice slapped Zhao so hard she nearly knocked him over, and then she bolted through the secret entryway and down the stairs.

CHAPTER 29

22$^{:53}$ Nicole Grant hit speed dial for Ron Hernandez's cell phone while scrambling down cement steps in the narrowest stairwell she'd ever been in. She touched her head and realized the wig was gone. Good, the bad guys will be on the lookout for a blonde. In seconds she reached the bottom of the short stairwell where an open door awaited. She felt scared but highly alert and in complete control of her movements.

"It's me," she gushed into the phone. "I'm being chased. There's some kind of secret stairway from Zhao's bedroom that goes down two flights. I'm about to walk into... I don't know what. A middle-aged blond woman came into his bedroom from these stairs. She knew who I was. They must be right behind me," she said, glancing over her shoulder, up the stairs.

She kept the connection open, put the phone in her purse, and stepped into a room that looked much like Zhao's bedroom. Okay, so maybe this condo had the same layout, but how to close the door? It was some kind of recessed sliding door. She heard footsteps on the stairs above now. There must be an electronic control. Crap, she had no time to search for hidden switches! Then she saw a remote control on a bookshelf. Shouts and footsteps closer now. She grabbed the remote and pressed...

...And the slowest moving door in the history of doors began to creep closed.

Part of her screamed "Run!" but she remained rooted in place, like a defender at the gates. She looked around for something to use a weapon. A red vase looked promising, and she hefted the heavy container. The doorway was halfway closed now when an Asian man bounded down the stairs and came into view: short, dyed black hair, a little chubby, sixties, looking completely disheveled. He locked eyes with her and raised his gun. But with the door now half closed, she simply stepped to the side as he fired into the opening, and then fired into the door itself. It sounded to Grant as if the bullets were striking metal. The chubby man tried to squeeze into the narrowing opening, but his girth hung him up.

He dropped his gun as he struggled to worm himself into the room without being crushed. Grunting from the effort, he just managed to pull free of the closing doorway and stumbled inside. As he looked up, Grant smashed the vase into the side of his head, shattering it and dropping him like a stone.

The door continued closing, but men shouted and reached their hands in to try and stop it. The sliding door was powered by a strong motor, but Grant had to get these intruding hands and arms out of the way. Someone stuck a gun into the opening and wildly fired several shots. Whoever it was then twisted their wrist and fired, spraying bullets all over the room.

Grant ducked and a bullet whizzed past just above her head. A strange sense of clarity then overtook her. She had to clear the hands and arms so the door could close. She noticed the thick pieces of broken glass all over the floor, then reached out, grabbed a nasty shard, lunged forward, and slashed the nearest hand holding the gun.

A man screamed and his gun skittered to the floor at her feet. She started slicing and stabbing hands and arms as men cried out curses in Mandarin. Another gun was thrust in, this one a Boberg XR9-L with a suppressor attached and held by a female, probably the blonde since the skin was pale white. Grant sliced extra deeply into the wrist and blood gushed everywhere. The woman screamed bloody murder and retracted her hand, allowing the door to continue sliding closed until it was sealed. More bullets were fired on the other side, but to no affect.

Grant slid down to the floor, relieved, and then bolted upright with a jolt of revelation. Maybe they can open the door from the other side. Not to mention that a simple elevator ride down two stories would put the bad guys right outside the condo she was now in. She checked the Chinese man; he was out cold. She grabbed his pistol, put it in her purse, and glanced around the room. An open closet door looked like it held woman's clothes. She wanted to ditch the LBD and everything it represented to her in terms of what had just happened in Zhao's bedroom.

She grabbed slacks, a blouse and a blazer that might be a little big, but would fit. It took less than fifteen seconds for her to throw off the dress, pull on the slacks, pull over the top, and get into the blazer. She grabbed her purse and ran forward. As she cleared the doorway into the next room, arms reached out and spun her into a bear hug. Grant screamed and flailed.

"Whoa cowgirl, I'm a friendly."

Then she looked up into the eyes of Ron Hernandez. Tears formed in her eyes, but she fought them back. Then she slapped him hard.

"I love you, too," he said.

She wrapped her arms around him and squeezed as hard as she could. He might only be one man, but it felt to her like Seal Team Six had just arrived. "Thanks for coming, but we need to get out of here."

He looked to the man lying on the floor and seemed to recognize him.

"We need to go," she said, trying to pull him away, riding an adrenaline rush from the last several minutes.

"I agree, but let's take the general with us."

"General?"

He crossed over to the still unconscious Ma and lifted him up and over his shoulders like a sack of rice, although he grimaced slightly due to pain from his knife wound. "Meet Major General Ma Ju, China's top military spy. He might come in handy."

• • • •

WITH AN UNCONSCIOUS General Ma slung over his shoulder, Hernandez stepped out of the CIA- owned condo into the hallway, followed by Grant. He had one plan: get to the elevators. Cars arrived quickly in this hotel and he was betting the Chinese would be on the stairs. He and Grant ran down the curving hall toward the elevator bank. His plan went out the window as a chime announced an arriving car carrying six of Ma's men.

"He's got the general!" yelled one of the men.

Hernandez and Grant stopped short as the Chinese erupted from the elevator.

"Drop your guns or I'll kill him!" yelled Grant in perfect Mandarin as she pressed a pistol to Ma's head.

The men halted and cast quick glances at each other, uncertainty etched on their faces. Hernandez was pleasantly surprised by the extent to which Grant had her head in the game. She'd changed so radically during the course of this one day.

"Each of you will be held responsible for his death! You know it's true," she said, continuing to speak in Chinese.

Hernandez's Chinese was almost as good as hers, and he could tell that her point hit home with Ma's men, because that's how things worked in Beijing. They would indeed be held accountable if something happened to the general. First one man slowly bent down and dropped his weapon, then another. The rest followed suit.

"Move back into the elevator and go!"

As the group of six started backing down the hallway, the chime of an arriving elevator car sounded. The men waited as doors opened and Kate Rice stormed out with a bloody handkerchief tied around her right wrist. She held the suppressed Boberg XR9-L in her left hand and raised it as soon as she spotted Grant and Hernandez.

Hernandez's eyes bored into the visage of Rice. He leveled the Kimber, intending to shoot her dead right now. He could avenge

Willie, avenge the dead families killed at the pool, and avenge the other dead Americans. He took aim as Rice screamed, "Kill them! Zhao wants them dead!" As soon as she fired the first shot, Ma's men scrambled forward to retrieve their guns.

Carrying Ma disrupted his aim, but Hernandez fired the Kimber until the slide locking back indicated the gun was empty. The big .45 sounded like a cannon in the enclosed space. Two of the Chinese men went down. Grant was shocked to find herself point the gun at Rice and fire off two rounds. Before she could consider what she'd done, Hernandez grabbed her and they retreated away from the elevators.

"Plan B!"

The nature of the curved hallway was such that as they ran, they were momentarily out of sight—and out of the line of fire—of their pursuers. At the stairwell, Grant flung open the door and crashed through. Hernandez tucked the empty Kimber into his pocket and they bounded down one flight, but then found themselves staring to the barrels of sub-machine guns held by four police officers tricked out in full black SWAT tactical assault gear. Hernandez spotted the Special Duties Unit shoulder patches they wore.

Grant put her hands in the air and Hernandez raised his free hand. His other hand held onto General Ma, still draped over his shoulder.

"You guys are SDU?" he asked quickly. "We're CIA. My ID is in my fanny pack. I've got a wounded man here I'd like to take downstairs. But I have to tell you, there's a half-dozen terrorists in the hallway up there who just tried to kill us. Seven counting the leader who's a blond female. They'll be coming through the door above us any second. I'm not joking, officers. *Any second.*"

Hernandez met the eyes of the man he guessed was the team leader. The leader motioned with his head for one of the other men to go up the stairs. That officer made it up just past Grant when the hallway door burst open and two of Ma's men charged in.

"Drop your weapons!" yelled the officer.

But Ma's men raised their guns... and were cut down by the SDU officer. The booming reports of the subgun firing in the stairwell rang like a bell tower. Two more officers now charged past Hernandez and Grant on the stairs. At the landing they fired again. The three police operators then entered the hallway and more gunfire erupted.

The team leader kept his weapon trained on Hernandez, but the veteran CIA spy could see the officer wanted to go to the aid of his men in the hallway.

"My ID is in my fanny pack. May I give it to you?"

"Slowly," said the team leader.

Hernandez gave the man his genuine CIA ID and the leader examined it closely. "This man needs help right now. Let me take him downstairs. Call it in and have paramedics waiting for us, okay? You guys can debrief me downstairs."

The team leader glanced at Ma, not knowing who he was, partly due to all of the blood covering the general's face. More gunfire sounded from the hallway and a man cried out, seeming to compel the team leader to action. "Okay, go!" he said, handing back Hernandez's ID. He then quickly called on his radio for backup and gave the information about shots fired and three people coming down the stairwell. The team leader raced up to join his men. Hernandez and Grant set off down the stairs, but there was no way he would lead them into the waiting arms of the police.

Meaning they were trapped.

CHAPTER 30

23$^{:03}$ General Ma Ju's head felt like a ripe durian that had been dropped from a third story terrace onto a cement alley filled with broken glass. He'd lost his gun, his hands were tied behind his back. He looked to be in some kind of office. Nicole Grant sat at a desk using a computer, and Ron Hernandez sat in an office chair next to her going through his things. *His* things, Major General Ma Ju's things. These two people—the last two Americans on the hit list—were not only alive and well but they had kidnapped him right under the nose of an elite Second Department security detail.

An electric clock on the wall told him that not much time had elapsed, so maybe they were still in the same building. Zhao would already be in a convoy to the airport to take either his jet or helicopter back to the Mainland. Ma's old friend would be furious, and there would be hell to pay here in Hong Kong. Fall guys and sacrificial lambs would be needed. Director Tang for sure. And yours truly, Ma Ju, for another. Of this there was no doubt. Even Barry Bergman had hinted at that in the emergency meeting.

Right now General Ma needed to send a text to the eldest of his five daughters. One word. A code for what she must hastily do to save the entire family and their fortune. Of course, Ma had already managed to squirrel tens of millions in ill-gotten gains out of China and into accounts in St. Lucia, Vanuatu and other tax havens that still provided a semblance of banking secrecy. But in a dire emergency there was still much to do.

Actually, he felt somewhat relieved. For years Ma suspected that one day he and Zhao would have an unpleasant parting of the ways. And from the moment Zhao had entered into a relationship with CIA spy Kate Rice, Ma began making certain arrangements. Yes, much valuable intelligence had been acquired from the woman over the years, but he calculated that Zhao's chances of becoming the next Chinese president had now dropped to no better than thirty percent.

So this was a good time for him to jump from a sinking death ship. But how could he bargain with these two Americans who sat just a few feet away from him? What could he offer? They surely wanted him dead even more that Zhao himself must now want him dead. Ma closed his eyes to think, but instead, drifted into unconsciousness.

• • • •

AFTER LEAVING THE SDU police in the stairwell, Hernandez and Grant had continued down, and then ducked onto this floor full of offices. General Ma's phone was clearly the most valuable item Ron Hernandez had gotten from searching the man. He'd quickly removed the battery and SIM card so the phone's location couldn't be tracked. There were no fancy spy tools or secret decoder watch on the general's person. Only the phone.

Hernandez glanced over at Grant. Moments earlier she'd told him about the Darknet files being corrupted and asked him to give her five minutes on a computer with high-speed Internet. So he waited, but it looked to him as if they'd lost any chance to recover the drone op files. Meaning a whole lot of time and effort had been wasted for nothing. He wanted to call a neighbor of his parents whom he could count on to deliver a discreet message, but didn't want to do it in front of her. He decided that if his death or capture appeared imminent, he'd call and tell them he loved them.

"Okay, there's a way," said Grant, interrupting his musings. "There's a way to get back the pieces of the files we lost on the Darknet. We can get the files reassembled properly." She turned to look at him.

"Can you do it quickly, from this office?"

"No."

He shook his head. "Grant. I promise you that this building is crawling with cops, security, the CIA, and Ma's men. We could split up, pretend we were working late in the office, or say we're hotel guests who got lost, but the cops will likely check our stories. Assuming we don't get shot first."

"But I have the blueprints in my tablet, remember? We can use crawlspaces for plumbing or conduit. Pipe chases, engineering spaces. We can get out," she said earnestly.

"The police and SWAT teams use blueprints, too," he said. "Trust me, they're already working with the building's facilities people to check all those places you just mentioned."

"I refuse to give up now," she said with a sharp edge, her face hardening into a mask of firm resolve.

"I'm not suggesting we surrender," he countered. Exhaling, he pulled the Kimber from his pocket, and fished out a loaded magazine from another pocket. He exchanged the gun's empty magazine for the loaded one and let the slide lock into place with an authoritative metallic clack. He looked over to where she sat patiently watching him. "Just for giggles, what exactly do you need to get the files fixed?"

"A supercomputer."

Hernandez burst out laughing. "A supercomputer?" The laugh became heartier as he shook his head. "Great, no problem," he managed to say. It felt good to laugh, even if it was due to gallows humor. Did she not get the preposterous nature of her suggestion?

"The world's most powerful supercomputer is Tianhe-2, located in Guangzhou," said Grant, as if the information were terribly significant.

"Uh oh, sounds like you have a plan."

"Always. Please understand that not all supercomputers are alike, and for some tasks, believe it or not, you'd be better off using your home computer. But for what we need, Tianhe-2 would be perfect, and Guangzhou is only eighty miles from here."

"I'm aware Guangzhou is close to Hong Kong. I'm also aware it's in China, as in the China that's trying to kill us," said Hernandez.

Undeterred, she leaned in closer toward him. "Carnegie Mellon University—you've heard of them?"

"Yeah, it's a U.S. school."

She nodded. "Full of very smart people. They partnered with SYSU—Sun Yat-sen University to operate a Joint Institute of Engineering."

"What kind of engineering?"

"The same kind I studied: electrical and computer engineering. The institute is in the same complex as Tianhe-2. Carnegie Mellon developed an algorithm specifically to be used with Tianhe-2 that I just downloaded. With some simple, fast modifications, I can use their algorithm to scour the Darknet and vacuum back pieces of the files that fell off."

Hernandez looked shocked. "You were able to download that algorithm?"

"Let's just say I borrowed it."

"So you can log into this Tianhe-2 supercomputer and use the Carnegie Mellon algorithm?"

"No. I need physical access."

Hernandez held up his hands and shook his head. "That's a nonstarter." He stood up, checked his watch. "Pull up the blueprints on your tablet, because we need to get our butts hidden until I can come up with something."

"I heard you mention the Tianhe-2 supercomputer in Guangzhou," said General Ma in perfect English, startling them as he blearily blinked his eyes.

Grant and Hernandez shot each other a quick look.

"That's right," she said.

"I know it well," said Ma. "I have loyal staff in that building at Sun Yat-sen University, right now. In a room adjacent to Tianhe-2."

"We need access to Tianhe-2," said Grant, before Hernandez could speak.

Ma raised his eyebrows. "I can get you into the building. But beyond that, I don't control access to the supercomputer."

"Why would you help us?" asked Hernandez, not trying to mask his skepticism.

"To save my life. The unfortunate turn of events here tonight have guaranteed my death. But since I'm not ready to die just yet, I have a helicopter waiting on the rooftop of the Peninsula Hotel, minutes from here. We can fly to Guangzhou. I have a lady friend there I'd like to pick up and take out of China."

The idea intrigued him, but seemed too good to be true. "Leave China, General? Defect?" asked Hernandez incredulously. "Assassination teams would track you to the ends of the earth."

"You forget I have run the Second Department for several years. I know the most sensitive secrets of the top cadre. I have no doubt that an understanding could be reached to prevent my murder."

Hernandez was starting to believe there was something here. And the truth was, he had no idea how to get them out of the Shangri-La tower. A quick study of Grant's face told him she was intrigued by the cooperation of Ma in getting her hands on Tianhe-2.

"I'd like to believe you," she said, "but fifteen minutes ago you were shooting bullets at me, so forgive me if I'm not so trusting."

"Fifteen minutes ago you nearly killed me with a red vase. I didn't become a major general by being inflexible," Ma countered. "Alliances shift. It's the way of war, and of the world. It always has been. Americans, who are terrible at history, who can't even seem to remember what happened last month, often overlook such facts. A few hours earlier I wanted you dead. Now, I'm proposing a truce and a temporary partnership."

"Forget about going to the Peninsula, could the helicopter fly here, land on the roof?" asked Hernandez.

"My personal pilots fly where I tell them. Our family relationships are intertwined, meaning they are unquestionably loyal." Ma appraised the two Americans carefully. "I will bring you to Guangzhou on one condition. I need to send a text to my eldest daughter. It's a simple code instructing her to flee China with the entire family."

"How do we know that?" asked Hernandez. "How do we know the text is going to your daughter?"

"How do you know it's not a trick?" asked Ma. "You don't. Nor can you be sure there won't be a division of troops in Guangzhou waiting to arrest you. Nor can I be sure you won't put a bullet into my head as revenge for everything that's happened."

"Before we agree to anything, answer me this: Who ran the wet teams in America, and where can I find them?" asked Hernandez. This was a test, since Chuck Wheeler had already given him the information. If Ma lied there would be no bond of trust, and whether Grant liked it or not he'd put a bullet into Ma Ju's brain as a measure of repayment.

"Ministry of State Security Special Projects Director Tang Jie ran the teams. You killed two of his people this afternoon on Tung Choi Street. None of my people took part in the murders. You can find him in his command post at the Marriott."

So Ma told the truth about Tang. Hernandez would like nothing better than to go find and kill the middle-aged man in the brown shirt who wore black-framed glasses, but he was in no position to do so. "Maybe your people didn't take part in the murders, General, but you approved those murders."

Ma shrugged. "I'm a soldier who follows orders. I advised against killing any Americans since we hadn't yet identified the leaker's identity. I was overruled."

Hernandez looked long and hard at the general. He shifted his gaze to Grant, who nodded very slightly.

"Get us into the building at Sun Yat-sen, but if it's a set-up, I won't put a bullet in your head, I'll put three in. As for your phone," said Hernandez, holding up Ma's cell, "it's not getting turned back on. Period."

"I don't care whose phone is used. I will tell you my daughter's number."

Hernandez found himself staring with his mouth slightly agape. He'd just agreed to fly on a Chinese military helicopter into China with a major general as hostage, and no clear means for escape. This play didn't even qualify as a Hail Mary, but he found himself nodding, because it was all they had.

CHAPTER 31

23 :29

Kate Rice made a series of calls, but couldn't reach any of the mercenary agents she'd assembled in Hong Kong. The bombing had probably scared them off. It was also possible that she was now a wanted woman. She removed the SIM cards and batteries from her phones, just to be on the safe side. Blowing the bomb had been a calculated risk. Hernandez and Grant might still be captured as a result of it. They'd better be.

Her nose and lip had stopped bleeding and moments earlier she used makeup to cover the spreading bruise on her face from where Zhao slugged her. The deep slash to her wrist delivered by Nicole Grant had been professionally patched up and bandaged by paramedics in a triage area hastily set up in response to the bombing and subsequent events at Pacific Place. A bullet from Grant's gun had sprayed paint chips and plaster into her right eye. The docs were going to take her to a hospital for further treatment, but Rice had easily slipped away in the confusion. She hid the gauze eye patch that now covered her right eye by wearing extra-large sunglasses.

Aside from the dark glasses, she had her hair tucked up into a rain hat she bought at a *Chat Jai*, the Hong Kong nickname for a 7-Eleven. Admiralty Station was jammed with people fleeing Pacific Place, so she moved in the shadows on the edge of the busy station. She was shaken. Zhao's alcoholism had gotten progressively worse over the last few years, but had largely been kept under wraps. Most Chinese top cadre, military generals, and powerful bureaucrats were heavy drinkers, due to nature of how the Chinese do business and accrue *guanxi*. While nowhere near being the kind of drunk Russia's Boris Yelstin had been before his death, Zhao's binges were getting longer and more violent. And he was on one tonight. Tonight of all nights.

The last thing she wanted was for him to go back to China in a drunken stupor where spies for his rivals might witness his behavior and tie it to the unfolding events here. As to the rest, the bombing and other murders would be papered over by the powers in D.C. if she could deliver Zhao into the Chinese presidency. But could she stay alive long enough for that to take place, since an Agency assassin would most likely be coming for her. That's just how these kind of deep black, one-off operations went when the crap hit the fan and the gutless desk jockeys and armchair commandos inside the Beltway faced having their illegal machinations exposed.

Zhao was the key. There might still be time.

* * * *

BARRY BERGMAN STOOD with Socorro Trujillo in a 15th floor vacant office in a high-rise on Queens Road East. He hitched his pants up to a more comfortable position on his expanding waistline as he peered across the street at the bedlam. The view of Justice Drive and the vehicular entrance into Pacific Place between the Marriott tower and the Conrad tower showed roads gridlocked with every kind of emergency vehicle imaginable. The westbound lanes of Queensway were closed and choked with fleeing pedestrians, many looking unsure of where to go. The media roamed everywhere, and the chaotic scene resembled a kind of slow motion disaster as a procession of cars inched out of the complex onto Justice Drive and then funneled onto a cloverleaf feeding them eastbound onto Queensway.

Bergman glanced at Trujillo. She'd been assigned to him six weeks ago, specifically to help him oversee the secret efforts to place Zhao into the Chinese presidency. He'd started having sex with her almost immediately and almost spent more Viagra-fueled time in the sack with her than he did taking care of business. She was a slick one who kept her own counsel and would do well in the sewer called Washington, D.C.

She's one cool customer, he thought as he watched her stoically take in the mayhem and the horrific mess still unfolding across the street. He looked back out the window and shook his head. Bergman usually kept this anger in check, but right now he was beyond livid.

"You're sure it was Rice?"

Trujillo nodded. "A South African freelancer put the device together for her. Wheeler was supposed to meet Hernandez and if he couldn't kill him, Rice would detonate."

"But instead she blows up a swimming pool full of civilians. And that's after the bloodbath in our field station," said Bergman, shaking his head. "She's completely off the reservation."

"Gail Roberts' body was found in our safehouse condo. Shot three times at close range. Had to be Rice."

"Roberts needed to die, but not in our safehouse."

The ground was metaphorically shifting beneath him like a magnitude eight quake. Bergman felt the need to say something out loud. "The Chief of Station here will put two and two together and blame all this on me. A horrible day, all the way around." He pulled out a small encrypted sat phone from his suit jacket pocket. "Where's Rice now?"

"Unknown."

"I'm going to recommend we bring in Agency teams to clean this mess up. Rice, Wheeler, Hernandez and Grant need to be terminated immediately."

Stone-faced, Trujillo stared at him, "Can Zhao salvage his candidacy?"

"I think our chances are still good that he can capture the Chinese presidency, so I'm going to tell the president that we should stay the course. Zhao's new Agency handler is waiting for him in Beijing. We close the loop and things will settle down."

Bergman put on reading glasses, and then looked at his phone.

"The president agrees with you that the loop needs to be closed."

Incredulous, Bergman gawked at his lover. "What did you say?"

"I was instructed to thank you for your service." Trujillo fixed Bergman with a look that sent chills down his spine.

It was the look of a killer that ran icy with contempt and annoyance. She moved her hand slowly into her purse.

Bergman's mouth went dry and perspiration appeared on his forehead. "This isn't funny." His eyes darted around the vacant office as Trujillo pulled out a suppressed semi-auto. He dropped the sat phone and raised his hands. "You're ambitious, we can make a deal!"

The worst night of his life was screeching downhill, and then two rounds tore into his heart.

• • • •

VICE PREMIER OF THE People's Republic of China Zhao Yiren had been known to move mountains, but he couldn't move the hundreds of vehicles blocking the road in front of his Rolls Royce and the rest of his large entourage. Since leaving the Island Shangri-La his progress could be measured in meters. That made him angry and he tended to drink when he got angry. So he opened up the recessed bar in the back seat of the Rolls and poured himself three fingers of Laphroiag single malt scotch.

The Americans were setting him up for something. He could feel it. Had they videotaped his sex sessions? Probably, but that wasn't really blackmail material. They wanted to have an ax hanging over his head, though. This whole business with Nicole Grant was a set-up, all the way back to Phoenix. Her computer and all of that. The CIA must have known she'd left the country but didn't inform Tang's people. So they had wanted Grant, and Hernandez, too, right here in Hong Kong. They had orchestrated all of this last-minute strife. Grant and Hernandez must be using an elaborate CIA support team. They'd even suckered Ma's men into an Agency field office.

Using the United States to further his goals had been risky, but not without precedent. Chairman Mao himself had once used relations with the U.S. to strengthen his position against political opponents in the Chinese military. But the Americans didn't want their friend as the Chinese president, they wanted their *asset*.

They wanted him to come begging to save himself. Fat chance. Zhao suddenly had a radical thought. *Kate Rice*. He needed to get her into China... and kill her. She was another loose end. Arrangements had already been made to eliminate Tang and Ma, so yes, he mustn't forget Rice. She could die in the explosion at the apartment of Ma's girlfriend, the hacker Oi Lam. The explosion, in fact, would be pinned on Rice. He could spin her to be a rogue agent who sought revenge upon the Chinese hacker who stole the American spy drone. Rice's death in this fashion would cement his carefully crafted story that it was his people, Zhao Yiren's people, who'd stolen the drone. He'd make it work.

Yes, yes he could do it. He smiled, lifted his glass, and drank to his success.

CHAPTER 32

23$^{:56}$ A number of copters circled above Pacific Place while a steady stream of medical helicopters took turns landing in the plaza near the Marriott to pick up critically wounded.General Ma's helicopter wasted no time in dropping into a tightly controlled hover just off the deck. Grant, Ma, and Hernandez sprinted under the slicing blades and through the rotor-wash of an Aerospatiale Gazelle SA 342 flown by the PLA Ground Force and painted in olive drab. The copter sat five, so Grant and Ma piled inside behind the female pilot and co-pilot—both of whom were nieces of the General—and onto a padded bench seat backed by the rear fuselage.

Grant saw Hernandez take a quick look up as a police helicopter appeared overhead. As soon as he climbed inside, before he even had the door closed, the pilot pulled up on the collective and the craft lurched into the air. Hernandez almost lost his balance, but got the door closed and locked. The three passengers buckled in and put on radio set headphones. The female pilot's voice came through almost immediately.

"We're being hailed by the police helicopter. They are ordering us to follow them."

"Ignore them and get us to Guangzhou!" said Ma, emphatically.

As the chopper gained altitude, Hernandez got Ma's attention in the noisy compartment and showed him a cell phone. Ma's code word was already typed in, the phone number of Ma's daughter already entered. Nicole watched as Hernandez made eye contact with the general, and then pressed SEND.

He's a man of his word, even with his enemies, thought Nicole. She hoped against hope that somehow, as crazy as this notion was of flying into China and breaking into that country's most precious computer, she hoped that somehow she'd be able to Skype with her mom tomorrow, and fly back to Phoenix with a bunch of genuine fake purses for her girlfriends, and, and maybe even get to know Ron Hernandez.

• • • •

GENERAL MA'S HELICOPTER had landed on the wide, multiple-lane road that serviced a cluster of five-story buildings—seven modern structures—making up the complex where Tianhe-2 was located just north of the Pearl River. As soon as Grant, Hernandez, and Ma disembarked the pilot took off to refuel. It had been a short, thirty-one-minute flight to Guangzhou from Hong Kong.

At this late hour the east campus was quiet, and this particular area of the school was more secluded. Few people noticed the brief landing and no one called the authorities. After all, it was a Chinese army helicopter that had landed and Tianhe-2 was built by the National University of Defense Technology—an engineering school for the military. A two-man security detail emerged from the building with visitor badges and escorted them inside. General Ma's standing as head of the feared Second Department was such that no questions were posed regarding his unusual arrival and Caucasian companions.

Ma scowled as they walked. The American woman had spent the entire flight madly working on her tiny computer. He was no expert, but it had looked like computer code to him. There was no way he'd let the U.S. agents sabotage Tianhe-2 or use it to their advantage. Even if he had to flee China, he was still loyal to the Motherland.

What he planned was to have the Americans killed, and then claim they kidnapped him and forced him to operate against his will. He'd assert he'd been plotting to get them all along. How marvelous the publicity would be from killing two American intelligence agents who'd beaten and kidnapped a Chinese general! He'd still flee China, of course, just to be on the safe side.

The range of his helicopter would take him all the way to Laos where he and Oi Lam would be most welcome. But he'd need to work out a settlement with the Standing Committee in Beijing. He hadn't lied to the two Americans earlier. He'd squirreled away enough blackmail material that an agreement to leave him alone should be fairly easy to reach. Otherwise, what Hernandez had said would be true—assassins would hunt him for the rest of his days.

As they wormed their way along brightly lit hallways with highly polished fake marble flooring, Ma noticed how few staffers were present. He'd never visited so late at night and the usual daytime hustle-bustle was nowhere to be seen. He frowned, realizing that the night shift security team was a skeleton force. The guards were armed with old-style Type 54 pistols and looked like retirees, so Ma wasn't sure how much help they'd be. How could he turn the tables on Hernandez? Then he thought of Oi Lam and got an idea.

• • • •

RON HERNANDEZ MEMORIZED the route he took with Nicole Grant and General Ma as they followed the guards through the modern campus building. He felt certain they'd be leaving under duress. If they left alive. The stab wound was bothering him but that was the least of his worries. Fatigue gnawed at his muscles and bones, affecting his concentration. He lacked sharp focus.

This incursion, the kidnapping of Ma to get to the supercomputer was audacious, but it was also madness. Why had he been going along with so many of Grant's ideas? How many times did he have to roll a boulder up a hill, only to have her tell him, "Whoops, sorry, there's a new problem," and then watch the boulder careen back down the hill? *How in the hell can we forcibly gain access to the fastest supercomputer in the world, set up shop, and then escape?* Since he didn't see an answer, he considered that this might be the place where he made his last stand. He'd cheated the Grim Reaper many times in his life, but his odds now were barely a blip. Maybe he'd call his parents in the next few minutes and tell them he'd be out of touch for a long time.

Then he caught himself and shook his head. *Improvise! Adapt! Overcome! You're not dead yet, Hernandez. There's a way. Look for the way.* He quickly latched onto a positive—he'd spent time in Guangzhou. There was advantage to being on the run in a gargantuan city, so if they could get off campus alive he had ideas about how to exfiltrate from China. After sending the text to General Ma's daughter, he'd texted Jaffir and told him to get to Guangzhou, pronto. Getting out of China would be difficult, but possible. In the meantime, he had to push another huge boulder up a hill for Grant. And look for a way.

CHAPTER 33

(S imulated rendering of the Tianhe-2 complex, Sun Yat-sen University, East Campus, Guangzhou, People's Republic of China)

00:28

The Hong Kong Business Aviation Center—BAC—facilities
served executive aircraft and sat tucked into a corner of Hong Kong
Airport, separate from the airport's public terminals. The sleek, upscale private terminal provided refuge for the rich, famous, and powerful, pampering them and keeping them isolated from the crass
huddled masses who had to fly commercial. Zhao's helicopter and executive jet were here now, prepped and ready to fly back to Beijing.

A cool night breeze heavy with moisture and redolent of jet fuel
enveloped Director Tang as he stood in the front gate area of the
BAC. Tang had good relations with Zhao's head of security, Chief
Lin. So he called Lin and explained that he needed to urgently speak
with Zhao about something so delicate it couldn't be done even on
an encrypted phone. He asked Lin not to alert Zhao about the matter, and said he'd be waiting for the Vice Premier outside the BAC
terminal.

Tang watched as jumbo jets executed precision landings on the
other side of the huge airport. He observed them, but wasn't really
looking; he was fixated on his desire to kill the Americans, Hernandez and Grant. Secondly, if the opportunity presented itself, he'd kill
General Ma as well. They all deserved to die, and they all needed to
die for Tang to feel confident that none of his team members would
be unfairly held accountable.

The arrival of Zhao's motorcade brought Tang out of his reverie.
The headlights of the third car in line flashed and Tang hurried over
to the black Rolls Royce Phantom. Chief Lin emerged from a rear
passenger door and held it open. Tang steeled himself as he eased into the luxury of the Rolls. He had bad news to deliver and knew that
when doing so one must always provide options.

Zhao was still drinking and didn't hide his displeasure with the
appearance of Tang, who got right to the point. "Vice Premier Zhao,
the two Americans, Grant and Hernandez boarded a PLA helicopter

with General Ma during an illegal rooftop landing on the Island Shangri-La tower."

"That can't be." Zhao set his drink down.

"It's true."

The vice premier of China then put his fingers to his temple as if he'd just heard the worst news of his life. This was the kind of reaction Tang expected. Now all he had to do was to convince the man to do something foolish.

"It's possible General Ma has made a deal with the Americans. But even if he hasn't, we must follow in your helicopter right now."

"Was Ma taken against his will?" asked Zhao. The man might be drunk, but knew how to ask incisive questions.

"That's unclear. His pilot didn't answer any radio hails. It appears they have landed in Guangzhou. Please take us there now, we haven't a moment to spare. I will kill Grant and Hernandez."

Zhao pursed he lips together as he seemed to digest the shocking information. "I can mobilize the Guangzhou Military Region Special Forces Unit. I've no doubt those troops could easily—"

"If you use that unit—the same unit you used two years ago to detain Wang Hongwei—President Li would learn of it almost immediately." Tang put his hand on Zhao's forearm. "Vice Premier Zhao, you, me and Chief Lin should go in your helicopter. We can assemble some local authorities once we're on the ground. Keep things quiet so Beijing doesn't get wind of these unfortunate developments... or how we resolve them."

Zhao appeared to consider this. "You're right that Beijing needs to stay in the dark. But my personal involvement may not be so wise." Zhao looked out the window. "Where are your men?"

"Detained by Hong Kong Police, caught in traffic, dead."

Zhao looked at him stoically.

"You think that getting personally involved in such dirty work will ruin your chance to become president. But I think that, on the contrary, after this catastrophe here in Hong Kong, your chances are now hanging in the balance. Your *personal involvement* in killing the assassin Hernandez and the spy Grant are your only hope of claiming the presidency. They are in league with Ma and must be stopped. After we kill them, you'll arrive in Beijing a conquering hero."

"What you're proposing is very risky."

"Risk has never stopped you from acting before. As I see it, the risk is to do nothing and watch your candidacy collapse into a pile of rubble."

Zhao simply sat there looking indecisive.

"You must decide now, before it's too late," said Tang. "If you chose to remain behind, I'll go with Chief Lin, but remember that the traitor General Ma wields more authority in Guangzhou than Lin or myself."

Zhao calmly looked toward the terminal building. "I was supposed to meet someone here at the BAC, but perhaps other arrangements can be made." Zhao fixed Tang with a dark look. "We'll take my helicopter to Guangzhou right now."

Unseen by anyone, Tang, the man with the even demeanor who never betrayed his feelings, allowed himself a slight smile. He was in the shadows again, in his element. Murder was in the air, of that he had no doubt.

· · · ·

KATE RICE WAS A FREQUENT flyer on private jets so she knew the BAC terminal well. She'd gotten a secure message from Zhao telling her to meet him here. What a stroke of good fortune that had been, since she didn't have to contact him herself. Maybe her luck was changing. She knew she could stop him from leaving for China tonight, if she could just get a moment with him alone.

She looked out a front window and saw Zhao's motorcade approach the gate. He'd be inside the terminal in minutes, so she turned away from the windows and rehearsed her spiel. She'd always been able to convince him to see things her way, and her inner confidence grew. This would be her swan song performance with Zhao, whose candidacy now hung by a thread. Who better to guide him during his final lap to victory than herself?

She glanced out into the parking lot again as the motorcade parked, but something looked wrong. What... where was the black Rolls? The hotel always provided the Phantom when Zhao visited Hong Kong. Hadn't she just seen it out at the gate?

Rice raced upstairs taking a carpeted stairway. She crossed an open space to a huge bank of windows giving her an elevated view of the entire executive ramp area. He eyes darted from jet to parked jet, most sitting in dim light. She saw tugs, fuel trucks, catering vehicles. Headlights far out on the macadam caught her eye. They pierced the dense, dark night, bobbing as they grew larger, more distinct, heading toward the BAC. She then spotted the running lights of some kind of small craft. Squinting, she could barely make out a row of helicopters parked at the far end of the ramp. A helicopter with its running lights on slowly lifted into the air just as the approaching headlights entered a well-lit area.

The headlights belonged to the Rolls, meaning Zhao was sitting in that helicopter rising into the night sky on its way to China. With him went eleven years of hard work, not to mention all of her dreams, her plans for retirement, her... everything. Rice noticed her reflection in the window just inches away. She looked old. It was a look that a thousand make-up touch-ups couldn't change. Everything had gone to hell. Zhao had left her, meaning others would come.

To kill her.

CHAPTER 34

00:46 Ron Hernandez and Major General Ma Ju slowed their gait in the main hallway of the gleaming computer complex at Sun Yat-sen University. Grant watched closely as one of the Chinese security officers peeled off from his escort of her and the others. She distinctly caught a whiff of piquant fermented fish sauce as the guard entered what appeared to be a break room. That left one escort remaining. The lone remaining guard motioned them forward and they made their way deeper into the brain of the seemingly deserted facility.

"General Ma, where are you taking us?" asked Grant, feeling slightly paranoid.

"To the room where my officers from the Fifty-seventh Research Institute are working."

"That's not our destination," said Hernandez with an edge to his voice.

"I have arrived with two foreigners in the middle of the night. It would raise suspicion to go anywhere except the room where my people are headquartered. And I only promised to get you into this building. I have done so, haven't I?"

Nicole couldn't argue the point. And yet a feeling that this was all too easy began to dog her.

Hernandez shot her a look and whispered, "You're about to meet the hackers who imaged your laptop and have been trying to break your encryption."

A wave of unease nipped at Grant like a persistent insect that wouldn't go away. The feeling of dread made her stomach queasy. It was some different kind of fear, unlike anything she'd felt today. At first she told herself there was nothing rational to it, but she quickly corrected herself. Considering the predicament, she had logical reasons to be scared out of her wits.

They stopped at a heavy steel door. The guard entered a four digit code, the lock clicked open, and they entered a changing room that contained a row of tall metal lockers and benches. A steel shelving unit held boxes of disposable clean room garb—gowns, booties, hair coverings, and even beard coverings. Windows provided a view into a computer room ten meters square, where a dozen encapsulated, six-foot-tall electronics racks formed two short rows. Computer workstations that could accommodate eight people lined the far wall, but only four hackers were present. They all sat facing the windows. To enter the computer room, one had to pass through a small airlock lined with nozzles that blew compressed air—an air shower—since the computer room was a clean room environment.

Of the four hackers present, three were men. It didn't take a theoretical physicist to determine that Ma's "lady friend," was the short-haired, bespectacled young woman looking at them with a cute smile on her porcelain face. Grant met the woman's gaze and wondered if she were looking at her counterpart.

Ma pressed up close to the glass as he stared into the computer room. The security guard slipped into the hallway, leaving them alone as he closed the door behind him. Grant and Hernandez huddled a few feet away so they could speak privately, without being heard.

"Look," said Nicole, quietly, indicating the large digital clock in the computer room. "That countdown clock is zeroed out. Maybe they broke my encryption."

"Maybe not," whispered Hernandez. "You said they didn't get the Darknet files."

"No they didn't. We have them. So they didn't get much at all."

Grant stared at the faces of the Chinese computer team. They looked befuddled. Her peripheral vision then picked up the image of

Ma's reflection in the window pane. She read his lips; he was silently mouthing in Mandarin, "Spies. Call police."

Grant's mouth dropped open in shock. She then forced a huge smile onto her face, quickly crossed to Ma and draped her arm around him like they were the best of friends. "Hernandez, smile, laugh, and slap the general on the back, right now!"

He joined them and obeyed instantly, without question.

"He was mouthing a message to them to call police, that we are spies," she said laughing.

Hernandez laughed even bigger and gently turned the general away from the window. He pointed at the hackers and gave them the thumbs up, laughing, as if they were in on the joke about being spies.

"General," said Hernandez with a huge smile on his face. "Since you have betrayed our trust, here's what's going to happen. Smile and motion for your girlfriend to join us. Then you will take us to Tian-he-2."

"I told you I do not control the access—"

Hernandez jammed the gun into Ma's ribs, unseen by the hackers. "I swear on my brother's grave I will kill you, and your girlfriend, too. Smile *húndàn*." Asshole.

With Hernandez's huge arm around his shoulder, Ma smiled and waved at the hackers, who immediately relaxed. He gestured for Oi Lam to come out. She opened the inner airlock door, got a brief, but loud, air shower, then opened the outer airlock door and stepped into the anteroom. She beamed with the kind of inner happiness endemic to pregnant women.

"We're old friends of General Ma," said Grant, by way of explanation. "Please join us to see Tianhe-2."

* * * *

ONE WOULD THINK THE world's fastest supercomputer would be booked solid, 24 hours a day, in the service of academia or industry. Exactly the opposite was true here in Guangzhou. As her group walked in the hallway escorted by the guard, Nicole knew why the place was largely empty. Supercomputers are specialized machines, not particularly adept at performing a wide variety of tasks. Slower and smaller machines might get a difficult job done cheaper and faster. To use Tianhe-2 efficiently, researchers could spend *years* rewriting software codes. Tianhe-2 quickly developed a reputation for software issues and so customers had stayed away.

Tianhe-2, like all supercomputers, was hugely expensive to build and costly to use and maintain. The irony was that most supercomputers remain idle for long periods, especially those in China where there was a "supercomputer bubble." China simply had more computing power than it required.

But China was obsessed with "face" and bragging rights and besting the West, especially America, in anything it could. As something of a Chinese scholar, she understood the chip China carried on her shoulder at having been subjugated for centuries by western powers. A collective, long-held inferiority complex was finally being overcome in the 21st Century due to China's explosive growth, new-found wealth, industrial might, and growing military power.So having the fastest supercomputer was an on-going priority. Even if it couldn't attract many customers and had a limited scope of what it was good for. For Guangzhou, Tianhe-2 was the supercomputer equivalent to having a trophy wife.

• • • •

AS OI LAM READILY EXPLAINED to General Ma that Tianhe-2 was largely disused, he grew angry. Grant, Hernandez, Ma, and Oi Lam all changed into clean room garb in a changing room adjacent to the supercomputer's control room, while the guard had remained outside in the hallway.

"Why was your team not allowed to use it?" asked Ma, as he tugged on a sheer white covering gown.

"Tianhe-2 is very much connected to Guangzhou—financially and in every other way. And your compatriot Zhao Yiren is not held in high esteem by the local cadres because of what happened to Wang Hongwei two years ago," she said simply, as she covered her head with a beanie-like cap. "So even though they could have given us full access, they gave us the small computer instead."

"Could you have used Tianhe-2 in your work here?" he asked fighting his anger.

"Yes, we could have broken the encryption quickly."

Grant and Hernandez carefully listened to the exchange as they pulled disposable booties over their shoes. It felt weird listening to her enemies talk about breaking her encryption, but a sense of poetic justice took hold. Perhaps Hernandez also felt it. Two years ago, they had personally witnessed, via a stealth spy drone, Zhao Yiren take down his main rival, Wang Hongwei, right here in Guangzhou. And because of what he did that night, Ma had subsequently been denied the use of a supercomputer that might have saved Zhao's candidacy. Hackers from the 57th could have used Tianhe-2 to break Grant's encryption and give Zhao and Ma and Tang and Rice the secret drone op files. But those same files would instead now destroy them. Her files.Nicole Grant's files.For she intended to fully restore them from their corrupted state, with the help of that same supercomputer.

"Payback is a bitch," interjected Hernandez.

Oi Lam seemed confused by the remark, but then, she was confused by the mere presence of the two Caucasians.

Suddenly, Ma sprinted across the changing room to the steel hallway door, catching Hernandez and Grant off guard. He threw open the door and called out, "Guard! These are American spies, kill them!" That was as far as he got. Hernandez grabbed him from behind and jerked so hard the general hurtled all the way across the changing room and crashed into the far wall.

Oi Lam raced for the general. The startled guard appeared in the hallway and went for his gun. Hernandez stood in the open doorway, popping open all the snaps on his clean room gown to grab the Kimber from his fanny pack. The guard got off two shots and one of them tore into Hernandez's shoulder. He managed to fire the Kimber once. He only needed one shot from the booming .45, and the guard dropped to the hallway floor.

Grant surprised herself by immediately drawing her pistol. She was covering Ma and Oi Lam, but spun when the door behind her flew open, the same door that led into the control room of Tianhe-2. Two technicians ran through the door into the changing room to see what was going on.

The bewildered technicians saw the guard in the hallway lying on the floor, Ma on the floor with Oi Lam, and a bleeding Hernandez. And Grant's gun was hard to miss.

"What are you doing here?" the younger techie demanded.

As Oi Lam administered to Ma, Hernandez dragged the dead guard into the room with them. He closed the hallway door, but kept an eye out through a small window in the door for anyone approaching.

"Grant, shoot anyone who moves." Hernandez tore off the white gown, then painfully reached under his navy blue blazer and probed his shoulder area.

"You've been shot!" she cried out. She started to take a step toward him.

"Stay where you are and cover me. Please, for once, do what I ask," he said softly, almost pleading with her.

Nicole felt herself flush and remained in place, duly admonished. Her sense of trepidation upon entering the building was unfortunately being vindicated. A guard was dead, Hernandez was shot. It was her idea to come here and now this was the result. With shots being fired, how could they possibly hope to escape? Somehow she kept the weapon leveled at the technicians. She stole a glance as Hernandez ripped the gown and created a compress. She watched his jaw tighten as he placed the makeshift bandage over the wound under his jacket.

"This will have to do," he muttered.

"Police are coming!" yelled the young techie, suddenly, startling Grant. "Give yourselves up!" He stepped toward Nicole, but she knew she couldn't shoot him. He was about to grab her gun, when Hernandez took a long stride forward and decked him with a right cross. The man staggered back into the wall and dropped to the floor unconscious.

"I will kill the next one of you who makes a problem," said Hernandez, making eye contact with each of the remaining Chinese. He turned to Nicole and gave a nod. "It's all yours, but make it fast." He pocketed the guard's pistol and herded everyone into the control room of the Tianhe-2 supercomputer, the fastest in the entire world.

"No problem," she said, swallowing hard.

CHAPTER 35

01 :00

She was a black beauty, thought Nicole. She'd been in a clean room once at Vandenberg Air Force Base in California, where a military satellite was being prepared for launch. She'd found it hard to stop looking at the satellite. The magnificent piece of technology had a mesmerizing effect that constantly drew her eyes to it.

And now, as she stared through the windows from the control room into the room that housed the computing beast, she felt the same kind of visceral pull. The computer room itself was nothing special, with a raised tile floor, drop ceiling, and fluorescent lighting. But the sprawling computer reminded Nicole of the movie *2001: A Space Odyssey,* where the astronaut couldn't stop looking at the black monolith. Instead of a single black monolith, however, here there were six of them.

Tianhe-2 was made up of scores of sleek, matte black, six-feet-high computer cabinets housing racks of electronics. The unseen, interior racks stood back-to-back to form a row, so each row of cabinets was a "double-wide." There were six rows of cabinets; two of the rows had gaps that allowed technicians to move from aisle to aisle without having to go all the way to the end of a row, creating something of a maze-like effect.

The cabinets connected almost seamlessly, so one could argue that there were only six incredibly long sleek cabinets, connected overhead in a grid pattern by sturdy black cable trays holding hundreds of cables. The six rows of cabinets encapsulated 125 racks jammed with 16,000 nodes (each node having two processor chips and three co-processor chips) circuit boards, switches, ports, 1,375 TiB[1] of memory, and the interconnected network, among other

---

1.   https://en.wikipedia.org/wiki/TiB

hardware. A water cooling system using Guangzhou city water kept everything cool, because the heat generated by this beast was enormous. At peak performance the system could draw something approaching 24 megawatts of power—24 million watts—enough to power a city of about 30,000.

Unlike the complexity of the supercomputer, the control room was simple and straightforward. A built-in counter ran the length of the wall just below the large windows that looked into the computer room. Four PCs with oversized flat screen monitors were spread out along the counter. An air lock with inner and outer doors, exactly the same as the one Oi Lam had usedearlier, lead into the computer room itself. Five inexpensive office chairs provided the seating, and Nicole sank into one of them in front of a PC on the long counter. She needed to focus on software and stop looking at the damn hardware.

She found her velvet pouch and retrieved a USB flash drive. She was about to insert it into a USB port on the PC when she stopped herself and looked over at the remaining technician, the older guy. "I need your help to set up my interface. I want to run a simple search program. My software is ready to use."

The older technician met her gaze. "Iwill not help you."

Grant and Hernandez exchanged a look. "You can't figure out how to do it yourself?" he asked.

"That might take a couple of hours."

"Take all the time you need. I'll send out for pizza."

His remark wasn't helpful, but could she blame him? Hernandez had gone to the mat for her, and right now stood dripping blood onto the control room floor. She'd told him she could do it, and he'd gotten her here. Was she going to deliver or not? She watched as he kept looking through the window in the door, looking into the changing room where two bodies lay on the floor.

Nicole didn't believe in "feminine intuition," but she instinctively keyed on the weak link in the room: Oi Lam. "You care for General Ma, I can see that," said Nicole gently. "But if I don't run this program that will restore my corrupted files—it's nothing that will hurt China—my partner will kill him. You see, the general was complicit in the death of my friend's brother, an innocent man. So my friend will take revenge if he has to."

"His brother? Who was that?" rasped Ma, with a disbelieving tone.

"Willie Taveras," said Hernandez, coldly. "You people killed him in Washington D.C."

"But your name is Hernandez."

"The Agency changed my name years ago."

"Taveras was your brother?" Ma shook his head like a man who keeps getting nothing but bad news.

Nicole riveted her eyes on Oi Lam. The young Chinese lady seemed to be listening carefully, trying to take it all in. "Too many people have died already over this," said Nicole. "American and Chinese. The general knows what I've said is true."

Oi Lam looked to him for confirmation, but Ma just stared at Grant. "What corrupted files are you talking about?" asked Ma.

"The files of the secret drone operation over this very city, two years ago.Files that will destroy Zhao Yiren.Files that will save my life, and my friend's life."

Ma scowled and cast his gaze downward. "Files that will not only destroy Zhao, but me as well."

"You told us you wanted to flee China with Oi Lam," Nicole gently reminded him. "You mentioned having blackmail material on the entire top cadre, so they'd have to let you live. You already have your blackmail material to keep you and your girlfriend alive, General. Now we want ours," said Nicole, gesturing with the flash drive. "Mister Hernandez and I want to live, the same as you do."

Ma started to speak but held his tongue. She could see how torn the man was.

"He planned to double-cross us all along. I ought to just put a bullet in him right now," said Hernandez, leveling his gun.

• • • •

OI LAM BLANCHED. THE last thing she could allow was for the American man to shoot General Ma, whom she now understood with certainty was her future meal ticket. No, more than a meal ticket, much more, since she knew Ma was worth hundreds of millions. She'd underestimated how important having a son would be to her lover. The American woman had just said, and Ma didn't dispute it, that he intended to flee China with her! She hadn't considered leaving China, but with that kind of money, so what?

Oi Lam had to do everything in her power right now to make sure General Ma remained unharmed. "Is she telling the truth?" asked Oi Lam as she touched Ma's arm.

Ma hesitated. "I imagine so."

Oi Lam turned to Nicole. "Then I will help you. If you promise not to hurt him." Oi Lam stood up. Ma looked completely vexed, but didn't try to stop her.

"You have my word," said Nicole.

The old technician narrowed his eyes and lurched forward, but Hernandez grabbed him and slammed him against the wall. "Don't get cute, pops." Hernandez drilled the man with a killer stare, and then backed up to his position next to the door. He pressed one hand over his shoulder wound, as if the amount of blood concerned him. Oi Lam knew that if a blood pathway had been nicked, the American would die.

She settled in next to Nicole, who sat in front of a PC at the long counter. "Let me see what you have," said General Ma's mistress.

• • • •

VICE PREMIER ZHAO YIREN, Zhao's Chief of Security Lin, and MSS Special Projects Director Tang Jie climbed out of the helicopter on the Tianhe-2 complex grounds at Sun Yat-sen University, East Campus in Guangzhou. Chinese military radar had tracked Ma's copter here, and Zhao knew why he'd come; his girlfriend was working inside.

Tang had a single earbud running from his cell phone to his ear as they all walked in a crouch from under the spinning rotor blades. The pilot took off again to refuel, just as General Ma's pilots had done. As the whine of the engines faded and the rotor wash abated, Zhao turned to Tang. "Well?"

"Same as the last call," said Tang, pulling the earbud from his ear. "You are hated in Guangzhou, so no one will unofficially help you. They all say the same thing. Make a request through official channels in Beijing."

Zhao lit a cigarette using his well-practiced ritual, sucked the nicotine deep into his lungs, then took in the surroundings. Instinct told him to act fast, and his mood was restless. He wanted to get back to his Beijing condo and get a massage and more from his new favorite girl, Qui Qui, since the non-fling with the non-blonde in Hong Kong had left him feeling randy.

"Then we'll do the job ourselves," said Zhao, a bit drunkenly, "just like I did in the old days. The campus police will help us kill the Americans, don't you agree, Chief Lin?"

"I should think so," said Lin, as he chambered a round into his semi-automatic pistol.

"Even though you are unpopular, every man with a gun in Guangzhou will come here to kill the Americans if they touch the supercomputer," said Tang.

"Better if we finish quickly. The fewer involved the better," said Zhao, flicking his cigarette and stepping toward the entrance.

• • • •

OI LAM DIDN'T NEED to set up a countdown clock; a digital countdown was built into Nicole Grant's software and displayed on one of the flat monitors. The algorithm Grant had stolen from Carnegie Mellon and then tweaked, was working—the files stored on the Darknet two years ago were being fully restored. But the countdown was cruel—sometimes it slowed or stopped, depending on progress, similar to running a scan or downloading a program on a home computer. The countdown display read 07:02.

Grant and Oi Lam nervously stared at the monitors as the sprawling supercomputer on the other side of the windows in front of them ramped up to full operating capacity. General Ma sat on a chair in the corner looking wrinkled and morose; the scowling older technician sat on the floor. The angry young technician was now bound and gagged but still unconscious. Ron Hernandez had also brought the body of the dead guard into the control room as a reminder to the Chinese present not to try anything.

Six minutes and change, now.An eternity, thought Hernandez, as he stole a glance at the countdown readout while standing guard at the door. The earlier three gunshots had brought out a few curious technicians working night shift in the big, mostly empty complex. They had approached the hallway door where he'd scared them off by brandishing the gun. That had been several minutes earlier. Now the building seemed still as stone. It had been more than twenty-five minutes since they first entered the building. Staying for six more minutes was insanity.

He had the Kimber with seven rounds remaining; the silenced Type-67 with one round remaining; and the guard's out-of-date Type-54 with six 7.62 x 25mm caliber rounds. Fourteen rounds in three different pistols. The gun Grant had gotten from General Ma in the CIA condo was a Chinese-made QSZ-92. She might have a dozen rounds left, but it was bad form to check your partner's weapon; she'd need that pistol.

"General Ma, are you still in the game?" asked Hernandez with a sharp edge. "Because if you are, your pilot needs to be circling the university, ready to land at a moment's notice."

Before Ma could respond, Hernandez heard the hallway door open that led into the changing room. He spun to look through the small doorway window and saw a group of men including two security guards holding pistols enter the changing room. A voice cried out, "That's him!" The men all raised their weapons.

Hernandez didn't hesitate. He fired one round through the window in the door, shattering it and sending glass spraying all over himself, then fired again. One guard went down, and for a millisecond, Ron Hernandez locked eyes with Zhao Yiren. The Chinese all returned fire and the rounds impacted into the steel control room door. Hernandez squeezed off two more unaimed shots without exposing his head through the window.

He chanced a quick look, and a guy wearing a suit standing in the doorway fired. The round grazed the side of Hernandez's skull and he started to bleed like a stuck pig. He'd seen one guard down on the floor, while the others had retreated from the changing room and regrouped in the hallway.

Hernandez glanced at the group in the control room. Grant and Oi Lam looked terrified and Ma and the old technician didn't look much better. Ten rounds left and the countdown clock read 05:57.

• • • •

ZHAO YIREN'S EYES HAD never been so wide open, thought Chief Lin as he looked at his boss, with his back pressed tight against the hallway wall. And the orbs looked extra bloodshot. Yes, the man was drunk, but that was nothing new. Alcoholic or not, Zhao was Lin's ticket to the top of the heap and he intended to reach that destination. Lin then shifted his gaze to Director Tang, who was taking quick looks into the changing room. Tang was a cool customer, Lin knew that. He'd take pride in killing him very soon, after Ma, Hernandez and Grant were erased. Those were his secret orders. Zhao had given him the assignment mere hours earlier. A little cleanup was in order before the doors to Lin's political future and fabulous reward would fully open.

"Is there another way into the computer room?" Tang asked the guard.

"An emergency exit through the rear airlock. But I have to get a key first."

Tang nodded and turned to Zhao and Lin. "If you handle this end, I'll take the other entrance."

Zhao waved them off. Once Tang and the guard were out of sight, Zhao leaned in close to his security chief. "Lin, I know you're ambitious. If you can get into that control room and kill everyone before soldiers or police arrive, it will be better for us. I'll be able to spin these events as I wish. And when I become president you can name your position in the Chinese government. Do it now, don't wait for Tang to get into place, because you must kill him, too."

Lin smiled. This was exactly what he wanted to hear. "Give me cover fire. The shooting will disguise any sounds I make."

The men checked their weapons, and then nodded to each other. Lin flung the hallway door open and Zhao opened fire, delivering a fusillade of lead as he emptied the magazine. With bullets whizzing overhead, the security chief scrambled in a fast crab walk across the changing room all the way to the control room door. He squatted just under the blown out doorway window that led into the control room.

• • • •

SUPERCOMPUTER CONTROL rooms are supposed to be sterile, hushed environments where important work is performed and talented scientists and researchers work with engineers to achieve breakthroughs in computing achievement, all to benefit mankind. Such control rooms are not supposed to be the scene of gunfights with dead people and broken glass strewn about.

Bullets screamed into the control room and Grant flinched as the flat panel monitor in front of her and Oi Lam was shattered by a ricochet. She instinctively crouched down onto the floor and pulled Oi Lam with her. Grant's cognition seemed to downshift into slow motion as she looked over to the door. As if in a dream, a gun appeared through the small window in the steel door. Ron Hernandez looked a bloody mess as he crouched next to the door. The deafening sound of the firing took away her hearing, and then her world shifted into even slower speed. The door opened and a large Chinese man hurtled in, grabbing Hernandez as he came. They tumbled into a heap. Her brain processed the recognition of the man. He was Lin, the cruel security chief she'd met at Zhao's condo.

Temporarily deaf, Grant found herself standing and was immediately slammed onto the counter, knocking a PC onto the floor as hands grabbed her throat. It was the old technician, strangling her. She twisted and fell, then somehow staggered to her feet, but he wouldn't let go.

She watched, in some kind of shock consciousness, as Hernandez and Lin wrestled around on the floor. Her partner struggled to break free and stand, but failed. Lin slammed him repeatedly in his face with his fist. Hernandez looked dazed and seemed to be the weaker fighter, but he managed to reach up and pull a keyboard from the counter and then jam it into Lin's face, breaking his nose.

In her ethereal-like vision, Grant saw General Ma moving now. Walking in some kind of half-time measure since her visual perception had been oddly slowed. Ma took Oi Lam by the arm and led her to the doorway. Smart man, getting out while he can.

Grant's eyes shifted to the black eyes of the man killing her. He held such hate, such anger. Fear. Every failure, every slight in his entire life was being avenged in this rage-filled moment as he tightened his grip on her neck. She thought of her mom, Jan. She loved her mom so much and wanted to see her again. Wanted to drink coffee and gossip and take her for a long drive in the mountains where they would remember old times and talk of her father. Her father who, in the last years of his life, she treated with such disrespect. With barely concealed contempt. He died having a daughter who'd turned her back on him. Shame washed over her. She barely noticed as her attacker's eyes bulged out and he squeezed her neck harder. Then a thought stabbed her with the headline that she had only seconds to act, if she wanted to live.

CHAPTER 36

01 :12   General Ma had never seen combat, but this was close enough. As soon as Lin started spraying lead into the control room, Ma was on the move. He had to practically drag Oi Lam with him, she was so terrified. Somehow, the four shots fired by Lin had missed hitting anyone. With Lin and Hernandez now fighting on the floor, it was a good time to leave. He'd already texted his pilot using Oi Lam's phone and ordered his refueled bird to land.

The steel control room door, now pock-marked with bullet slugs, closed behind them. They were almost clear. He ripped off his clean room gown and pulled the covering from his head. He and Oi Lam had hurried half way across the changing room floor when Zhao, looking quite insane and holding a pistol, stepped into the doorway and blocked them from exiting into the hall.

"Zhao!" shouted Ma, pretending to be relieved to see his old friend. "The Americans kidnapped me! Lin needs help in there! Give me your gun and I'll kill Hernandez and Grant. No need for you to bloody your hands this close to the election, old friend."

"You weren't kidnapped, *old friend*. You're a traitor." Zhao sprayed spittle as he spoke the words, slurring.

"No, you misunderstand!"

Zhao fired four times, two bullets into each of them. Oi Lam screamed and her legs gave out slowly, as if she didn't want to fall hard and hurt her baby. General Ma, in utter disbelief, swayed on his feet as he tried to comprehend what happened. The woman who carried his unborn son had just been shot right next to him. It couldn't possibly be true. Ma's eyes rolled upward and he collapsed into a rumpled unconscious pile.

• • • •

STRANGELY, IT WAS GRANT'S father who came to her. After the way she'd disowned him, how could he possibly care about her? Back in college she'd stopped taking his calls, never answered his letters. Not even the ones he'd written on his deathbed. She'd kept the letters, but for the first few years, she never reread them. She'd kept them like one might keep old legal documents, papers that may or may not ever be referenced again. But in the last few years, she'd started to reread the letters every so often. They made her sad because she realized how much she missed and loved him.

And right now her father seemed to be here, his voice in her head was emphatic and loud. "Break free!" It was a command, not a request. When she was a headstrong, highly opinionated teen, he would gently urge her to break free of rigid judgments that seemed to allow little tolerance of her parents.

"Break free!"

Obeying the command, Grant brought her palms together at her waist, laced her fingers together, and then raised her hands forcefully, straight up. Her laced fingers were like a double fist that cracked into the bottom of the technician's chin and rocked his head back. He loosened his grip, but when she forced her arms open wide, the move broke his grip entirely. She delivered a sharp blow from her flat right hand—a judo chop—to his throat, and he collapsed to the floor, retching.

She gulped down air, rubbed her neck, and surveyed the room. Her perception returned to normal speed, but she was now possessed with a strange serenity. She reached into her purse, found the gun she'd gotten from Ma, and crossed to the door, which was again closed. She saw Zhao through the small, broken window. And he saw her. Zhao fired, Grant fired, and then he turned tail and ran back out into the hall, leaving the bodies of Ma and Oi Lam on the changing room floor.

She turned to Hernandez. He lay flat on his back, but was strangling Lin with a black keyboard cable. Gritting his teeth, his face a mask of grim determination, Hernandez pulled the cord tighter. Lin's feet kicked at empty air, his eyes popped out like a gasping frog, and then he died. Hernandez rolled the big man off him. He looked up at Nicole as blood ran down his cheek.

In an unspoken union of concern, they both looked at the countdown clock: 02:47

• • • •

KATE RICE DUCKED THROUGH a service entrance of the Grand Hyatt and took a rear stairway up several flights before picking up an elevator. One swipe of her magnetic key card and the door opened into herdarkened hotel suite. The main room was as still as a church on Monday morning. She couldn't be certain whether Chinese or Agency killers were already after her, but held her suppressed Boberg semi-auto as she silently checked the main room. Everything appeared undisturbed, so she slithered into the bedroom.

A splash of awareness hit her like a hot shower suddenly turning cold. A killer was here. Somewhere in her hotel suite. A shiver ran up her arm as the fuzz on the back of her neck stood up. Rice felt tingly, but wasn't afraid. No lights were on in the suite, but ambient light from a city blazing with them filtered through the floor-to-ceiling windows in the bedroom and living rooms. No one was in the bedroom and no one had been in the main room.That left the bathroom. The half-closed doorway was only a few steps away.

A lighting control panel for the entire suite was recessed in the wall next to the bed. Rice trained her gun on the bathroom doorway, crouched down, reached over, and pushed a button causing the bathroom light to come on.

Now who's scared?

She grabbed a pillow from the bed, keeping her gun leveled. The plush carpet underfoot gave away no creaks. Stalking a killer wasn't in her job description, but Rice was a hands-on operator. Hyper-alive with certainty that the advantage was all hers, she silently closed in and flung the pillow hard at the partially open door.

Two soft puffts and the sounds of wood splintering as two shots from a suppressed automatic blew holes in the wooden bathroom door. Rice answered six times as she moved forward, firing her equally quiet weapon. Six 9mm slugs tore through the door and then three more for good measure as she kicked at the disintegrating wood. Something heavy crashed to the floor.

Rice stormed in as Socorro Trujillo crumbled to the floor, limbs akimbo. She'd been shot multiple times but still managed to raise her suppressed handgun. Without missing a beat Rice kicked the gun away, bent down and placed the tip of her suppressor against the woman's forehead.

Trujillo's mouth was open as she tried to suck in air. Her glassy black eyes displayed the shock of realization that her life span now numbered in mere seconds.

"Who do you work for?"

"Take a guess," gasped Trujillo, weakly.

"What are your orders regarding me?"

"You're a dead bitch walking." Trujillo's lips curled into a snarl.

The woman was a pro and had real balls. Rice took satisfaction in having bested her. "You're a dead bitch in a toilet." Rice pulled the trigger. Time to get far away from Hong Kong.

• • • •

HERNANDEZ LOOKED BAD and felt worse as he sat on the floor of the control room of the supercomputer Tianhe-2. His shoulder burned and his suit jacket around the gunshot wound was soaked with blood. He touched his face—half of it was sticky and red from the graze to his scalp and from the bloody nose Lin had given him. He felt weak and fatigued, but there was no time to rest. Grant stood at the door holding a gun. He stood on wobbly legs and crossed to her.

"Zhao is out there in the hallway."

Hernandez nodded, chanced a quick look out, and immediately came under fire. "Get down!" he said, pushing her clear. As she scrambled away he stood there trading fire with Zhao. He tossed the empty Kimber aside, then fired the last bullet from the Type 67 silenced pistol and tossed it aside. He retrieved the last pistol from his fanny pack, and fired three times at Zhao.

"I'm going to rush him before the whole Chinese army shows up," said Hernandez.

"Please don't do that."

"It's time to move, files or no files. I only have three rounds left." He started to open the door.

"Wait!" shouted Grant, as her eyes darted to the countdown display. It read 01:51, then jumped down to 01:22, then jumped again to 00:37. In the IT world, digital countdown clocks could be cruel, or they could be beautiful. Right now it looked glorious.

Hernandez registered shock. The countdown display had zeroed out: 00:00.

"We got it?!" he asked, almost not believing it.

"We got it!" she gushed, snatching her flash drive from the PC. "And look." She pointed to an emergency evacuation diagram sign mounted on the wall. "There are two ways into the supercomputer room. Let's use the rear exit in case Zhao isn't alone."

He turned and fired three more times toward Zhao's position, to discourage any approach. The pistol clicked empty and he tossed it. They hurried to the door leading into the airlock. A bright red sign with white letters was mounted on it in Chinese and English:

WHEN ALARM SOUNDS
VACATE AT ONCE

HALON 1301 BEING RELEASED

He flung open the door and ran with Grant into the airlock toward Tianhe-2.

• • • •

ZHAO YIREN STOOD IN the hallway, at the open doorway leading into the changing room that led into the control room that lead into Tianhe-2. While normally he might complain about the delay in a police response to a shooting, in this instance he was glad. Lin had obviously failed. Perhaps he himself could do the deed before police arrived.

Zhao stepped into the changing room, while pointing his weapon at the much shot-up door. He stepped around the bodies of General Ma and his girlfriend and crossed to the door. He hesitated only for a moment, and then looked in through the shot-out window.

He counted three bodies: Lin and two technicians. Where were the Americans? Zhao angrily flung open the door and barged into the control room.

He saw 00:00 displayed on a flat panel monitor. Zhao's booze addled brain perked up. Why had they come here, to Tianhe-2? Ma only wanted to save his girlfriend. No, it was Grant and Hernandez. They needed to use the supercomputer, something about her files on the laptop in his condo. He was simply too drunk and couldn't put it together. No matter, if he killed them now, he'd not only solve his problems, but be a hero to all of China. Since they could only be in the computer room itself, he stormed into the airlock.

• • • •

WHEN GENERAL MA REGAINED consciousness, pain shot into his brain like a white hot poker. He sprawled on the floor confused and nauseous. He'd been knocked unconscious not by being shot, but by hitting his head as he fell. He'd taken some bullets, and it took a few seconds to find the wet, sticky places on his shirt. Ma didn't feel pain, but felt woozy. He got to all fours and when he saw Oi Lam his face contorted like he was about to cry. The general crawled to her, ripped open her clean room gown and recoiled at the sight of the blood covering her chest. "Oi Lam! Oi Lam!"

She didn't respond. Ma literally gasped, *My son! Please let him live!* Without thinking, he scooped his arms under her and stood up unsteadily. Horrible pain from the gunshot wound now coiled up through his torso, and he broke out into a sweat, but he calmly walked out through the open door and into the hallway holding his lover, with the fetus of his unborn son in her belly.

CHAPTER 37

01 :21

Grant and Hernandez made a bee line to the rear of the chilly room housing the rows of elegant metal cabinets that comprised the supercomputer. She tried the door leading into the rear airlock, but it wouldn't budge. This airlock stood in the opposite corner from the front airlock, and from here, they couldn't see the control room windows. The six long black consoles shielded them from view while emanating a low hum, like an electronic mantra to the gods of computation.

Grant tried the door again. "It must be stuck."

Hernandez pulled hard but the door remained frozen in place. "It's not stuck, it's locked from the inside. He winced from pain as he bent down to examine the door handle more closely. Then a shot rang out and a bullet pinged into the door frame right in front of them. He reached up and pulled her with him to the floor. Another shot, and then the sound of a slide locking back on an empty semi-automatic pistol, indicating that the gun was out of ammunition.

Hernandez caught a glimpse of Zhao standing at the opposite end of the room, backlit by soft light. "Give me your gun," he whispered.

She looked confused. "I must have left it in the control room."

Hernandez could just make out the sight of Zhao ejecting his empty magazine. "Quick, he's reloading."

They scrambled to their feet and hustled along the rear wall. Searing pain from the knife wound stabbed him all over again as they ran into the space between the first two rows of consoles. Another shot rang out and splintered into a tower of electronics recessed in the wall behind them. Hernandez pulled her to him as they took cover at the end of the second row of cabinets.

Six perfectly parallel, long rows of wide and tall consoles comprised Tianhe-2. Hernandez and Grant stood at one end of a console, Zhao at the other end. If he committed to any particular aisle to come after them, they could simply choose a different aisle and try to reach the front airlock. But he had a weapon and they didn't. As Hernandez looked up to the top of a console, she followed his gaze.

"These things will support our weight?"

"Yes. Technicians spend a lot of time on top of consoles to run wires."

"Alright, here's the plan." He put his hands on her shoulders so she had to face him. He locked his gaze into her eyes. "We go up. You first. Crawl quickly but quietly toward the front door. I'll do the same on the next console over. When you get to the other end, drop down, go through the airlock, and don't stop for anything. Head for the river. Jaffir should be in Guangzhou any minute. His number's in your phone. We'll call him and get out of this mess."

He couldn't tell if she believed him, but her eyes moistened. "We're not going to make it, are we?" she managed to say.

"Hell yes, we'll make it! I'm just giving you the plan. I thought you liked plans," he joked, trying to give her hope in a hopeless situation. "I've given you how many today? Be thankful."

"I am thankful. I'm so thankful for you, for everything you've done. I want us to—"

He took her face and kissed her passionately. He broke off, and then stroked her cheek. "Grant, listen. You're an amazing woman. I can't believe I'm saying it, but it's the truth. You're one of the best partners I've ever had. You taught me a lot today. And I very much look forward to spending some relaxed time with you, even if you do have two left feet."

She held him tight and drilled her eyes into his. "Why don't we—?"

"Please do what I ask, and trust me." He gently turned her around then squatted slightly, offering his right thigh as a step. "Put your foot here like you're using a step-stool." She pushed off from him and grabbed the raised edges of the console. He grabbed her thighs and lifted, giving her enough momentum to pull herself on top of the console.

Hundreds of yellow and orange cables snaked along the top—the raised edges of the consoles were designed to act as "cable trays" keeping all of the cabling from spilling over the sides, but right now they provided her with cover—she couldn't be seen by anyone walking along the aisle below.

Waves of pain from lifting Grant raked his upper body and left leg. Hernandez fought to stay standing as he clutched his gunshot wound. A shower of sweat coursed down from his forehead. His stab wound felt like a white hot tear, the gunshot wound radiated an inner burn. Clammy and feverish, anemic from blood loss and lack of sleep, spent from too many adrenalin rushes, he felt dead on his feet. He wanted to go to sleep for a week. He wanted a cold one and a nice cigar and a beach chair in Antigua. Too weak to hoist himself atop a console, he battled to shake off dizziness and chanced a look down an aisle as fever sweat dripped from his chin and spattered onto the floor.

The dark silhouette of Zhao stood lurking at the other end of the long console like a final reaper at the Ninth Gate of Hell. A shot rang out, and then Hernandez stumbled wearily along the far wall, drawing Zhao away from Nicole Grant.

• • • •

IT WASN'T THAT THE police response was slow, local police and Sun Yat-sen University security guards simply couldn't get into the secure building that housed Tianhe-2. None of the campus cops had the right key card, since they didn't work in this section of the university. About twenty-five officers stood around the main entrance with their guns drawn. They'd already checked the perimeter, and all of the heavy steel doors were locked. An officer spoke into his cell phone, trying to get someone to bring the right key card, since the guards inside were presumed to be dead.

A campus security supervisor then drove up in a small white car. The chubby man ran panting to the door, swiped a key card and the door clicked open. All of the officers from various departments ran into the building, leaving the perimeter unguarded.

• • • •

TEARS STREAMED DOWN his face as Major General Ma Ju shoved his hips against the push bar of an emergency exit. He ignored the pain from his gunshots as he trotted out onto the lawn of the Tianhe-2 complex. His helicopter touched down only thirty yards away. Ma seemed to gain strength as he neared the roaring whine of the engine, and he powered through the rotor wash from the spinning overhead blades. He jogged the last few yards, strengthened by the lure of escape. The co-pilot emerged and helped get the body of Oi Lam inside, where Ma held his lover's hand, trying to will his *chi*—his life energy—into her. He glanced out for a last look at the campus as the bird lifted into the night sky. His face muscles tightened into a facade of hate. Hate for Guangzhou and the local cadre who had refused to help. Hate for his childhood friend Zhao who betrayed him. But mostly, hate for Nicole Grant and Ron Hernandez, the American spies who had ruined his life.

• • • •

GRANT SLITHERED OVER cabling running along the top of the console until she reached the end. She lifted her head and saw the front airlock door only fifteen feet away. Movement from inside the control room caught her eye, as police arrived. When some cops peered into the computer room she ducked back down. Hernandez had told her to get through the airlock, but that plan had lasted less than a minute.

Gunfire rang out from the far corner of the room. She instinctively knew—instinctively, there was a new concept for her—that Hernandez had lured Zhao away from the airlock door to give her a chance to make a run for it. He was sacrificing himself for her freedom.

She bit down on her lip as her mind raced. Every problem has a solution, what's the solution here? It came to her in a flash—the sign on the airlock door! Halon gas! She reached into her fake Celine bag and found the phony Cartier cigarette lighter she'd bought for her smoker friend back in Phoenix. She tugged at an orange cable and positioned it over the lighter's flame. Black smoke curled up toward the ceiling. Heat sensors and smoke detectors in rooms such as this were numerous and extremely sensitive. After only a moment, a loud shrieking alarm pierced the room. Fire alarm!

Institutions with a $400 million investment to protect don't want a fire. And they don't want a sprinkler system to spray water and ruin all the electronics. Fire suppression systems for supercomputers and other facilities full of costly electronics were usually comprised of gasses that were pumped into the sealed room once a sensor detected too much heat. The fast-acting, invisible, odorless gasses reduced the oxygen content in a sealed space, such as a computer clean room, to less than ten percent, well below the level of combustion. The sensitivity of the sensors could detect heat before combustion took place, and the gas solved the problem before an actual fire broke out.

But people need oxygen to breathe, and many human fatalities had been racked up over the years when personnel were not able to exit fast enough from a room filled with the fire suppression gasses, especially Halon gas, now banned in the United States.

Respirators! She'd seen respirators next to the locked rear airlock door.

· · · ·

COPS HAULED THE OLDER, unconscious technician from the control room. Chief Lin and the security guard were dead. The angry young technician had regained consciousness and they had him sitting in a chair. Two cops were about to enter the airlock to get into the supercomputer room when the piercing fire alarm went off.

"Wait!" shouted the young technician to the cops. "Don't go in there unless you want to die."

The two policemen stopped just short of the airlock. "Someone's inside!" a cop called out.

Everyone turned to look through the windows with surprise as Grant stood atop the second of the long row of consoles. The six rows of consoles were all connected by sturdy overhead cable trays and she scurried over a cable tray to get to the first console, and then ran toward the rear of the room.

"For our safety, we should all move into the hallway now," said the technician.

"What about her?" asked a cop.

The angry young technician smiled. "The gas will reduce the oxygen level in there to five percent. She'll be dead in less than a minute."

· · · ·

RON HERNANDEZ WASN'T the type to give up, ever. But he felt incredibly weak. He listened carefully, trying to isolate any sounds not created by the humming electronics, the HVAC system, or the chilled water under high pressure that coursed through pipes and helped keep the equipment cool. He listened for Zhao's footsteps, for Grant opening the airlock door. He couldn't make a break for it until she made her move.

No weapons meant improvising, so he took stock of his gear. A cell phone and tablet computer, but not much else. The only other things in his fanny pack were the items he took from General Ma: fingernail clipper, address book, a small tin of what smelled like ginseng powder.

He looked again at the phone, wanting to call his parents, but then heard movement on the other side of the console. Zhaocould step around the corner any second. He tried to shake off a dizzy feeling when a bleating fire alarm ripped the air like a blast of trouble. What the hell? Grant! It had to be. Then, as if on cue, he heard her scream, "Hernandez!" The screeching alarm made it hard to hear. "Meet me at the place that was stuck, RIGHT NOW!"

WTF? He'd brought Zhao over to this side of the room to give her a chance, and now she was changing the plan on him. As usual. She must have a good reason, she always did, so with what little energy he had left, he broke into a run, ducked through a gap in the sixth console, and crossed into the next aisle...

...where Zhao was waiting. As Zhao raised his gun, Hernandez flung the ginseng powder toward his face but kept his momentum going, crossing through the next gap in the fifth console—the last gap—and then barreling to his right, limping up an aisle toward the rear wall. He doubted he'd make it, and braced himself for a bullet to enter his back.

• • • •

ZHAO KNEW SOMETHING was wrong. Yes, he'd had too much to drink, he admitted that now. Drunk or not, he could have shot Hernandez if his gun hadn't jammed. Wasn't his fault the gun jammed. The last spent cartridge failed to clear the ejection port. *Cheap Chinese crap!* The QSZ-92 was a rip-off design of the Beretta 92F that had been used by the U.S. military in its most recent wars. He struggled to free the steel case, but couldn't dislodge it. *Cheap steel case Chinese garbage ammo, not even decent brass rounds.* Zhao would never own such a cheap weapon or inferior ammunition.

He moved into the gaps, but which row had Hernandez taken? And did he go right or left? The man had thrown some kind of powder at him; it was all over the front of his clothes. And where was that bitch, Nicole Grant? His lips then formed into a frown of rage and he stumbled forward.

• • • •

THE SHRIEKING FIRE alarm was too loud in this hallway, thought Tang, who watched with concealed contempt as the guard fiddled with a massive key ring and finally got the correct key into the lock. It had taken the guard several minutes just to locate the key ring in the security office, so a frustrated Tang didn't wait for permission and swung the heavy door open, revealing the first of two airlock doors just beyond. This was the rear entrance into the supercomputer room. The airlock doors had windows in them so he should be able to see into the computer room, but the bright light angling in from the hall reflected off the window and turned it opaque, obstructing his view.

"I advise you not to go in there," said the guard, backing away.

"Get lost." Tang pointed his pistol at the guard, who turned and ran.

Tang lowered his pistol and looked to the airlock. The last two of twenty Americans would be dead within minutes. Grant he would kill quickly. Hernandez, however, merited special treatment.

He stepped forward, opened the white outer door and entered. The small airlock was only six feet long and narrow so only one person could pass through at a time. The explosive sound of compressed air suddenly blasting all over him was loud enough to wake the dead, but maybe the air would blow away any bad *chi*, bad energy. Six people lost today! Tang brimmed with anxiousness as he pulled his semi-automatic handgun.

He walked the length of the airlock and tried opening the inner airlock door, the door that lead into the supercomputer room, but it was locked. He checked, and then lifted up a simple latch. He looked through the window and saw the insistent glow of flashing red warning lights and sharp stabs of white strobe beams reflect off a sleek black console. He tugged at his earlobe as he reached for the door handle with his pistol at the ready.

• • • •

FEELING LIGHT-HEADED and fighting to focus, Hernandez took quick, short breaths. Something was terribly wrong. He staggered to the far rear corner of the supercomputer room, near the rear airlock door. With blurred peripheral vision he saw a hand reach out and grab him. He tried to block it, but couldn't, he didn't have the strength. Completely startled, it took him a second to realize the humanoid wearing the odd-looking breathing device was Grant. She slipped one over his head, adjusted the straps and he took deep sweet breaths of good air, oxygenating his brain and bloodstream.

Because they were standing right next to the locked airlock door, and only because of that, they heard the loud, distinctive sound of the air-blowers engage from inside the airlock. Someone was coming. He grabbed Grant and pressed her flat against the wall. Hernandez pivoted to face the door and squatted slightly just as Director Tang entered.

Tang was turning his head toward him when Hernandez slammed his full weight into the thin man in the brown shirt, the man in his forties with black-framed eyeglasses, the man who had murdered his brother at the Foggy Bottom Metro Station. The screeching fire alarm seemed to fade away as he entered his own personal killing zone of consciousness and used his last ounces of strength to ram Tang's face into the wall, knocking out two teeth and shattering his nose, while simultaneously stripping the gun from Tang's hand. He pressed the gun barrel into the back of the MSS man's neck.

"Director Tang!" yelled Hernandez, his voice muffled by the respirator. "You killed my brother, Willie Taveras in Washington D.C. So here's a little something from me to you."

Red blood splattered the wall in front of Tang as rounds tore into the lower rear of his skull and blew out through the front. Hernandez watched as Tang blinked in shock, and then collapsed.

As Hernandez teetered over Tang's body, he fought tears because at this moment he felt the spirit of his brother Willie was with him. Tang had murdered Willie in cold blood, and now payback had been delivered. But there was no feeling of satisfaction, no joyful glee, no gloating. There was only tremendous sadness for the huge hole that had been created in his family, a hole that could never be filled.

• • • •

GRANT TOOK HERNANDEZ by the hand and led him into the airlock. The air blowers came on and they ripped off their respirators. She closed the inner door behind them and saw the door's locking latch. Just as she tripped it, Zhao's enraged face appeared in the window as his body slammed into the door. He tried the door, but she'd just locked it. He was trapped in the supercomputer room, unless he could make it to the front airlock.

Zhao threw his jammed gun against the window, but it bounced off the thick glass. Did he know he was about to be asphyxiated? He lasered Grant with his fiery eyes. He weakly pounded on the glass as he cursed her, and since she read lips, it was as if she heard every ugly word.

You cheap tart! You whore with a bloody vagina! I'll bloody your vagina! Open this door, woman! Open it, slut! We Han are better than your ilk This century is our century, the Pacific Century, the Chinese Century, my century I will make you all crawl on your knees...

Grant stood fast, her eyes locked on Zhao's. She sensed his hate, his laser-sharp wrath. Hernandez put his hand in hers and gently squeezed her fingers, but didn't intervene, didn't say a word. She looked at Zhao with no pity, no remorse, no guilt. Even though, my God, she was killing a human being. She could simply open the door and Hernandez would gladly do the deed. But instead, she watched with righteous satisfaction as Zhao faded. His eyes rolled up in his head and he dropped to the floor, unconscious. Unless someone came to his aid right now, his nomination was withdrawn.

Rapist, killer, world leader. To die like this... he was getting off easy.

• • • •

GRANT AND HERNANDEZ slammed against the pushbars of heavy steel crash-out doors—emergency exits for fire or haz-mat situations—and darted out into the night air. They raced across the lawn, crossed the double-lane roadway and disappeared into the dark trees on the banks of the meandering Pearl River.

Hernandez had spotted a dock and boats when they were coming in for a landing in Ma's helicopter. As they approached it now, it appeared the small dock was for student use. Kayaks, ratty-looking skiffs, and a few two-person plastic canoes floated loosely tied to the dock. Since plastic canoes were virtually unsinkable, Hernandez selected a dark-colored one.

In less than a minute, with Grant in the front seat, they'd silently slipped into the inky waters, each holding a plastic paddle as the current drew them swiftly toward the sea. Not that they were going that far. With luck, Jaffir would pick them up long before they reached Jinxing Bay and the ocean beyond.

They stayed quiet, bent over low in the canoe to reduce their profile. In a matter of minutes they glided below a massive bridge and skirted the creaking, rusting hulks of ocean-going cargo ships docked on the river banks. The current inexorably drew them toward the heart of the city and sounds of street traffic, snippets of Cantonese music from riverside karaoke bars, and shards of laughter from fisherman trolling the black water. Musky scents of garbage and sewage and dead fish mixed with the tickling aroma of pork and garlic frying in palm oil from open air stalls on the bank. Life, they had found life, leaving the university killing ground far behind.

"You okay to steer this thing, Grant?" asked Hernandez, weakly.

"I am, and my friends call me Nicole. What's your real first name, Mr. Taveras?"

"Nicole, my real first name is Manny."

"Manny, after we get you to a doctor and when you've had time to recover, I'd like to take you out for dinner and drinks and dancing, although, as I've said before, I don't know how to dance."

"You're a fast learner. I'll teach you."

"I'd like that." There wasn't much wiggle room in the canoe. She placed the paddle across her lap and reached blindly behind her with her right hand.

He leaned forward, gently took her hand in his, and laced their fingers together.

ABOUT ED KOVACS

E d Kovacs is the author of the critically-acclaimed Detective Cliff St. James mystery/crime series, as well as stand-alone espionage and action thrillers. Ed has studied martial arts, holds many weapons-related licenses, certifications and permits, and is a certified medical First Responder.

Using various pen names, he has worked professionally around the world as a screenwriter, journalist, and media consultant. He is a member of the Association of Former Intelligence Officers, American Legion Post 299, the International Thriller Writers association, and Mystery Writers of America.

Mr. Kovacs graduated from Southern Illinois University, having paid his tuition by working in a steel mill, driving a truck, and spinning records as a late-night jazz DJ on local radio. He lives in Asia with his wife and children.

Please visit his Website[1] at https://edkovacs.com. Follow him on Facebook[2] and Goodreads. [3]

If you are a BookBub subscriber, please click here[4] for Ed's books.

Book reviews are hugely important, both to authors and to other readers. Please leave an honest online review of this or any of Ed's other books on the page of your favorite bookseller.

---

1.   http://www.edkovacs.com/

2.   https://www.facebook.com/ed.kovacs.888/

3.   https://www.goodreads.com/author/show/1344624.Ed_Kovacs

4.   https://www.bookbub.com/authors/ed-kovacs

COPYRIGHT

THIS BOOK IS A WORK of fiction. Names, characters, places, and incidents are either the product of the author's imagination or used fictitiously. Any resemblance to actual events or locales or persons, living or dead, is entirely coincidental.

PRINTING HISTORY

First edition: The Phoenix Group August 2016
ISBN: XXXXXXXXXXXX (e-book edition)
ISBN: 978-1-3933993-5-3 (print edition 2021)

• • • •

Cover design: Bookdesign
Photo of Ed Kovacs © Neungreuthai Chanphonsean

Don't miss out!

Visit the website below and you can sign up to receive emails whenever ED KOVACS publishes a new book. There's no charge and no obligation.

https://books2read.com/r/B-A-LKBD-IFIL

BOOKS 2 READ

Connecting independent readers to independent writers.

Did you love *Locked Down*? Then you should read *Unseen Forces*[5] by
ED KOVACS!

Maverick archeologist Dr. Sky Wilder has never been able to prove
any of his outside-the-box fringe theories... until now. When he
breaks what had been an impenetrable code, he unearths a long-
buried Egyptian stone tablet in Arizona's Red Rock country. Whoever possesses all three hidden tablets holds the key to locate an an-
cient alchemical text containing a formula for physical immortali-
ty. The bodies pile up as Wilder realizes he's been set-up as a pawn,
caught between opposing covert agencies and secret brotherhoods
that have been warring for centuries.

---

5. https://books2read.com/u/brw7z3

6. https://books2read.com/u/brw7z3